THE SINS OF THE FATHER

JEFFREY ARCHER, whose novels and short stories include *Kane and Abel*, *A Prisoner of Birth* and *Cat O' Nine Tales*, has topped the bestseller lists around the world for over thirty years, with sales of more than 270 million copies.

He is the only author ever to have been a number one bestseller in fiction (fifteen times), short stories (four times) and non-fiction (*The Prison Diaries*).

The author is married with two sons and lives in London and Cambridge.

www.jeffreyarcher.com

ALSO BY JEFFREY ARCHER

NOVELS

Not a Penny More, Not a Penny Less

Shall We Tell the President?   Kane and Abel

The Prodigal Daughter   First Among Equals

A Matter of Honour   As the Crow Flies   Honour Among Thieves

The Fourth Estate   The Eleventh Commandment

Sons of Fortune   False Impression

The Gospel According to Judas
(*with the assistance of Professor Francis J. Moloney*)

A Prisoner of Birth   Paths of Glory

Only Time Will Tell

SHORT STORIES

A Quiver Full of Arrows   A Twist in the Tale

Twelve Red Herrings   The Collected Short Stories

To Cut a Long Story Short   Cat O' Nine Tales

And Thereby Hangs a Tale

PLAYS

Beyond Reasonable Doubt   Exclusive   The Accused

PRISON DIARIES

Volume One – Belmarsh: Hell

Volume Two – Wayland: Purgatory

Volume Three – North Sea Camp: Heaven

SCREENPLAYS

Mallory: Walking Off the Map   False Impression

JEFFREY ARCHER

THE CLIFTON CHRONICLES

VOLUME TWO

THE SINS OF THE FATHER

PAN BOOKS

First published 2012 by Macmillan

This edition first published 2012 by Pan Books
an imprint of Pan Macmillan, a division of Macmillan Publishers Limited
Pan Macmillan, 20 New Wharf Road, London N1 9RR
Basingstoke and Oxford
Associated companies throughout the world
www.panmacmillan.com

ISBN 978-1-4472-0922-5

A CIP catalogue record for this book is available from
the British Library.

Typeset by SetSystems Ltd, Saffron Walden, Essex
Printed and bound in India by Replika Press Pvt. Ltd.

Visit **www.panmacmillan.com** to read more about all our books
and to buy them. You will also find features, author interviews and
news of any author events, and you can sign up for e-newsletters
so that you're always first to hear about our new releases.

SIR TOMMY MACPHERSON

CBE, MC**, TD, DL

Chevalier de la Légion d'Honneur,
Croix de Guerre with 2 Palms and a Star,
Medaglia d'Argento and Resistance Medal, Italy,
Kt of St Mary of Bethlehem

My thanks go to the following people for their invaluable advice and research:

Simon Bainbridge, Eleanor Dryden, Dr Robert Lyman FRHistS, Alison Prince, Mari Roberts and Susan Watt

THE BARRINGTONS

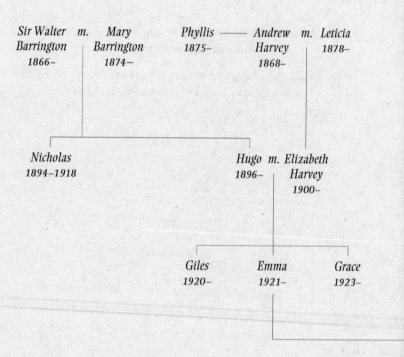

Sir Walter Barrington 1866– m. Mary Barrington 1874–

Phyllis 1875– —— Andrew Harvey 1868– m. Leticia 1878–

Nicholas 1894–1918

Hugo 1896– m. Elizabeth Harvey 1900–

Giles 1920–

Emma 1921–

Grace 1923–

THE CLIFTONS

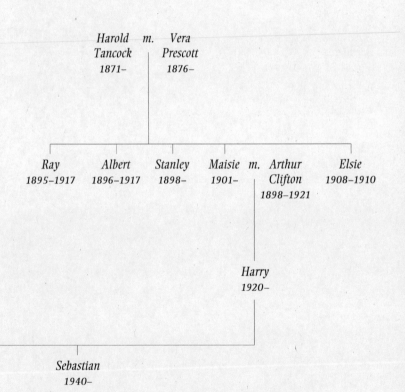

Harold Tancock 1871–   *m.*   Vera Prescott 1876–

Ray 1895–1917   Albert 1896–1917   Stanley 1898–   Maisie 1901–   *m.*   Arthur Clifton 1898–1921   Elsie 1908–1910

Harry 1920–

Sebastian 1940–

'For I the Lord thy God am a jealous God, and visit the sins of the fathers upon the children unto the third and fourth generation . . .'

Book of Common Prayer

HARRY CLIFTON

1939–1941

1

'My name is Harry Clifton.'

'Sure, and I'm Babe Ruth,' said Detective Kolowski as he lit a cigarette.

'No,' said Harry, 'you don't understand, there's been a terrible mistake. I'm Harry Clifton, an Englishman from Bristol. I served on the same ship as Tom Bradshaw.'

'Save it for your lawyer,' said the detective, exhaling deeply and filling the small cell with a cloud of smoke.

'I don't have a lawyer,' protested Harry.

'If I was in the trouble you're in, kid, I'd consider having Sefton Jelks on my side to be about my only hope.'

'Who's Sefton Jelks?'

'You may not have heard of the sharpest lawyer in New York,' said the detective as he blew out another plume of smoke, 'but he has an appointment to see you at nine o'clock tomorrow morning, and Jelks don't leave his office unless his bill has been paid in advance.'

'But—' began Harry, as Kolowski banged the palm of his hand on the cell door.

'So when Jelks turns up tomorrow morning,' Kolowski continued, ignoring Harry's interruption, 'you'd better come up with a more convincing story than we've arrested the wrong man. You told the immigration officer that you were

Tom Bradshaw, and if it was good enough for him, it's going to be good enough for the judge.'

The cell door swung open, but not before the detective had exhaled another plume of smoke that made Harry cough. Kolowski stepped out into the corridor without another word and slammed the door behind him. Harry collapsed on to a bunk that was attached to the wall and rested his head on a brick-hard pillow. He looked up at the ceiling and began to think about how he'd ended up in a police cell on the other side of the world on a murder charge.

◄O►

The door opened long before the morning light could creep through the bars of the window and into the cell. Despite the early hour, Harry was wide awake.

A warder strolled in carrying a tray of food that the Salvation Army wouldn't have considered offering a penniless hobo. Once he'd placed the tray on the little wooden table, he left without a word.

Harry took one look at the food before beginning to pace up and down. With each step, he grew more confident that once he explained to Mr Jelks the reason he'd exchanged his name with Tom Bradshaw, the matter would quickly be sorted out. Surely the worst punishment they could exact would be to deport him, and as he'd always intended to return to England and join the navy, it all fitted in with his original plan.

At 8.55 a.m., Harry was sitting on the end of the bunk, impatient for Mr Jelks to appear. The massive iron door didn't swing open until twelve minutes past nine. Harry leapt up as a prison guard stood to one side and allowed a tall, elegant man with silver grey hair to enter. Harry thought he must have been about the same age as Grandpa. Mr Jelks wore a dark blue pinstripe, double-breasted suit, a white shirt and a striped tie. The weary look on his face suggested that little would surprise him.

'Good morning,' he said, giving Harry a faint smile. 'My name is Sefton Jelks. I am the senior partner of Jelks, Myers and Abernathy, and my clients, Mr and Mrs Bradshaw, have asked me to represent you in your upcoming trial.'

Harry offered Jelks the only chair in his cell, as if he was an old friend who had dropped in to his study at Oxford for a cup of tea. He perched on the bunk and watched the lawyer as he opened his briefcase, extracted a yellow pad and placed it on the table.

Jelks took a pen from an inside pocket and said, 'Perhaps you might begin by telling me who you are, as we both know you're not Lieutenant Bradshaw.'

If the lawyer was surprised by Harry's story he showed no sign of it. Head bowed, he wrote copious notes on his yellow pad while Harry explained how he'd ended up spending the night in jail. Once he'd finished, Harry assumed his problems must surely be over, as he had such a senior lawyer on his side – that was, until he heard Jelks's first question.

'You say that you wrote a letter to your mother while you were on board the *Kansas Star*, explaining why you had assumed Tom Bradshaw's identity?'

'That's correct, sir. I didn't want my mother to suffer unnecessarily, but at the same time I needed her to understand why I'd made such a drastic decision.'

'Yes, I can understand why you might have considered that changing your identity would solve all your immediate problems, while not appreciating that it could involve you in a series of even more complicated ones,' said Jelks. His next question surprised Harry even more. 'Do you recall the contents of that letter?'

'Of course. I wrote and rewrote it so many times I could reproduce it almost verbatim.'

'Then allow me to test your memory,' Jelks said and, without another word, tore off a sheet from his yellow pad and handed it and his fountain pen to Harry.

Harry spent some time recalling the exact words, before he set about rewriting the letter.

My dearest mother,

I have done everything in my power to make sure you receive this letter before anyone can tell you that I died at sea. As the date on this letter shows, I did not perish when the Devonian was sunk on September 4th. In fact, I was plucked out of the sea by a sailor from an American ship and thanks to him, I'm still very much alive. However, an unexpected opportunity arose for me to assume another man's identity, and I did so willingly, in the hope it would release Emma from the many problems I seem to have unwittingly caused her and her family over the years.

It is important that you realize my love for Emma has in no way diminished; far from it. I cannot believe I shall ever experience such love again. But I do not feel I have the right to expect her to spend the rest of her life clinging on to the vain hope that at some time in the future I might be able to prove that Hugo Barrington is not my father, and that I am, in fact, the son of Arthur Clifton. At least this way, she can consider a future with someone else. I envy that man.

I plan to return to England on the first available ship, so should you receive any communication from a Tom Bradshaw, you can assume it's me. I'll be in touch with you the moment I set foot in Bristol, but in the meantime, I must beg you to keep my secret as steadfastly as you kept your own for so many years.

Your loving son,

Harry

When Jelks had finished reading the letter, he once again took Harry by surprise. 'Did you post the letter yourself, Mr Clifton,' he asked, 'or did you give that responsibility to someone else?'

For the first time Harry felt suspicious, and decided not to mention that he'd asked Dr Wallace to deliver the letter to his mother when he returned to Bristol in a fortnight's time. He feared that Jelks might persuade Dr Wallace to hand over the letter and then his mother would have no way of knowing he was still alive.

'I posted the letter when I came ashore,' he said.

The elderly lawyer took his time before he responded. 'Do you have any proof that you are Harry Clifton, and not Thomas Bradshaw?'

'No, sir, I do not,' said Harry without hesitation, painfully aware that no one on board the *Kansas Star* had any reason to believe he wasn't Tom Bradshaw, and the only people who could verify his story were on the other side of the ocean, more than three thousand miles away, and it would not be long before they were all informed that Harry Clifton had been buried at sea.

'Then I may be able to assist you, Mr Clifton. That's assuming you still wish Miss Emma Barrington to believe you are dead. If you do,' said Jelks, an insincere smile on his face, 'I may be able to offer a solution to your problem.'

'A solution?' said Harry, looking hopeful for the first time.

'But only if you felt able to retain the persona of Thomas Bradshaw.'

Harry remained silent.

'The district attorney's office has accepted that the charge against Bradshaw is at best circumstantial, and the only real evidence they are clinging on to is that he left the country the day after the murder had been committed. Aware of the weakness of their case, they have agreed to drop the charge of murder if you felt able to plead guilty to the lesser charge of desertion while serving in the armed forces.'

'But why would I agree to that?' asked Harry.

'I can think of three good reasons,' replied Jelks. 'Firstly, if you don't, you're likely to end up spending six years in prison for entering the United States on false pretences. Secondly, you would retain your anonymity, so the Barrington family would have no reason to believe you are still alive. And thirdly, the Bradshaws are willing to pay you ten thousand dollars if you take their son's place.'

Harry realized immediately that this would be an opportunity to repay his mother for all the sacrifices she'd made for him over the years. Such a large sum of money would transform her life, making it possible for her to escape the two-up-two-down in Still House Lane, along with the weekly knock on the door from the rent collector. She might even consider giving up her job as a waitress at the Grand Hotel and start living an easier life, although Harry thought that was unlikely. But before he agreed to fall in with Jelks's plans, he had some questions of his own.

'Why would the Bradshaws be willing to go through with such a deception, when they must now know that their son was killed at sea?'

'Mrs Bradshaw is desperate to have Thomas's name cleared. She will never accept that one of her sons might have killed the other.'

'So is that what Tom is accused of – murdering his brother?'

'Yes, but as I said, the evidence is flimsy and circumstantial, and certainly wouldn't stand up in court, which is why the DA's office is willing to drop the charge, but only if we agree to plead guilty to the lesser charge of desertion.'

'And how long might my sentence be, if I agreed to that?'

'The DA has agreed to recommend to the judge that you're sentenced to one year, so with good behaviour you could be free in six months; quite an improvement on the six years you can expect if you go on insisting that you're Harry Clifton.'

'But the moment I walk into the courtroom, someone's bound to realize that I'm not Bradshaw.'

'Unlikely,' said Jelks. 'The Bradshaws hail from Seattle, on the west coast, and although they're well off, they rarely visit New York. Thomas joined the navy when he was seventeen, and as you know to your cost, he hasn't set foot in America for the past four years. And if you plead guilty, you'll only be in the courtroom for twenty minutes.'

'But when I open my mouth, won't everyone know I'm not an American?'

'That's why you won't be opening your mouth, Mr Clifton.' The urbane lawyer seemed to have an answer for everything. Harry tried another ploy.

'In England, murder trials are always packed with journalists, and the public queue up outside the courtroom from the early hours in the hope of getting a glimpse of the defendant.'

'Mr Clifton, there are fourteen murder trials currently taking place in New York, including the notorious "scissors stabber". I doubt if even a cub reporter will be assigned to this case.'

'I need some time to think about it.'

Jelks glanced at his watch. 'We're due in front of Judge Atkins at noon, so you have just over an hour to make up your mind, Mr Clifton.' He called for a guard to open the cell door. 'Should you decide not to avail yourself of my services I wish you luck, because we will not be meeting again,' he added before he left the cell.

Harry sat on the end of the bunk, considering Sefton Jelks's offer. Although he didn't doubt that the silver-haired counsel had his own agenda, six months sounded a lot more palatable than six years, and who else could he turn to, other than this seasoned lawyer? Harry wished he could drop into Sir Walter Barrington's office for a few moments and seek his advice.

◄०►

An hour later, Harry, dressed in a dark blue suit, cream shirt, starched collar and a striped tie, was handcuffed, marched from his cell to a prison vehicle and driven to the courthouse under armed guard.

'No one must believe you're capable of murder,' Jelks had pronounced after a tailor had visited Harry's cell with half a dozen suits, shirts and a selection of ties for him to consider.

'I'm not,' Harry reminded him.

Harry was reunited with Jelks in the corridor. The lawyer gave him that same smile before pushing his way through the swing doors and walking down the centre aisle, not stopping until he reached the two vacant seats at counsel's table.

Once Harry had settled into his place and his handcuffs had been removed, he looked around the almost empty courtroom. Jelks had been right about that. Few members of the public, and certainly no press, seemed interested in the case. For them, it must have been just another domestic murder, where the defendant was likely to be acquitted; no 'Cain and Abel' headlines while there was no possibility of the electric chair in court number four.

As the first chime rang out to announce midday, a door opened on the far side of the room and Judge Atkins appeared. He walked slowly across the court, climbed the steps and took his place behind a desk on the raised dais. He then nodded in the direction of the DA, as if he knew exactly what he was about to say.

A young lawyer rose from behind the prosecutor's desk and explained that the state would be dropping the murder charge, but would be pursuing Thomas Bradshaw on a charge of desertion from the US Navy. The judge nodded, and turned his attention to Mr Jelks, who rose on cue.

'And on the second charge, of desertion, how does your client plead?'

'Guilty,' said Jelks. 'I hope your honour will be lenient with my client on this occasion, as I don't need to remind you, sir, that this is his first offence, and before this uncharacteristic lapse he had an unblemished record.'

Judge Atkins scowled. 'Mr Jelks,' he said, 'some may consider that for an officer to desert his post while serving his country is a crime every bit as heinous as murder. I'm sure I don't have to remind *you* that until recently such an offence would have resulted in your client facing a firing squad.'

Harry felt sick as he looked up at Jelks, who didn't take his eyes off the judge.

'With that in mind,' continued Atkins, 'I sentence Lieutenant Thomas Bradshaw to six years in jail.' He banged his gavel and said, 'Next case,' before Harry had a chance to protest.

'You told me—' began Harry, but Jelks had already turned his back on his former client and was walking away. Harry was about to chase after him, when the two guards grabbed him by the arms, thrust them behind his back and quickly handcuffed the convicted criminal, before marching him across the courtroom towards a door Harry hadn't noticed before.

He looked back to see Sefton Jelks shaking hands with a middle-aged man who was clearly congratulating him on a job well done. Where had Harry seen that face before? And then he realized – it had to be Tom Bradshaw's father.

2

HARRY WAS MARCHED unceremoniously down a long, dimly lit corridor and out of an unmarked door into a barren courtyard.

In the middle of the yard stood a yellow bus that displayed neither number nor any hint of its destination. A muscle-bound conductor clutching a rifle stood by the door, and nodded to indicate that Harry should climb on board. His guards gave him a helping hand, just in case he was having second thoughts.

Harry took a seat and stared sullenly out of the window as a trickle of convicted prisoners were led up to the bus, some with their heads bowed, while others, who had clearly trodden this path before, adopted a jaunty swagger. He assumed it wouldn't be long before the bus set off for its destination, wherever that might be, but he was about to learn his first painful lesson as a prisoner: once you've been convicted, no one is in any hurry.

Harry thought about asking one of the guards where they were going, but neither of them looked like helpful tour guides. He turned anxiously when a body slumped into the seat next to him. He didn't want to stare at his new companion, but as the man introduced himself immediately, Harry took a closer look at him.

'My name's Pat Quinn,' he announced with a slight Irish accent.

'Tom Bradshaw,' said Harry, who would have shaken hands with his new companion if they hadn't both been hand-cuffed.

Quinn didn't look like a criminal. His feet barely touched the ground, so he couldn't have been an inch over five feet, and whereas most of the other prisoners on the bus were either muscle-bound or simply overweight, Quinn looked as if a gust of wind would blow him away. His thinning red hair was beginning to grey, although he couldn't have been a day over forty.

'You're a first-timer?' said Quinn confidently.

'Is it that obvious?' asked Harry.

'It's written all over your face.'

'What's written all over my face?'

'You haven't got a clue what's going to happen next.'

'So *you're* obviously not a first-timer?'

'This is the eleventh time I've been on this bus, or it could be the twelfth.'

Harry laughed for the first time in days.

'What are you in for?' Quinn asked him.

'Desertion,' Harry replied, without elaboration.

'Never heard of that one before,' said Quinn. 'I've deserted three wives, but they never put me in the slammer for it.'

'I didn't desert a wife,' said Harry, thinking about Emma. 'I deserted the Royal Navy— I mean the navy.'

'How long did you get for that?'

'Six years.'

Quinn whistled through his two remaining teeth. 'Sounds a bit rough. Who was the judge?'

'Atkins,' said Harry with feeling.

'Arnie Atkins? You got the wrong judge. If you're ever on trial again, make sure you pick the right judge.'

'I didn't know you could pick your judge.'

'You can't,' said Quinn, 'but there are ways of avoiding the worst ones.' Harry looked more closely at his companion, but didn't interrupt. 'There are seven judges who work the circuit, and you need to avoid two of them at all costs. One is Arnie Atkins. He's short on humour and long on sentencing.'

'But how could I have avoided him?' asked Harry.

'Atkins has presided over court four for the past eleven years, so if I'm heading in that direction, I have an epileptic fit and the guards take me off to see the court doctor.'

'You're an epileptic?'

'No,' said Quinn, 'you're not paying attention.' He sounded exasperated, and Harry fell silent. 'By the time I've staged a recovery, they will have allocated my case to another court.'

Harry laughed for the second time. 'And you get away with it?'

'No, not always, but if I end up with a couple of rookie guards, I'm in with a chance, though it's getting more difficult to pull the same stunt again and again. I didn't need to bother this time because I was taken straight to court two, which is Judge Regan's territory. He's Irish – like me, just in case you hadn't noticed – so he's more likely to give a fellow countryman a minimum sentence.'

'What was your offence?' asked Harry.

'I'm a pickpocket,' Quinn announced, as if he were an architect or a doctor. 'I specialize in race meetings in the summer and boxing halls in the winter. It's always easier if the marks are standing up,' he explained. 'But my luck's been running short recently because too many stewards recognize me, so I've had to work the subway and the bus depots, where the pickings are slim and you're more likely to be caught.'

Harry had so much he wanted to ask his new tutor and,

like an enthusiastic student, he concentrated on the questions that would help him pass the entrance exam, rather pleased that Quinn hadn't questioned his accent.

'Do you know where we're going?' he asked.

'Lavenham or Pierpoint,' said Quinn. 'All depends on whether we come off the highway at exit twelve or fourteen.'

'Have you been to either of them before?'

'Both, several times,' said Quinn matter-of-factly. 'And before you ask, if there was a tourist guide to prisons, Lavenham would get one star and Pierpoint would be closed down.'

'Why don't we just ask the guard which one we're going to?' said Harry, who wanted to be put out of his misery.

'Because he'd tell us the wrong one, just to piss us off. If it's Lavenham, the only thing you need to worry about is which block they put you on. As you're a first-timer you'll probably end up on A block, where life is a lot easier. The old-timers, like me, are usually sent to D block, where there's no one under thirty and no one with a record for violence, so it's the ideal set-up if you just want to keep your head down and do your time. Try to avoid B and C block – they're both full of hopheads and psychos.'

'What do I have to do to make sure I end up on A block?'

'Tell the reception officer you're a devout Christian, don't smoke and don't drink.'

'I didn't know you were allowed to drink in prison,' said Harry.

'You aren't, you stupid fucker,' said Quinn, 'but if you can supply the greenbacks,' he added, rubbing a thumb against the tip of his index finger, 'the guards suddenly become barmen. Even prohibition didn't slow them down.'

'What's the most important thing for me to watch out for on my first day?'

'Make sure you get the right job.'

'What's the choice?'

'Cleaning, kitchen, hospital, laundry, library, gardening and the chapel.'

'What do I have to do to get in the library?'

'Tell 'em you can read.'

'What do you tell them?' asked Harry.

'That I trained as a chef.'

'That must have been interesting.'

'You still haven't caught on, have you?' said Quinn. 'I never trained as a chef, but it means I'm always put in the kitchen, which is the best job in any prison.'

'Why's that?'

'You're let out of your cell before breakfast, and you don't go back to it until after dinner. It's warm, and you have the best choice of food. Ah, we're going to Lavenham,' said Quinn as the bus turned off the highway at exit 12. 'That's good, 'cause now I won't have to answer any dumb questions about Pierpoint.'

'Anything else I ought to know about Lavenham?' asked Harry, unperturbed by Quinn's sarcasm, as he suspected that the old-timer was enjoying delivering a master class to such a willing pupil.

'Too much to tell you,' he sighed. 'Just remember to stick close by me once we've been registered.'

'But won't they automatically send you to D block?'

'Not if Mr Mason's on duty,' Quinn said without explanation.

Harry managed several more questions before the bus finally drew up outside the prison. In fact, he felt he'd learnt more from Quinn in a couple of hours than he'd managed in a dozen tutorials at Oxford.

'Stick with me,' repeated Quinn as the massive gates swung open. The bus moved slowly forward and on to a desolate piece of scrubland that had never seen a gardener. It stopped in front of a vast brick building that displayed rows of small filthy windows, some with eyes staring out of them.

Harry watched as a dozen guards formed a corridor that led all the way to the entrance of the prison. Two armed with rifles had planted themselves on either side of the bus door.

'Leave the bus in twos,' one of them announced gruffly, 'with a five-minute interval between each pair. No one moves an inch unless I say so.'

Harry and Quinn remained on the bus for another hour. When they were finally ushered off, Harry looked up at the high walls topped with barbed wire that surrounded the entire prison and thought even the world record holder for the pole vault wouldn't have been able to escape from Lavenham.

Harry followed Quinn into the building, where they came to a halt in front of an officer who was seated behind a table and wearing a well-worn shiny blue uniform with buttons that didn't shine. He looked as if he'd already served a life sentence as he studied the list of names on his clipboard. He smiled when he saw the next prisoner.

'Welcome back, Quinn,' he said. 'You won't find much has changed since you were last here.'

Quinn grinned. 'It's good to see you too, Mr Mason. Perhaps you'd be kind enough to ask one of the bell hops to take my luggage up to my usual room.'

'Don't push your luck, Quinn,' said Mason, 'otherwise I might be tempted to tell the new doc you're not an epileptic.'

'But, Mr Mason, I've got a medical certificate to prove it.'

'From the same source as your chef's certificate no doubt,' said Mason, turning his attention to Harry. 'And who are you?'

'This is my buddy, Tom Bradshaw. He doesn't smoke,

drink, swear or spit,' said Quinn before Harry had a chance to speak.

'Welcome to Lavenham, Bradshaw,' said Mason.

'Captain Bradshaw actually,' said Quinn.

'It used to be Lieutenant,' said Harry. 'I was never a captain.' Quinn looked disappointed with his protégé.

'A first-timer?' asked Mason, taking a closer look at Harry.

'Yes, sir.'

'I'll put you on A block. After you've showered and collected your prison clothes from the store, Mr Hessler will take you to cell number three-two-seven.' Mason checked his clipboard before turning to a young officer who was standing behind him, a truncheon swinging from his right hand.

'Any hope of joining my friend?' asked Quinn once Harry had signed the register. 'After all, Lieutenant Bradshaw might need a batman.'

'You're the last person he needs,' said Mason. Harry was about to speak as the pickpocket bent down, removed a folded dollar bill from inside his sock and slipped it into Mason's top pocket in the blink of an eye. 'Quinn will also be in cell three-two-seven,' said Mason to the junior officer. If Hessler had witnessed the exchange, he didn't comment. 'You two, follow me,' was all he said.

Quinn chased after Harry before Mason could change his mind.

The two new prisoners were marched down a long green brick corridor until Hessler stopped outside a small shower room that had two narrow wooden benches fixed to the wall, littered with discarded towels.

'Strip,' said Hessler, 'and take a shower.'

Harry slowly removed the tailored suit, smart cream shirt, stiff collar and striped tie that Mr Jelks had been so keen for him to wear in court to impress the judge. The trouble was, he'd picked the wrong judge.

Quinn was already under the shower before Harry had unlaced his shoes. He turned on the tap and a trickle of water reluctantly dripped down on to his balding head. He then picked up a sliver of soap from the floor and began to wash. Harry stepped under the cold water of the only other shower, and a moment later Quinn passed him what was left of the soap.

'Remind me to speak to the management about the facilities,' said Quinn as he picked up a damp towel, not much bigger than a dishcloth, and attempted to dry himself.

Hessler's lips remained pursed. 'Get dressed and follow me,' he said, before Harry had finished soaping himself.

Once again Hessler marched off down the corridor at a brisk pace, with a half-dressed, still wet Harry chasing after him. They didn't stop until they came to a double door marked STORES. Hessler rapped firmly and a moment later it was pulled open to reveal a world-weary officer, elbows on the counter, smoking a rolled cigarette. The officer smiled when he saw Quinn.

'I'm not sure we've got your last lot back from the laundry yet, Quinn,' he said.

'Then I'll need a new set of everything, Mr Newbold,' said Quinn, who bent down and removed something from inside his other sock, and once again it disappeared without trace. 'My requirements are simple,' he added. 'One blanket, two cotton sheets, one pillow, one pillowcase . . .' The officer selected each item from the shelves behind him, before placing them in a neat pile on the counter. '. . . Two shirts, three pairs of socks, six pairs of pants, two towels, one bowl, one plate, one knife, fork and spoon, one razor, one toothbrush and one tube of toothpaste – I prefer Colgate.'

Newbold made no comment as Quinn's pile grew larger

and larger. 'Will there be anything else?' he eventually asked, as if Quinn were a valued customer who was likely to return.

'Yes, my friend Lieutenant Bradshaw will require the same order, and as he is an officer and a gentleman, be sure that he gets only the best.'

To Harry's surprise, Newbold began to build another pile, seeming to take his time selecting each item, and all because of the prisoner who'd sat next to him on the bus.

'Follow me,' said Hessler when Newbold had completed his task. Harry and Pat grabbed their piles of clothes and charged off down the corridor. There were several stops on the way, as a duty officer had to unlock and lock barred gates as they came nearer to the cells. When they eventually stepped on to the wing, they were greeted by the noise of a thousand prisoners.

Quinn said, 'I see we're on the top floor, Mr Hessler, but I won't be taking the elevator, as I need the exercise.' The officer ignored him and continued past the shouting prisoners.

'I thought you said this was the quiet wing,' said Harry.

'It's clear Mr Hessler is not one of the more popular officers,' whispered Quinn, just before the three of them reached cell 327. Hessler unlocked the heavy iron door and pulled it open to allow the new con and the old con to enter the home Harry had a lease on for the next six years.

Harry heard the door slam behind him. He looked around the cell, and noticed there was no handle on the inside of the door. Two bunks, one on top of the other, a steel wash basin attached to the wall, a wooden table, also attached to the wall, and a wooden chair. His eyes finally settled on a steel bowl under the lower bunk. He thought he was going to be sick.

'You get the top bunk,' said Quinn, interrupting his thoughts, 'on account of you being a first-timer. If I get out before you, you'll move down to the bottom one, and your new cellmate will get the top. Prison etiquette,' he explained.

Harry stood on the bottom bunk and slowly made up his bed, then climbed up, lay down and placed his head on the thin, hard pillow, painfully aware that it might be some time before he managed a night's sleep. 'Can I ask you one more question?' he said to Quinn.

'Yes, but don't speak again until lights on tomorrow morning.' Harry recalled Fisher saying almost the same words on his first night at St Bede's.

'It's obvious you've been able to smuggle in a considerable amount of cash, so why didn't the guards confiscate it as soon as you got off the bus?'

'Because if they did,' said Quinn, 'no con would ever bring in any money again, and the whole system would break down.'

3

Harry lay on the top bunk and stared at the one-coated white ceiling that he could touch by reaching up with his fingers. The mattress was lumpy and the pillow so hard that he could only manage to sleep for a few minutes at a time.

His thoughts turned to Sefton Jelks and how easily he had been duped by the old advocate. Get my son off the murder charge, that's all I care about, he could hear Tom Bradshaw's father telling Jelks. Harry tried not to think about the next six years, which Mr Bradshaw didn't care about. Had it been worth $10,000?

He dismissed his lawyer and thought about Emma. He missed her so much, and wanted to write and tell her he was still alive, but he knew he couldn't. He wondered what she would be doing on an autumn day in Oxford. How was her work progressing as she began her freshman year? Was she being courted by another man?

And what of her brother, Giles, his closest friend? Now that Britain was at war, had Giles left Oxford and signed up to fight the Germans? If he had, Harry prayed that he was still alive. He thumped the side of the bunk with a clenched fist, angry that he was not being allowed to play his part. Quinn didn't speak, assuming that Harry was suffering 'first-night-itis'.

And what of Hugo Barrington? Had anyone seen him

since he disappeared on the day Harry should have married his daughter? Would he find a way of creeping back into favour, when everyone believed Harry was dead? He dismissed Barrington from his mind, still unwilling to accept the possibility that the man might be his father.

When his thoughts turned to his mother, Harry smiled, hoping that she would make good use of the $10,000 Jelks had promised to send her once he'd agreed to take the place of Tom Bradshaw. With over £2,000 in the bank, Harry hoped she would give up her job as a waitress at the Grand Hotel and buy that little house in the country she'd always talked about; that was the only good thing that would come out of this whole charade.

And what of Sir Walter Barrington, who had always treated him like a grandchild? If Hugo was Harry's father, then Sir Walter *was* his grandfather. If that turned out to be the case, Harry would be in line to inherit the Barrington estate and the family title, and would in time become Sir Harry Barrington. But not only did Harry want his friend Giles, Hugo Barrington's legitimate son, to inherit the title, even more important, he was desperate to *prove* that his real father was Arthur Clifton. That would still give him an outside chance of being able to marry his beloved Emma. Harry tried to forget where he'd be spending the next six years.

—◆—

At seven o'clock a siren sounded to wake those prisoners who had served long enough to enjoy a night's sleep. You're not in prison when you're asleep, were the last words Quinn had muttered before falling into a deep slumber, then snoring. It didn't bother Harry. As a snorer, his uncle Stan was in a different class.

Harry had made up his mind about several things during his long, sleepless night. To help pass the numbing cruelty of wasted time, 'Tom' would be a model prisoner, in the hope that his sentence would be reduced for good behaviour. He would get a job in the library, and write a diary about what had happened before he was sentenced, and everything that took place while he was behind bars. He would keep himself fit, so that if war was still raging in Europe, he would be ready to sign up the moment he was released.

Quinn was already dressed by the time Harry climbed down from the top bunk.

'What now?' asked Harry, sounding like a new boy on his first day of term.

'Breakfast,' said Quinn. 'Get dressed, grab your plate and mug, and make sure you're ready when the screw unlocks the door. If you're a few seconds late, some officers get a kick out of slamming the door in your face.' Harry began to pull on his trousers. 'And don't talk on your way down to the canteen,' added Quinn. 'It draws attention to yourself, which annoys the old-timers. In fact, don't talk to anyone you don't know until your second year.'

Harry would have laughed, but he wasn't sure if Quinn was joking. He heard a key turning in the lock, and the cell door swung open. Quinn shot through like a greyhound out of the slips, with his cellmate only a stride behind. They joined a long line of silent prisoners who were making their way across the landing past the open doors of empty cells, before walking down a spiral staircase to the ground floor, where they would join their fellow inmates for breakfast.

The line came to a halt long before they reached the canteen. Harry watched the servers in their short white coats, standing behind the hotplate. A guard carrying a truncheon and wearing a long white coat was keeping an eye on them, making sure no one got an extra portion.

'How nice to see you again, Mr Siddell,' Pat said quietly

to the guard once they reached the front of the queue. The two men shook hands as if they were old friends. This time Harry couldn't see any money changing hands, but a curt nod from Mr Siddell indicated that a deal had been struck.

Quinn moved along the line as his tin plate was filled with a fried egg with a solid yolk, a pile of potatoes more black than white and the regulation two slices of stale bread. Harry caught up with him as he was having his mug half filled with coffee. The servers looked puzzled when Harry thanked them one by one, as if he were a guest at a vicarage tea party.

'Damn,' he said when the last server offered him coffee. 'I left my mug in the cell.'

The server filled Quinn's mug to the brim. 'Don't forget next time,' said Harry's cellmate.

'No talking in line!' yelled Hessler, slamming his truncheon into a gloved hand. Quinn led Harry to the end of a long table and sat on the bench opposite him. Harry was so hungry he devoured every morsel on his plate, including the greasiest egg he'd ever tasted. He even considered licking his plate, and then he recalled his friend Giles, on another first day.

When Harry and Pat had finished their five-minute breakfast, they were marched back up the spiral staircase to the top floor. Once their cell door had been slammed shut, Quinn washed his plate and mug, and placed them neatly under his bunk.

'When you live in an eight by four for years on end, you make use of every inch of space,' he explained. Harry followed his lead, and could only wonder how long it would be before he was able to teach Quinn something.

'What next?' asked Harry.

'Work allocation,' said Quinn. 'I'll be joining Siddell in the kitchen, but we've still got to make sure they put you in the library. And that'll depend on which officer is on duty. Trouble is, I'm running out of cash.' Quinn had hardly got the words out of his mouth before the door was pulled open again and Hessler was silhouetted in the doorway, the truncheon thumping into his gloved hand.

'Quinn,' he said, 'report to the kitchen immediately. Bradshaw, go to station nine and join the other wing cleaners.'

'I was hoping to work in the library, Mr—'

'I don't give a fuck what you were hoping, Bradshaw,' said Hessler. 'As wing officer, I make the rules around here. You can go to the library on Tuesdays, Thursdays and Sundays between six and seven, like any other inmate. Is that clear enough for you?' Harry nodded. 'You're not an officer any longer, Bradshaw, just a con, like everyone else in this place. And don't waste your time thinking you can bribe me,' he added, before marching off to the next cell.

'Hessler's one of the few officers you can't bribe,' whispered Quinn. 'Your only hope now is Mr Swanson, the prison warden. Just remember that he considers himself a bit of an intellectual, which probably means he can manage joined-up writing. He's also a Fundamental Baptist. Hallelujah!'

'When will I get the chance to see him?' asked Harry.

'Could be any time. Just be sure to let him know you want to work in the library, because each new prisoner only gets five minutes of his time.'

Harry slumped down on the wooden chair and placed his head in his hands. If it wasn't for the $10,000 Jelks had promised to send to his mother, he'd use his five minutes to tell the warden the truth about how he'd ended up in Lavenham.

'Meantime, I'll do what I can to get you into the kitchen,' added Quinn. 'It may not be what you hoped for, but it's sure better than being a wing cleaner.'

'Thanks,' said Harry. Quinn scurried off to the kitchens, not needing directions. Harry took the stairs back down to the ground floor and went in search of station nine.

Twelve men, all first-timers, stood in a huddle and waited for instructions. Initiative was frowned on in Lavenham – it smacked of rebellion, or the suggestion that a prisoner just might be cleverer than an officer.

'Pick up a bucket, fill it with water, and get yourself a mop,' said Hessler. He smiled at Harry as he ticked off his name on yet another clipboard. 'As you were last down, Bradshaw, you'll be working in the shit house for the next month.'

'But I wasn't the last down,' protested Harry.

'I think you were,' said Hessler, the smile not leaving his face.

Harry filled his bucket with cold water and grabbed a mop. He didn't need to be told in which direction to go, he could smell the latrines from a dozen paces. He began retching before he'd even entered the large square room with thirty holes in the ground. He held his nose, but he had to continually leave the room to gasp for air. Hessler stood some way off, laughing.

'You'll get used to it, Bradshaw,' he said, 'in time.'

Harry regretted having eaten such a large breakfast, which he brought up within minutes. It must have been about an hour later that he heard another officer bellowing his name. 'Bradshaw!'

Harry staggered out of the latrines, white as a sheet. 'That's me,' he said.

'The warden wants to see you, so let's get movin'.'

Harry was able to breathe more deeply with each step he took, and by the time he'd reached the warden's office, he felt almost human.

'Wait there until you're called for,' said the officer.

Harry took a spare seat between two other prisoners,

who quickly turned away. He couldn't blame them. He tried to gather his thoughts as each new prisoner went in and out of the warden's office. Quinn was right, the interviews lasted for about five minutes, some even less. Harry couldn't afford to waste one second of his allotted time.

'Bradshaw,' said the officer, and opened the door. He stood aside as Harry entered the warden's office. Harry decided not to get too close to Mr Swanson, and remained several paces from his large leather-topped desk. Although the warden was seated, Harry could see that he was unable to do up the middle button of his sports jacket. His hair had been dyed black in an attempt to make him look younger, but it only made him look slightly ridiculous. What did Brutus say of Caesar's vanity? Offer him garlands, and praise him as if he were a god, and that will be his downfall.

Swanson opened Bradshaw's file and studied it for a few moments before looking up at Harry.

'I see you were sentenced to six years for desertion. Haven't come across that one before,' he admitted.

'Yes, sir,' said Harry, not wanting to waste any of his precious time.

'Don't bother telling me you're innocent,' Swanson continued, 'because only one in a thousand is, so the odds are stacked against you.' Harry had to smile. 'But if you keep your nose clean' – Harry thought about the latrines – 'and don't cause any trouble, I can't see why you would have to serve the full six years.'

'Thank you, sir.'

'Do you have any special interests?' Swanson asked, looking as if he wasn't at all interested if Harry did.

'Reading, art appreciation and choral singing, sir.'

The warden gave Harry a disbelieving look, not sure if he was trying to get a rise out of him. He pointed to a sign hanging on the wall behind his desk and asked, 'Can you tell me the next line, Bradshaw?'

Harry studied the embroidered sampler: *I will lift up mine eyes unto the hills*. He gave silent thanks to Miss Eleanor E. Monday, and the hours he'd spent at her choir practices. 'From whence cometh my help, sayeth the Lord. Psalm one hundred and twenty-one.'

The warden smiled. 'Tell me, Bradshaw, who are your favourite authors?'

'Shakespeare, Dickens, Austen, Trollope and Thomas Hardy.'

'None of our own countrymen good enough?'

Harry wanted to curse out loud, having made such an obvious blunder. He glanced across at the warden's half-filled bookshelf. 'Of course,' he said. 'I consider F. Scott Fitzgerald, Hemingway and O. Henry to be anyone's equal, and I believe Steinbeck is America's finest modern writer.' He hoped he'd pronounced the name correctly. He'd make sure he had read *Of Mice and Men* before he came across the warden again.

The smile returned to Swanson's lips. 'What job has Mr Hessler allocated to you?' he asked.

'Wing cleaner, although I'd like to work in the library, sir.'

'Would you indeed?' said the warden. 'Then I'll have to see if there's a vacancy.' He made a note on the pad in front of him.

'Thank you, sir.'

'If there is, you'll be informed later today,' said the warden as he closed the file.

'Thank you, sir,' repeated Harry. He left quickly, aware that he'd taken longer than his allotted five minutes.

Once he was out in the corridor, the duty officer escorted him back to the wing. Harry was thankful that Hessler was nowhere to be seen, and that the cleaners had moved on to the second floor by the time he rejoined them.

Long before the siren sounded for lunch, Harry was

exhausted. He joined the line for the hotplate, and found Quinn already ensconced behind the counter, serving his fellow inmates. Large portions of potato and over-cooked meat were dropped on to Harry's plate. He sat alone at the long table and picked at his food. He feared that if Hessler were to reappear that afternoon, he would be dispatched back to the latrines, and so would his lunch.

Hessler was not on duty when Harry reported back to work, and a different officer put another first-timer on the latrines. Harry spent the afternoon sweeping corridors and emptying trash cans. His only thought was whether the warden had given an order to reallocate him to the library. If he hadn't, Harry would have to hope for a job in the kitchen.

When Quinn returned to their cell after dinner, the expression on his face left Harry in no doubt that he wouldn't be joining his friend.

'There was one place available for a washer-up.'

'I'll take it,' said Harry.

'But when Mr Siddell put your name forward, Hessler vetoed it. Said you'd have to do at least three months as a wing cleaner before he'd consider a transfer to kitchen duty.'

'What is it with that man?' asked Harry desperately.

'Rumour has it he signed up to be a naval officer, but failed the board exam and had to settle for the prison service. So Lieutenant Bradshaw has to suffer the consequences.'

4

HARRY SPENT the next twenty-nine days cleaning the latrines on A block, and it wasn't until another first-timer appeared on the wing that Hessler finally released him from his duties and began to make someone else's life hell.

'Damn man's a psycho,' said Quinn. 'Siddell's still willing to offer you a job in the kitchen, but Hessler's vetoed it.' Harry didn't comment. 'But the news isn't all bad,' Quinn suggested, 'because I've just heard that Andy Savatori, the deputy librarian, has been granted parole. He's due to be released next month and, even better, no one else seems to want his job.'

'Deakins would,' said Harry under his breath. 'So what do I have to do, to make sure I get it?'

'Nothing. In fact, try to give the impression you're not that interested, and keep out of Hessler's way, because we know the warden's on your side.'

The next month dragged on, each day seeming longer than the one before. Harry visited the library every Tuesday, Thursday and Sunday between six and seven, but Max Lloyd, the senior librarian, gave him no reason to believe he was being considered for the post. Savatori, his deputy, remained tight-lipped, although he clearly knew something.

'I don't think Lloyd wants me to be his deputy,' said Harry after lights out one evening.

'Lloyd won't have a say about it,' said Quinn. 'That's the warden's decision.'

But Harry wasn't convinced. 'I suspect Hessler and Lloyd are working together to make sure I don't get the job.'

'You're becoming para— what's the word?' said Quinn.

'Paranoid.'

'Yeah, that's what you're becoming, not that I'm sure what it means.'

'Suffering from unfounded suspicions,' said Harry.

'Couldn't have put it better myself!'

Harry wasn't convinced that his suspicions were unfounded and, a week later, Savatori took him to one side and confirmed his worst fears.

'Hessler's put up three cons for the warden's consideration, and your name isn't on the list.'

'Then that's that,' said Harry, thumping the side of his leg. 'I'm going to be a wing cleaner for the rest of my days.'

'Not necessarily,' said Savatori. 'Come and see me the day before I'm due to be discharged.'

'But by then it will be too late.'

'I don't think so,' said Savatori, without explanation. 'Meanwhile, study every page of this very carefully.' He handed Harry a heavy, leather-bound tome that rarely left the library.

◄◦►

Harry sat on the top bunk and opened the cover of the 273-page prison handbook. Before he'd reached page 6, he began to make notes. Long before he'd started reading the book a second time, a plan had begun to form in his mind.

He knew his timing would be critical, and both acts would have to be rehearsed, particularly as he would be on stage when the curtain went up. He accepted that he couldn't go ahead with his plan until after Savatori had been released, even though a new deputy librarian had already been appointed.

When Harry carried out a dress rehearsal in the privacy of their cell, Quinn told him that he was not only paranoid, but crazy, because, he assured him, his second performance would be in solitary.

◄○►

The warden made his monthly rounds of each block on a Monday morning, so Harry knew that he'd have to wait for three weeks after Savatori had been discharged, before he would reappear on A block. Swanson always took the same route, and prisoners knew that if they valued their skin, they disappeared out of sight the moment he came into view.

When Swanson stepped on to the top floor of A block that Monday morning, Harry was waiting to greet him, mop in hand. Hessler slipped in behind the warden, and waved his truncheon to indicate that if Bradshaw valued his life, he should step aside. Harry didn't budge, leaving the warden with no choice but to stop in his tracks.

'Good morning, warden,' said Harry, as if they bumped into each other regularly.

Swanson was surprised to come face-to-face with a prisoner on his rounds, and even more surprised when one spoke to him. He looked more closely at Harry. 'Bradshaw, isn't it?'

'You have a good memory, sir.'

'I also remember your interest in literature. I was surprised when you turned down the job as deputy librarian.'

'I was never offered the job,' said Harry. 'If I had been, I would have accepted it with alacrity,' he added, which clearly took the warden by surprise.

Turning to Hessler, Swanson said, 'You told me Bradshaw didn't want the job.'

Harry jumped in before Hessler could reply. 'Probably my fault, sir. I didn't realize I had to apply for the position.'

'I see,' said the warden. 'Well, that would explain it. And

I can tell you, Bradshaw, that the new man doesn't know the difference between Plato and Pluto.' Harry burst out laughing. Hessler remained tight-lipped.

'A good analogy, sir,' said Harry as the warden attempted to move on. But Harry hadn't finished. He thought Hessler would explode when he removed an envelope from his jacket and handed it to the warden.

'What's this?' Swanson asked suspiciously.

'An official request to address the board when they make their quarterly visit to the prison next Tuesday, which is my prerogative under statute thirty-two of the penal code. I've sent a copy of the request to my lawyer, Mr Sefton Jelks.' For the first time, the warden looked anxious. Hessler could barely contain himself.

'Will you be making a complaint?' asked the warden cautiously.

Harry stared directly at Hessler before replying, 'Under statute one-one-six, it is my right not to disclose to any member of the prison staff why I wish to address the board, as I'm sure you're aware, warden.'

'Yes, of course, Bradshaw,' said the warden, sounding flustered.

'But it is my intention, among other things, to inform the board of the importance you place on including literature and religion as part of our daily lives.' Harry stood aside to allow the warden to continue on his way.

'Thank you, Bradshaw,' he said. 'That's good of you.'

'I'll be seeing you later, Bradshaw,' hissed Hessler under his breath.

'I'll look forward to that,' said Harry, loud enough for Mr Swanson to hear.

◄◦►

Harry's confrontation with the warden was the main topic of conversation among the prisoners in the dinner queue, and when Quinn returned from the kitchen later that evening, he warned Harry that the rumour on the block was that once lights were out, Hessler was likely to kill him.

'I don't think so,' said Harry calmly. 'You see, the problem with being a bully is that on the flipside of that particular coin, you'll find the imprint of a coward.'

Quinn didn't look convinced.

Harry didn't have long to wait to prove his point, because within moments of lights out, the cell door swung open and Hessler strolled in, swinging his truncheon.

'Quinn, out,' he said, not taking his eyes off Harry. Once the Irishman had scurried on to the landing, Hessler closed the cell door and said, 'I've been looking forward to this all day, Bradshaw. You're about to discover how many bones you've got in your body.'

'I don't think so, Mr Hessler,' said Harry, not flinching.

'And what do you think will save you?' asked Hessler, advancing. 'The warden isn't around to rescue you this time.'

'I don't need the warden,' said Harry. 'Not while you're being considered for promotion,' he added, meeting Hessler's stare. 'I'm reliably informed that you'll be appearing before the board next Tuesday afternoon at two o'clock.'

'So what?' said Hessler, now less than a foot away.

'You've clearly forgotten that *I'll* be addressing the board at ten o'clock that morning. One or two of them may be curious to find out how so many of my bones came to be broken after I dared to speak to the warden.' Hessler slammed his truncheon down on the side of the bunk, only inches from Harry's face, but Harry didn't flinch.

'Of course,' Harry continued, 'it's possible that you want to remain a wing officer for the rest of your life, but somehow I doubt it, because even you can't be so stupid as to ruin your one chance of promotion.' Hessler raised his truncheon once again, but hesitated when Harry took a thick exercise book from under his pillow.

'I've made a comprehensive list of the regulations you've broken over the past month, Mr Hessler, some of them several times. I'm confident that the board will find it interesting reading. This evening I'll be adding two more indiscretions: being alone in a cell with a prisoner while the cell door is closed, statute four-one-nine, and making physical threats when that prisoner has no way of defending himself, statute five-one-two.' Hessler took a pace back. 'But I'm confident that what will most influence the board when they come to consider your promotion, will be the question of why you had to leave the navy at such short notice.' The blood drained from Hessler's face. 'It certainly wasn't because you failed the exam when you applied to be an officer.'

'Who squealed?' said Hessler, his words barely a whisper.

'One of your former shipmates, who unfortunately ended up in here. You made sure he kept his mouth shut by giving him the job as deputy librarian. I expect nothing less.'

Harry handed his past month's work to Hessler, pausing to allow this latest piece of information to sink in before adding, 'I'll keep my mouth shut until the day I'm released – unless, of course, you give me some reason not to. And if you ever lay as much as a finger on me, I'll have you thrown out of the prison service even quicker than you were drummed out of the navy. Do I make myself clear?' Hessler nodded, but didn't speak. 'Also, should you decide to pick on any other unfortunate first-timers, all bets are off. Now get out of my cell.'

5

WHEN LLOYD STOOD to greet him at nine o'clock on his first morning as deputy librarian, Harry realized that he'd only ever seen the man sitting down. Lloyd was taller than he'd expected, well over six feet. Despite the unhealthy prison food he had a spare frame, and was one of the few prisoners who shaved every morning. With his swept-back, jet-black hair, he resembled an ageing matinee idol, rather than a man who was serving five years for fraud. Quinn didn't know the details of his crime, which meant that nobody other than the warden knew the full story. And the rule in jail was simple: if a prisoner didn't volunteer what he was in for, you didn't ask.

Lloyd took Harry through the daily routine, which the new deputy librarian had mastered by the time they went down for supper that evening. During the next few days he continued to quiz Lloyd with questions about matters like collecting overdue books, fines, and inviting prisoners to donate their own books to the library when they were released, which Lloyd hadn't even considered. Most of Lloyd's answers were monosyllabic, so Harry finally allowed him to return to a resting position at his desk, well hidden behind a copy of the *New York Times*.

Although there were nearly a thousand prisoners locked up in Lavenham, fewer than one in ten of them could read and write, and not all of those who could bothered to visit the library on a Tuesday, Thursday or Sunday.

Harry soon discovered that Max Lloyd was both lazy and devious. He didn't seem to mind how many initiatives his new deputy came up with, as long as it didn't involve him in any extra work.

Lloyd's main task seemed to be to keep a pot of coffee on the go, just in case an officer dropped by. Once the warden's copy of the previous day's *New York Times* had been delivered to the library, Lloyd settled down at his desk for the rest of the morning. He first turned to the book review section, and when he finished perusing it, he turned his attention to the classified ads, followed by the news, and finally sports. After lunch he would make a start on the crossword puzzle, which Harry would complete the following morning.

By the time Harry got the newspaper, it was already two days out of date. He always began with the international news pages, as he wanted to find out how the war in Europe was progressing. That was how he learned about the fall of France, and a few months later that Neville Chamberlain had resigned as Prime Minister, and Winston Churchill had succeeded him. Not everyone's first choice, although Harry would never forget the speech Churchill had made when he presented the prizes at Bristol Grammar School. He wasn't in any doubt that Britain was being led by the right man. Time and again Harry cursed the fact that he was a deputy librarian in an American prison, and not an officer in the Royal Navy.

During the last hour of the day, when even Harry couldn't find anything new to do, he brought his diary up to date.

‹◊›

It took Harry just over a month to reorganize all the books into their correct categories: first fiction, then non-fiction.

During the second month, he broke them down into even smaller classifications, so that prisoners didn't have to waste time searching for the only three books on woodwork that were on the shelves. He explained to Lloyd that when it came to non-fiction, the category was more important than the author's name. Lloyd shrugged.

On Sunday mornings, Harry would push the library cart around the four blocks, retrieving overdue books from prisoners, some of which hadn't been returned for more than a year. He had expected a few of the old-timers on D block to be resentful, even to take offence at the intrusion, but they all wanted to meet the man who'd got Hessler transferred to Pierpoint.

After his interview with the board, Hessler had been offered a senior post at Pierpoint, and he accepted the promotion as it was nearer his home town. While Harry never suggested he'd had anything to do with Hessler's transfer, that wasn't the story Quinn peddled from ear to ear until it became legend.

During his trips around the blocks in search of missing books, Harry often picked up anecdotes that he would record in his diary that evening.

The warden occasionally dropped into the library, not least because when Harry had appeared before the board, he'd described Mr Swanson's attitude to the education of inmates as bold, imaginative and far-seeing. Harry couldn't believe how much undeserved flattery the warden was quite happy to soak up.

After his first three months, loans were up by 14 per cent. When Harry asked the warden if he could instigate a reading class in the evenings, Swanson hesitated for a moment, but gave in when Harry repeated the words *bold, imaginative* and *far-seeing.*

Only three prisoners attended Harry's first class, and one of them was Pat Quinn, who could already read and write.

But by the end of the following month the class had grown to sixteen, even if several of them would have done almost anything to get out of their cells for an hour in the evening. But Harry managed to notch up one or two notable successes among the younger prisoners, and was continually reminded that just because you hadn't gone to the 'right' school, or hadn't gone to school at all, it didn't mean you were stupid – or the other way round, Quinn reminded him.

Despite all the extra activity Harry had initiated, he found he was still left with time on his hands, so he set himself the task of reading two new books a week. Once he'd conquered the few American classics in the library, he turned his attention to crime, by far the most popular category with his fellow inmates, taking up seven of the library's nineteen shelves.

Harry had always enjoyed Conan Doyle, and he was looking forward to turning his attention to his American rivals. He began with *The Bigger They Come* by Erle Stanley Gardner, before moving on to Raymond Chandler's *The Big Sleep*. He felt a little guilty about enjoying them so much. What would Mr Holcombe think?

During the last hour before the library closed, Harry would continue to bring his diary up to date. He was taken by surprise one evening when Lloyd, having finished the paper, asked if he could read it. Harry knew that Lloyd had been a literary agent in New York on the outside, which was how he'd landed the job in the library. He sometimes dropped the names of authors he'd represented, most of whom Harry had never heard of. Lloyd only spoke about how he'd ended up in Lavenham on one occasion, watching the door to make sure no one overheard.

'A bit of bad luck,' Lloyd explained. 'In good faith I invested some of my clients' money on the Stock Exchange, and when things didn't go quite according to plan, I was left carrying the bag.'

When Harry repeated the story to Quinn that night, he raised his eyes to the heavens.

'More likely he spent the money on slow nags and fast dames.'

'Then why go into such detail,' asked Harry, 'when he's never mentioned the reason he's in here to anyone else?'

'You're so naïve sometimes,' said Quinn. 'With you as the messenger, Lloyd knows there's a far better chance of the rest of us believing his story. Just be sure you never make a deal with that man, because he's got six fingers on each hand' – a pickpocket's expression that Harry recorded in his diary that night. But he didn't take much notice of Quinn's advice, partly because he couldn't imagine any circumstances in which he would make a deal with Max Lloyd, other than about whose turn it was to pour the coffee when the warden dropped in.

◄o►

By the end of his first year at Lavenham, Harry had filled three exercise books with his observations on prison life, and could only wonder how many more pages of this daily chronicle he'd manage before he completed his sentence.

He was surprised by how enthusiastic Lloyd was, always wanting to read the next instalment. He even suggested he might be allowed to show Harry's work to a publisher. Harry laughed.

'I can't imagine anyone would be interested in my ramblings.'

'You'd be surprised,' said Lloyd.

EMMA BARRINGTON

1939–1941

6

'SEBASTIAN ARTHUR CLIFTON,' said Emma, handing the sleeping child to his grandmother.

Maisie beamed as she took her grandson in her arms for the first time.

'They wouldn't let me come and see you before I was packed off to Scotland,' said Emma, making no attempt to hide her scorn. 'That's why I called you the moment I got back to Bristol.'

'That was kind of you,' said Maisie, as she stared intently at the little boy, trying to convince herself that Sebastian had inherited her husband's fair hair and clear blue eyes.

Emma sat at the kitchen table, smiled and sipped her tea: Earl Grey, how typical of Maisie to remember. And cucumber and salmon sandwiches, Harry's favourite, which must have emptied her ration book. As she looked around the room, her eyes settled on the mantelpiece, where she spotted a sepia photograph of a private soldier from the first war. How Emma wished she could see the shade of his hair, hidden under the helmet, or even the colour of his eyes. Were they blue, like Harry's, or brown, like hers? Arthur Clifton cut a dashing figure in his army uniform. The square jaw and the determined looked showed Emma that he'd been proud to serve his country. Her gaze moved on to a more recent photo of Harry singing in the St Bede's school choir, just before his voice broke, and next to that, propped against the wall, was an envelope displaying Harry's unmistakable hand. She assumed it was the last letter he had written to his mother before he died. She wondered if Maisie would allow her to read it. She stood up and walked across to the mantelpiece, and was surprised to find that the envelope hadn't been opened.

'I was so sorry to hear you had to leave Oxford,' Maisie ventured, when she saw Emma staring at the envelope.

'Given the choice of continuing with my degree or having Harry's child, there was no contest,' said Emma, her eyes still fixed on the letter.

'And Sir Walter tells me that your brother Giles joined the Wessex regiment, but has sadly been—'

'I see you had a letter from Harry,' interrupted Emma, unable to contain herself.

'No, it's not from Harry,' said Maisie. 'It's from a Lieutenant Thomas Bradshaw who served with him on the SS *Devonian*.'

'What does Lieutenant Bradshaw have to say?' asked Emma, aware that the envelope hadn't been opened.

'I've no idea,' said Maisie. 'A Dr Wallace delivered it to me, and said it was a letter of condolence. I didn't feel I needed any more reminders of Harry's death, so I never opened it.'

'But isn't it possible that it might throw some light on what happened on the *Devonian*?'

'I doubt it,' Maisie replied, 'after all, they'd only known each other for a few days.'

'Would you like me to read the letter to you, Mrs Clifton?' Emma asked, aware that Maisie might be embarrassed by having to admit she couldn't read.

'No, thank you, my dear,' Maisie replied. 'After all, it's not going to bring Harry back, is it?'

'I agree,' said Emma, 'but perhaps you would allow me to read it for my own peace of mind,' she said.

'With the Germans targeting the docks at night,' said Maisie, 'I hope Barrington's hasn't been too badly affected.'

'We've escaped a direct hit,' said Emma, reluctantly accepting that she wasn't going to be allowed to read the letter. 'Mind you, I doubt even the Germans would dare to drop a bomb on Gramps.'

Maisie laughed, and for a moment Emma considered snatching the envelope from the mantelpiece and ripping it open before Maisie could stop her. But Harry would never have approved of that. If Maisie were to leave the room, even for a moment, Emma would use the steaming kettle to unseal the envelope, check the signature and make sure it was back in its place before she returned.

But it was almost as if Maisie could read her thoughts, because she remained by the mantelpiece and didn't budge.

'Gramps tells me congratulations are in order,' said Emma, still refusing to give up.

Maisie blushed, and began to chat about her new appointment at the Grand Hotel. Emma's eyes remained on the envelope. She carefully checked the M, the C, the S, the H and the L in the address, knowing that she would have to keep the image of those letters in her mind's eye, like a photograph, until she returned to the Manor House. When Maisie handed little Sebastian back to her, explaining that sadly she had to get back to work, Emma reluctantly stood up, but not before she had given the envelope one last look.

On the way back to the Manor House, Emma tried to keep the image of the handwriting in her mind, thankful that Sebastian had fallen into a deep sleep. As soon as the car came to a halt on the gravel outside the front steps, Hudson opened the back door to allow Emma to get out and carry her son into the house. She took him straight up to the nursery, where Nanny Barrington was waiting for them. To Nanny's surprise, Emma kissed him on the forehead and left without a word.

Once she was in her own room, Emma unlocked the centre drawer of her writing desk and pulled out a stack of letters that Harry had written to her over the years.

The first thing she checked was the capital H of Harry's signature, so plain and bold, just like the H in Still House Lane on Maisie's unopened envelope. This gave her confidence to carry on with the quest. She next searched for a capital C, and eventually found one on a Christmas card, with the bonus of the capital M of Merry: the same M and the same C as Mrs Clifton on the envelope. Harry must surely be alive, she kept repeating out loud. Finding a Bristol was easy, but England was more difficult, until she came across a letter he'd written to her from Italy when they were both still at school. It took her over an hour to neatly cut out the thirty-nine letters and two numbers, before she was able to reproduce the address on the envelope.

> *Mrs M. Clifton*
> *27 Still House Lane*
> *Bristol*
> *England*

Emma collapsed exhausted on to her bed. She had no idea who Thomas Bradshaw was, but one thing was certain: the unopened letter propped on Maisie's mantelpiece had been written by Harry, and for some reason, best known to himself, he didn't want her to know he was still alive. She wondered if he would have thought differently had he known she was pregnant with his child, before he set off on that fateful voyage.

Emma was desperate to share the news that Harry might not be dead with her mother, Gramps, Grace and of course

Maisie, but she realized she would have to remain silent until she had more conclusive proof than an unopened letter. A plan began to form in her mind.

◄○►

Emma didn't go down for dinner that evening, but remained in her room and continued to try to fathom out why Harry would want everyone except his mother to believe he'd died that night.

When she climbed into bed just before midnight, she could only assume that it must have been for what he considered a matter of honour. Perhaps he imagined, poor, foolish, disillusioned man, that it would release her from any obligation she might feel towards him. Didn't he realize that from the first moment she'd set eyes on him, at her brother's birthday party when she was only ten years old, there was never going to be another man in her life?

Emma's family had been delighted when she and Harry became engaged eight years later, with the exception of her father, who had for so long been living a lie – a lie that wasn't exposed until the day of their wedding. The two of them were standing at the altar, about to take their vows, when Old Jack had brought the ceremony to an unrehearsed and unexpected close. The revelation that Emma's father might also be Harry's father didn't stop her loving Harry, and it never would. No one was surprised that Harry behaved like a gentleman, while Emma's father had remained true to his character, and behaved like a cad. One stood and faced the music, while the other slunk out of the back door of the vestry and hadn't been seen since.

Harry had made it clear, long before he asked Emma to be his wife, that if war was declared he wouldn't hesitate to leave Oxford and join the Royal Navy. He was a stubborn man at the best of times, and these were the worst of times. Emma realized there was no point in trying to dissuade him, as nothing she could say or do would have changed his mind. He had also warned her that he would not consider returning to Oxford until the Germans had surrendered.

Emma had also left Oxford early, but unlike Harry, she hadn't been given a choice. For her there would be no chance of returning. Pregnancy was frowned upon at Somerville, and even more so when you weren't married to the father. The decision must have broken her mother's heart. Elizabeth Barrington had so wanted her daughter to achieve the academic accolades that she had been denied for no other reason than her sex. A rare glimmer of light appeared on the horizon a year later, when Emma's younger sister Grace won an open scholarship to Girton College, Cambridge, and from the day she'd arrived in that seat of learning she had outshone the brightest men.

Once it became obvious that Emma was pregnant, she was whisked off to her grandfather's estate in Scotland, to give birth to Harry's child. Barringtons don't produce illegitimate offspring, at least not in Bristol. Sebastian was crawling around the castle before the prodigal daughter was allowed to return to the Manor House. Elizabeth had wanted them to remain at Mulgelrie until the war was over, but Emma had had more than enough of being hidden away in a remote Scottish castle.

One of the first people she visited after returning to the West Country was her grandfather, Sir Walter Barrington. It had been he who had told her that Harry had joined the crew of the SS *Devonian*, and planned to return to Bristol within the month, as he intended to sign up as an ordinary seaman on HMS *Resolution*. Harry never returned, and six weeks went by before she learned that her lover had been buried at sea.

Sir Walter had taken it upon himself to visit each

member of the family one by one, to inform them of the tragic news. He'd begun with Mrs Clifton, although he knew she had already heard what had happened from Dr Wallace, who had passed on Thomas Bradshaw's letter. He next travelled up to Scotland to break the news to Emma. Sir Walter was surprised that his granddaughter didn't shed a tear, but then Emma simply refused to accept that Harry was dead.

Once he'd returned to Bristol, Sir Walter visited Giles and told him the news. Harry's closest friend had sunk into a desolate silence, and there was nothing any of the family could say or do to console him. When Lord and Lady Harvey heard the news of Harry's death, they were stoical. A week later, when the family attended Captain Jack Tarrant's memorial service at Bristol Grammar School, Lord Harvey remarked that he was glad Old Jack had never found out what had happened to his protégé.

The only person in the family Sir Walter refused to visit was his son, Hugo. He made an excuse about not knowing how to get in touch with him, but when Emma returned to Bristol he admitted to her that even if he had known, he wouldn't have bothered, and added that her father was probably the one person who would be pleased that Harry was dead. Emma said nothing, but didn't doubt that he was right.

For several days after her visit to Maisie in Still House Lane, Emma had spent hours alone in her room endlessly considering what she might do with her new-found knowledge. She concluded that there was no way she could hope to discover the contents of the letter that had rested on the mantelpiece for more than a year, without harming her relationship with Maisie. However, Emma resolved not only to prove to the whole world that Harry was still alive, but to find him, wherever he might be. With that in mind, she made another appointment to see her grandfather. After all, Sir Walter Barrington was the only person other than Maisie who'd met Dr Wallace, so he must surely be her best chance of unravelling the mystery of exactly who Thomas Bradshaw was.

7

ONE THING Emma's grandfather had instilled in her from an early age was never to be late for an appointment. It gives the wrong impression, he told her; that is, if you want to be taken seriously.

With that in mind, Emma left the Manor House at 9.25 that morning, and was driven through the gates of Barrington's shipyard at exactly eight minutes to ten. The car parked outside Barrington House at six minutes to ten. By the time she stepped out of the lift on the fifth floor and walked down the corridor to the chairman's office, it was two minutes to ten.

Sir Walter's secretary, Miss Beale, opened the door of his office as the clock on his mantelpiece began to chime ten. The chairman smiled, rose from behind his desk and walked across the room to greet Emma with a kiss on both cheeks.

'And how is my favourite granddaughter?' he asked as he guided her to a comfortable chair by the fire.

'Grace is just fine, Gramps,' said Emma. 'Doing brilliantly at Cambridge, I'm told, and sends her love.'

'Don't get cheeky with me, young lady,' he said, returning her smile. 'And Sebastian, my favourite great-grandson, how's he coming along?'

'Your only great-grandson,' Emma reminded him as she settled back into a deep leather chair.

'As you haven't brought him with you, I assume you have something serious to discuss.'

The small talk had already been dispensed with. Emma knew that Sir Walter would have allocated a certain amount of time for the meeting. Miss Beale had once told her that visitors were granted fifteen minutes, thirty minutes or an hour, depending on how important he considered they were. Family were not exempt from this rule, except on Sunday. Emma had a number of questions she needed answered, so hoped he'd allotted her at least half an hour.

She sat back and tried to relax, because she didn't want Gramps to work out the real reason she wanted to see him.

'Do you remember when you kindly travelled up to Scotland,' she began, 'to let me know that Harry had been killed at sea? I'm afraid I was in such a state of shock that I didn't take it all in, so I hoped you might tell me a little more about the last few days of his life.'

'Of course, my dear,' said Sir Walter sympathetically. 'Let's hope my memory is up to it. Is there anything in particular you want to know?'

'You told me that Harry signed up as the fourth officer on the *Devonian* after he'd come down from Oxford.'

'That's right. It was my old friend Captain Havens who made it possible, and he was among the few survivors of the tragedy. When I visited him recently, he could not have spoken more warmly of Harry. He described him as a courageous young man, who not only saved his life after the ship had been hit by a torpedo, but sacrificed his own when he attempted to rescue the chief engineer.'

'Was Captain Havens also picked up by the *Kansas Star*?'

'No, by another ship that was in the vicinity, so sadly he never saw Harry again.'

'So he didn't witness Harry being buried at sea?'

'No. The only officer from the *Devonian* who was with

Harry when he died was an American, called Lieutenant Thomas Bradshaw.'

'You told me that a Dr Wallace delivered a letter from Lieutenant Bradshaw to Mrs Clifton.'

'That's correct. Dr Wallace was the chief medical officer on the *Kansas Star*. He assured me that he and his team did everything in their power to save Harry's life.'

'Did Bradshaw write to you as well?'

'No, only to the next of kin, if I recall Dr Wallace's words.'

'Then don't you find it strange that he didn't write to me?'

Sir Walter fell silent for some time. 'You know, I've never really given it any thought. Perhaps Harry never mentioned you to Bradshaw. You know how secretive he could be.'

Emma had often thought about it, but moved quickly on. 'Did you read the letter he sent to Mrs Clifton?'

'No, I didn't. But I saw it on the mantelpiece when I visited her the following day.'

'Do you think Dr Wallace had any idea what Bradshaw had written in that letter?'

'Yes. He told me it was a letter of condolence from a fellow officer who had served with Harry on the *Devonian*.'

'If only I could meet Lieutenant Bradshaw,' said Emma, fishing.

'I don't know how you'll manage that, my dear,' said Sir Walter, 'unless Wallace kept in touch with him.'

'Do you have an address for Dr Wallace?'

'Only care of the *Kansas Star*.'

'But surely they must have stopped sailing to Bristol when war was declared.'

'Not as long as there are Americans stranded in England who are willing to pay through the nose to get home.'

'Isn't that taking an unnecessary risk, with so many German U-boats patrolling the Atlantic?'

'Not while America remains neutral,' said Sir Walter. 'The last thing Hitler wants is to start a war with the Yanks simply because one of his U-boats sank an American passenger ship.'

'Do you know if the *Kansas Star* is expected to return to Bristol in the near future?'

'No, but I can easily find out.' The old man heaved himself out of his chair and walked slowly across to his desk. He began to flick through page after page of the monthly timetable of dockings.

'Ah, here it is,' he eventually said. 'She's due out of New York in four weeks' time, and is expected in Bristol on the fifteenth of November. If you're hoping to get in touch with anyone on board, be warned, she won't be hanging around for long, as it's the one place she'll be vulnerable to attack.'

'Will I be allowed on board?'

'Not unless you're a crew member or looking for a job, and frankly I can't see you as either a deckhand or a cocktail waitress.'

'So how can I get to see Dr Wallace?'

'You'll just have to wait on the dockside in the hope that he'll come ashore. Almost everyone does after a week-long voyage. So if he's on the ship, I'm sure you'll catch him. But don't forget, Emma, it's more than a year since Harry died, so Wallace may no longer be the ship's medical officer.' Emma bit her lip. 'But if you'd like me to arrange a private meeting with the captain, I'd be happy—'

'No, no,' said Emma quickly, 'it's not that important.'

'If you change your mind—' began Sir Walter, suddenly realizing just how important Emma considered it to be.

'No, thank you, Gramps,' she said as she rose from her place. 'Thank you for giving me so much of your time.'

'Not nearly enough,' said the old man. 'I only wish you'd

drop in more often. And make sure you bring Sebastian with you next time,' he added as he accompanied her to the door.

Sir Walter was no longer in any doubt why his grand-daughter had come to see him.

—◦—

In the car on the way back to the Manor House, one sentence remained etched in Emma's mind. She played the words over and over, like a gramophone needle stuck in a groove.

Once she had returned home, she joined Sebastian in the nursery. He had to be coaxed off his rocking horse, but not before a few tears had been shed. After lunch he curled up like a satisfied cat, and fell into a deep sleep. Nanny put him to bed while Emma rang for the chauffeur.

'I'd like to be driven back into Bristol, Hudson.'

'Anywhere in particular, miss?'

'The Grand Hotel.'

—◦—

'You want me to do what?' said Maisie.

'Take me on as a waitress.'

'But why?'

'I'd prefer not to tell you.'

'Do you have any idea how hard the work is?'

'No,' admitted Emma, 'but I won't let you down.'

'And when do you want to start?'

'Tomorrow.'

'Tomorrow?'

'Yes.'

'For how long?'

'One month.'

'Now let me try and get this straight,' said Maisie. 'You want me to train you as a waitress, starting tomorrow, and you'll be leaving in a month's time, but you won't tell me why?'

'That's about it.'

'Are you expecting to be paid?'

'No,' said Emma.

'Well, that's a relief.'

'So when do I start?'

'Six o'clock tomorrow morning.'

'Six o'clock?' repeated Emma in disbelief.

'This may come as a surprise, Emma, but I have customers who need to be fed by seven, and at work by eight, so you'll have to make sure you're at your station by six – every morning.'

'My station?'

'I'll explain if you turn up before six.'

--◦--

Emma wasn't late for work once in the next twenty-eight days, possibly because Jenkins tapped on her door at 4.30 every morning, and Hudson dropped her off a hundred yards from the staff entrance of the Grand Hotel by 5.45.

Miss Dickens, as she was known by the rest of the staff, took advantage of her acting skills to make sure that no one worked out that she was a Barrington.

Mrs Clifton showed Emma no favours when she spilt some soup over a regular customer, and even less when she dropped a stack of plates that shattered in the middle of the dining room. The cost would normally have been deducted from her pay packet, if she'd had one. And it was some time before Emma got the knack of using her shoulder to barge through the swing doors that led in and out of the kitchen without colliding with another waitress coming from the opposite direction.

Despite this, Maisie quickly discovered that she only had to tell Emma something once, and she never forgot it. She was also impressed how quickly Emma could turn a table round, although she'd never laid one before in her life. And while most trainees took several weeks to master the skill of silver service, some never managing it, Emma didn't need any further supervision by the end of her second week.

By the end of her third, Maisie wished she wasn't leaving, and by the end of the fourth, so did several regulars, who were insisting that only Miss Dickens must serve them.

Maisie was becoming anxious about how she was going to explain to the hotel manager that Miss Dickens had given in her notice after only a month.

'You can tell Mr Hurst that I've been offered a better job, with more pay,' said Emma as she began folding up her uniform.

'He's not going to be pleased,' said Maisie. 'It might have been easier if you'd turned out to be useless, or at least been late a few times.' Emma laughed, and placed her little white cap neatly on top of her clothes for the last time.

'Is there anything else I can do for you, Miss Dickens?' asked Maisie.

'Yes please,' said Emma. 'I need a reference.'

'Applying for another unpaid job, are you?'

'Something like that,' replied Emma, feeling a little guilty that she wasn't able to take Harry's mother into her confidence.

'Then I'll dictate a reference, you write it, and I'll sign it,' she said, passing Emma a sheet of the hotel's headed notepaper. 'To whom it may concern,' Maisie began. 'During the short time—'

'Could I possibly leave out "short"?' asked Emma.

Maisie smiled.

'During the time Miss Dickens has been with us at the Grand' – Emma wrote 'Miss Barrington', but didn't tell her – 'she has proved hard-working, efficient and popular with both the customers and staff. Her skills as a waitress are impressive, and her ability to learn on the job convinces me that any establishment would be fortunate to have her as a member of their staff. We will be sorry to lose her, and should she ever want to return to this hotel, we would welcome her back.'

Emma smiled as she handed the sheet of paper back. Maisie scribbled her signature above the words *Restaurant Manageress*.

'Thank you,' said Emma, wrapping her arms around her.

'I have no idea what you're up to, my dear,' said Maisie, once Emma had released her, 'but whatever it is, I wish you luck.'

Emma wanted to tell her, I'm going in search of your son, and I won't return until I've found him.

8

EMMA HAD BEEN standing on the dockside for over an hour when she spotted the *Kansas Star* nosing its way into port, but it was another hour before the ship finally docked.

During that time, Emma thought about the decision she'd made, and was already beginning to wonder if she had the courage to go through with it. She tried to dismiss from her thoughts the sinking of the *Athenia* a few months before, and the possibility of never even making it to New York.

She had written a long letter to her mother, trying to explain why she'd be away for a couple of weeks – three at the most – and only hoped she would understand. But she couldn't write a letter to Sebastian to let him know that she was going in search of his father, and was already missing him. She kept trying to convince herself that she was doing it as much for her son as for herself.

Sir Walter had once again offered to introduce her to the captain of the *Kansas Star*, but Emma had politely declined, as it didn't fit in with her plan to remain anonymous. He'd also given her a vague description of Dr Wallace, and certainly no one who looked remotely like that had disembarked from the ship that morning. However, Sir Walter was able to pass on two other valuable pieces of information. The *Kansas Star* would be departing on the last tide that evening. And the purser could usually be found in his office between the hours of two and five every afternoon, completing embarkation forms. More important, he was responsible for the employment of non-crew members of staff.

Emma had written to her grandfather the day before to thank him for his help, but she still didn't let him know what she was up to, although she had a feeling he'd worked it out.

After the clock on Barrington House had struck twice, and there was still no sign of Dr Wallace, Emma picked up her small suitcase and decided the time had come to walk the gangplank. When she stepped nervously on to the deck, she asked the first person she saw in uniform the way to the purser's office, and was told lower deck aft.

She spotted a passenger disappearing down a wide staircase, and followed her to what she assumed must be the lower deck, but as she had no idea where aft was, she joined a queue at the information desk.

Behind the counter stood two girls, dressed in dark blue uniforms and white blouses. They were attempting to answer every passenger's query while keeping smiles etched on their faces.

'How can I help you, miss?' one of them asked when Emma eventually reached the front of the queue. The girl clearly assumed she was a passenger, and in fact Emma had considered paying for her passage to New York, but had decided she was more likely to find out what she needed to know if she signed on as a member of the crew.

'Where will I find the purser's office?' she asked.

'Second door on the right down that companionway,' replied the girl. 'You can't miss it.'

Emma followed her pointing finger, and when she reached a door marked *Purser* she took a deep breath and knocked.

'Come in.'

Emma opened the door and stepped inside to find a smartly dressed officer seated behind a desk that was strewn with forms. He wore a crisp, open-necked white shirt which had two gold epaulettes on each shoulder.

'How can I help you?' he asked in an accent she'd never heard before, and could hardly decipher.

'I'm looking for a job as a waitress, sir,' said Emma, hoping she sounded like one of the maids at the Manor House.

'Sorry,' he said, looking back down. 'Don't need any more waitresses. The only available position is on the information desk.'

'I'd be happy to work there,' said Emma, reverting to her normal voice.

The purser gave her a closer look. 'The pay's not good,' he warned her, 'and the hours are worse.'

'I'm used to that,' said Emma.

'And I can't offer you a permanent position,' continued the purser, 'because one of my girls is on shore leave in New York, and will be rejoining the ship after this crossing.'

'That's not a problem,' said Emma without explanation.

The purser still didn't look convinced. 'Can you read and write?'

Emma would like to have told him that she'd won a scholarship to Oxford, but simply said, 'Yes, sir.'

Without another word, he pulled open a drawer and extracted a long form, passed her a fountain pen and said, 'Fill this in.' As Emma began to answer the questions, he added, 'And I'll also need to see a reference.'

Once Emma had completed the form, she opened her bag and handed over Maisie's letter of recommendation.

'Very impressive,' he said. 'But are you sure you're suited to being a receptionist?'

'It was going to be my next job at the Grand,' Emma said. 'All part of my training to be a manageress.'

'Then why give up that opportunity to join us?'

'I have a great-aunt who lives in New York, and my mother wants me to stay with her until the war is over.'

This time the purser did look convinced, as it wasn't the first time someone had wanted to work their passage in order to get away from England. 'Then let's get you started,' he said, jumping up. He marched out of the office and led her on the short journey back to the information desk.

'Peggy, I've found someone to replace Dana on this voyage, so you better get her started straight away.'

'Thank God for that,' said Peggy, lifting a flap so Emma could join her behind the counter. 'What's your name?' she asked in the same almost impenetrable accent. For the first time Emma understood what Bernard Shaw had meant when he suggested that the English and the Americans were divided by a common language.

'Emma Barrington.'

'Well, Emma, this is my assistant, Trudy. As we're so busy, perhaps you could just observe for now, and we'll try to fill you in as we go along.'

Emma took a pace back and watched as the two girls handled everything that was thrown at them, while somehow managing to keep smiling.

Within an hour, Emma knew at what time and where passengers should report for lifeboat drill, which deck the grill room was on, how far out to sea they had to be before passengers could order a drink, where they might find a partner for a round of bridge after dinner, and how to get to the upper deck if you wanted to watch the sunset.

For the next hour, Emma listened to most of the same questions being asked again and again, and during the third, she took a step forward and began to respond to the passengers' queries herself, only occasionally needing to refer to the other two girls.

Peggy was impressed, and when the queue had dwindled

to a few latecomers, she said to Emma, 'Time to show you your quarters and grab some supper while the passengers are having a pre-dinner drink.' She turned to Trudy and added, 'I'll be back around seven to relieve you,' then lifted the flap and stepped out from behind the desk. Trudy nodded as another passenger came forward.

'Can you tell me if we have to dress for dinner tonight?'

'Not on the first night, sir,' came back the firm reply, 'but every other night.'

Peggy never stopped chatting as she led Emma down a long corridor, arriving at the top of some roped-off steps with a sign declaring in bold red letters, CREW ONLY.

'This leads to our quarters,' she explained as she un-hooked the rope. 'You're going to have to share a cabin with me,' Peggy added as they walked down, 'because Dana's bunk is the only one available at the moment.'

'That's fine,' said Emma.

Down, down and down they went; the stairwells becoming more cramped with each deck. Peggy only stopped talking when a crew member stood aside to let them pass. Occasionally she would reward them with a warm smile. Emma had never come across anyone like Peggy in her life: so fiercely independent, yet somehow she managed to remain feminine, with her bobbed fair hair, skirt that only just fell below the knees, and tight jacket that left you in no doubt how good her figure was.

'This is our cabin,' she said finally. 'It's where you'll be sleeping for the next week. I hope you weren't expecting anything palatial.'

Emma entered a cabin that was smaller than any room at the Manor House, including the broom cupboard.

'Ghastly, isn't it?' said Peggy. 'In fact, this old tub has only one thing going for it.' Emma didn't need to ask what that might be, because Peggy was only too happy to answer her own questions, as well as Emma's. 'The male to female ratio is better than almost anywhere else on earth,' said Peggy, laughing, before she added, 'That's Dana's bunk, and this is mine. As you can see, there isn't enough room for two people in here at the same time, unless one of them is in bed. I'll leave you to get unpacked, and come back in half an hour to take you down to the staff canteen for supper.'

Emma wondered how they could go any further down, but Peggy had disappeared before she could ask. She sat on her bunk in a daze. How could she get Peggy to answer all of her questions if she never stopped talking? Or might that turn out to be an advantage; would she, given time, reveal everything Emma needed to know? She had a whole week to find out, so felt she could afford to be patient. She began to stuff her few possessions into a drawer that Dana had made no attempt to empty.

Two long blasts on the ship's horn, and a moment later she felt a little shudder. Although there was no porthole to look through, she could feel that they were on the move. She sat back down on her bunk and tried to convince herself she'd made the right decision. Although she planned to return to Bristol within a month, she was already missing Sebastian.

She began to look more carefully at what would be her residence for the next week. On each side of the cabin a narrow bunk was attached to the wall, whose dimensions assumed that any occupant would be below average height. She lay down and tested a mattress that didn't give, because it hadn't any springs, and rested her head on a pillow that was filled with foam rubber, not feathers. There was a small washbasin with two taps, both of which delivered the same trickle of tepid water.

She put on Dana's uniform, and tried not to laugh. When Peggy returned, she did laugh. Dana must have been at least three inches shorter and certainly three sizes larger than Emma. 'Be thankful it's only for a week,' said Peggy as she led Emma off for supper.

They descended even further into the bowels of the ship to join the other members of the crew. Several young men and one or two older ones invited Peggy to join them at their table. She favoured a tall young man who, she told Emma, was an engineer. Emma wondered if that explained why it wasn't only his hair that was covered in oil. The three of them joined the queue at the hotplate. The engineer filled his plate with almost everything on offer. Peggy managed about half, while Emma, feeling a little queasy, satisfied herself with a biscuit and an apple.

After supper, Peggy and Emma returned to the information desk to relieve Trudy. As the passengers' dinner was served at eight, few of them appeared at the desk, other than those who needed to ask for directions to the dining room.

During the next hour, Emma learnt a great deal more about Peggy than she did about the SS *Kansas Star*. When they came to the end of their shift at ten o'clock, they pulled down the grille and Peggy led her new companion back towards the lower deck staircase.

'Do you want to join us for a drink in the staff canteen?' she asked.

'No, thank you,' said Emma. 'I'm exhausted.'

'Do you think you can find your way back to the cabin?'

'Lower deck seven, room one-one-three. If I'm not in bed by the time you get back, send out a search party.'

As soon as Emma had entered her cabin, she quickly undressed, washed and slipped under the single sheet and blanket provided. She lay on the bunk trying to settle, her knees almost tucked under her chin, while the irregular bobbing of the vessel meant that she couldn't remain in the same position for more than a few moments. Her last thoughts before she drifted into a fitful sleep were of Sebastian.

Emma woke with a start. It was so dark she had no way of checking the time on her watch. At first she assumed the swaying was caused by the movement of the ship, until her eyes focused and she was able to make out two bodies in the bunk on the other side of the cabin, moving rhythmically up and down. One of the bodies had legs that stretched far beyond the end of the bunk and were braced against the wall; it had to be the engineer. Emma wanted to laugh, but she just lay very still until Peggy let out a long sigh and the movement stopped. A few moments later, the feet attached to the long legs touched the floor and began to wriggle into some old overalls. Not long afterwards, the cabin door opened and closed quietly. Emma fell into a deep sleep.

9

When Emma woke the following morning, Peggy was already up and dressed.

'I'm off for breakfast,' she announced. 'I'll see you at the desk later. By the way, we're expected on duty at eight.'

The moment the door closed, Emma jumped out of bed, and after she'd washed slowly and dressed quickly, she realized there wouldn't be any time for breakfast if she hoped to be behind the information desk on time.

Once she'd reported for work, Emma quickly discovered that Peggy took her job very seriously and put herself out to assist any passenger who needed her help. During their morning coffee break Emma said, 'One of the passengers asked me about doctor's surgery hours.'

'Seven to eleven in the morning,' replied Peggy, 'four to six in the afternoon. In case of an emergency, dial one-one-one on the nearest telephone.'

'And the doctor's name?'

'Parkinson. Dr Parkinson. He's the one man every girl on board has a crush on.'

'Oh – one of the passengers thought it was a Dr Wallace.'

'No, Wally retired about six months ago. Sweet old thing.'

Emma asked no more questions during the break, just drank coffee.

'Why don't you spend the rest of the morning finding your way around, so you know where you're sending everyone,' Peggy suggested once they'd reported back to the desk. She handed Emma a guide to the ship. 'See you for lunch.'

With the guidebook open, Emma began her quest on the upper deck: the dining rooms, the bars, the card room, a library, and even a ballroom with a resident jazz band. She only stopped to take a closer look when she came across the infirmary on lower deck two, tentatively opening the double doors and poking her head inside. Two neatly made, unoccupied beds stood against the wall on the far side of the room. Had Harry slept in one and Lieutenant Bradshaw in the other?

'Can I help you?' said a voice.

Emma swung round to see a tall man in a long white coat. She immediately understood why Peggy had a crush on him.

'I've just started on the information desk,' she blurted out, 'and I'm meant to be finding out where everything is.'

'I'm Simon Parkinson,' he said, giving her a friendly smile. 'Now you've found out where I am, you're most welcome to drop in at any time.'

'Thank you,' said Emma. She quickly stepped back into the corridor, closed the door behind her and hurried away. She couldn't remember the last time someone had flirted with her, but she wished it had been Dr Wallace. She spent the rest of the morning exploring each deck until she felt she'd mastered the ship's layout and would be able to tell any passenger where everything was with more confidence.

She was looking forward to spending the afternoon testing out her new skills, but Peggy asked her to go over the passenger files in the same way she'd studied the ship. Emma sat alone in the back office, learning about people she would never see again in her life.

In the evening she made an attempt to eat supper, beans on toast and a glass of lemonade, but she was back in her cabin soon afterwards, hoping to catch some sleep in case the engineer returned.

When the door opened, the light in the corridor woke her. Emma couldn't make out who it was that entered the cabin, but it certainly wasn't the engineer, because his feet didn't reach the wall. She lay awake for forty minutes, and didn't get back to sleep until the door had opened and closed again.

<o>

Emma quickly became accustomed to the routine of the daily work followed by the nocturnal visits. These visits didn't vary greatly, only the men, although on one occasion the amorous visitor headed for Emma's bunk and not Peggy's.

'Wrong girl,' said Emma firmly.

'Sorry,' came back the reply, before he changed direction. Peggy must have assumed she had fallen asleep, because after the couple had made love, Emma could hear every word of their whispered conversation.

'Do you think your friend's available?'

'Why, have you taken a shine to her?' giggled Peggy.

'No, not me, but I know someone who'd like to be the first man to unbutton Dana's uniform.'

'Not a hope. She's got a boyfriend back home in Bristol, and I'm told even Dr Parkinson didn't make an impression on her.'

'Pity,' said the voice.

<o>

Peggy and Trudy often talked about the morning that nine sailors from the *Devonian* had been buried at sea before breakfast. With some subtle prompts, Emma was able to gain information that neither her grandfather nor Maisie could possibly have known. But with only three days left before they reached New York, she was no nearer to discovering if it was Harry or Lieutenant Bradshaw who'd survived.

On the fifth day, Emma took charge of the desk for the first time, and there were no surprises. The surprise came on the fifth night.

When the cabin door opened at whatever hour it was, a man once again headed for Emma's bunk, but this time when she said, 'Wrong girl,' firmly, he left immediately. She lay awake wondering who it could possibly have been.

On the sixth day, Emma learnt nothing new about Harry or Tom Bradshaw, and was beginning to fear that she might arrive in New York without any leads to follow up. It was during dinner that night that she decided to ask Peggy about 'the one that survived'.

'I only met Tom Bradshaw once,' said Peggy, 'when he was roaming around the deck with his nurse. Well, come to think of it, he wasn't exactly roaming, because the poor man was on crutches.'

'Did you speak to him?' asked Emma.

'No, he seemed very shy. In any case, Kristin didn't let him out of her sight.'

'Kristin?'

'She was the hospital nurse at the time, worked alongside Dr Wallace. Between them, they undoubtedly saved Tom Bradshaw's life.'

'So you never saw him again?'

'Only when we docked in New York, and I spotted him going ashore with Kristin.'

'He left the ship with Kristin?' said Emma anxiously. 'Was Dr Wallace with them?'

'No, just Kristin and her boyfriend Richard.'

'Richard?' said Emma, sounding relieved.

'Yes, Richard something. I can't remember his surname. He was the third officer. Not long afterwards he married Kristin, and we never saw either of them again.'

'Was he a good-looking man?' asked Emma.

'Tom or Richard?' asked Peggy.

'Can I get you a drink, Peg?' asked a young man Emma had never seen before, but had a feeling she would be seeing in profile later that night.

Emma was right, and she didn't sleep before, during or after the visit, as she had something else on her mind.

–◦–

The following morning, for the first time on the voyage, Emma was standing behind the information desk waiting for Peggy to appear.

'Shall I prepare the passenger list for disembarkation?' she asked when Peggy finally arrived and lifted the counter flap.

'You're the first person I've ever known to volunteer for that job,' said Peggy, 'but be my guest. Someone has to make sure it's up to date in case immigration decides to double-check any of the passengers' details once we've docked in New York.'

Emma went straight through to the back office. Putting aside the current passenger list, she turned her attention to the files of past crew members, which she found in a separate cabinet that looked as if it hadn't been opened for some time.

She began a slow, meticulous search for the names Kristin and Richard. Kristin proved easy, because there was only one person with that name, and she'd worked as a senior staff nurse on the *Kansas Star* from 1936 to 1939. However, there were several Richards, Dicks and Dickies, but the address of one of them, Lieutenant Richard Tibbet, was in the same Manhattan apartment building as Miss Kristin Craven.

Emma made a note of the address.

10

'WELCOME TO the United States, Miss Barrington.'

'Thank you,' said Emma.

'How long do you plan to be in the United States?' asked the immigration officer as he checked her passport.

'A week, two at the most,' said Emma. 'I'm visiting my great-aunt, and then I'll be returning to England.' It was true that Emma had a great-aunt who lived in New York, Lord Harvey's sister, but she had no intention of visiting her, not least because she didn't want the rest of the family to find out what she was up to.

'Your great-aunt's address?'

'Sixty-fourth and Park.'

The immigration officer made a note, stamped Emma's passport and handed it back to her.

'Enjoy your stay in the Big Apple, Miss Barrington.'

Once Emma had passed through immigration, she joined a long queue of passengers from the *Kansas Star*. It was another twenty minutes before she climbed into the back of a yellow cab.

'I require a small, sensibly priced hotel, located near Merton Street in Manhattan,' she told the driver.

'You wanna run that past me again, lady?' said the cabbie, the stub of an unlit cigar protruding from the corner of his mouth.

As Emma had found it difficult to understand a word he said, she assumed he was having the same problem. 'I'm looking for a small, inexpensive hotel near Merton Street, on Manhattan Island,' she said, slowly enunciating each word.

'Merton Street,' repeated the driver, as if it was the only thing he'd understood.

'That's right,' said Emma.

'Why didn't you say so the first time?'

The driver took off, and didn't speak again until he'd dropped his fare outside a red-brick building that flew a flag proclaiming *The Mayflower Hotel*.

'That'll be forty cents,' said the cabbie, the cigar bobbing up and down with each word.

Emma paid the fare from the wage packet she'd earned while on the ship. Once she'd checked into the hotel, she took the lift to the fourth floor and went straight to her room. The first thing she did was to get undressed and run herself a hot bath.

When she reluctantly climbed out, she dried herself with a large fluffy towel, dressed in what she considered a demure frock and made her way back down to the ground floor. She felt almost human.

Emma found a quiet table in the corner of the hotel coffee shop and ordered a cup of tea – they hadn't heard of Earl Grey – and a club sandwich, something she'd never heard of. While she waited to be served, she began to write out a long list of questions on a paper napkin, hoping there would be someone living at 46 Merton Street who was willing to answer them.

Once she'd signed the check, another new word, Emma asked the receptionist for directions to Merton Street. Three blocks north, two blocks west, she was told. She hadn't realized that every New Yorker possessed a built-in compass.

Emma enjoyed the walk, stopping several times to

admire windows filled with merchandise she had never seen in Bristol. She arrived outside a high-rise apartment block just after midday, unsure what she would do if Mrs Tibbet wasn't at home.

A smartly dressed doorman saluted and opened the door for her. 'Can I help you?'

'I've come to see Mrs Tibbet,' Emma said, trying to sound as if she was expected.

'Apartment thirty-one, on the third floor,' he said, touching the rim of his cap.

It was true, an English accent did appear to open doors.

As the elevator made its way slowly up to the third floor, Emma rehearsed some lines she hoped would open another door. When the elevator stopped, she pulled back the grille, stepped out into the corridor and went in search of number 31. There was a tiny circle of glass set in the middle of the Tibbets' door, which reminded Emma of a Cyclops eye. She couldn't see in, but she assumed the occupants could see out. A more familiar buzzer was on the wall beside the door. She pressed it and waited. It was some time before the door eventually opened, but only a few inches, revealing a brass chain. Two eyes peered out at her.

'What do you want?' asked a voice that she could at least understand.

'I'm sorry to bother you, Mrs Tibbet,' said Emma, 'but you may be my last chance.' The eyes looked suspicious. 'You see, I'm desperately trying to find Tom.'

'Tom?' repeated the voice.

'Tom Bradshaw. He's the father of my child,' said Emma, playing her last door-opening card.

The door closed, the chain was removed and the door opened once again to reveal a young woman carrying a baby in her arms.

'I'm sorry about that,' she said, 'but Richard doesn't like me opening the door to strangers. Please come in.' She led

Emma through to the living room. 'Have a seat while I put Jake back in his cot.'

Emma sat down and glanced around the room. There were several photographs of Kristin with a young naval officer who she assumed must be her husband, Richard.

Kristin returned a few minutes later carrying a tray of coffee. 'Black or white?'

'White please,' said Emma, who'd never drunk coffee in England, but was quickly learning that Americans don't drink tea, even in the morning.

'Sugar?' enquired Kristin after she'd poured two coffees.

'No, thank you.'

'So, is Tom your husband?' asked Kristin as she sat down opposite Emma.

'No, I'm his fiancée. To be fair, he had no idea I was pregnant.'

'How did you find me?' asked Kristin, still sounding a little apprehensive.

'The purser on the *Kansas Star* said you and Richard were among the last people to see Tom.'

'That's true. We were with him until he was arrested a few moments after he stepped on shore.'

'Arrested?' said Emma in disbelief. 'What could he possibly have done to get himself arrested?'

'He was accused of murdering his brother,' said Kristin. 'But surely you knew that?'

Emma burst into tears, her hopes shattered by the realization that it must have been Bradshaw who'd survived, and not Harry. If Harry had been accused of murdering Bradshaw's brother, it would have been so easy for him to prove they'd arrested the wrong man.

If only she'd ripped open the letter on Maisie's mantelpiece, she would have discovered the truth and not put herself through this ordeal. She wept, accepting for the first time that Harry was dead.

GILES BARRINGTON

1939–1941

11

When Sir Walter Barrington visited his grandson to tell him the terrible news that Harry Clifton had been killed at sea, Giles felt numb, as if he'd lost a limb. In fact, he would have been happy to lose a limb if it would have brought Harry back. The two of them had been inseparable since childhood, and Giles had always assumed they would both score one of life's centuries. Harry's pointless, unnecessary death made Giles even more determined not to make the same mistake himself.

Giles was in the drawing room listening to Mr Churchill on the radio when Emma asked, 'Do you have any plans to join up?'

'Yes, I shan't be returning to Oxford. I intend to sign up immediately.'

His mother was clearly surprised, but told him that she understood. Emma gave him a huge hug, and said, 'Harry would be proud of you.' Grace, who rarely displayed any emotion, burst into tears.

Giles drove into Bristol the following morning and parked his yellow MG ostentatiously outside the front door of the recruiting office. He marched in with what he hoped was resolution written across his face. A sergeant major from the Gloucesters – Captain Jack Tarrant's old regiment – stood smartly to attention the moment he saw young Mr

Barrington. He handed Giles a form which he dutifully filled in, and an hour later he was invited to step behind a curtain and be examined by an army doctor.

The doctor placed a tick in every box after he'd thoroughly checked this latest recruit – ears, nose, throat, chest and limbs – before finally testing his eyesight. Giles stood behind a white line and recited the letters and numbers on demand; after all, he could dispatch a leather ball coming straight at him at ninety miles an hour, to the most distant boundary. He was confident he would pass with flying colours, until the doctor asked him if he was aware of any hereditary ailments or diseases in his family. Giles replied truthfully, 'Both my father and grandfather are colour-blind.'

The doctor carried out a further series of tests, and Giles noticed that the ums and ahs turned into tut-tuts.

'I'm sorry to have to tell you, Mr Barrington,' he said when he came to the end of his examination, 'that given your family's medical history, I will not be able to recommend you for active service. But of course, there's nothing to stop you joining up and doing a desk job.'

'Can't you just tick the relevant box, doctor, and forget I ever raised the damn subject?' said Giles, trying to sound desperate.

The doctor ignored his protest, and in the final box on the form he wrote 'C3': unfit for active service.

Giles was back at the Manor House in time for lunch. His mother, Elizabeth, didn't comment on the fact that he drank almost a bottle of wine. He told everyone who asked, and several who didn't, that he'd been rejected by the Gloucesters because he suffered from colour-blindness.

'It didn't stop Grandfather fighting the Boers,' Grace reminded him after he'd been served with a second helping of pudding.

'They probably had no idea the condition existed back then,' said Giles, trying to make light of her barb.

Emma followed up with a punch below the belt. 'You never intended to sign up in the first place, did you?' she said, looking her brother in the eye. Giles was staring down at his shoes when she delivered the knock-out blow. 'Pity your friend from the docks isn't here to remind you that he was also colour-blind.'

When Giles's mother heard the news she was clearly relieved, but didn't comment. Grace didn't speak to her brother again before she returned to Cambridge.

—◦—

Giles drove back to Oxford the following day trying to convince himself that everyone would accept the reason he'd been unable to sign up and intended to continue his life as an undergraduate. When he strolled through the college gates, he found that the quad resembled a recruiting centre rather than a university, with young men in uniform outnumbering those wearing subfusc. In Giles's opinion, the only good thing to come out of all this was that for the first time in history there were as many women as men up at the university. Unfortunately, most of them were only willing to be seen on the arm of someone in uniform.

Giles's old school friend Deakins was one of the few undergraduates who didn't seem uncomfortable about not signing up. Mind you, there wouldn't have been much point in Deakins taking a medical. It would have been one of the rare exams in which he failed to get a tick in any box. But then he suddenly disappeared, to somewhere called Bletchley Park. No one could tell Giles what they got up to there, except it was all 'hush-hush', and Deakins warned Giles that he wouldn't be able to visit him at any time, under any circumstances.

As the months passed, Giles began to spend more time alone in the pub than in the crowded lecture theatre, while Oxford began to fill up with servicemen returning from the Front, some with one arm, others with one leg, a few who were blind, and they were just in his college. He tried to carry on as if he hadn't noticed, but the truth was, by the end of term, he began to feel more and more out of place.

◄○►

Giles drove up to Scotland at the end of term to attend the christening of Sebastian Arthur Clifton. Only the immediate family and one or two close friends were invited to the ceremony that took place in the chapel at Mulgelrie Castle. Emma and Giles's father was not among them.

Giles was surprised and delighted when Emma asked him to be a godfather, although he was somewhat taken aback when she admitted that the only reason she'd even considered him was that, despite everything, she had no doubt he would have been Harry's first choice.

As he was going down to breakfast the following morning, Giles noticed a light coming from his grandfather's study. As he passed the door on his way to the dining room, Giles heard his name come up in conversation. He stopped in his tracks, and took a step nearer to the half-open door. He froze in horror when he heard Sir Walter saying, 'It pains me to have to say this, but like father, like son.'

'I agree,' replied Lord Harvey. 'And I'd always thought so highly of the boy, which makes the whole damn business all the more distasteful.'

'No one,' said Sir Walter, 'could have been prouder than I was, as chairman of the governors, when Giles was appointed head boy of Bristol Grammar School.'

'I'd assumed,' said Lord Harvey, 'that he would put those remarkable talents of leadership and courage he displayed so often on the playing field to good use on the battlefield.'

'The only good thing to come out of all this,' suggested Sir Walter, 'is that I no longer believe that Harry Clifton could possibly be Hugo's son.'

Giles strode across the hallway, past the breakfast room and out of the front door. He climbed into his car and began the long journey back to the West Country.

The following morning, he parked the car outside a recruiting office. Once again he stood in line, not for the Gloucesters this time, but on the other side of the Avon, where the Wessex regiment were signing up new recruits.

After he'd filled in the form, he was put through another rigorous medical. This time when the doctor asked him, 'Are you aware of any hereditary ailments or diseases in your family that might prevent you from carrying out active service?' he replied, 'No, sir.'

12

AT NOON the following day, Giles left one world and entered another.

Thirty-six raw recruits, with nothing in common other than the fact that they had signed up to take the King's shilling, clambered aboard a train with a corporal acting as their nanny. As the train pulled out of the station, Giles stared through the grimy third-class window and was certain of only one thing: they were heading south. But not until the train shunted into Lympstone four hours later did he realize just how far south.

During the journey, Giles remained silent, and listened attentively to all those men around him who would be his companions for the next twelve weeks. A bus driver from Filton, a policeman from Long Ashton, a butcher from Broad Street, a builder from Nailsea and a farmer from Winscombe.

Once they disembarked from the train, the corporal ferried them on to a waiting bus.

'Where are we going?' asked the butcher.

'You'll find out soon enough, laddie,' replied the corporal, revealing his birthplace.

For an hour the bus trundled across Dartmoor until there was no sign of houses or people, just the occasional hawk flying overheard in search of prey.

They eventually stopped outside a desolate group of

buildings, displaying a weathered sign that announced *Ypres Barracks: Training camp for the Wessex Regiment*. It didn't lift Giles's spirits. A soldier marched out of the gatehouse and raised the barrier to allow the bus to continue for another hundred yards before coming to a halt in the middle of a parade ground. A solitary figure stood waiting for them to disembark.

When Giles climbed off the bus, he came face to face with a giant of a man, barrel-chested and dressed in a khaki uniform, who looked as if he had been planted on the parade ground. There were three rows of medals on his chest and a pace stick under his left arm, but what struck Giles most about him was the knife-edge crease in his trousers and the fact that his boots were so highly polished he could see his reflection in them.

'Good afternoon, gentlemen,' the man said in a voice that boomed around the parade ground; not someone who would find any use for a megaphone, thought Giles. 'My name is Sergeant Major Dawson – sir, to you. It's my responsibility to turn you from a shambolic rabble into a fighting force in just twelve weeks. By then, you will be able to call yourselves members of the Wessex, the finest regiment of the line. For the next twelve weeks I will be your mother, your father and your sweetheart and, let me assure you, I only have one purpose in life, and that is to make sure that when you meet your first German, you'll be able to kill him before he kills you. That process will begin at five tomorrow morning.' A groan went up which the sergeant major ignored. 'Until then, I'll leave Corporal McCloud to take you to the canteen, before you settle into your barracks. Be sure to get a good night's rest, because you'll need every ounce of energy you possess when we meet again. Carry on, corporal.'

Giles sat down in front of a fishcake whose ingredients had never seen salt water, and after one sip of lukewarm brown water, posing as tea, he put his mug back on the table.

'If you're not going to eat your fishcake, can I have it?' asked the young man sitting next to him. Giles nodded, and they swapped plates. He didn't speak again until he'd devoured Giles's offering.

'I know your mum,' the man said.

Giles gave him a closer look, wondering how that could be possible.

'We supply the meat for the Manor House and Barrington Hall,' the man continued. 'I like your mum,' he said. 'Very nice lady. I'm Bates, by the way, Terry Bates.' He shook Giles firmly by the hand. 'Never thought I'd end up sitting next to you.'

'Right, chaps, let's be 'avin' you,' said the corporal. The new recruits leapt up from the benches and followed the corporal out of the canteen and across the parade ground to a Nissen hut with MARNE painted on the door. Another Wessex battle honour, the corporal explained before opening the door to reveal their new home.

Thirty-six beds, eighteen on each side, had been crammed into a space no larger than the dining room at Barrington Hall. Giles had been placed between Atkinson and Bates. Not unlike prep school, he thought, though he did come across one or two differences during the next few days.

'Right, chaps, time to get undressed and have a kip.'

Long before the last man had climbed into bed, the corporal switched off the lights and bellowed, 'Make sure you get some shut-eye. You've got a busy day ahead of you tomorrow.' It wouldn't have surprised Giles if, like Fisher, his old school prefect, he'd added, 'No talking after lights out.'

As promised, the lights came back on at five o'clock the following morning; not that Giles had a chance to look at his watch after Sergeant Major Dawson entered the hut and bellowed, 'The last man with both feet on the ground will be first to be bayoneted by a Kraut!'

A large number of feet quickly hit the floor as the sergeant major marched down the centre of the hut, his pace stick banging the end of any bed whose incumbent still didn't have both feet on the ground.

'Now listen, and listen carefully,' he continued. 'I'm going to give you four minutes to wash and shave, four minutes to make your bed, four minutes to get dressed and eight minutes to have breakfast. Twenty minutes in all. I don't recommend any talking, on account of the fact you can't afford to waste the time, and in any case, I'm the only one who's allowed to talk. Is that understood?'

'It most certainly is,' said Giles, which was followed by a ripple of surprised laughter.

A moment later the sergeant major was standing in front of him. 'Whenever you open your mouth, sonny,' he barked, placing his pace stick on Giles's shoulder, 'all I want to hear is yes, sir, no, sir, three bags full, sir. Is that clear?'

'Yes, sir,' said Giles.

'I don't think I heard you, sonny.'

'Yes, sir!' shouted Giles.

'That's better. Now get yourself in the washroom, you horrible little man, before I put you on jankers.'

Giles had no idea what jankers was, but it didn't sound enticing.

Bates was already on his way out of the washroom when Giles walked in. By the time he'd shaved, Bates had made his bed, dressed and was on his way to the canteen. When Giles eventually caught up with him, he took a seat on the bench opposite.

'How do you manage it?' asked Giles in admiration.

'Manage what?' asked Bates.

'To be so wide awake, when the rest of us are still half asleep.'

'Simple really. I'm a butcher, like me dad. Up every mornin' at four, and off to the market. If I want the best cuts I have to be waitin' for them the moment they're delivered from the docks or the station. Only have to be a few minutes late, and I'm gettin' second best. Half an hour late, and it's scrag-ends, and your mum wouldn't thank me for that, would she?'

Giles laughed as Bates leapt up and began heading back to the barracks, only to discover that the sergeant major hadn't allowed any time for cleaning teeth.

Most of the morning was spent fitting up the 'sprogs', as they were referred to, with uniforms, one or two of which looked as if they'd had a previous owner. Berets, belts, boots, tin hats, blanco, Brasso and boot polish followed. Once they had been kitted out, the recruits were taken on to the parade ground for their first drill session. Having served, if somewhat inattentively, in the school's Combined Cadet Force, Giles started with a slight advantage, but he had a feeling it wouldn't be too long before Terry Bates caught up with him.

At twelve, they were marched off to the canteen. Giles was so hungry he ate almost everything on offer. After lunch, they returned to the barracks and changed into their gym kit before being herded across to the gymnasium. Giles silently thanked his prep school PT instructor for having taught him how to climb a rope, how to balance on a beam and how to use the wall bars for stretching. He couldn't help noticing that Bates shadowed his every move.

The afternoon ended with a five-mile run across the Devon moors. Only eight of the thirty-six raw recruits came back through the barracks gates at the same time as their gym instructor. One even managed to get lost and a search party had to be sent out to look for him. Tea was followed by what the sergeant major described as recreation, which for most of the lads turned out to be collapsing on their bunks and falling into a deep sleep.

—◦—

At five the following morning, the door to the barracks flew open once again, and this time several pairs of feet were already on the ground before the sergeant major had switched the lights on. Breakfast was followed by another hour of marching on the parade ground, and by now almost everyone was in step. The new recruits then sat in a circle on the grass and learnt how to strip, clean, load and fire a rifle. The corporal pulled a 4 by 2 through the barrel in one clean movement, reminding them that the bullet doesn't know which side it's on, so give it every chance to leave the barrel from the front and kill the enemy, and not backfire and kill you.

The afternoon was spent on the rifle range, where the instructors taught each recruit to nestle the butt of the rifle firmly into their shoulder, line up the foresight and rearsight with the centre circle of the target, and squeeze the trigger gently, never snatch at it. This time Giles thanked his grandfather for the hours spent on his grouse moor that ensured he kept hitting the bullseye.

The day ended with another five-mile run, tea and recreation, followed by lights out at ten. Most of the men had collapsed on their beds long before that, wishing the sun would fail to rise the next morning, or at least that the sergeant major would die in his sleep. They didn't get lucky. The first week felt like a month to Giles, but by the end of the second he was beginning to master the routine, although he never once got to the washroom ahead of Bates.

Although he didn't enjoy basic training any more than the next man, Giles did relish the challenge of competition. But he had to admit that as each day went by, he was finding it more and more difficult to shake off the butcher from Broad Street. Bates was able to match him punch for punch in the boxing ring, trade bullseyes on the rifle range, and when they started wearing heavy boots and having to carry a rifle on the five-mile run, the man who for years had been hauling carcasses of beef around on his shoulder, morning, noon and night, suddenly became a lot harder to beat.

—◦—

At the end of the sixth week, no one was surprised that it was Barrington and Bates who were selected for promotion to lance corporal, and each given a section of their own.

No sooner had they sewn on their stripes than the two sections they led became deadly rivals; not just on the parade ground or in the gymnasium, but whenever they went out on night ops or were involved in field exercises and troop movements. At the end of each day, like a couple of schoolboys, Giles and Bates would both declare themselves the winner. Often the sergeant major would have to prise them apart.

As they approached the day of the passing-out parade, Giles could sense the pride in both sections, who'd begun to believe they might just be worthy of calling themselves Wessexions by the time they passed out; although the sergeant major repeatedly warned them that it wouldn't be long before they had to take part in a real battle, against a real enemy with real bullets. He also reminded them that he wouldn't be around to hold their hands. For the first time Giles accepted that he was going to miss the damn man.

'Bring 'em on,' was all Bates had to say on the subject.

When they finally passed out on the Friday of the twelfth week, Giles assumed that he would be returning to Bristol with the other lads, to enjoy a weekend's leave before reporting to the regimental depot the following Monday. But when he walked off the parade ground that afternoon, the sergeant major took him to one side.

'Corporal Barrington, you're to report to Major Radcliffe immediately.'

Giles would have asked why, but he knew he wouldn't get an answer.

He marched across the parade ground and knocked on the office door of the adjutant, a man he'd only ever seen at a distance.

'Enter,' said a voice. Giles walked in, stood to attention and saluted. 'Barrington,' Major Radcliffe said after he'd returned the salute, 'I have some good news for you. You've been accepted for officer training school.'

Giles didn't even realize he was being considered for a commission.

'You'll have to travel straight to Mons tomorrow morning, where you will begin an induction course on Monday. Many congratulations, and good luck.'

'Thank you, sir,' said Giles, before asking, 'Will Bates be joining me?'

'Bates?' said Major Radcliffe. 'Do you mean Corporal Bates?'

'Yes, sir.'

'Good heavens, no,' replied the adjutant. 'He's not officer material.'

Giles could only hope that the Germans were just as short-sighted when it came to selecting their officers.

‹o›

When Giles reported to the Mons Officer Cadet Training Unit in Aldershot the following afternoon, he was unprepared for how quickly his life would change again. It took him some time to get used to corporals, sergeants, even the sergeant major calling him 'sir'.

He slept in a single room where the door didn't fly open at five in the morning with an NCO banging the end of his bed with a stick, demanding he place both feet on the ground. The door only opened when Giles chose to open it. He had breakfast in the mess with a group of young men who didn't need to be taught how to hold a knife and fork, although one or two of them looked as if they would never learn how to handle a rifle, let alone fire it in anger. But in a few weeks' time these same men would be in the front line, leading inexperienced volunteers whose lives would depend on their judgement.

Giles joined these men in a classroom where they were taught military history, geography, map reading, battle tactics, German and the art of leadership. If he'd learnt one thing from the butcher from Broad Street, it was that the art of leadership couldn't be taught.

Eight weeks later, the same young men stood on a passing-out parade and were awarded the King's Commission. They were presented with two crowned pips, one for each shoulder, a brown leather officer's cane and a letter of congratulations from a grateful King.

All Giles wanted to do was to rejoin his regiment and team up with his old comrades, but he knew that wouldn't be possible, because when he walked off the parade ground that Friday afternoon, the corporals, the sergeants and, yes, even the sergeant major saluted him.

Sixty young second lieutenants left Aldershot that afternoon for every corner of the land, to spend a weekend with their families, some of them for the last time.

⋖◦⋗

Giles spent most of Saturday jumping on and off trains, as he made his way back to the West Country. He arrived at the Manor House just in time to join his mother for dinner.

When she first saw the young lieutenant standing in the hallway, Elizabeth made no attempt to hide her pride.

Giles was disappointed that neither Emma nor Grace was at home to see him in uniform. His mother explained that Grace, who was in her second term at Cambridge, rarely came home, even during the vacation.

Over a one-course meal served by Jenkins – several of the staff were now serving on the frontline, not at the dinner table, his mother explained – Giles told his mother about what they'd got up to in training camp on Dartmoor. When she heard about Terry Bates she sighed, 'Bates and Son, they used to be the best butchers in Bristol.'

'Used to be?'

'Every shop in Broad Street was razed to the ground, so we've been deprived of Bates the butcher. Those Germans have a lot to answer for.'

Giles frowned. 'And Emma?' he asked.

'Couldn't be better . . . except – '

'Except?' repeated Giles. It was some time before his mother quietly added, 'How much more convenient it would have been if Emma had produced a daughter, rather than a son.'

'Why is that important?' asked Giles, as he refilled his glass.

His mother bowed her head, but said nothing.

'Oh God,' said Giles, as the significance of her words sank in. 'I had assumed that when Harry died, I would inherit—'

'I'm afraid you can't assume anything, darling,' said his mother looking up. 'That is, not until it can be established that your father is not also Harry's father. Until then, under the terms of your great-grandfather's will, it will be Sebastian who eventually inherits the title.'

Giles hardly spoke again during the meal while he tried

to take in the significance of his mother's words. Once coffee had been served, his mother said she felt tired and went to bed.

When Giles climbed the stairs to his room a few moments later, he couldn't resist dropping into the nursery to see his godson. He sat alone with the heir to the Barrington title. Sebastian gurgled in blissful sleep, clearly untroubled by war, and certainly not giving a thought to his grandfather's will, or the significance of the words, *and all that therein is*

The following day Giles joined his grandfathers for lunch at the Savage Club. It was a very different atmosphere from the weekend they'd shared five months earlier at Mulgelrie Castle. The only thing the two old men seemed keen to find out was where his regiment would be posted.

'I've no idea,' replied Giles, who would like to have known himself; but he would have given the same response even if he had been briefed, despite the fact that these two venerable old gentlemen were Boer War veterans.

◂◦▸

Lieutenant Barrington rose early on the Monday morning and, after breakfast with his mother, was driven by Hudson to the headquarters of the 1st Wessex regiment. He was held up by a steady stream of armoured vehicles and lorries filled with troops pouring out of the main gate. He got out of the car and walked to the guard house.

'Good morning, sir,' said a corporal, after giving him a crisp salute; something Giles still hadn't got used to. 'The adjutant has requested that you report to his office as soon as you arrive.'

'I'd be happy to do so, corporal,' said Giles, returning his salute, 'if I knew where Major Radcliffe's office was.'

'Far side of the square, sir, green door. You can't miss it.'

Giles marched across the square, returning several more salutes before he reached the adjutant's office.

Major Radcliffe looked up from behind his desk as Giles entered the room.

'Ah, Barrington, old chap. Good to see you again,' he said. 'We weren't certain if you'd make it in time.'

'In time for what, sir?' asked Giles.

'The regiment's been posted abroad, and the colonel felt you should be given the opportunity of joining us, or staying behind and waiting for the next shindig.'

'Where are we going, sir?'

'Haven't a clue, old chap; way above my rank. But I can tell you one thing for certain, it will be a damn sight closer to the Germans than Bristol.'

HARRY CLIFTON

1941

13

HARRY WOULD NEVER FORGET the day Lloyd was released from Lavenham and, although he wasn't disappointed
to see him go, he was surprised by Max's parting words.

'Would you do me a favour, Tom?' Lloyd said as they
shook hands for the last time. 'I'm enjoying your diaries so
much, I'd like to go on reading them. If you'd send them
to this address,' he said, handing Harry a card as if he
were already on the outside, 'I'll return them to you within
a week.'

Harry was flattered, and agreed to send Max each
exercise book once he'd completed it.

The following morning Harry took his place behind the
librarian's desk, but didn't consider reading the previous
day's newspaper before he'd completed his duties. He
continued to update his diaries every evening, and whenever
he came to the end of a notebook, he would post his latest
efforts to Max Lloyd. He was relieved, and a little surprised,
when they were always returned, as promised.

As the months passed, Harry began to accept the fact
that prison life was mostly routine and mundane, so when
the warden charged into the library one morning bran-
dishing his copy of the *New York Times* he was taken by
surprise. Harry put down the stack of books he had been
replacing on the shelves.

'Do we have a map of the United States?' Swanson demanded.

'Yes, of course,' Harry replied. He walked quickly over to the reference section and extracted a copy of *Hubert's Map of America*. 'Anywhere in particular, warden?' he asked.

'Pearl Harbor.'

For the next twenty-four hours, there was only one subject on everyone's lips, prisoners and guards alike. When would America enter the war?

Swanson returned to the library the following morning.

'President Roosevelt has just announced on the radio that the United States has declared war on Japan.'

'That's all very well,' said Harry, 'but when will the Americans help us defeat Hitler?'

Harry regretted the word 'us' the moment he'd uttered it. He looked up to find Swanson staring at him quizzically, and quickly returned to shelving the previous day's books.

Harry found out the answer some weeks later, when Winston Churchill boarded the *Queen Mary* and sailed to Washington to conduct discussions with the President. By the time the Prime Minister had arrived back in Britain, Roosevelt had agreed that the United States would turn their attention to the war in Europe, and the task of defeating Nazi Germany.

Harry filled page after page of his diary with the reaction of his fellow prisoners to the news that their country was at war. He concluded that most of them fell into one of two distinct categories, the cowards and the heroes: those who were relieved to be safely locked up in jail, and only hoped the hostilities would be over long before they were released, and those who couldn't wait to get out and take on an enemy they hated even more than the prison guards. When Harry asked his cellmate which category he fell into, Quinn replied, 'Have you ever met an Irishman who didn't relish a scrap?'

For his part, Harry became even more frustrated, convinced that now the Americans had entered the war, it would be over long before he'd been given the chance to play his part. For the first time since being locked up, he thought about trying to escape.

—◦—

Harry had just finished reading a book review in the *New York Times* when an officer marched into the library and said, 'The warden wants to see you in his office immediately, Bradshaw.'

Harry wasn't surprised, although after glancing once again at the advertisement at the bottom of the page, he still wondered how Lloyd imagined he would get away with it. He folded the paper neatly, placed it back in the rack, and followed the officer out of the room.

'Any idea why he wants to see me, Mr Joyce?' Harry asked as they walked across the yard.

'Don't ask me,' said Joyce, not attempting to hide his sarcasm. 'I've never been one of the warden's confidants.'

Harry didn't speak again until they were standing outside the warden's office. Joyce gave a quiet tap on the door.

'Enter,' said an unmistakable voice. Joyce opened the door, and Harry walked into the room. He was surprised to find another man he'd never seen before seated opposite the warden. The man was wearing an army officer's uniform, and looked as smart as Harry felt unkempt. He never took his eyes off the prisoner.

The warden rose from behind his desk. 'Good morning, Tom.' It was the first time Swanson had addressed him by his Christian name. 'This is Colonel Cleverdon, of the Fifth Texas Rangers.'

'Good morning, sir,' said Harry.

Cleverdon stood up and shook hands with Harry; another first.

'Have a seat, Tom,' said Swanson. 'The colonel has a proposition he wants to put to you.'

Harry sat down.

'It's good to meet you, Bradshaw,' began Colonel Cleverdon as he sat back down. 'I'm the commanding officer of Rangers.' Harry gave him a quizzical look. 'You won't find us listed in any recruitment manuals. I train groups of soldiers who will be dropped behind enemy lines with the purpose of causing as much mayhem for the enemy as possible, so the infantry will have a better chance to do their job. Nobody knows yet where or when our troops will be landing in Europe, but I'll be among the first to be told, as my boys will be parachuted into the target area a few days before the invasion.'

Harry was sitting on the edge of his seat.

'But before that balloon goes up, I'll be putting together a small specialist unit to prepare for any eventuality. This unit will consist of three groups, each comprising ten men: one captain, one staff sergeant, two corporals and six private soldiers. During the past few weeks I've been in touch with several prison wardens to ask if they had any exceptional men, who they felt might be suited for such an operation. Your name was one of the two put forward by Mr Swanson. Once I checked your record, from when you served in the navy, I had to agree with the warden that you'd be better off in uniform rather than wasting your time in here.'

Harry turned to the warden. 'Thank you, sir, but may I ask who the other person is?'

'Quinn,' said Swanson. 'The two of you have caused me so many problems during the past couple of years, I thought it was the Germans' turn to be subjected to your special brand of subterfuge.' Harry smiled.

'If you decide to join us, Bradshaw,' continued the colonel, 'you will begin an eight-week basic training course immediately, followed by a further six weeks with special operations. Before I go any further, I need to know if the idea appeals to you.'

'When do I start?' said Harry.

The colonel smiled. 'My car's outside in the yard, and I left the engine running.'

'I've already arranged for your civilian clothes to be collected from the stores,' said the warden. 'Obviously we need to keep the reason you've left at such short notice between ourselves. Should anyone ask, I'll say you and Quinn have been transferred to another prison.'

The colonel nodded. 'Any questions, Bradshaw?'

'Has Quinn agreed to join you?' asked Harry.

'He's sitting in the back seat of my car, probably wondering what's taking you so long.'

'But you do know the reason I'm in prison, colonel?'

'Desertion,' said Colonel Cleverdon. 'So I'll have to keep a close eye on you, won't I?' Both men laughed. 'You'll be joining my group as a private soldier, but I can assure you, your past record won't hinder your chances of promotion. However, while we're on that subject, Bradshaw, a change of name might be appropriate, given the circumstances. We wouldn't want some smart-ass in records to get their hands on your navy files and start asking embarrassing questions. Any ideas?'

'Harry Clifton, sir,' he said a little too quickly.

The warden smiled. 'I've always wondered what your real name was.'

EMMA BARRINGTON

1941

14

EMMA WANTED TO LEAVE Kristin's apartment as soon as possible, escape from New York and return to England. Once she was back in Bristol she could grieve alone and devote her life to bringing up Harry's son. But escape wasn't proving to be that easy.

'I'm so sorry,' said Kristin, placing an arm around Emma's shoulders. 'I had no idea you didn't know what had happened to Tom.'

Emma smiled weakly.

'I want you to know,' continued Kristin, 'that Richard and I never doubted even for a moment that he was innocent. The man I nursed back to life wasn't capable of murder.'

'Thank you,' said Emma.

'I have some photographs of Tom while he was with us on the *Kansas Star*. Would you like to see them?' asked Kristin.

Emma nodded politely, although she had no interest in seeing any photographs of Lieutenant Thomas Bradshaw. She decided that once Kristin had left the room, she would quietly slip out of the apartment and return to her hotel. She had no desire to continue making such a fool of herself in front of a complete stranger.

As soon as Kristin went out, Emma jumped up. As she

did so, she knocked her cup off the table and on to the floor, spilling some coffee on the carpet. She fell to her knees and began weeping again, just as Kristin came back into the room, clutching a handful of photographs.

When she saw Emma on her knees in tears, she tried to comfort her. 'Please don't worry about the carpet, it's not important. Here, why don't you look at these, while I find something to clear it up?' She handed the photographs to Emma and quickly left the room again.

Emma accepted she could no longer make good her escape, so she returned to her chair and reluctantly began to look at the photos of Tom Bradshaw.

'Oh my God,' she said out loud. She stared in disbelief at a picture of Harry standing on the deck of a ship with the Statue of Liberty in the background, and then at another with the skyscrapers of Manhattan as the backdrop. Tears came to her eyes once again, even if she was unable to explain how it was possible. She waited impatiently for Kristin to return. It wasn't long before the conscientious housewife reappeared, knelt down and began to remove the small brown stain with a damp cloth.

'Do you know what happened to Tom after he was arrested?' Emma asked anxiously.

'Didn't anyone tell you?' asked Kristin, looking up. 'Apparently there wasn't enough evidence to try him for murder, and Jelks got him off. He was charged with desertion from the navy, pleaded guilty, and was sentenced to six years.'

Emma just didn't understand how Harry could have ended up in jail for a crime he obviously hadn't committed. 'Did the trial take place in New York?'

'Yes,' Kristin replied. 'As his lawyer was Sefton Jelks, Richard and I assumed he wasn't in need of any financial help.'

'I'm not sure I understand.'

'Sefton Jelks is the senior partner of one of New York's most prestigious law practices, so at least Tom was being well represented. When he came to see us about Tom, he seemed genuinely concerned. I know he also visited Dr Wallace and the ship's captain, and he assured all of us that Tom was innocent.'

'Do you know which prison they sent him to?' Emma asked quietly.

'Lavenham, in upstate New York. Richard and I tried to visit him, but Mr Jelks told us he didn't want to see anyone.'

'You've been so kind,' said Emma. 'Perhaps I can ask one more small favour before I leave. May I be allowed to keep one of these photographs?'

'Keep them all. Richard took dozens, he always does. Photography is his hobby.'

'I don't want to waste any more of your time,' said Emma, rising unsteadily to her feet.

'You're not wasting my time,' Kristin replied. 'What happened to Tom never made sense to either of us. When you see him, please pass on our best wishes,' she said as they walked out of the room. 'And if he'd like us to visit him, we'd be happy to.'

'Thank you,' said Emma as the chain was removed once again. As Kristin opened the door she said, 'We both realized Tom was desperately in love, but he didn't tell us you were English.'

15

EMMA SWITCHED ON the bedside light and once again studied the photographs of Harry standing on the deck of the *Kansas Star*. He looked so happy, so relaxed, and clearly unaware what awaited him when he stepped ashore.

She drifted in and out of sleep as she tried to work out why Harry would be willing to face a murder trial, and would plead guilty to desertion from a navy he'd never signed up for. She concluded that only Sefton Jelks could provide the answers. The first thing she needed to do was make an appointment to see him.

She glanced again at the bedside clock: 3.21. She got out of bed, put on a dressing gown, sat down at the little table and filled several sheets of hotel stationery with notes in preparation for her meeting with Sefton Jelks. It felt like prepping for an exam.

At six, she showered and dressed, then went downstairs to breakfast. A copy of the *New York Times* had been left on her table and she quickly turned the pages, only stopping to read one article. The Americans were becoming pessimistic about Britain being able to survive a German invasion, which was looking increasingly likely. Above a photograph of Winston Churchill standing on the white cliffs of Dover staring defiantly out across the Channel, his trademark cigar in place, was the headline, 'We will fight them on the beaches'.

Emma felt guilty about being away from her homeland. She must find Harry, get him released from prison and together they would return to Bristol.

The hotel receptionist looked up Jelks, Myers & Abernathy in the Manhattan telephone directory, wrote out an address on Wall Street and handed it to Emma.

The cab dropped her outside a vast steel and glass building that stretched high into the sky. She pushed through the revolving doors and checked a large board on the wall that listed the names of every firm on the forty-eight floors. Jelks, Myers & Abernathy was located on floors 20, 21 and 22; all enquiries at reception on the twentieth floor.

Emma joined a horde of grey-flannel-suited men who filled the first available elevator. When she stepped out on the twentieth floor, she was greeted by the sight of three smart women dressed in open-neck white blouses and black skirts, who sat behind a reception desk, something else she hadn't seen in Bristol. She marched confidently up to the desk. 'I'd like to see Mr Jelks.'

'Do you have an appointment?' the receptionist asked politely.

'No,' admitted Emma, who'd only ever dealt with a local solicitor, who was always available whenever a member of the Barrington family dropped in.

The receptionist looked surprised. Clients didn't just turn up at the front desk hoping to see the senior partner; they either wrote, or their secretary phoned to make an appointment in Mr Jelks's crowded diary. 'If I could take your name, I'll have a word with his assistant.'

'Emma Barrington.'

'Please have a seat, Miss Barrington. Someone will be with you shortly.'

Emma sat alone in a little alcove. 'Shortly' turned out to be more than half an hour, when another grey-suited man appeared carrying a yellow pad.

'My name is Samuel Anscott,' he said, offering his hand. 'I understand that you wish to see the senior partner.'

'That is correct.'

'I'm his legal assistant,' said Anscott as he took the seat opposite her. 'Mr Jelks has asked me to find out why you want to see him.'

'It's a private matter,' said Emma.

'I'm afraid he won't agree to see you unless I'm able to tell him what it's about.'

Emma pursed her lips. 'I'm a friend of Harry Clifton.'

She watched Anscott closely, but it was obvious that the name meant nothing to him, although he did make a note of it on his yellow pad.

'I have reason to believe that Harry Clifton was arrested for the murder of Adam Bradshaw, and that Mr Jelks represented him.'

This time the name did register, and the pen moved more swiftly across the pad.

'I wish to see Mr Jelks, in order to find out how a lawyer of his standing could have allowed my fiancé to take Thomas Bradshaw's place.'

A deep frown appeared on the young man's face. He clearly wasn't used to anyone referring to his boss in this way. 'I have no idea what you're talking about, Miss Barrington,' he said, which Emma suspected was true. 'But I will brief Mr Jelks, and come back to you. Perhaps you could give me a contact address.'

'I'm staying at the Mayflower Hotel,' said Emma, 'and I'm available to see Mr Jelks at any time.'

Anscott made another note on his pad, stood up, gave a curt nod, but this time didn't offer to shake hands. Emma felt confident that she wouldn't have to wait long before the senior partner agreed to see her.

She took a taxi back to the Mayflower Hotel, and could

hear the phone ringing in her room even before she'd opened the door. She ran across the room, but by the time she picked up the receiver, the line had gone dead.

She sat down at the desk and began to write to her mother to say she'd arrived safely although she didn't mention the fact that she was now convinced Harry was alive. Emma would only do that when she'd seen him in the flesh. She was on the third page of the letter when the phone rang again. She picked it up.

'Good afternoon, Miss Barrington.'

'Good afternoon, Mr Anscott,' she said, not needing to be told who it was.

'I've spoken to Mr Jelks concerning your request for a meeting, but I'm afraid he's unable to see you, because it would create a conflict of interest with another client he represents. He is sorry not to be more helpful.'

The line went dead.

Emma remained at the desk, stunned, still clutching the phone, the words 'conflict of interest' ringing in her ears. Was there really another client and, if so, who could it be? Or was that just an excuse not to see her? She placed the receiver back in its cradle and sat still for some time, wondering what her grandfather would have done in these circumstances. She recalled one of his favourite maxims: there's more than one way to skin a cat.

Emma opened the desk drawer, thankful to find a fresh supply of stationery, and made a list of people who might be able to fill in some of the gaps created by Mr Jelks's supposed conflict of interest. She then went downstairs to reception, knowing that she was going to be fully occupied for the next few days. The receptionist tried to hide her surprise when the softly spoken young lady from England asked for the address of a courthouse, a police station and a prison.

Before she left the Mayflower, Emma dropped into the hotel's shop and purchased a yellow pad of her own. She walked out on to the pavement and hailed another cab.

It dropped her in a very different part of town to the one Mr Jelks inhabited. As she climbed the courthouse steps, Emma thought about Harry, and how he must have felt when he'd entered that same building, in very different circumstances. She asked the guard on the door where the reference library was, in the hope of finding out what those circumstances were.

'If you mean the records room, miss, it's in the basement,' the guard said.

After walking down two flights of stairs, Emma asked a clerk behind the counter if she could see the records for the case of the State of New York *v.* Bradshaw. The clerk handed her a form to fill in, which included the question, *Are you a student?* to which she answered yes. A few minutes later Emma was handed three large box files.

'We close in a couple hours,' she was warned. 'When the bell goes, you must return the records to this desk immediately.'

Once Emma had read a few pages of documents, she couldn't understand why the State hadn't proceeded with Tom Bradshaw's trial for murder, when they seemed to have such a strong case against him. The brothers had been sharing a hotel room; the whiskey decanter had Tom's bloody fingerprints all over it, and there was no suggestion anyone else had entered the room before Adam's body had been found lying in a pool of blood. But, worse, why had Tom fled the scene of the crime, and why had the state attorney settled for a guilty plea on the lesser charge of desertion? Even more puzzling was how Harry had ever become involved in the first place. Might the letter on Maisie's mantelpiece contain the answers to all these questions, or was it simply that Jelks knew something he didn't want her to find out?

Her thoughts were interrupted by a clanging bell, demanding that she return the files to the desk. Some questions had been answered, but far more remained unanswered. Emma made a note of two names she hoped could supply most of those answers, but would *they* also claim a conflict of interest?

She emerged from the courthouse just after five, clutching several more sheets of paper covered in her neat long-hand. She grabbed something called a Hershey Bar and a Coke from a street vendor, before she hailed another cab and asked the driver to take her to the 24th precinct police station. She ate and drank on the move, something her mother would never have approved of.

On arrival at the police station, Emma asked to speak to either Detective Kolowski or Detective Ryan.

'They're both on nights this week,' she was told by the desk sergeant, 'so won't be back on duty until ten.'

Emma thanked him and decided to return to the hotel and have supper before going back to the 24th precinct at ten.

After a Caesar salad and her first knickerbocker glory, Emma returned to her room on the fourth floor. She lay down on the bed and thought about what she needed to ask Kolowski or Ryan, assuming either of them agreed to see her. Did Lieutenant Bradshaw have an American accent . . . ?

Emma fell into a deep sleep, to be jolted back to consciousness by the unfamiliar sound of a police siren blaring from the street below. Now she understood why the rooms on the upper floors were more expensive. She checked her watch. It was 1.15.

'Damn,' she cursed as she leapt off the bed, ran to the bathroom, soaked a flannel under the cold tap and covered her face. She quickly left the room and took the lift to the ground floor. When she stepped out of the hotel, she was surprised to find the street was just as busy, and the pavement every bit as crowded, as it had been at midday.

She hailed another cab and asked the driver to take her back to the 24th precinct. The New York cabbies were beginning to understand her, or was she beginning to understand them?

She climbed the steps to the police station a few minutes before two. Another desk sergeant asked her to take a seat, and promised to let Kolowski or Ryan know she was waiting in reception.

Emma settled down for a long wait, but to her surprise, a couple of minutes later she heard the desk sergeant say, 'Hey, Karl, there's some lady sitting over there who says she wants to see you.' He gestured in Emma's direction.

Detective Kolowski, a coffee in one hand, a cigarette in the other, walked across and gave Emma a half smile. She wondered how quickly that smile would disappear when he discovered why she wanted to see him.

'How can I help you, ma'am?' he asked.

'My name is Emma Barrington,' she said, exaggerating her English accent, 'and I need to seek your advice on a private matter.'

'Then let's go to my office, Miss Barrington,' Kolowski said, and began to walk down a corridor until he came to a door which he kicked open with the heel of his shoe. 'Have a seat,' he said pointing to the only other chair in the room. 'Can I get you a coffee?' he asked as Emma sat down.

'No, thank you.'

'A wise decision, ma'am,' he said as he placed his mug on the table, lit his cigarette and sat down. 'So, how can I help?'

'I understand that you were one of the detectives who arrested my fiancé.'

'What's his name?

'Thomas Bradshaw.'

She was right. The look, the voice, the demeanour, everything about him changed. 'Yes, I was. And I can tell you, ma'am, it was an open and shut case until Sefton Jelks became involved.'

'But the case never came to trial,' Emma reminded him.

'Only because Bradshaw had Jelks as his lawyer. If that guy had defended Pontius Pilate, he would have convinced the jury that he was simply assisting a young carpenter who wanted to buy some nails for a cross he was working on.'

'Are you suggesting that Jelks—'

'No,' said Kolowski sarcastically before Emma could finish her sentence. 'I always thought it was a coincidence that the DA was coming up for re-election that year, and some of Jelks's clients were among his biggest campaign contributors. Anyway,' he continued after exhaling a long cloud of smoke, 'Bradshaw ended up getting six years for desertion, when the precinct's sweepstakes had him down for eighteen months – two years tops.'

'What are you suggesting?' asked Emma.

'That the judge accepted Bradshaw was guilty –' Kolowski paused and blew out another cloud of smoke before adding – 'of murder.'

'I agree with you and the judge,' said Emma. 'Tom Bradshaw probably was guilty of murder.' Kolowski looked surprised. 'But did the man you arrested ever tell you that you'd made a mistake, and that he wasn't Tom Bradshaw, but Harry Clifton?'

The detective gave Emma a closer look, and thought for a moment. 'He did say something like that early on, but Jelks must have told him that it wouldn't fly, because he never mentioned it again.'

'Would you be interested, Mr Kolowski, if I was able to prove that it would fly?'

'No, ma'am,' said Kolowski firmly. 'That case was closed a long time ago. Your fiancé is doin' six years for a crime he pleaded guilty to, and I've got too much work on my desk –' he placed a hand on a stack of files – 'to be reopening old wounds. Now, unless you got anything else I can help you with . . .'

'Will they allow me to visit Tom at Lavenham?'

'I can't see why not,' said Kolowski. 'Write to the warden. He'll send you a visiting order. After you've filled it in and sent it back, they'll give you a date. It shouldn't take more than six to eight weeks.'

'But I haven't got six weeks,' protested Emma. 'I need to return to England in a couple of weeks' time. Isn't there anything I can do to speed up the process?'

'That's only possible on compassionate grounds,' said the detective, 'and that's limited to wives and parents.'

'What about the mother of the prisoner's child?' countered Emma.

'In New York, ma'am, that gives you the same rights as a wife, as long as you can prove it.'

Emma produced two photos from her handbag, one of Sebastian and one of Harry standing on the deck of the *Kansas Star*.

'That's good enough for me,' said Kolowski handing back the picture of Harry without commenting. 'If you promise to leave me in peace I'll speak to the warden and see if anything can be done.'

'Thank you,' said Emma.

'How do I reach you?'

'I'm staying at the Mayflower Hotel.'

'I'll be in touch,' said Kolowski, making a note. 'But I don't want you to be in any doubt, ma'am, that Tom Bradshaw killed his brother. I'm sure of it.'

'And I don't want you to be in any doubt, officer, that the man locked up in Lavenham is not Tom Bradshaw. I'm sure of that.' Emma placed the photographs back in her bag and rose to leave.

A frown appeared on the detective's face as she walked out of the room.

Emma returned to her hotel, undressed and went straight back to bed. She lay awake wondering if Kolowski might be having second thoughts about whether he'd arrested the right man. She still couldn't work out why Jelks had allowed Harry to be sentenced to six years, when it would have been so easy for him to prove that Harry wasn't Tom Bradshaw.

She finally fell asleep, grateful not to be woken by any nocturnal visitors.

—◦—

The phone rang when she was in the bathroom, but by the time she'd picked it up, there was only a dial tone.

The second call came just as she was closing the door of her room on her way down to breakfast. She dashed back inside and grabbed the phone, to hear a voice she recognized on the other end of the line.

'Good morning, Officer Kolowski,' she replied.

'The news isn't good,' said the detective, who didn't deal in small talk. She collapsed on to the bed, fearing the worst. 'I spoke to the warden of Lavenham just before I came off duty, and he told me that Bradshaw has made it clear he doesn't want any visitors, no exceptions. It seems that Mr Jelks has issued an order that he's not even to be informed when someone asks to see him.'

'Couldn't you try to get a message to him somehow?' begged Emma. 'I'm sure that if he knew it was me—'

'Not a hope, lady,' said Kolowski. 'You have no idea how far Jelks's tentacles reach.'

'He can overrule a prison warden?'

'A prison warden is small fry. The DA and half the

judges in New York are under his thumb. Just don't tell anyone I said so.'

The line went dead.

Emma didn't know how much time had passed before she heard a knock on the door. Who could it possibly be? The door opened and a friendly face peered in.

'Can I clean the room, miss?' asked a woman pushing a trolley.

'I'll only be a couple of minutes,' said Emma. She checked her watch and was surprised to find it was ten past ten. She needed to clear her head before she could consider her next move, and decided to take a long walk in Central Park.

She strolled around the park before making a decision. The time had come to visit her great-aunt and seek her advice about what she should do next.

Emma headed off in the direction of 64th and Park, and was so deep in thought about how she was going to explain to Great-aunt Phyllis why she hadn't visited her earlier, that what she saw didn't fully register. She stopped, turned and retraced her steps, checking every window until she reached Doubleday's. A pyramid of books dominated the centre window, alongside a photograph of a man with slicked-back black hair and a pencil moustache. He was smiling out at her.

THE DIARY OF A CONVICT:

My time at Lavenham maximum security prison

by

Max Lloyd

The author of the runaway bestseller
will be signing books in this store
at 5.00 p.m. on Thursday

Don't miss this opportunity to meet the author

GILES BARRINGTON

1941

16

GILES HAD NO IDEA where the regiment was going. For days he seemed to be perpetually on the move, never able to sleep for more than a couple of hours at a time. First he boarded a train, followed by a truck, before he climbed up the gangway of a troop carrier that ploughed through the ocean waves at its own pace, until it finally disgorged 1,000 soldiers from the Wessex at the Egyptian port of Alexandria on the North African coast.

During the voyage, Giles had been reunited with his chums from Ypres camp on Dartmoor, who he had to accept were now under his command. One or two of them, Bates in particular, didn't find it easy to call him sir, and found it even more difficult to salute him every time they bumped into each other.

A convoy of army vehicles awaited the Wessex Regiment as they disembarked from the ship. Giles had never experienced such intense heat and his fresh khaki shirt was soaked in sweat within moments of him stepping on foreign soil. He quickly organized his men into three groups before they climbed on board the waiting trucks. The convoy progressed slowly along a narrow, dusty coastal road, not stopping for several hours until they finally reached the outskirts of a badly bombed town that Bates announced in a loud voice, 'Tobruk! Told you so,' and money began to change hands.

Once they'd entered the town, the convoy dropped the men at various points. Giles and the other officers jumped off outside the Majestic Hotel, which had been requisitioned by the Wessex as their company HQ. Giles pushed his way through the revolving doors and quickly discovered there wasn't much majestic about the hotel. Makeshift offices had been crammed into every available space. Charts and maps were pinned on walls where paintings had once hung, and the plush red carpet that welcomed VIPs from all over the world had worn thin with the continual tramping of studded boots.

The reception area was the only feature to remind them this might once have been a hotel. A duty corporal checked off Second Lieutenant Barrington's name on a long list of new arrivals.

'Room two-one-nine,' he said, handing him an envelope. 'You'll find everything you need in there, sir.'

Giles strode up the wide staircase to the second floor and let himself into the room. He sat on the bed, opened the envelope and read his orders. At seven o'clock he was to report to the ballroom, when the colonel of the regiment would address all officers. Giles unpacked his suitcase, took a shower, put on a clean shirt and went back downstairs. He grabbed a sandwich and a cup of tea from the officers' mess and made his way to the ballroom just before seven.

The large room, with its high imperial ceiling and magnificent chandeliers, was already filled with boisterous officers, who were being reunited with old friends and introduced to new ones as they waited to find out which square on the chessboard they would be moved to. Giles caught a glimpse of a young lieutenant on the far side of the room whom he thought he recognized, but then lost sight of him.

At one minute to seven, Lieutenant Colonel Robertson marched up on to the stage, and everyone else in the room quickly fell silent and sprang to attention. He stopped in the centre of the stage and waved the men down. Feet apart, hands on hips, he began to address them.

'Gentlemen, it must seem strange to you to have travelled from all parts of the empire to do battle with the Germans in North Africa. However, Field Marshal Rommel and his Afrika Korps are also here, with the purpose of maintaining a supply of oil for their troops in Europe. It is our responsibility to send him back to Berlin with a bloody nose, long before their last tank has run out of petrol.'

Cheers erupted around the hall, accompanied by the stamping of feet.

'General Wavell has granted the Wessex the privilege of defending Tobruk, and I have told him that we will all sacrifice our lives before Rommel books a suite at the Majestic Hotel.'

This was greeted with even louder cheers and more stamping of feet.

'Now I want you all to report to your company commanders, who will brief you on our overall plan to defend the town, and the responsibilities each of you will be expected to carry out. Gentlemen, we haven't a moment to waste. Good luck, and happy hunting.'

The officers all sprang to attention again as the colonel left the stage. Giles checked his orders once more. He'd been allocated to 7 Platoon, C company, which was to meet in the hotel library following the colonel's address for a briefing by Major Richards.

'You must be Barrington,' said the major when Giles walked into the library a few minutes later. Giles saluted. 'It was good of you to join us so soon after being commissioned. I've put you in charge of seven platoon as understudy to your old friend. You will have three sections of twelve men, and your responsibility will be to patrol the west perimeter of the city. You will have a sergeant and three corporals to assist you. The lieutenant will brief you on the finer details. As you were at school together, you won't have to spend too much time getting to know each other.'

Giles wondered who it could be. And then he recalled the familiar lone figure on the other side of the ballroom.

◄○►

Second Lieutenant Giles Barrington would have liked to give Lieutenant Fisher the benefit of the doubt, although he would never be able to erase the memory of him as a prefect at St Bede's, when he thrashed Harry every night during his first week for no reason other than that he was a docker's son.

'It's good to catch up with you, Barrington, after such a long time,' said Fisher. 'I can't see any reason why we shouldn't work well together, can you?' He obviously also recalled his treatment of Harry Clifton. Giles managed a weak smile.

'We've got over thirty men under our command, along with three corporals and a sergeant. Some of them you'll remember from your days at training camp. In fact, I've already put Corporal Bates in charge of number one section.'

'Terry Bates?'

'Corporal Bates,' repeated Fisher. 'Never use a Christian name when you're referring to the other ranks. In the mess, and when we're on our own, Giles, you can call me Alex, but never in front of the men. I'm sure you understand.'

You always were an arrogant little shit, and clearly nothing has changed, thought Giles. This time he didn't smile.

'Now, it's our responsibility to patrol the western perimeter of the town in four-hour watches. Don't underestimate the importance of our task, because if Rommel does attack Tobruk, intelligence is that he'll try and enter the city from the west. So we have to remain vigilant at all times. I'll leave it to you to fix the rotas. I usually manage a couple of shifts a day, but I can't do a lot more because of my other responsibilities.'

Like what, Giles wanted to ask him.

Giles enjoyed patrolling the west side of the town with his men, and quickly got to know all thirty-six of them, not least because Corporal Bates kept him so well informed. And although he tried to keep them on perpetual alert following Fisher's warning, as the weeks passed without incident, he began to wonder if they'd ever come face to face with the enemy.

◄○►

It was on a hazy evening in early April, when all three of Giles's patrols were out on an exercise, that a volley of bullets came from nowhere. The men instantly hit the ground, and quickly crawled to the nearest building to find whatever cover they could.

Giles had been with the leading section when the Germans presented their calling card, then fired off a second volley. The bullets fell nowhere near their target, but he knew it wouldn't be long before the enemy identified his position.

'Don't fire until I say so,' he ordered as he slowly scanned the horizon with his binoculars. He decided to brief Fisher before he made a move. He picked up the field phone and got an immediate response.

'How many of them are there, do you think?' Fisher asked.

'I'd guess no more than seventy, at most eighty. If you bring forward number two and three sections, that should be more than enough to hold them off until reinforcements arrive.'

A third volley followed, but after Giles had scanned the horizon, he once again gave the order, 'Hold your fire.'

'I'll send up Two Section under Sergeant Harris to support you,' said Fisher, 'and if you keep me briefed, I'll decide whether to join you with Three Section.' The phone went dead.

A fourth volley quickly followed the third, and this time when Giles focused his binoculars, he could see a dozen men crawling across the open ground towards them.

'Take aim, but don't fire until the target is in range, and make sure every bullet counts.'

Bates was the first to squeeze his trigger. 'Got you,' he said as a German collapsed into the desert sand. As he reloaded, he added, 'That'll teach you to bomb Broad Street.'

'Shut up, Bates, and concentrate,' said Giles.

'Sorry, sir.'

Giles continued to scan the horizon. He could see two, possibly three men who'd been hit and were lying face down in the sand a few yards from their dugouts. He gave the order to fire another volley and Giles watched as several more Germans scampered back to safety, like ants scurrying down a hole.

'Cease fire!' shouted Giles, aware that they couldn't afford to waste precious ammunition. He looked to his left and could see 2 Section already in position under Sergeant Harris, awaiting their orders.

He picked up the field phone and Fisher came back on the line. 'My ammunition won't last much longer, sir. My left flank's now covered by Sergeant Harris, but my right flank's exposed. If you were able to come forward, we'd have a better chance of holding them off.'

'Now that you've got Two Section to strengthen your position, Barrington, I'd better stay back and cover you, in case they break through.'

Another volley of bullets flew in their direction. The Germans had clearly worked out exactly where they were positioned, but Giles still instructed his two sections to hold fire. He cursed, put down the phone and ran across the open gap to join Sergeant Harris. A volley followed his trouble.

'What do you think, sergeant?'

'It's a half-company, sir, about eighty men in all. But I think they're just a reconnaissance party, so all we have to do is bed down and be patient.'

'I agree,' said Giles. 'What do you think they'll do?'

'The Krauts will know that they outnumber us, so they'll want to mount an attack before any reinforcements arrive. If Lieutenant Fisher brought up Three Section to cover our right flank, it would strengthen our position.'

'I agree,' repeated Giles as another volley greeted them. 'I'll go back and speak to Fisher. Await my orders.'

Giles zigzagged across the open terrain. This time the bullets were a little too close to risk that trick again. He was just about to call Fisher when the field phone rang. He grabbed it.

'Barrington,' said Fisher. 'I believe the time has come for us to take the initiative.'

Giles needed to repeat Fisher's words to be sure he'd heard them correctly. 'You want me to lead an attack on the Germans' position, while you bring forward Three Section to cover me.'

'If we do that,' said Bates, 'we'd be like sitting ducks on a rifle range.'

'Shut up, Bates.'

'Yes, sir.'

'Sergeant Harris thinks, and I agree with him,' continued Giles, 'that if you bring up Three Section to cover our right flank, the Germans will have to mount an attack, and then we could—'

'I'm not interested in what Sergeant Harris thinks,' said Fisher. 'I give the orders and you'll carry them out. Is that clear?'

'Yes, sir,' Giles said as he slammed down the phone.

'I could always kill him, sir,' said Bates.

Giles ignored him as he loaded his pistol and attached six hand grenades to his webbed belt. He stood up so that both platoons could see him, and said in a loud voice, 'Fix bayonets and prepare to advance.' He then stepped out from behind his cover and shouted, 'Follow me!'

As Giles began to run across the deep scorching sand with Sergeant Harris and Corporal Bates only a stride behind him, he was greeted with yet another volley of bullets and wondered how long he would survive against such overwhelming odds. With forty yards still to cover, he could see exactly where the three enemy dugouts were situated. He snatched a hand grenade from his belt, removed the pin and tossed it towards the centre dugout, as if he was returning a cricket ball from the deep boundary into the wicketkeeper's gloves. It landed just above the stumps. Giles saw two men fly into the air, while another fell back.

He swung round and hurled a second grenade to his left, a definite run-out, because the enemy's firepower suddenly dried up. The third grenade took out a machine gun. As Giles charged on, he could see the men who had him in their sights. He took his pistol out of its holster and began to fire as if he was on a shooting range but this time the bullseyes were human beings. One, two, three went down, and then Giles saw a German officer lining him up in his sights. The German pulled the trigger just a moment too late, and collapsed on the ground in front of him. Giles felt sick.

When he was only a yard from the dugout, a young German dropped his rifle on the ground, while another threw his arms high into the air. Giles stared into the desperate eyes of the defeated men. He didn't need to speak German to know they didn't want to die.

'Cease fire!' screamed Giles, as what was left of 1 and 2 sections quickly overwhelmed the enemy positions. 'Round them up and disarm them, Sergeant Harris,' he added, then turned back to see Harris, head down in the sand, blood trickling out of his mouth, only yards from the dugout.

Giles stared back across the open terrain they had crossed and tried not to count the number of soldiers who had sacrificed their lives because of one man's weak decision. Stretcher bearers were already removing the dead bodies from the battlefield.

'Corporal Bates, line up the enemy prisoners in threes, and march them back to camp.'

'Yes, sir,' said Bates, sounding as if he meant it.

A few minutes later, Giles and his depleted band headed back across the open ground. They had covered about fifty yards when Giles saw Fisher running towards him, with 3 Section following in his wake.

'Right, Barrington, I'll take over,' he shouted. 'You bring up the rear. Follow me,' he ordered as he led the captured German soldiers triumphantly back towards the town.

By the time they reached the Majestic Hotel, a small crowd had gathered to cheer them. Fisher returned the salutes of his brother officers.

'Barrington, see that the prisoners are interned, then take the lads off to the canteen for a drink; they've earned it. Meanwhile, I'll report to Major Richards.'

'Can I kill him, sir?' asked Bates.

17

When Giles came down for breakfast the following morning, several officers, some of whom he'd never spoken to before, went out of their way to shake hands with him.

As he strolled into the mess, several heads turned and smiled in his direction, which he found slightly embarrassing. He grabbed a bowl of porridge, two boiled eggs and an out-of-date copy of *Punch*. He sat alone, hoping to be left in peace, but a few moments later three Australian officers he didn't recognize joined him. He turned a page of *Punch*, and laughed at an E.H. Shepard cartoon of Hitler retreating from Calais on a penny farthing.

'An incredible act of courage,' said the Australian on his right.

Giles could feel himself turning red.

'I agree,' said a voice from the other side of the table. 'Quite remarkable.'

Giles wanted to leave before they . . .

'What did you say the fellow's name was?'

Giles took a spoonful of porridge.

'Fisher.'

Giles nearly choked.

'It seems that Fisher, against all odds, led his platoon over open terrain and, with only hand grenades and a pistol, took out three dugouts full of German soldiers.'

'Unbelievable!' said another voice.

At least Giles could agree with that.

'And is it true that he killed a Hun officer and then took fifty of the bastards prisoner, with only twelve men to back him up?'

Giles removed the top of his first boiled egg. It was hard.

'It must be true,' said another voice, 'because he's been promoted to captain.'

Giles sat and stared at the yolk of his egg.

'I'm told he'll be recommended for a Military Cross.'

'That's the least he deserves.'

The least he deserved, thought Giles, was what Bates had recommended.

'Anyone else involved in the action?' asked the voice from the other side of the table.

'Yes, his second in command, but I'm damned if I can remember his name.'

Giles had heard enough and decided to let Fisher know exactly what he thought of him. Leaving his second egg untouched, he marched out of the mess and headed straight for the ops room. He was so angry that he barged in without knocking. The moment he entered the room, he sprang to attention and saluted. 'I do apologize, sir,' he said. 'I had no idea you were here.'

'This is Mr Barrington, colonel,' said Fisher. 'You'll remember that I told you he assisted me in yesterday's action.'

'Ah, yes. Barrington. Good show. You may not have seen company orders this morning, but you've been promoted to full lieutenant, and having read Captain Fisher's report, I can tell you that you'll also be mentioned in dispatches.'

'Many congratulations, Giles,' said Fisher. 'Well deserved.'

'Indeed,' said the colonel. 'And while you're here, Barrington, I was just saying to Captain Fisher, now that he's identified Rommel's preferred route into Tobruk, we'll need to double our patrols on the west side of the city and deploy a full squadron of tanks to back you up.' He jabbed the map spread out on the table with his finger. 'Here, here and here. I hope you both agree?'

'I do, sir,' said Fisher. 'I'll set about getting the platoon in place immediately.'

'Can't be too soon,' said the colonel, 'because I have a feeling it won't be long before Rommel returns, and this time he won't be on a reconnaissance mission but leading the full force of the Afrika Korps. We must be lying in wait and be sure that he walks straight into our trap.'

'We'll be ready for him, sir,' said Fisher.

'Good. Because I'm putting you in charge of our new patrols, Fisher. Barrington, you will remain second in command.'

'I'll have my report on your desk by midday, sir,' said Fisher.

'Good show, Fisher. I'll leave you to work out the details.'

'Thank you, sir,' said Fisher, standing to attention and saluting as the colonel left the room.

Giles was about to speak, but Fisher quickly jumped in. 'I've put in a recommendation that Sergeant Harris should be awarded a posthumous military medal, and Corporal Bates should also be mentioned in dispatches. I hope you'll support me.'

'Am I also to understand that you've been put up for a Military Cross?' asked Giles.

'That's not in my hands, old fellow, but I'm happy to go along with whatever the commanding officer sees fit. Now, let's get down to business. With six patrols now under our command, I propose that we . . .'

◄○►

After what had become known by 1 and 2 sections as 'Fisher's Fantasy', everyone from the colonel downwards was on red alert. Two platoons patrolled the western edge of the town, one on, one off, night and day, no longer wondering if, only when, Rommel would appear over the horizon at the head of his Afrika Korps.

Even Fisher, in his newly elevated state as hero, had to appear occasionally on the outer perimeter, if simply to maintain the myth of his heroic deed, but only long enough to be sure everyone had seen him. He would then report back to the tank squadron commander, three miles to the rear, and set up his field phones.

❖

The Desert Fox chose April 11th, 1941 to begin his assault on Tobruk. The British and Australians couldn't have fought more bravely when defending the perimeter against the German onslaught. But as the months passed and supplies of food and ammunition began to run low, few doubted – though it was never voiced – that it could only be a matter of time before the sheer size of Rommel's army would overwhelm them.

It was a Friday morning, just as the desert haze was clearing, that Lieutenant Barrington scanned the horizon with his binoculars and focused on rows and rows of German tanks.

'Shit,' he said. He grabbed the field phone as a shell hit the building he and his men had selected as their observation post. Fisher came on the other end of the line. 'I can see forty, possibly fifty tanks heading towards us,' Giles told him, 'and what looks like a full regiment of soldiers to back them up. Permission to withdraw my men to a more secure position where we can regroup and take up battle formation?'

'Hold your ground,' said Fisher, 'and once the enemy's within range, engage them.'

'Engage them?' said Giles. 'What with, bows and arrows? This isn't Agincourt, Fisher. I've got barely a hundred men facing a regiment of tanks, with nothing more than rifles to protect ourselves. For God's sake, Fisher, allow me to decide what's best for my men.'

'Hold your ground,' repeated Fisher, 'and engage the enemy when they come within range. That's an order.'

Giles slammed the phone down.

'For some reason best known to himself,' said Bates, 'that man doesn't want you to survive. You should have let me shoot him.'

Another shell hit the building while masonry and rubble began to fall around them. Giles no longer needed binoculars to see just how many tanks were advancing towards them, and to accept that he only had moments left to live.

'Take aim!' He suddenly thought of Sebastian, who would inherit the family title. If the boy turned out to be half as good as Harry had been, the Barrington dynasty need have no fear for its future.

The next shell hit the building behind them, and Giles could clearly see a German soldier returning his stare from the turret of his tank. 'Fire!'

As the building began to collapse around him, Giles thought about Emma, Grace, his father, his mother, his grandfathers, and ... The next shell brought the entire edifice crashing down. Giles looked up, to see a large piece of masonry falling, falling, falling. He leapt on top of Bates, who was still firing at an advancing tank.

The last image Giles saw was Harry swimming to safety.

EMMA BARRINGTON

1941

18

EMMA SAT ALONE in her hotel room reading *The Diary of a Convict* from cover to cover. She didn't know who Max Lloyd was, but she was sure of one thing: he wasn't the author.

Only one man could have written this book. She recognized so many familiar phrases, and Lloyd hadn't even bothered to change all the names, unless of course he had a girlfriend called Emma whom he still adored.

Emma turned the last page just before midnight, and decided to make a phone call to someone who would still be at work.

'Just one more favour,' she begged when his voice came on the line.

'Try me,' he said.

'I need the name of Max Lloyd's parole officer.'

'Max Lloyd the author?'

'No less.'

'I'm not even going to ask why.'

She began to read the book a second time, making pencil notes in the margin, but long before the new deputy librarian had started, she had fallen asleep. She woke around five the next morning, and didn't stop reading until a prison officer entered the library and said, 'Lloyd, the warden wants to see you.'

Emma took a long, lazy bath, and considered the fact

that all the information she'd been trying so hard to discover had been available for a dollar fifty from any bookstore.

Once she was dressed, she went down to breakfast and picked up a copy of the *New York Times*. She was taken by surprise as she turned the pages to come across a review of *The Diary of a Convict*.

> We should be grateful to Mr Lloyd for bringing to our attention what is happening in our prisons today. Lloyd is a gifted writer with real talent, and we must hope that now he's been released, he will not put down his pen.

He never picked it up in the first place, thought Emma indignantly as she signed her bill.

Before going back up to her room, she asked the receptionist to recommend a good restaurant near Doubleday's bookstore.

'The Brasserie, madam. It has a first-class reputation. Would you like me to book a table for you?'

'Yes, please,' said Emma. 'I'd like a table for one at lunch today, and another for two this evening.'

The receptionist was quickly learning not to be surprised by the lady from England.

Emma returned to her room and settled down to read the diary once more. She was puzzled why the narrative opened with Harry's arrival at Lavenham, despite the fact that there were several references scattered throughout the book which suggested that his previous experiences had also been recorded, even if they hadn't been seen by the publisher, and certainly not the public. In fact, this convinced Emma that there had to be another notebook in existence, which would not only describe Harry's arrest and trial, but might explain why he had put himself through such an ordeal, when a lawyer of Mr Jelks's standing must have known that he was not Tom Bradshaw.

After reading marked pages of the diaries for a third time, Emma decided another long stroll in the park was required. As she walked up Lexington Avenue, she dropped into Bloomingdales and placed an order that she was assured would be ready for collection by three o'clock. In Bristol, the same order would have taken a fortnight.

As she walked through the park, a plan was beginning to form in her mind, but she needed to return to Doubleday's and take a closer look at the store's layout before she could apply the finishing touches. When she walked into the bookstore, the staff were already preparing for the author signing. A table was in place and a roped-off area showed clearly where the line should form. The poster in the window now had a bold red banner across it declaring, **TODAY**.

Emma selected a gap between two rows of shelves from which she would have a clear view of Lloyd while he was signing, and would be able to observe her prey while setting him a trap.

She left Doubleday's just before 1 p.m., and made her way across Fifth Avenue to the Brasserie. A waiter showed her to a table that would never have been considered acceptable by either of her grandfathers. But the meal was, as promised, first class, and when the bill was presented, she took a deep breath, and left a large tip.

'I've booked a table for this evening,' she said to the waiter. 'Would it be possible to be seated in an alcove?' The waiter looked doubtful, until Emma produced a dollar bill, which seemed to remove any doubt. She was getting the hang of how things worked in America.

'What's your name?' Emma asked as she passed him the note.

'Jimmy,' the waiter replied.

'And another thing, Jimmy.'

'Yes, ma'am?'

'May I keep a copy of the menu?'

'Of course, ma'am.'

On the way back to the Mayflower, Emma called in at Bloomingdales and picked up her order. She smiled when the clerk showed her an example of the card. 'I hope it's satisfactory, madam.'

'Couldn't be better,' said Emma. Once she was back in her room, she went over her prepared questions again and again, and after deciding on the best possible order, she pencilled them neatly on to the back of the menu. Exhausted, she lay down on the bed and fell into a deep sleep.

When the persistent ringing of the phone woke her, it was already dark outside. She checked her watch: 5.10 p.m.

'Damn,' she said as she picked up the phone.

'I know the feeling,' said a voice on the other end of the line, 'even if that wasn't the four-letter word I would have chosen.' Emma laughed. 'The name you're looking for is Brett Elders . . . I didn't tell you.'

'Thank you,' said Emma. 'I'll try not to bother you again.'

'I wish,' said the detective, and the line went dead.

Emma wrote the name 'Brett Elders' neatly in pencil at the top right-hand corner of the menu. She would like to have taken a quick shower and changed her clothes, but she was already running late and she couldn't afford to miss him.

She grabbed the menu and three of the cards. Stuffing them into her bag, she then dashed out of the door and down the staircase, not waiting for the elevator. She hailed a cab and leapt into the back. 'Doubleday's on Fifth,' she said, 'and make it snappy.'

Oh no, Emma thought, as the taxi sped away. What's happening to me?

◄○►

Emma entered the crowded bookstore and took her chosen spot between politics and religion, from where she could observe Max Lloyd at work.

He was signing each book with a flourish, basking in the glow of his adoring fans. Emma knew it should have been Harry sitting there receiving the accolades. Did he even know his work had been published? Would she find out tonight?

As it turned out, she needn't have rushed, because Lloyd went on signing his runaway bestseller for another hour, until the line began to dwindle. He was taking longer and longer with each message, in the hope that it might entice others to join the queue.

As he was chatting expansively to the last customer in the line, Emma deserted her post and strolled across.

'And how is your dear mother?' the customer was asking effusively.

'Very well, thank you,' said Lloyd. 'No longer having to work in a hotel,' he added, 'following the success of my book.'

The customer smiled. 'And Emma, dare I ask?'

'We're going to be married in the fall,' said Lloyd after he'd signed her copy.

Are we indeed? thought Emma.

'Oh, I'm so glad,', said the customer. 'She sacrificed so much for you. Do give her my best wishes.'

Why don't you turn around and do it in person, Emma wanted to say.

'I most certainly will,' said Lloyd, as he handed her the book and gave her his back-cover smile.

Emma stepped forward and handed a card to Lloyd. He studied it for a moment before the same smile reappeared.

'A fellow agent,' he said, standing to greet her.

Emma shook his outstretched hand, and somehow managed to return his smile. 'Yes,' she said, 'and several publishers in London are showing considerable interest in the rights to your book. Of course, if you've already signed a contract, or are represented by another agent in England, I wouldn't want to waste your time.'

'No, no, dear lady, I'm very happy to consider any proposal you might have.'

'Then perhaps you would join me for dinner, so we can talk further?'

'I think they're expecting me to have dinner with them,' whispered Lloyd, waving an expansive hand in the direction of some of the members of the Doubleday staff.

'What a pity,' said Emma. 'I'm flying to LA tomorrow to visit Hemingway.'

'Then I'll have to disappoint them, won't I?' said Lloyd. 'I'm sure they'll understand.'

'Good. Shall we meet at the Brasserie, then, when you've finished signing?'

'You'll do well to get a table at such short notice.'

'I don't think that will be a problem,' said Emma, before one last customer stepped forward, still hoping to get a signature. 'I'll look forward to seeing you later, Mr Lloyd.'

'Max, please.'

Emma made her way out of the bookstore and walked across Fifth Avenue to the Brasserie. This time she wasn't kept waiting.

'Jimmy,' she said as the waiter accompanied her to an alcove table, 'I have a very important client joining me, and I want it to be an evening he won't forget.'

'You can rely on me, madam,' the waiter said as Emma sat down. After he'd gone she opened her bag, took out the menu and went over her list of questions once more. When she saw Jimmy heading towards her with Max Lloyd in his wake, she turned the menu over.

'You're obviously well known here,' said Lloyd as he slipped into the seat opposite her.

'It's my favourite New York restaurant,' said Emma, returning his smile.

'Can I get you a drink, sir?'

'Manhattan, on the rocks.'

'And you, madam?'

'My usual, Jimmy.'

The waiter hurried off. Emma was curious to discover what he would come back with. 'Why don't we order,' said Emma, 'and then we can get down to business.'

'Good idea,' replied Lloyd. 'Although I know exactly what I want,' he added as the waiter reappeared and placed a Manhattan in front of him and a glass of white wine by Emma's side; the drink she'd ordered at lunch. Emma was impressed.

'Jimmy, I think we're ready to order.' The waiter nodded and turned to Emma's guest.

'I'll have one of your juicy sirloin steaks. Make it medium, and don't spare on the trimmings.'

'Certainly, sir.' Turning to Emma, he asked, 'What can I tempt you with this evening, madam?'

'A Caesar salad please, Jimmy, but light on the dressing.'

Once the waiter was out of earshot, she turned her menu back over, although she didn't need to be reminded of the first question. 'The diary only covered eighteen months of your incarceration,' she said. 'But you served more than two years, so I hope we can look forward to another volume.'

'I still have a notebook full of material,' said Lloyd, relaxing for the first time. 'I've been thinking about incorporating some of the more extraordinary events I experienced in a novel that I have planned.'

Because if you ever wrote them as a diary, any publisher would realize you weren't the author, Emma wanted to say.

The sommelier appeared by Lloyd's side, summoned by the demand of an empty glass.

'Would you care to see the wine list, sir? Something to complement the steak, perhaps?'

'Good idea,' said Lloyd, opening the thick, leather-bound book as if he were the host. He ran his finger down a long list of burgundies, and paused near the bottom. 'A bottle of the thirty-seven, I think.'

'An excellent choice, sir.'

Emma presumed that meant it wasn't cheap. But this was not an occasion to quibble over price.

'And what a nasty piece of work Hessler turned out to be,' she said, glancing at her second question. 'I thought that sort of person only existed in trashy novels, or B-movies.'

'No, he was real enough,' said Lloyd. 'But I did get him transferred to another prison, if you remember.'

'I do,' said Emma, as a large steak was placed in front of her guest and a Caesar salad on her side of the table. Lloyd picked up his knife and fork, clearly ready for the challenge.

'So tell me, what sort of proposal do you have in mind?' he asked as he dug into the steak.

'One where you get exactly what you're worth,' said Emma, the tone of her voice changing, 'and not a penny more.' A puzzled look appeared on Lloyd's face, and he put down his knife and fork as he waited for Emma to continue. 'I am well aware, Mr Lloyd, that you didn't write one word of *The Diary of a Convict*, other than to replace the real author's name with your own.' Lloyd opened his mouth, but before he had time to protest, Emma continued, 'If you're foolish enough to keep up the pretence that you wrote the book, my first visit in the morning will be to Mr Brett Elders, your parole officer, and it won't be to discuss how well your rehabilitation is going.'

The sommelier reappeared, uncorked a bottle, and waited to be told who would be tasting the wine. Lloyd was staring at Emma like a rabbit caught in the glare of headlights, so she gave a slight nod. She took her time swirling the wine around in her glass before taking a sip.

'Excellent,' she eventually said. 'I particularly like the thirty-seven.' The sommelier bowed slightly, poured two glasses and went off in search of another victim.

'You can't prove I didn't write it,' said Lloyd defiantly.

'Yes I can,' said Emma, 'because I represent the man who did.' She took a sip of wine before adding, 'Tom Bradshaw, your deputy librarian.' Lloyd sank back into his seat and lapsed into a sullen silence. 'So let me outline the deal I'm proposing, Mr Lloyd, while at the same time making it clear that there is no room for negotiation, unless, of course, you want to go back to prison on a charge of fraud, as well as theft. Should you end up in Pierpoint, I have a feeling Mr Hessler will be only too happy to escort you to your cell, as he doesn't come out of the book very well.'

Lloyd didn't look as if the idea appealed to him.

Emma took another sip of wine before continuing. 'Mr Bradshaw has generously agreed to allow you to continue the myth that you wrote the diary, and he won't even expect you to give back the advance you were paid, which in any case I suspect you've already spent.' Lloyd pursed his lips. 'However, he wishes to make it clear that should you be foolish enough to attempt to sell the rights in any other country, a writ for copyright theft will be issued against you and the publisher concerned. Is that clear?'

'Yes,' mumbled Lloyd, clutching the arms of his chair.

'Good. Then that's settled,' said Emma, and after taking another sip of wine added, 'I feel sure you'll agree, Mr Lloyd, that there's no purpose in us continuing this conversation, so perhaps the time has come for you to leave.'

Lloyd hesitated.

'We'll meet again at ten o'clock tomorrow morning, at forty-nine Wall Street.'

'Forty-nine Wall Street?'

'The office of Mr Sefton Jelks, Tom Bradshaw's lawyer.'

'So it's Jelks who's behind this. Well that explains everything.'

Emma didn't understand what he meant, but said, 'You will bring every single notebook with you, and hand them over. Should you be even one minute late, I will instruct Mr Jelks to call your probation officer and tell him what you've been up to since you left Lavenham. Stealing a client's earnings is one thing, but claiming you wrote his book . . .' Lloyd continued to grip the arms of his chair, but said nothing. 'You may go now, Mr Lloyd,' said Emma. 'I look forward to seeing you in the lobby of forty-nine Wall Street at ten tomorrow morning. Don't be late, unless you want your next appointment to be with Mr Elders.'

Lloyd rose unsteadily to his feet and made his way slowly across the restaurant, leaving one or two customers wondering if he was drunk. A waiter held the door open for him, then hurried over to Emma's table. Seeing the untouched steak and a full glass of wine, he asked anxiously, 'I hope everything was all right, Miss Barrington?'

'It couldn't have gone better, Jimmy,' she said, pouring herself another glass of wine.

19

ONCE EMMA had returned to her hotel room, she checked the back of her lunch menu, and was delighted to confirm that she'd been able to tick off almost every question. She thought her demand that the notebooks should be handed over in the lobby of 49 Wall Street was inspired, because it must have left Lloyd with the distinct impression that Mr Jelks was her lawyer, which would have put the fear of God into a perfectly innocent man. Although she was still puzzled by what Lloyd had meant when he'd let slip the words *So it's Jelks who's behind this. Well that explains everything.* She switched off the light and slept soundly for the first time since she'd left England.

Emma's morning routine followed much the same pattern as previous days. After a leisurely breakfast, shared only with the *New York Times*, she left the hotel and took a cab to Wall Street. She had planned to be a few minutes early, and the cab dropped her off outside the building at 9.51 a.m. As she handed the driver a quarter, she was relieved that her visit to New York was coming to an end; it had turned out to be far more expensive than she had anticipated. Two meals at the Brasserie with a five-dollar bottle of wine plus tips didn't help.

However, she wasn't in any doubt that the trip had been worthwhile. Not least because the photographs taken on board the *Kansas Star* had confirmed her belief that Harry was still alive and had, for some reason, assumed Tom Bradshaw's identity. Once she'd got her hands on the missing notebook, the rest of the mystery would unravel, and surely she would now be able to convince Officer Kolowski that Harry should be released. She didn't intend to return to England without him.

Emma joined a stampede of office workers as they made their way into the building. They all headed towards the nearest available elevator, but Emma didn't join them. She placed herself strategically between the reception desk and the bank of twelve lifts, which allowed her an unimpeded view of everyone who entered 49 Wall Street.

She checked her watch: 9.54. No sign of Lloyd. She checked it again at 9.57, 9.58, 9.59, and 10 o'clock. He must have been held up by traffic. 10.02, her eyes rested for a split second on every person who came in. 10.04, had she missed him? 10.06, she glanced towards reception; still no sign of him. 10.08, she tried to stop negative thoughts from entering her mind. 10.11, had he called her bluff? 10.14, would her next appointment have to be with Mr Brett Elders? 10.17, how much longer was she willing to hang about? 10.21, and a voice behind her said, 'Good morning, Miss Barrington.'

Emma swung round and came face to face with Samuel Anscott, who said politely, 'Mr Jelks wonders if you'd be kind enough to join him in his office.'

Without another word, Anscott turned and walked towards a waiting elevator. Emma only just managed to jump in before the doors closed.

Conversation was out of the question as the packed elevator made its slow, interrupted journey to the 22nd floor, where Anscott stepped out and led Emma down a long oak-panelled, thickly carpeted corridor, lined with portraits of previous senior partners and their colleagues on the board, giving an impression of honesty, integrity and propriety.

Emma would have liked to question Anscott before she met Jelks for the first time, but he remained several paces ahead of her. When he reached a door at the end of the corridor, Anscott knocked, and opened it without waiting for a response. He stood aside to allow Emma to enter, then closed the door, but didn't join them.

There, sitting in a comfortable high-backed chair by the window, was Max Lloyd. He was smoking a cigarette, and gave Emma the same smile he'd bestowed on her when they had first met at Doubleday's.

She turned her attention to a tall, elegantly dressed man, who rose slowly from behind his desk. No hint of a smile, or any suggestion that they should shake hands. Behind him was a wall of glass, beyond which skyscrapers towered into the sky, suggesting unfettered power.

'It's kind of you to join us, Miss Barrington,' he said. 'Please have a seat.'

Emma sank into a leather chair so deep that she almost disappeared from sight. She noticed a stack of notebooks on the senior partner's desk.

'My name is Sefton Jelks,' he began, 'and I have the privilege of representing the distinguished and acclaimed author, Mr Max Lloyd. My client visited me earlier this morning, to tell me that he had been approached by someone claiming to be a literary agent from London, who was making an accusation, a slanderous accusation, that he was not the author of *The Diary of a Convict*, which bears his name. It may interest you to know, Miss Barrington,' continued Jelks, 'that I am in possession of the original manuscript, every word of which is written in Mr Lloyd's hand.' He placed a fist firmly on top of the notebooks, and allowed himself the suggestion of a smile.

'May I be allowed to see one?' asked Emma.

'Of course,' replied Jelks. He removed the book on top of the pile and handed it to her.

Emma opened it and began to read. The first thing she saw was that it wasn't written in Harry's bold hand. But it was Harry's voice. She handed the book back to Mr Jelks, who replaced it at the top of the pile. 'May I have a look at one of the others?' she asked.

'No. We've proved our point, Miss Barrington,' said Jelks. 'And my client will take advantage of every remedy the law provides should you be foolish enough to repeat your slander.' Emma kept her eyes on the pile of notebooks, while Jelks continued in full flow. 'I also felt it appropriate to have a word with Mr Elders to warn him you might be in touch, and to let him know that should he agree to see you, he would undoubtedly be called as a witness, were this matter to end up in court. Mr Elders felt, on balance, that his best course of action would be to avoid meeting you. A sensible man.'

Emma continued to look at the pile of notebooks.

'Miss Barrington, it didn't take a lot of research to discover that you are the granddaughter of Lord Harvey and Sir Walter Barrington, which would account for your misplaced confidence when dealing with Americans. Allow me to suggest that if you intend to continue trying to pass yourself off as a literary agent, perhaps I can offer you some free advice, which is a matter of public record. Ernest Hemingway left America to live in Cuba in 1939—'

'How very generous of you, Mr Jelks,' interrupted Emma, before he could continue. 'Allow me to offer you some free advice in return. I know perfectly well that it was Harry Clifton' – Jelks's eyes narrowed – 'and not your client, who wrote *The Diary of a Convict*. If you were foolish enough, Mr Jelks, to issue a writ for slander against me, you might well find yourself in court having to explain why you defended a man on a charge of murder who you knew wasn't Lieutenant Tom Bradshaw.'

Jelks began frantically pressing a button underneath his desk. Emma rose from her chair, smiled sweetly at both of them, and left the room without another word. She marched quickly down the corridor towards the elevator, as Mr Anscott and a security guard hurried past her on their way to Mr Jelks's office. At least she'd avoided the humiliation of being escorted off the premises.

When she stepped into the lift, the attendant enquired, 'Which floor, miss?'

'Ground, please.'

The attendant chuckled. 'You must be English.'

'Why do you say that?'

'In America, we call it the first floor.'

'Of course you do,' said Emma, giving him a smile as she stepped out of the elevator. She walked across the lobby, pushed through the revolving doors and ran down the steps and out on to the pavement, quite clear what she had to do next. There was only one person left she could turn to. After all, any sister of Lord Harvey had to be a formidable ally. Or would Great-aunt Phyllis turn out to be a close friend of Sefton Jelks, in which case Emma would be taking the next boat back to England.

She hailed a cab, but when she jumped in, she almost had to shout to make herself heard above the blare of the radio.

'Sixty-fourth and Park,' she said, working out how she might explain to her great-aunt why she hadn't visited her earlier. She leant forward and would have asked the driver to turn the volume down, if she hadn't heard the words, 'President Roosevelt will address the nation from the Oval Office at twelve thirty this afternoon, Eastern Time'.

GILES BARRINGTON

1941–1942

20

THE FIRST THING Giles saw was his right leg hitched to a pulley and encased in plaster.

He could dimly remember a long journey, during which the pain had become almost unbearable, and he had assumed he would die long before they got him to a hospital. And he would never forget the operation, but then how could he, when they'd run out of anaesthetic moments before the doctor made the first incision?

He turned his head very slowly to the left and saw a window with three bars across it, then to the right; that's when he saw him.

'No, not you,' Giles said. 'For a moment I thought I'd escaped and gone to heaven.'

'Not yet,' said Bates. 'First you have to do a spell in purgatory.'

'For how long?'

'At least until your leg's mended, possibly longer.'

'Are we back in England?' Giles asked hopefully.

'I wish,' said Bates. 'No, we're in Germany, Weinsberg PoW camp, which is where we all ended up after being taken prisoner.'

Giles tried to sit up, but could only just raise his head off the pillow; enough to see a framed picture on the wall of Adolf Hitler giving him a Nazi salute.

'How many of our boys survived?'

'Only a handful. The lads took the colonel's words to heart. "We will all sacrifice our lives before Rommel books a suite at the Majestic Hotel".'

'Did anyone else from our platoon make it?'

'You, me and—'

'Don't tell me, Fisher?'

'No. Because if they'd sent him to Weinsberg, I'd have asked for a transfer to Colditz.'

Giles lay still, staring up at the ceiling. 'So how do we escape?'

'I wondered how long it would be before you asked that.'

'And what's the answer?'

'Not a chance while your leg's still in plaster, and even after that it won't be easy, but I've got a plan.'

'Of course you have.'

'The plan's not the problem,' said Bates. 'The problem is the escape committee. They control the waiting list, and you're at the back of the queue.'

'How do I get to the front?'

'It's like any queue in England, you just have to wait your turn . . . unless—'

'Unless?'

'Unless Brigadier Turnbull, the senior ranking officer, thinks there's a good reason why you should be moved up the queue.'

'Like what?'

'If you can speak fluent German, it's a bonus.'

'I picked up a bit when I was at OTS – just wish I'd con- centrated more.'

'Well, there are lessons twice a day, so someone of your intelligence shouldn't find that too difficult. Unfortunately even that list is still fairly long.'

'So what else can I do to get bumped up the escape-list faster?'

'Find yourself the right job. That's what got me moved up three places in the past month.'

'How did you manage that?'

'As soon as the Krauts found out I was a butcher, they offered me a job in the officers' mess. I told them to fuck off, excuse my French, but the brigadier insisted I took the job.'

'Why would he want you to work for the Germans?'

'Because occasionally I can manage to steal some food from the kitchen, but more important, I pick up the odd piece of information that's useful to the escape committee. That's why I'm near the front of the queue, and you're still at the back. You're going to have to get both feet on the ground if you're still hoping to make it to the washroom before me.'

'Any idea how long it will be before I can do that?' asked Giles.

'The prison doc says it'll be at least another month, possibly six weeks before they can remove the plaster.'

Giles settled back on the pillow. 'But even when I do get up, how can I hope to be offered a job in the officers' mess? Unlike you, I don't have the right qualifications.'

'But you do,' said Bates. 'In fact, you can go one better than me, and get yourself a job in the camp commandant's dining room, because I know they're looking for a wine waiter.'

'And what makes you think I'm qualified to be a wine waiter?' asked Giles, making no attempt to hide the sarcasm in his voice.

'If I remember correctly,' said Bates, 'you used to have a butler called Jenkins working for you at the Manor House.'

'Still do, but that hardly qualifies me—'

'And your grandfather, Lord Harvey, is in the wine trade. Frankly, you're over-qualified.'

'So what are you suggesting?'

'Once you get out of here, they'll make you fill in a labour form, listing your previous employment. I've already told them you were a wine waiter at the Grand Hotel, Bristol.'

'Thanks. But they'll know within minutes—'

'Believe me, they don't have a clue. All you have to do is get your German up to scratch, and try to remember what Jenkins did. Then if we can come up with a decent plan to present to the escape committee, we'll march to the front of the queue in no time. Mind you, there's a catch.'

'There has to be, if you're involved.'

'But I've found a way round it.'

'What's the catch?'

'You can't get a job workin' for the Krauts if you take German lessons, because they're not that stupid. They make a list of everyone who attends the classes, because they don't want no one eavesdropping on their private conversations.'

'You said you'd found a way around that?'

'You'll have to do what all toffs do to keep ahead of people like me. Take private lessons. I've even found you a tutor; a bloke who taught German at Solihull Grammar School. It's only his English you'll find difficult to understand.' Giles laughed. 'And since you'll be locked up in here for another six weeks, and haven't anything better to do, you can start straight away. You'll find a German–English dictionary under your pillow.'

'I'm in your debt, Terry,' said Giles, grasping his friend by the hand.

'No, I owe you, don't I? On account of the fact that you saved my life.'

21

BY THE TIME Giles was released from the sick bay five
weeks later, he knew a thousand German words but he
hadn't been able to work on his pronunciation.

He'd also spent countless hours lying in bed, trying to
recall how Jenkins had gone about his job. He practised
saying *Good morning, sir,* with a deferential nod of the
head, and *Would you care to sample this wine, colonel,*
while pouring a jug of water into a specimen bottle.

'Always appear modest, never interrupt and don't speak
till you're spoken to,' Bates reminded him. 'In fact, do
exactly the opposite of everythin' you've always done in the
past.'

Giles would have hit him, but he knew he was right.

Although Bates was only allowed to visit Giles twice a
week for thirty minutes, he used every one of those minutes
to brief him about the day-to-day workings of the commandant's private dining room. He taught him the names and
ranks of each officer, their particular likes and dislikes, and
warned him that Major Müller of the SS, who was in charge
of camp security, was not a gentleman, and was certainly
not susceptible to charm, especially old-school.

Another visitor was Brigadier Turnbull, who listened
with interest to what Giles told him he had in mind for
when he was moved out of the sick bay and into the camp.

The brigadier went away impressed, and returned a few days later with some thoughts of his own.

'The escape committee aren't in any doubt that the Krauts will never allow you to work in the commandant's dining room if they think you're an officer,' he told Giles. 'For your plan to have any chance of succeeding, you'll need to be a private soldier. Since Bates is the only man to have served under you, he's the only one who'll have to keep his mouth shut.'

'He'll do what I tell him,' said Giles.

'Not any longer he won't,' warned the brigadier.

◄◦►

When Giles finally emerged from the sick bay and moved into camp, he was surprised to find how disciplined the life was, especially for a private soldier.

It brought back memories of his days at Ypres training camp on Dartmoor – feet on the floor at six every morning, with a sergeant major who certainly didn't treat him like an officer.

Bates still beat him to the washroom and to breakfast every morning. There was full parade on the square at seven, when the salute was taken by the brigadier. Once the sergeant major had screamed, 'Parade dismissed!' everyone became engaged in frantic activity for the rest of the day.

Giles never missed the five-mile run, twenty-five times around the perimeter of the camp, or an hour's quiet conversation in German with his private tutor while sitting in the latrines.

He quickly discovered that the Weinsberg PoW camp had a lot of other things in common with Ypres barracks: cold, bleak, barren terrain, and dozens of huts with wooden bunks, horsehair mattresses and no heating other than the sun, which, like the Red Cross, only made rare visits to Weinsberg. They also had their own sergeant major who endlessly referred to Giles as an idle little sod.

As on Dartmoor, there was a high wire fence surrounding the compound, and only one way in and out. The problem was that there were no weekend passes, and the guards, armed with rifles, certainly didn't salute as you drove out of the gates in your yellow MG.

When Giles was asked to fill in the camp labour form, under 'name', he wrote Private Giles Barrington, and under 'previous occupation', sommelier.

'What the hell's that when it's at home?' asked Bates.

'Wine waiter,' said Giles in a superior tone.

'Then why not bloody well say so?' Bates said as he tore up the form, 'unless of course you were hoping to get a job at the Ritz. You'll have to fill in another one of these,' he added, sounding exasperated.

Once Giles had handed in the second form, he waited impatiently to be interviewed by someone in the commandant's office. He used the endless hours to keep fit in both mind and body. 'Mens sana in corpore sano' was about the only Latin he could still remember from his schooldays.

Bates kept him informed about what was happening on the other side of the fence, and even managed to smuggle out the odd potato or crust of bread, and on one occasion half an orange.

'Can't overdo it,' he explained. 'The last thing I need is to lose my job.'

❧

It was about a month later that they were both invited to appear before the escape committee and present the Bates/Barrington plan, which quickly became known as the bed and breakfast plan – bed in Weinsberg, breakfast in Zurich.

Their clandestine presentation went well, and the committee agreed that they should be allowed to climb a few more places up the order, but no one was yet suggesting that they should open the batting. In fact, the brigadier told them bluntly that until Private Barrington had landed a job in the commandant's dining room, they were not to bother the committee again.

'Why is it taking so long, Terry?' asked Giles after they'd left the meeting.

Corporal Bates grinned. 'I'm quite happy for you to call me Terry,' he said, 'that is, when we're on our own, but never in front of the men, you understand?' he added, giving a passable imitation of Fisher.

Giles punched him on the arm.

'Court martial offence, that,' Bates reminded him, 'a private soldier attacking a non-commissioned officer.'

Giles punched him again. 'Now answer my question,' he demanded.

'Nothing moves quickly in this place. You'll just have to be patient, Giles.'

'You can't call me Giles until we're sitting down for breakfast in Zurich.'

'Suits me, if you're payin'.'

Everything changed the day the camp commandant had to host lunch for a group of visiting Red Cross officials, and needed an extra waiter.

◄○►

'Don't forget you're a private soldier,' said Bates when Giles was escorted to the other side of the wire for his interview with Major Müller. 'You have to try to think like a servant, not someone who's used to being served. If Müller suspects, even for a moment, that you're an officer, we'll both be out on our arses, and you'll go back to the bottom of the snakes and ladders board. I can promise you one thing, the briga-dier won't ever invite us to throw the dice again. So act like a servant, and never even hint that you understand a word of German. Got it?'

'Yes, sir,' said Giles.

Giles returned an hour later with a large grin on his face.

'You got the job?' asked Bates.

'I got lucky,' said Giles. 'The commandant interviewed me, not Müller. I start tomorrow.'

'And he never suspected you were an officer and a gentleman?'

'Not after I told him I was a friend of yours.'

—◦—

Before the lunch for the visiting Red Cross officials was served, Giles uncorked six bottles of merlot to allow them to breathe. Once the guests were seated, he poured half an inch of wine into the commandant's glass and waited for his approval. After a nod, he served the guests, always pouring from the right. He then moved on to the officers, according to rank, finally returning to the commandant, as host.

During the meal he made sure no one's glass was ever empty, but he never served anyone while they were speaking. Like Jenkins, he was rarely seen and never heard. Everything went as planned, although Giles was well aware that Major Müller's suspicious eyes rarely left him, even when he tried to melt into the background.

After the two of them had been escorted back to the camp later that afternoon, Bates said, 'The commandant was impressed.'

'What makes you say that?' asked Giles, fishing.

'He told the head chef that you must have worked for a grand household, because although you were obviously from the lower classes, you'd been well taught by a consummate professional.'

'Thank you, Jenkins,' said Giles.

'So what does consummate mean?' asked Bates.

—◦—

Giles became so skilled in his new vocation that the camp commandant insisted on being served by him even when he dined alone. This allowed Giles to study his mannerisms, the inflections in his voice, his laugh, even his slight stutter.

Within weeks, Private Barrington had been handed the keys to the wine cellar, and allowed to select which wines would be served at dinner. And after a few months, Bates overheard the commandant telling the chef that Barrington was *erstklassig*.

Whenever the commandant held a dinner party, Giles quickly assessed which tongues could be loosened by the regular topping up of glasses, and how to make himself invisible whenever one of those tongues began to wag. He passed on any useful information he'd picked up the previous evening to the brigadier's batman while they were out on the communal five-mile run. These titbits included where the commandant lived, the fact that he'd been elected to the town council at the age of thirty-two, and been appointed mayor in 1938. He couldn't drive, but he had visited England three or four times before the war and spoke fluent English. In return, Giles learnt that he and Bates had climbed several more rungs up the escape committee's ladder.

Giles's main activity during the day was to spend an hour chatting to his tutor. Never a word of English was spoken, and the man from Solihull even told the brigadier that Private Barrington was beginning to sound more and more like the commandant.

⊸◦⊷

On December 3rd 1941, Corporal Bates and Private Barrington made their final presentation to the escape committee. The brigadier and his team listened to the bed and breakfast plan with considerable interest, and agreed that it had a far better chance of succeeding than most of the half-baked schemes that were put before them.

'When would you consider the best time to carry out your plan?' asked the brigadier.

'New Year's Eve, sir,' said Giles without hesitation. 'All the officers will be joining the commandant for dinner to welcome in the New Year.'

'And as Private Barrington will be pouring the drinks,' added Bates, 'there shouldn't be too many of them who are still sober by the time midnight strikes.'

'Except for Müller,' the brigadier reminded Bates, 'who doesn't drink.'

'True, but he never fails to toast the Fatherland, the Führer and the Third Reich. If you add in the New Year, and his host, I have a feeling he'll be pretty sleepy by the time he's driven home.'

'What time are you usually escorted back to camp after one of the commandant's dinner parties?' asked a young lieutenant who had recently joined the committee.

'Around eleven,' said Bates, 'but as it's New Year's Eve, it won't be before midnight.'

'Don't forget, gentlemen,' Giles chipped in, 'I have the keys to the wine cellar, so I can assure you several bottles will find their way to the guard house during the evening. We wouldn't want them to miss out on the celebrations.'

'That's all very well,' said a wing commander who rarely spoke, 'but how do you plan to get past them?'

'By driving out through the front gate in the commandant's car,' said Giles. 'He's always a dutiful host and never leaves before his last guest, which should give us at least a couple of hours' start.'

'Even if you are able to steal his car,' said the brigadier, 'however drunk the guards are, they'll still be able to tell the difference between a wine waiter and their commanding officer.'

'Not if I'm wearing his greatcoat, hat, scarf and gloves, and holding his baton,' said Giles.

The young lieutenant clearly wasn't convinced. 'And is it part of your plan for the commandant to meekly hand all his clothes over to you, Private Barrington?'

'No, sir,' said Giles to an officer he outranked. 'The commandant always leaves his coat, cap and gloves in the cloakroom.'

'But what about Bates?' said the same officer. 'They'll spot him a mile off.'

'Not if I'm in the boot of the car, they won't,' said Bates.

'What about the commandant's driver, who we must assume will be stone-cold sober?' said the brigadier.

'We're working on it,' said Giles.

'And if you do manage to overcome the problem of the driver and get past the guards, how far is it to the Swiss border?' The young lieutenant again.

'One hundred and seventy-three kilometres,' said Bates. 'At a hundred kilometres an hour, we should reach the border in just under two hours.'

'That's assuming there are no hold-ups on the way.'

'No escape plan can ever be foolproof,' interjected the brigadier. 'In the end, it all comes down to how you cope with the unforeseen.'

Both Giles and Bates nodded their agreement.

'Thank you, gentlemen,' said the brigadier. 'The committee will consider your plan, and we'll let you know our decision in the morning.'

'What's that young sprog got against us?' asked Bates once they'd left the meeting.

'Nothing,' said Giles. 'On the contrary, I suspect he wishes he was the third member of our team.'

◄◦►

On December 6th, the brigadier's batman told Giles during the five-mile run that their plan had been given the green light, and the committee wished them bon voyage. Giles quickly caught up with Corporal Bates and passed on the news.

Barrington and Bates went over their B&B plan again and again, until, like Olympic athletes, they became bored with the endless hours of preparation and longed to hear the starter's pistol.

At six o'clock on December 31st, 1941, Corporal Terry Bates and Private Giles Barrington reported for duty in the commandant's quarters, aware that if their plan failed, at best they would have to wait for another year, but if they were caught red-handed . . .

22

'YOU-COME-BACK-at-six-thirty,' Terry almost shouted at the German corporal who had escorted them from the camp to the commandant's quarters.

The blank look on the corporal's face left Giles in little doubt that he was never going to make sergeant.

'Come-back-at-six-thirty,' repeated Terry, enunciating each word slowly. He grabbed the corporal's wrist and pointed to the six on his watch. Giles only wished he could say to the corporal, in his own language, 'If you return at six-thirty, corporal, there'll be a crate of beer for you and your friends in the guard house.' But he knew that if he did, he would be arrested and be spending New Year's Eve in solitary confinement.

Terry once again pointed to the corporal's watch, and imitated a man drinking. This time the corporal smiled and mimicked the same action.

'I think he's finally got the message,' said Giles as they made their way into the commandant's quarters.

'We still have to make sure he picks the beer up before the first officer arrives. So we'd better get a move on.'

'Yes, sir,' said Terry as he headed off in the direction of the kitchen. Natural order restored.

Giles went to the cloakroom, removed the waiter's uniform from its peg and changed into the white shirt, black tie, black trousers and white linen jacket. He spotted a pair of black leather gloves on the bench that an officer must have left behind on some previous occasion, and tucked them into his pocket thinking they might prove useful later. He closed the cloakroom door and made his way to the dining room. Three waitresses from the town – including Greta, the only one he'd ever been tempted to flirt with, but he knew Jenkins wouldn't have approved – were laying a table for sixteen.

He checked his watch: 6.12 p.m. He left the dining room and went downstairs to the wine cellar. A single bulb lit a room that had once stored filing cabinets full of archives. Since Giles's arrival, they had been replaced by wine racks.

Giles had already decided he would need at least three cases of wine for the dinner that night, as well as a crate of beer for the thirsty corporal and his comrades in the guard house. He studied the racks carefully before selecting a couple of bottles of sherry, a dozen bottles of Italian pinot grigio, two cases of French burgundy and a crate of German beer. Just as he was leaving, his eyes settled on three bottles of Johnnie Walker Red Label, two bottles of Russian vodka, half a dozen bottles of Rémy Martin and a flagon of vintage port. Giles felt that a visitor might be forgiven for not being sure who was at war with whom.

For the next fifteen minutes he lugged the cases of wine and beer up the stairs, constantly stopping to check his watch, and at 6.29 he opened the back door to find the German corporal jumping up and down and slapping his sides in an effort to keep warm. Giles raised the palms of both hands to indicate that he should stay put for a moment. He then moved swiftly back down the corridor – Jenkins never ran – picked up the crate of beer, returned and handed it to him.

Greta, who was clearly running late, watched the handover

and grinned at Giles. He returned her smile, before she disappeared into the dining room.

'The guard house,' said Giles firmly, pointing towards the outer perimeter. The corporal nodded, and headed off in the right direction. Terry had asked Giles earlier if he should smuggle some food from the kitchen for the corporal and his friends in the guard house.

'Certainly not,' Giles had replied firmly. 'We want them drinking all night on an empty stomach.'

Giles closed the door and returned to the dining room, where the waitresses had almost finished laying the table.

He uncorked the dozen bottles of merlot, but only placed four on the sideboard, discreetly hiding the other eight underneath it. He didn't need Müller to work out what he was up to. He also put a bottle of whisky and two of sherry at one end of the sideboard, before lining up, like soldiers on parade, a dozen tumblers and half a dozen sherry glasses. Everything was in place.

Giles was polishing a tumbler when Colonel Schabacker walked in. The commandant checked the table, made one or two adjustments to the seating plan, then turned his attention to the array of bottles on the sideboard. Giles wondered if he might comment, but he simply smiled and said, 'I'm expecting the guests to arrive around seven-thirty, and I have told the chef we will sit down for dinner at eight.'

Giles could only hope that in a few hours' time, his German would prove as fluent as Colonel Schabacker's English.

The next person to enter the dining room was a young lieutenant who had recently joined the officers' mess and was attending his first commandant's dinner. Giles noticed him eyeing the whisky and stepped forward to serve him, pouring him half a glass. He then handed the commandant his usual sherry.

The second officer to make an appearance was Captain

Henkel, the camp's adjutant. Giles handed him his usual glass of vodka, and spent the next thirty minutes serving each new guest, always having their favourite tipple to hand.

By the time the guests sat down for dinner, several empty bottles had been replaced by the reserves Giles had secreted under the sideboard.

Moments later waitresses appeared carrying plates of borscht, while the commandant sampled the white wine.

'Italian,' said Giles, showing him the label.

'Excellent,' he murmured.

Giles then filled every glass except that of Major Müller, who continued to sip his water.

Some of the guests drank more quickly than others, which kept Giles moving around the table, always making sure that no one had an empty glass. Once the soup bowls had been whisked away, Giles melted into the background because Terry had warned him what would happen next. With a flourish, the double doors opened and the chef entered carrying a large boar's head on a silver salver. The waitresses followed and placed dishes of vegetables and potatoes, along with jugs of thick gravy, in the centre of the table.

As the chef began to carve, Colonel Schabacker sampled the burgundy, which caused another smile to appear on his face. Giles returned to the task of topping up any half-empty glasses, with one exception. He'd noticed that the young lieutenant hadn't spoken for some time, so he left his glass untouched. One or two of the other officers were beginning to slur their words, and he needed them to stay awake until at least midnight.

The chef returned later to serve second helpings, and Giles obliged when Colonel Schabacker demanded that everyone's glasses should be replenished. By the time Terry made his first appearance to remove what was left of the boar's head, Major Müller was the only officer still sober.

A few minutes later, the chef made a third entrance, this

time carrying a black forest gateau, which he placed on the table in front of the commandant. The host plunged a knife into the cake several times, and the waitresses distributed generous portions to each of the guests. Giles continued topping up their glasses, until he was down to the last bottle.

As the waitresses cleared the dessert plates, Giles removed the wine glasses from the table, replacing them with brandy balloons and port glasses.

'Gentlemen,' announced Colonel Schabacker just after eleven, 'please charge your glasses, as I would like to propose a toast.' He rose from his place, held his glass high in the air and said, 'The Fatherland!'

Fifteen officers rose at various speeds, and repeated, 'The Fatherland!' Müller glanced towards Giles, and tapped his glass to indicate that he would require something for the toast.

'Not wine, you idiot,' said Müller. 'I want some brandy.' Giles smiled, and filled his glass with burgundy.

Müller had failed to trap him.

Loud, convivial chatter continued as Giles carried a humidor around the table and invited the guests to select a cigar. The young lieutenant was now resting his head on the table, and Giles thought he detected a snore.

When the commandant rose a second time, to drink the health of the Führer, Giles poured Müller some more red wine. He raised his glass, clicked his heels together and gave a Nazi salute. A toast to Frederick the Great followed, and this time Giles made sure Müller's glass had been topped up long before he rose.

At five minutes to midnight, Giles checked that every glass was full. When the clock on the wall began to chime, fifteen officers cried almost in unison, 10, 9, 8, 7, 6, 5, 4, 3, 2, 1, and then broke into 'Deutschland, Deutschland über alles', slapping each other on the back as they welcomed in the New Year.

It was some time before they resumed their places. The commandant remained standing and tapped his glass with a spoon. Everyone fell silent in anticipation of his annual speech.

He began by thanking his colleagues for their loyalty and dedication during a difficult year. He then spoke for some time about the destiny of the Fatherland. Giles remembered that Schabacker had been the local mayor before he took over as commandant of the camp. He ended by declaring that he hoped the right side would have won the war by this time next year. Giles wanted to scream, Hear, Hear! in any language, but Müller swung round to see if the colonel's words had evoked any reaction. Giles stared blankly ahead, as if he hadn't understood a word. He had passed another of Müller's tests.

23

IT WAS A FEW MINUTES after 1.00 a.m. when the first guest rose to leave. 'I'm on duty at six in the morning, colonel,' he explained. This was greeted with mock applause, as the officer bowed low and left without another word.

Several other guests departed during the next hour, but Giles knew he couldn't consider executing his own well-rehearsed exit while Müller was still on the premises. He became a little anxious when the waitresses started to clear away the coffee cups, a sign that their evening was coming to an end and he might be ordered back to the camp. Giles kept himself busy, continuing to serve those officers who didn't seem in any hurry to leave.

Müller finally rose as the last waitress left the room and bade goodnight to his colleagues, but not before clicking his heels and giving his comrades another Nazi salute. Giles and Terry had agreed that their plan couldn't be put into motion until at least fifteen minutes after Müller had departed and they had checked that his car was no longer in its usual place.

Giles refilled the glasses of the six officers who remained seated around the table. They were all close friends of the commandant. Two of them had been at school with him, another three had served on the town council, and only the camp adjutant was a more recent acquaintance; information Giles had picked up during the past few months.

It must have been about twenty past two when the commandant beckoned Giles over. 'It's been a long day,' he said in English. 'Go and join your friend in the kitchen, and take a bottle of wine with you.'

'Thank you, sir,' said Giles, placing a bottle of brandy and a decanter of port in the centre of the table.

The last words he heard the commandant say before he left were to the adjutant, who was seated on his right. 'When we've finally won this war, Franz, I intend to offer that man a job. I can't imagine he'll want to return to England while a Swastika flies over Buckingham Palace.'

Giles removed the only bottle of wine still on the sideboard, left the room and closed the door quietly behind him. He could feel the adrenaline pumping through his body, and was well aware that the next fifteen minutes would decide their fate. He took the back stairs down to the kitchen where he found Terry chatting to the chef, a half-empty bottle of cooking sherry by his side.

'Happy New Year, chef,' said Terry as he rose from his chair. 'Got to dash, otherwise I'll be late for breakfast in Zurich.'

Giles tried to keep a straight face as the chef just about raised a hand in acknowledgement.

They ran up the stairs, the only two sober people in the building. Giles passed the bottle of wine to Terry and said, 'Two minutes, no more.'

Terry walked down the corridor and slipped out of the back door. Giles withdrew into the shadows at the top of the stairs, just as an officer came out of the dining room and headed for the lavatory.

Moments later, the back door reopened and a head appeared. Giles waved furiously at Terry and pointed to the lavatory. Terry ran over to join him in the shadows, just before the officer emerged to make his way unsteadily back to the dining room. Once the door had closed behind him, Giles asked, 'How's our tame German, corporal?'

'Half asleep. I gave him the bottle of wine and warned him we could be at least another hour.'

'Do you think he understood?'

'I don't think he cared.'

'Good enough. Your turn to act as lookout,' said Giles as he stepped back out into the corridor. He clenched his fists to stop his hands trembling, and was just about to open the cloakroom door when he thought he heard a voice coming from inside. He froze, put his ear to the door and listened. It only took him a moment to realize who it must be. For the first time, he broke Jenkins's golden rule and charged back down the corridor to rejoin Terry in the shadows at the top of the stairs.

'What's the problem?'

Giles put a finger up to his lips, as the cloakroom door opened and out stepped Major Müller, doing up his fly buttons. Once he'd pulled on his greatcoat, he glanced up and down the corridor to make sure no one had spotted him, then slipped through the front door and out into the night.

'Which girl?' asked Giles.

'Probably Greta. I've had her a couple of times, but never in the cloakroom.'

'Isn't that fraternizing?' whispered Giles.

'Only if you're an officer,' said Terry.

They only had to wait for a few moments before the door opened again and Greta appeared, looking a little flushed. She walked calmly out of the front door without bothering to check if anyone had seen her.

'Second attempt,' said Giles, who moved swiftly back down the corridor, opened the cloakroom door and disappeared inside just as another officer came out of the dining room.

Don't turn right, don't turn right, Terry begged silently. The officer turned left and headed for the lavatory. Terry prayed for the longest pee in history. He began counting the seconds, but then the cloakroom door opened and out stepped the commandant in all but name. Get back inside, Terry waved frantically. Giles ducked back into the cloakroom and pulled the door closed.

When the adjutant reappeared, Terry feared he would go to the cloakroom to collect his cap and coat, and find Giles dressed as the commandant, in which case the game would be up before it had even begun. Terry followed each step, fearing the worst, but the adjutant stopped at the dining room door, opened it and disappeared inside. Once the door had closed, Terry bolted down the corridor and opened the cloakroom door to find Giles dressed in a greatcoat, scarf, gloves and peaked cap and carrying a baton, beads of sweat on his forehead.

'Let's get out of here before one of us has a heart attack,' said Terry.

Terry and Giles left the building even more quickly than Müller or Greta had.

'Relax,' said Giles once they were outside. 'Don't forget we're the only two people who are sober.' He tucked the scarf around his neck so that it covered his chin, pulled down his cap, gripped the baton firmly and stooped slightly, as he was a couple of inches taller than the commandant.

As soon as the driver heard Giles approaching, he leapt out of the car and opened the back door for him. Giles had rehearsed a sentence he'd heard the colonel say to his driver many times, and as he fell into the back seat, he pulled his cap even further down and slurred, 'Take me home, Hans.'

Hans returned to the driver's seat, but when he heard a

click that sounded like the boot closing, he looked back suspiciously, only to see the commandant tapping his baton on the window.

'What's holding you up, Hans?' Giles asked with a slight stutter.

Hans switched on the ignition, put the car into first gear and drove slowly towards the guard house. A sergeant emerged from the sentry box when he heard the vehicle approaching. He tried to open the barrier and salute at the same time. Giles raised his baton in acknowledgement, and nearly burst out laughing when he noticed that the top two buttons of the sentry's tunic were undone. Colonel Scha-backer would never have let that pass without comment, even on New Year's Eve.

Major Forsdyke, the escape committee's intelligence officer, had told Giles that the commandant's house was approximately two miles from the compound, and the last two hundred yards were down a narrow, unlit lane. Giles remained slumped into the corner of the back seat, where he couldn't be seen in the rear-view mirror, but the moment the car swung into the lane, he sat bolt upright, tapped the driver on the shoulder with his baton and ordered him to stop.

'I can't wait,' he said, before jumping out of the car and pretending to undo his fly buttons.

Hans watched as the colonel disappeared into the bushes. He looked puzzled; after all, they were only a hundred metres from his front door. He stepped out of the car and waited by the back door. When he thought he heard his master coming back, he turned around just in time to see a clenched fist, an instant before it broke his nose. He slumped to the ground.

Giles ran to the back of the car and opened the boot. Terry leapt out, walked across to Hans's prostrate body and began to unbutton the driver's uniform, before pulling off his own clothes. Once Bates had finished putting on his new uniform, it became clear just how much shorter and fatter Hans was.

'It won't matter,' said Giles, reading his thoughts. 'When you're behind the wheel, no one will give you a second look.'

They dragged Hans to the back of the car and bundled him into the boot.

'I doubt if he'll wake up before we sit down for breakfast in Zurich,' said Terry as he tied a handkerchief around Hans's mouth.

The commandant's new driver took his place behind the wheel, and neither of them spoke again until they were back on the main road. Terry didn't need to stop and check any signposts, as he'd studied the route to the border every day for the past month.

'Stay on the right-hand side of the road,' said Giles, unnecessarily, 'and don't drive too fast. The last thing we need is to be pulled over.'

'I think we've made it,' Terry said as they passed a signpost for Schaffhausen.

'I won't believe we've made it until we're being shown to our table at the Imperial Hotel and a waiter hands me the breakfast menu.'

'I won't need a menu,' said Terry. 'Eggs, bacon, beans, sausage and tomato, and a pint of beer. That's my usual down at the meat market every morning. How about you?'

'A kipper, lightly poached, a slice of buttered toast, a spoonful of Oxford marmalade and a pot of Earl Grey tea.'

'It didn't take you long to go back from butler to toff.'

Giles smiled. He checked his watch. There were few cars on the road that New Year's morning, so they continued to make good progress. That was, until Terry spotted the convoy ahead of them.

'What do I do now?' he said.

'Overtake them. We can't afford to waste any time. They'll have no reason to be suspicious – you're driving a senior officer who wouldn't expect to be held up.'

Once Terry caught up with the rear vehicle, he eased out into the centre of the road and began to overtake a long line of armoured trucks and motorcycles. As Giles had predicted, no one took any interest in a passing Mercedes that was clearly going about official business. When Terry overtook the leading vehicle, he breathed a sigh of relief, but he didn't fully relax until he swept round a corner and could no longer see any headlights in his rear-view mirror.

Giles continued to check his watch every few minutes. The next signpost confirmed they were making good time, but Giles knew they had no control over when the commandant's last guest would leave and Colonel Schabacker would go in search of his car and driver.

It was another forty minutes before they reached the outskirts of Schaffhausen. They were both so nervous that hardly a word had passed between them. Giles was exhausted just sitting in the back seat, doing nothing, but he knew they couldn't afford to relax until they had crossed the Swiss border.

When they entered the town, the locals were just beginning to wake up; the occasional tram, the odd car, a few bicycles ferrying people who were expected to work on New Year's Day. Terry didn't need to look for signs to the border, as he could see the Swiss Alps dominating the skyline. Freedom felt as if it was touching distance away.

'Bloody hell!' said Terry as he slammed on the brakes.

'What's the problem?' said Giles, leaning forward.

'Look at that queue.'

Giles stuck his head out of the window to see a line of about forty vehicles, bumper to bumper, ahead of them, all waiting to cross the border. He checked to see if any of them were official cars. When he was sure there were none, he said, 'Drive straight to the front. That's what they'd expect us to do. If we don't, we'll only draw attention to ourselves.'

Terry drove slowly forward, only stopping when he reached the barrier.

'Get out and open the door for me, but don't say anything.'

Terry turned off the engine, got out and opened the back door. Giles marched up to the customs post.

A young officer leapt up from behind his desk and saluted when he saw the colonel enter the room. Giles handed over two sets of papers that the camp forger had assured him would pass muster at any border post in Germany. He was about to find out if he'd exaggerated. As the officer flicked through the documents, Giles tapped the side of his leg with his baton and glanced repeatedly at his watch.

'I have an important meeting in Zurich,' he snapped, 'and I'm running late.'

'I'm sorry, colonel. I'll get you on your way as soon as possible. It should only take me a few moments.'

The officer checked the photograph of Giles on his papers, and looked puzzled. Giles wondered if he'd have the nerve to ask him to remove his scarf, because if he did, he would immediately realize that he was too young to be a colonel.

Giles stared defiantly at the young man, who must have been weighing up the possible consequences of holding up a senior officer by asking him unnecessary questions. The scales came down in Giles's favour. The officer nodded his head, stamped the papers and said, 'I hope you won't be late for your meeting, sir.'

'Thank you,' said Giles. He put the documents back in an inside pocket and was walking towards the door when the young officer stopped him in his tracks.

'Heil Hitler!' he shouted.

Giles hesitated, turned slowly around and said, 'Heil Hitler,' giving a perfect Nazi salute. As he walked out of the building, he had to suppress his laughter when he noticed that Terry was holding open the back door with one hand, and holding up his trousers with the other.

'Thank you, Hans,' said Giles as he slumped into the back seat.

That was when they heard a banging noise coming from the boot.

'Oh my God,' said Terry. 'Hans.'

The brigadier's words came back to haunt them; no escape plan can ever be foolproof. In the end, it all comes down to how you cope with the unforeseen.

Terry closed the back door and returned to his place behind the wheel as quickly as he could, as he feared the guards would hear the banging. He tried to remain calm as the barrier rose inch by inch, and the banging became louder and louder.

'Drive slowly,' said Giles. 'Don't give them any reason to become suspicious.'

Terry eased the gear lever into first and drove slowly under the barrier. Giles glanced out of the side window as they passed the customs post. The young officer was speaking on the phone. He looked out of the window, stared directly at Giles, jumped up from his desk and ran out on to the road.

Giles estimated that the Swiss border post was no more than a couple of hundred yards away. He looked out of the back window to see the young officer waving frantically, as guards carrying rifles poured out of the customs post.

'Change of plan,' said Giles. 'Step on the accelerator,' he shouted as the first bullets hit the back of the car.

Terry was changing gear when the tyre burst. He tried desperately to keep the car on the road, but it swerved from side to side, careered into the side railings and came to a standstill midway between the two border posts. Another volley of shots quickly followed.

'My turn to beat you to the washroom,' said Giles.

'Not a hope,' said Terry, who had both feet on the ground before Giles had dived out of the back door.

They both began running flat out towards the Swiss border. If either of them was ever going to run a ten-second hundred, it would be today. Although they were dodging and changing direction in their attempt to avoid the bullets, Giles still felt confident that he would cross the finishing line first. The Swiss border guards were cheering them on, and when Giles dipped at the tape, he raised his arms in triumph, having finally defeated his greatest rival.

He turned around to gloat, and saw Terry lying in the middle of the road about thirty yards away, a bullet wound in the back of his head and blood trickling from his mouth.

Giles fell on his knees and began to crawl towards his friend. More shots rang out as two Swiss border guards grabbed him by the ankles and pulled him back to safety.

He wanted to explain to them that he didn't care to have breakfast alone.

HUGO BARRINGTON

1939–1942

24

HUGO BARRINGTON COULDN'T remove the smile from his face when he read in the *Bristol Evening News* that Harry Clifton had been buried at sea within hours of war being declared.

At last the Germans had done something worthwhile. A U-boat commander had single-handedly solved his biggest problem. Hugo began to believe it might even be possible that, given time, he could return to Bristol and resume his place as deputy chairman of the Barrington Shipping Line. He would begin to work on his mother with regular phone calls to Barrington Hall, but only after his father had left for work each day. That night he went out to celebrate, and arrived home as drunk as a lord.

When Hugo first migrated to London following his daughter's aborted wedding, he rented a basement flat in Cadogan Gardens for a pound a week. The only good thing about the three-roomed accommodation was the address, which created the impression that he was a man of means.

Although he still had a few bob in the bank, it soon dwindled, while he had time on his hands and no regular source of income. It wasn't long before he had to let go of the Bugatti, which kept him solvent for a few more weeks, but only until the first cheque bounced. He couldn't turn to his father for help, because he'd cut him off, and frankly Sir

Walter would have given Maisie Clifton a helping hand before he'd lift a finger to assist his son.

After a fruitless few months in London, Hugo tried to find a job. But it wasn't easy; if any potential employer knew his father, he never even got an interview, and when he did, his new boss expected him to work hours he hadn't realized existed, and for a wage that wouldn't have covered his bar bill at the club.

Hugo began to dabble what little he had left on the stock exchange. He listened to too many old school chums telling him about deals that couldn't fail, and even got involved in one or two more shady enterprises that brought him into contact with what the press described as spivs, and his father would have considered crooks.

Within a year, Hugo had resorted to borrowing money from friends, and even friends of friends. But when you don't have any means of repaying your debts, you are quickly dropped from most dinner-party guest lists, and are no longer invited to join country-house shooting parties at the weekend.

Whenever he was desperate, Hugo would ring his mother, but not until he was sure his father was at the office. Mama could always be relied on for a tenner, just as she'd been for ten bob when he was at school.

An old school chum, Archie Fenwick, was also good for the occasional lunch at his club or an invitation to one of his fashionable Chelsea cocktail parties. And that was where Hugo first met Olga. It wasn't her face or figure that immediately attracted his attention, but the pearls, three rows of them, that were draped around her neck. Hugo cornered Archie and asked if they were real.

'They most certainly are,' he said. 'But be warned, you're not the only person hoping to dip your paw into that honey pot.'

Olga Piotrovska, Archie told him, had recently arrived in

London, having escaped from Poland after the German invasion. Her parents had been taken away by the Gestapo, for no other reason than that they were Jewish. Hugo frowned. Archie wasn't able to tell Hugo much more about her, except that she lived in a magnificent townhouse on Lowndes Square and possessed a fine art collection. Hugo had never taken a great deal of interest in art, but even he'd heard of Picasso and Matisse.

Hugo strolled across the room and introduced himself to Miss Piotrovska. When Olga told him why she'd had to leave Germany, he expressed outrage and assured her that his family had been proud to do business with the Jews for over a hundred years. After all, his father, Sir Walter Barrington, was a friend of the Rothschilds and the Hambros. Long before the party was over, he had invited Olga to join him for lunch at the Ritz the following day, but as he was no longer allowed to sign the bill, he had to cadge another fiver from Archie.

The lunch went well, and for the next few weeks Hugo courted Olga assiduously, within the limits of his resources. He told her that he'd left his wife after she'd admitted having an affair with his best friend, and he'd asked his lawyer to instigate divorce proceedings. In fact, Elizabeth had already divorced him, and the judge had awarded her the Manor House, and everything Hugo hadn't removed after he'd left in such a hurry.

Olga was very understanding, and Hugo promised her that the moment he was free, he would ask her to marry him. He never stopped telling her how beautiful she was and how her rather lifeless efforts in bed were so exciting compared to Elizabeth. He continually reminded her that when his father died, she would become Lady Barrington, and his temporary financial difficulties would be resolved when he inherited the Barrington estate. He may have given her the impression that his father was a lot older and less robust than he actually was. 'Fading fast' was the expression he used.

◄o►

A few weeks later Hugo moved into Lowndes Square, and over the next few months he returned to a lifestyle he assumed was his by right. Several chums commented on how lucky he was to have the company of such a charming and beautiful woman, and some of them couldn't resist adding, 'And she's not short of a bob or two.'

Hugo had almost forgotten what it was like to eat three meals a day, wear new clothes and be chauffeured around town. He paid off most of his debts, and it wasn't too long before doors began to reopen that had until recently been slammed in his face. However, he was beginning to wonder how long it could last, because he certainly had no intention of marrying a Jewish refugee from Warsaw.

◄o►

Derek Mitchell climbed on board the express train from Temple Meads to Paddington. The private detective was back working full time for his old employer, now that his stipend was once again paid on the first day of the month, and his expenses were redeemed on presentation. Hugo expected Mitchell to report to him once a month on what the Barrington family were up to. In particular, Hugo was interested in the comings and goings of his father, his ex-wife, Giles, Emma and even Grace, but he was still paranoid about Maisie Clifton, and expected Mitchell to brief him on everything she got up to, and he meant everything.

Mitchell would travel to London by train, and the two of them would meet in the waiting room opposite platform seven at Paddington Station. An hour later Mitchell would take the train back to Temple Meads.

That was how Hugo knew that Elizabeth continued to

live at the Manor House, while Grace rarely came home since she'd won a scholarship to Cambridge. Emma had given birth to a son, whom she'd christened Sebastian Arthur. Giles had enlisted in the Wessex Regiment as a private soldier, and after completing a twelve-week basic training course, had been sent to Mons Officer Cadet Training Unit.

This came as a surprise to Hugo, as he knew Giles had been passed unfit for active service by the Gloucesters shortly after the outbreak of war, because, like him and his father, he was colour-blind. Hugo had used the same excuse to avoid being called up in 1915.

―◦―

As the months passed, Olga began to ask more and more frequently when Hugo's divorce would be finalized. He always tried to make it sound as if it were imminent, but it wasn't until she suggested he move back into his flat in Cadogan Square until he could confirm that papers had been lodged with the court that he decided to do something about it. He waited another week before he told her his lawyers had begun proceedings.

A few more months of domestic harmony followed. What he hadn't told Olga was that he'd given his landlord in Cadogan Square a month's notice on the day he moved in with her. If she threw him out, he would have nowhere to live.

―◦―

It was about a month later that Mitchell phoned Hugo and said he needed to see him urgently, a most unusual request. They agreed to meet at four o'clock the following afternoon at their usual rendezvous.

When Mitchell walked into the station waiting room, Hugo was already sitting on a bench, hidden behind a copy of the London *Evening News*. He was reading about Rommel's sacking of Tobruk, not that he could have placed Tobruk on a map. He continued reading when Mitchell sat down beside him. The private detective spoke softly and never once looked in Hugo's direction.

'I thought you'd want to know that your eldest daughter took a job as a waitress at the Grand Hotel, using the name Miss Dickens.'

'Isn't that where Maisie Clifton works?'

'Yes, she's the restaurant's manageress, and was your daughter's boss.'

Hugo couldn't imagine why Emma could possibly want to work as a waitress. 'Does her mother know?'

'She must, because Hudson dropped her a hundred yards from the hotel every morning at five forty-five. But that isn't the reason I needed to see you.'

Hugo turned the page of his newspaper to see a photograph of General Auchinleck standing outside his tent in the desert, addressing the troops.

'Your daughter took a taxi to the docks yesterday morning. She was carrying a suitcase, when she boarded a passenger ship called the *Kansas Star*, where she was given a job in reception. She told her mother she was going to New York to visit her great-aunt Phyllis, who I believe is Lord Harvey's sister.'

Hugo would have been fascinated to know how Mitchell had picked up that particular piece of information, but he was still trying to work out why Emma would want to take a job on the ship Harry Clifton had died on. None of this made any sense. He instructed Mitchell to dig deeper and let him know immediately he picked up any more information about what Emma was up to.

Just before Mitchell left to catch the train back to Temple Meads, he told Hugo that German bombers had razed Broad Street to the ground. Hugo couldn't imagine why this would be of any interest to him, until Mitchell reminded him that it was the street on which Tilly's tea shop had stood. He thought Mr Barrington ought to know that some developers were taking an interest in Mrs Clifton's old site. Hugo thanked Mitchell for the information, without suggesting that it was of any real interest to him.

◄○►

Hugo telephoned Mr Prendergast at the National Provincial Bank the moment he got back to Lowndes Square.

'I expect you're calling about Broad Street,' were the bank manager's opening words.

'Yes, I heard the site of Tilly's tea shop might be up for sale.'

'The whole street's up for sale following the bombing,' said Prendergast. 'Most of the shopkeepers have lost their livelihoods, and because it was an act of war, they can't claim insurance.'

'So could I pick up the Tilly's site for a reasonable price?'

'Frankly, you could pick up the whole street for next to nothing. In fact, if you have any spare cash, Mr Barrington, I would recommend it as a shrewd investment.'

'That's assuming we're going to win the war,' Hugo reminded him.

'I admit it's a gamble, but it could show a handsome return.'

'How much are we talking about?'

'For Mrs Clifton's site, I think I could talk her into accepting two hundred pounds. In fact, as half the traders in that street bank with me, I suspect you could pick up the whole shooting match for around three thousand. It's like playing Monopoly with loaded dice.'

'I'll look into it,' Hugo said before putting the phone down. What he couldn't tell Prendergast was that he didn't even have Monopoly money.

He tried to think of some way of raising that amount, when all his usual contacts were unwilling to lend him even a fiver. He couldn't ask Olga for any more money, unless he was willing to walk down the aisle with her, and that was out of the question.

He wouldn't have given the matter another thought if he hadn't bumped into Toby Dunstable at one of Archie's parties.

Toby and Hugo had been contemporaries at Eton. Hugo couldn't remember much about Dunstable, except that he regularly helped himself to the younger boys' tuck. When he was finally caught removing a ten-shilling note from one of the boys' lockers, everyone assumed he would be expelled, and possibly he would, if he hadn't been the second son of the Earl of Dunstable.

When Hugo asked Toby what he was up to nowadays, he said rather vaguely that he dabbled in property. Hugo told him about the investment opportunity Broad Street presented, but he didn't seem that interested. In fact, Hugo couldn't help noticing that Toby didn't take his eyes off the diamond necklace that sparkled around Olga's neck.

Toby handed Hugo his card, saying, 'If you're ever in need of some ready cash, it shouldn't prove too difficult, if you get my drift, old fellow.'

Hugo got his drift, but didn't take his hinted proposal at all seriously, until Olga asked him over breakfast one morning if a date had been fixed for the decree nisi. Hugo assured her it was imminent.

He left the house, went straight to his club, checked Toby's card and gave him a call. They agreed to meet at a pub in Fulham, where they sat alone in a corner, drinking double gins and chatting about how our lads were faring in the Middle East. They only changed the subject when they were certain they couldn't be overheard.

'All I'll need is a key to the flat,' said Toby, 'and the exact location of her jewellery.'

'That shouldn't prove difficult,' Hugo assured him.

'The only thing you'll have to do, old chum, is make sure you're both off the premises long enough for me to carry out the job.'

When Olga suggested over breakfast that she would like to see a production of *Rigoletto* at Sadler's Wells, Hugo agreed to book a couple of tickets. He would usually have made some excuse, but on this occasion he readily agreed, and even suggested that they have dinner at the Savoy afterwards to celebrate.

'Celebrate what?' she asked.

'My decree nisi has been granted,' he said casually. She threw her arms around him. 'Just another six months, my darling, and you'll be Mrs Barrington.'

Hugo took a small leather box out of his pocket and presented her with an engagement ring he'd bought on approval in Burlington Arcade the previous day. She approved. He intended to return it in six months' time.

The opera seemed to last for three months, rather than the three hours suggested in the programme. However, Hugo didn't complain, as he knew Toby would be making good use of the time.

Over dinner in the River Room, Hugo and Olga discussed where they might spend their honeymoon, as they couldn't travel abroad. Olga favoured Bath, which was a little too close to Bristol for Hugo's liking, but as it was never going to happen, he happily went along with her suggestion.

In the taxi on the way back to Lowndes Square, Hugo wondered how long it would be before Olga discovered that her diamonds were missing. Sooner than he'd bargained for, because when they opened the front door, they found the whole place had been ransacked. All that was left on the walls where the paintings had once hung were clear outlines to show what size they had been.

While Olga broke down in hysterics, Hugo picked up the phone and dialled 999. It took the police several hours to complete an inventory of everything that was missing, because Olga couldn't remain calm enough to answer their questions for more than a few moments at a time. The chief inspector in charge of the case assured them that the details of the stolen items would be circulated to all the leading diamond merchants and art dealers in London within forty-eight hours.

Hugo hit the roof when he caught up with Toby Dunstable in Fulham the following afternoon. His old school chum calmly took it on the chin like a heavyweight boxer. When Hugo was finally spent, Toby pushed a shoebox across the table.

'I don't need a new pair of shoes,' Hugo snapped.

'Perhaps not, but you'll be able to buy a shoe shop with what's inside there,' he said tapping the box.

Hugo lifted the lid and stared into the box, which contained no shoes, but was packed with five-pound notes.

'You needn't bother to count them,' said Toby. 'You'll find there's ten thousand pounds in readies.'

Hugo smiled, suddenly calm again. 'You're a good fellow,' he said as he placed the lid back and ordered another two double gin-and-tonics.

As the weeks passed, and the police failed to come up with any suspects, the chief inspector didn't leave Hugo in much doubt that he thought it was an inside job, an expression he used again and again whenever they met. However, Toby reassured him that they would never consider arresting the son of Sir Walter Barrington, unless they had cast-iron proof of his guilt that would convince a jury beyond reasonable doubt.

Olga asked Hugo where his new suits had come from and how he could possibly afford a Bugatti. He showed her the car's logbook, which confirmed that he'd owned it before they met. What he didn't tell her was how fortunate he'd been that the dealer he'd reluctantly sold it to still had it on his books.

As the end of the period after which the decree absolute would be granted was fast approaching, Hugo began to prepare for what they call in military circles an exit strategy. That was when Olga announced that she had some wonderful news to share with him.

Wellington once told a junior officer that timing was everything in life, and who was Hugo to disagree with the victor of Waterloo, especially when the great man's prophecy was about to apply to him?

He was reading *The Times* over breakfast, when he turned to the obituaries and saw a picture of his father staring out at him. He tried to read it without Olga discovering that both their lives were about to change.

In Hugo's opinion, the Thunderer had given the old man a good send-off, but it was the last paragraph of his record that most interested him. *Sir Walter Barrington is succeeded by his only surviving son, Hugo, who will inherit the title.*

However, what *The Times* didn't add was, *and all that therein is.*

MAISIE CLIFTON

1939–1942

25

MAISIE COULD STILL REMEMBER the pain she'd experienced when her husband didn't come home at the end of his evening shift. She knew Arthur was dead, even though it would be years before her brother Stan was willing to tell her the truth about how her husband had died at the dockyard that afternoon.

But that pain was nothing compared to being told that her only son had been buried at sea after the *Devonian* had been struck by a German torpedo, hours after war had been declared.

Maisie could still recall the last time she'd seen Harry. He'd come to visit her at the Grand Hotel that Thursday morning. The restaurant was packed, with a long queue of customers waiting to be seated. He'd stood in line, but when he saw his mother bustling in and out of the kitchen without a moment to spare, he slipped away, assuming she hadn't noticed him. He was always a thoughtful boy, and he knew she didn't approve of being interrupted at work, and, if the truth be told, he also knew she wouldn't have wanted to hear that he'd left Oxford to join the navy.

Sir Walter Barrington dropped by the next day to let Maisie know that Harry had sailed on the morning tide as fourth officer on the SS *Devonian*, and would be back within the month to join the crew of HMS *Resolution* as an ordinary seaman, as he intended to go off in search of German U-boats in the Atlantic. What he didn't realize was that they were already searching for him.

Maisie planned to take the day off when Harry returned, but it was not to be. Knowing how many other mothers had lost their offspring because of this evil and barbaric war didn't help.

Dr Wallace, the senior medical officer on the SS *Kansas Star*, was waiting by her front door in Still House Lane when she returned home after work that October evening. He didn't need to tell her why he was there. It was etched on his face.

They sat in the kitchen, and the doctor told her he'd been responsible for the welfare of those sailors who'd been dragged from the ocean following the sinking of the *Devonian*. He assured her that he'd done everything in his power to save Harry's life, but unhappily he'd never regained consciousness. In fact, of the nine sailors he tended to that night, only one had survived, a Tom Bradshaw, the *Devonian's* third officer, who was evidently a friend of Harry's. Bradshaw had written a letter of condolence which Dr Wallace had promised to deliver to Mrs Clifton as soon as the *Kansas Star* returned to Bristol. He had kept his word. Maisie felt guilty the moment the doctor had left to return to his ship. She hadn't even offered him a cup of tea.

She placed Tom Bradshaw's letter on the mantelpiece next to her favourite photograph of Harry singing in the school choir.

When she returned to work the following day, her colleagues at the hotel were kind and solicitous, and Mr Hurst, the hotel manager, suggested she took a few days off. She told him that was the last thing she needed. Instead she took on as much overtime as she could handle, in the hope that it might dull the pain.

It didn't.

—◦—

Many of the young men who worked at the hotel were leaving to join the armed forces, and their places were being taken by women. It was no longer considered a stigma for a young lady to work, and Maisie found herself taking on more and more responsibility as the number of male staff dwindled.

The restaurant manager was due to retire on his sixtieth birthday, but Maisie assumed that Mr Hurst would ask him to stay on until the end of the war. It came as a shock when he called her into his office and offered her the job.

'You've earned it, Maisie,' he said, 'and head office agrees with me.'

'I'd like a couple of days to think about it,' she replied before leaving the office.

Mr Hurst didn't raise the subject for another week, and when he did, Maisie suggested that perhaps she should be put on a month's trial. He laughed.

'It's usual,' he reminded her, 'for the employer, not the employee, to insist on a month's trial.'

Within a week, they'd both forgotten about the trial period, because although the hours were long and her new responsibilities were onerous, Maisie had never felt more fulfilled. She knew that when the war was over and the lads returned from the front, she'd go back to being a waitress. She'd have gone back to being a prostitute, if it had meant Harry would be among those who came home.

—◦—

Maisie didn't need to be able to read a newspaper to know that the Japanese air force had destroyed the American fleet at Pearl Harbor, and the citizens of the United States had risen as one against a common enemy and joined the Allies, because for days it was the only subject on everyone's lips.

It wasn't long before Maisie met her first American.

Thousands of Yanks found their way to the West Country over the next couple of years, and many of them were billeted in an army camp on the outskirts of Bristol. Some of the officers began to dine in the hotel restaurant, but no sooner had they become regulars than they would disappear, never to be seen again. Maisie was continually, painfully, reminded that some of them were no older than Harry.

But that changed when one of them did return. Maisie didn't immediately recognize him when he wheeled himself into the restaurant and asked for his usual table. She had always thought she was good at remembering names, and even better when it came to faces – you have to be when you can't really read and write. But the moment she heard that Southern drawl, the penny dropped. 'It's Lieutenant Mulholland, isn't it?'

'No, Mrs Clifton. It's Major Mulholland now. I've been sent back here to recuperate before they pack me off home to North Carolina.'

She smiled and showed him to his usual table, although he wouldn't allow her to assist him with his wheelchair. Mike, as he insisted Maisie call him, did become a regular, turning up twice, even three times a week.

Maisie laughed when Mr Hurst whispered, 'You know he's sweet on you.'

'I think you'll find my courting days are over,' she replied.

'Don't kid yourself,' he countered. 'You're in your prime, Maisie. I can tell you, Major Mulholland's not the first man who's asked me if you're walking out with anyone.'

'Try not to forget, Mr Hurst, that I'm a grandmother.'

'I wouldn't tell him that if I was you,' said the manager.

Maisie failed to recognize the major a second time when he came in one evening on crutches, the wheelchair clearly having been abandoned. Another month, and the crutches were replaced by sticks, and it wasn't much longer before they too became relics of the past.

One evening, Major Mulholland telephoned to book a table for eight; he had something to celebrate, he told Maisie. She assumed he must be returning to North Carolina, and for the first time she realized how much she would miss him.

She didn't consider Mike a handsome man, but he had the warmest smile and the manners of an English gentleman, or, as he once pointed out, a Southern gentleman. It had become fashionable to bad-mouth the Americans since they'd taken up residence on bases in Britain, and the oft repeated jibe that they were over-sexed, over-paid and over here could be heard on the lips of many Bristolians who'd never even met an American; not least, Maisie's brother Stan, and nothing she could say would change his mind.

By the time the major's celebration dinner had come to an end, the restaurant was almost empty. On the stroke of ten, a fellow officer rose to toast Mike's health and congratulate him.

As the party was about to leave and return to camp before curfew, Maisie told him, on behalf of the whole staff, how pleased they all were that he had fully recovered and was well enough to go home.

'I'm not going home, Maisie,' he said, laughing. 'We were celebrating my promotion to deputy commander of the base. I'm afraid you're stuck with me until this war is over.' Maisie was delighted by the news, and was taken by surprise when he added, 'It's the regimental dance next Saturday, and I wonder if you would do me the honour of being my guest.'

Maisie was speechless. She couldn't remember the last

time she'd been asked out on a date. She wasn't sure how long he stood there waiting for her to respond, but before she could do so he said, 'I'm afraid it will be the first time I've stepped on to a dance floor for several years.'

'Me too,' Maisie admitted.

26

MAISIE ALWAYS deposited her wages and her tips in the bank on Friday afternoon.

She didn't take any money home, because she didn't want Stan to find out she was earning more than he was. Her two accounts were always in credit, and every time the current account showed a balance of ten pounds, five would be transferred to her savings account – her little nest egg, as she described it, just in case something went wrong. After her financial setback with Hugo Barrington, she always assumed that something would go wrong.

That Friday she emptied her purse out on to the counter, and the teller began to sort the coins into neat little piles, as he did every week.

'That's four shillings and nine pence, Mrs Clifton,' he said, filling in her account book.

'Thank you,' said Maisie, as he slid the book under the grille. She was putting it back in her purse when he added, 'Mr Prendergast wondered if he could have a word with you.'

Maisie's heart sank. She considered bank managers and rent collectors a breed who only ever dispensed bad news, and she had good cause in Mr Prendergast's case, because the last time he'd asked to see her, it was to remind her there were insufficient funds in her account to cover Harry's fees for his last term at Bristol Grammar School. She reluctantly headed off in the direction of the manager's office.

'Good morning, Mrs Clifton,' said Mr Prendergast, rising from behind his desk as Maisie entered his office. He motioned her to a seat. 'I wanted to speak to you about a private matter.'

Maisie felt even more apprehensive. She tried to recall if she'd written any cheques during the past couple of weeks that might have caused her account to be overdrawn. She had bought a smart dress for the dance Mike Mulholland had invited her to on the American base, but it was second-hand, and well within her budget.

'A valued client of the bank,' Mr Prendergast began, 'has enquired about your plot of land in Broad Street, where Tilly's tea shop once stood.'

'But I assumed I'd lost everything when the building was bombed.'

'Not everything,' said Prendergast. 'The deeds of the land remain in your name.'

'But what could it possibly be worth,' said Maisie, 'now that the Germans have flattened most of the neighbourhood? When I last walked down Chapel Street, it was nothing more than a bomb site.'

'That may well be the case,' replied Mr Prendergast, 'but my client is still willing to offer you two hundred pounds for the freehold.'

'Two hundred pounds?' repeated Maisie as if she'd won the pools.

'That is the sum he is willing to pay,' confirmed Prendergast.

'How much do you think the land is worth?' asked Maisie, taking the bank manager by surprise.

'I've no idea, madam,' he replied. 'I'm a banker, not a property speculator.'

Maisie remained silent for a few moments. 'Please tell your client that I'd like a few days to think about it.'

'Yes, of course,' said Prendergast. 'But you ought to be aware that my client has instructed me to leave the offer on the table for one week only.'

'Then I'll have to make my decision by next Friday, won't I?' said Maisie defiantly.

'As you wish, madam,' said Prendergast, when Maisie rose to leave. 'I'll look forward to seeing you next Friday.'

When Maisie left the bank, she couldn't help thinking that the manager had never addressed her as madam before. During her walk home past black-curtained houses – she only ever took the bus when it was raining – she started to think about how she might spend two hundred pounds, but these thoughts were soon replaced by wondering who could advise her as to whether it was a fair price.

Mr Prendergast had made it sound like a reasonable offer, but which side was he on? Perhaps she'd have a word with Mr Hurst, but long before she reached Still House Lane she decided that it would be unprofessional to involve her boss in a personal matter. Mike Mulholland seemed a shrewd, intelligent man, but what would he know about the value of land in Bristol? As for her brother Stan, there would be absolutely no point in seeking his opinion, as he'd be sure to say, 'Take the money and run, girl.' And come to think about it, the last person she wanted to know about her potential windfall was Stan.

By the time Maisie had turned into Merrywood Lane, darkness was falling and the residents were preparing for blackout. She was no closer to resolving the problem. As she passed the gates of Harry's old primary school, a flood of happy memories returned, and she silently thanked Mr Holcombe for all he'd done for her son while he was growing up. She stopped on the spot. Mr Holcombe was a clever man; after all he'd been to Bristol University and got a degree. Surely he could advise her?

Maisie turned back and walked towards the school gates, but when she entered the playground there was no one to be seen. She checked her watch; a few minutes past five. All the children would have gone home some time ago, so Mr Holcombe had probably already left for the day.

She walked across the playground, opened the school door and stepped into a familiar corridor. It was as if time had stood still; the same red brick walls, just a few more initials etched into them, the same colourful paintings pinned up on the wall, just by different children, the same football cups, just won by another team. Although, where school caps had once hung, gas masks had taken their place. She recalled the first time she'd come to see Mr Holcombe, to complain about the red marks she'd found on Harry's backside at bath-time. He'd remained calm while she lost her temper, and Maisie had left an hour later in no doubt who the guilty party was.

Maisie noticed a light coming from under the door of Mr Holcombe's classroom. She hesitated, took a deep breath and knocked softly on the pebbled glass.

'Come on in,' said the cheerful voice she remembered so well.

She entered the room to find Mr Holcombe seated behind a large pile of books, pen scratching across paper. She was about to remind him who she was when he leapt up and said, 'This is a pleasant surprise, Mrs Clifton, especially if it's me you're looking for.'

'Yes it is,' Maisie replied, a little flustered. 'I'm sorry to bother you, Mr Holcombe, but I need some advice, and I didn't know who else to turn to.'

'I'm flattered,' said the schoolmaster, offering her a tiny chair, normally occupied by an eight-year-old. 'How can I help?'

Maisie told him about her meeting with Mr Prendergast, and the offer of £200 for her piece of land on Broad Street. 'Do you think it's a fair price?' she asked.

'I've no idea,' said Mr Holcombe, shaking his head. 'I have no experience of such matters, and I'd be worried about giving you the wrong advice. Actually, I thought it might be another matter you'd come to see me about.'

'Another matter?' repeated Maisie.

'Yes. I hoped you'd seen the notice on the board outside the school, and wanted to apply.'

'Apply for what?' she asked.

'One of the government's new schemes for night classes, designed to help people like you, who are clearly intelligent, but haven't had the opportunity to continue their education.'

Maisie didn't want to admit that even if she'd seen the notice, she would have struggled to read it. 'I'm too overworked to consider taking on anything else at the moment,' she said, 'what with the hotel, and . . . and—'

'I'm sorry to hear that,' said Mr Holcombe, 'because I think you'd be an ideal candidate. I'll be taking most of the classes myself and it would have given me particular pleasure to teach the mother of Harry Clifton.'

'It's just that—'

'It would only be for an hour, twice a week,' he continued, refusing to give up. 'The classes are in the evenings, and there's nothing to stop you dropping out if you decided they weren't for you.'

'It was kind of you to think of me, Mr Holcombe. Perhaps when I haven't got quite so much on my plate.' She stood up and shook hands with the schoolmaster.

'I'm sorry I couldn't help you with your problem, Mrs Clifton,' he said as he accompanied her to the door. 'Mind you, it's a nice problem to have.'

'It was good of you to spare the time, Mr Holcombe,'

she replied before leaving. Maisie walked back down the corridor, across the playground and out through the school gates. She stood on the pavement and stared at the notice board. How she wished she could read.

27

MAISIE HAD ONLY taken a taxi a couple of times in her life: once to Harry's wedding in Oxford, and then only from the local station, and on a second occasion, quite recently, when she'd attended her father's funeral. So when an American staff car drew up outside 27 Still House Lane, she felt a little embarrassed, and only hoped the neighbours had their curtains drawn.

As she came down the staircase wearing her new red silk dress with padded shoulders and belted at the waist – very fashionable before the war – she spotted her mother and Stan staring out of the window.

The driver got out of the car and knocked on the front door. He looked unsure that he'd come to the right address. But when Maisie opened the door, he understood immediately why the major had invited this particular belle to the regimental dance. He gave Maisie a smart salute and opened the back door of the car.

'Thank you,' she said, 'but I'd prefer to sit in the front.'

Once the driver had found his way back on to the main road, Maisie asked him how long he'd been working for Major Mulholland.

'All my life, ma'am. Man and boy.'

'I'm not sure I understand,' said Maisie.

'We both come from Raleigh, North Carolina. Once this war's over, I'll be goin' home to my old job in the major's factory.'

'I didn't know the major owned a factory.'

'Several, ma'am. In Raleigh, he's known as the Corn-on-the-Cob King.'

'Corn on the cob?' queried Maisie.

'You ain't seen nothin' like it in Bristol, ma'am. To truly appreciate corn on the cob, it has to be boiled, covered in melting butter and eaten straight after it's picked – and preferably in North Carolina.'

'So who's running the factories while the Corn-on-the-Cob King is away fighting the Germans?'

'Young Joey, his second son, with a little help from his sister Sandy, would be my guess.'

'He has a son and a daughter back home?'

'Had two sons and a daughter, ma'am, but sadly Mike Junior was shot down over the Philippines.'

Maisie wanted to ask the corporal about Mike senior's wife, but felt that the young man might have been embarrassed by questions on that subject, so she moved on to safer ground and asked about his home state. 'Finest in the forty-eight,' he replied, and didn't stop talking about North Carolina until they reached the camp gate.

When the guard spotted the car, he immediately raised the barrier and gave Maisie a smart salute as they drove on into the compound. 'The major asked me to take you straight to his quarters, ma'am, so you can have a drink before going across to the dance.'

The car drew up outside a small prefabricated house and she spotted Mike standing on the doorstep waiting to greet her. She jumped out of the car before the driver could open the door, and walked quickly up the path to join him. He bent down, kissed her on the cheek and said, 'Come on in, honey, I'd like you to meet some of my colleagues.' He took her coat and added, 'You look just swell.'

'Like one of your corn on the cobs?' suggested Maisie.

'More like one of our North Carolina peaches,' he said as he guided her towards a noisy room, full of laughter and animated voices. 'Now let's make everyone jealous, because they're about to find out that I'm escorting the belle of the ball.'

Maisie entered a room filled with officers and their dates. She couldn't have been made to feel more welcome. She couldn't help wondering, if she'd been the guest of an English major a few miles up the road at the Wessex regimental HQ, would they also have treated her as their equal?

Mike guided her around the room, introducing her to all his colleagues, including the camp commander, who clearly approved. As she moved from group to group, she couldn't help noticing several photographs scattered around the room, on tables, bookshelves and the mantelpiece, of what could only have been Mike's wife and children.

Just after nine o'clock, the guests made their way to the gymnasium, where the dance was being held, but not before the dutiful host had helped all the ladies on with their coats. This gave Maisie the opportunity to look more closely at one of the photographs of a beautiful young woman.

'My wife Abigail,' said Mike when he came back into the room. 'A great beauty, like you. I still miss her. She died of cancer almost five years ago. Now that's something all of us should be declaring war on.'

'I'm so sorry,' said Maisie. 'I didn't mean . . .'

'No. Now you've discovered just how much we have in common. I understand exactly how you feel, having lost a husband and a son. But hell, this is an evening to celebrate, not to feel sorry for ourselves, so come on, honey, now you've made all the officers jealous, let's go and make the other ranks sore.'

Maisie laughed as she took his arm. They left the house and joined a stream of boisterous young people who were all heading in the same direction.

Once she was on the dance floor, the youthful and exuberant Americans made Maisie feel as if she'd known them all her life. During the evening, several of the officers asked her for a dance, but Mike rarely let her out of his sight. When the band struck up the last waltz, she couldn't believe how quickly the evening had flown by.

Once the applause had died down, everyone remained on the floor. The band played a number unfamiliar to Maisie, but which served to remind everyone else in the room that their country was at war. Many of the young men who stood to attention with hand on heart, lustily singing 'The Star-Spangled Banner', would not live to celebrate their next birthday. Like Harry. What an unnecessary waste of life, Maisie thought.

As they walked off the dance floor, Mike suggested that they return to his quarters and enjoy a glass of Southern Comfort before the corporal drove her home. It was the first bourbon Maisie had ever drunk, and it quickly loosened her tongue.

'Mike, I have a problem,' she said once she'd settled on the sofa and her glass had been refilled. 'And as I've only got a week to solve it, I could do with a dollop of your Southern common sense.'

'Fire away, honey,' said Mike. 'But I ought to warn you that if limeys are involved, I've never been able to get on their wavelength. In fact, you're the first one I've been able to relax with. Are you sure you're not an American?'

Maisie laughed. 'That's sweet of you, Mike.' She took another swig of bourbon, by which time she felt ready to do far more than just tell him her immediate problems. 'It all began many years ago, when I owned a tea shop in Broad Street called Tilly's. It's now nothing more than a derelict bomb site, but someone is offering me two hundred pounds for it.'

'So what's the problem?' asked Mike.

'I have no idea what it's really worth.'

'Well, one thing's for certain, as long as there's a chance the Germans might return and continue their bombing raids, no one is going to be rebuilding anything on that site, at least not until the war is over.'

'Mr Prendergast described his client as a property speculator.'

'Sounds more like a profiteer to me,' said Mike, 'someone who buys derelict land on the cheap, so when the war is over they'll be able to make a quick killing. Frankly, that sort of spiv will do anything to make a fast buck, and ought to be strung up.'

'But isn't it just possible that two hundred pounds is a fair price?'

'Depends on your marriage value.'

Maisie sat bolt upright, not sure she'd heard him correctly. 'I don't understand what you mean.'

'You say the whole of Broad Street was bombed, and not one building survived?'

'Yes, but why would that make my little plot any more valuable?'

'If this speculator guy has already got his hands on every other bit of land in the street, you're in a strong position to strike a bargain. In fact, you should demand a dowry, because your plot may be the one piece of land that, withheld, will prevent him from rebuilding the entire block, although that's the last thing he'd want you to find out.'

'So how do I discover if my little site has marriage value?'

'Tell your bank manager that you won't settle for less than four hundred pounds, and you'll find out soon enough.'

'Thank you, Mike,' said Maisie, 'that's good advice.' She smiled, took another swig of Southern Comfort, and passed out in his arms.

28

When Maisie came down for breakfast the following morning, she couldn't remember who'd driven her home, or how she'd got upstairs to her room.

'I put you to bed,' said her mother as she poured her a cup of tea. 'A nice young corporal drove you home. He even helped me get you up the stairs.'

Maisie sank into a chair, before taking her mother slowly through the evening, leaving her in no doubt how much she'd enjoyed Mike's company.

'And you're sure he's not married?' asked her mother.

'Hold your horses, Mum, it was only our first date.'

'Did he seem keen?'

'I think he asked me to the theatre next week, but I'm not sure which day, or which theatre,' she said as her brother Stan came into the room.

Stan plonked himself down at the end of the table and waited for a bowl of porridge to be placed in front of him, before gulping down the contents like a dog drinking water on a hot day. When he'd finished, he flicked off the top of a bottle of Bass and drank it in one draught. 'I'll have another,' he said. 'As it's Sunday,' he added, burping loudly.

Maisie never spoke during Stan's morning ritual, and she usually slipped off to work before he had time to air his opinions on anything that crossed his mind. She rose from her place and was just about to leave for the morning service at St Mary's, when he bellowed, 'Sit down, woman! I want a word with you before you go to church.'

Maisie would have liked to walk out without responding, but Stan wasn't beyond dragging her back and giving her a black eye if the mood took him. She sat back down.

'So what are you doin' about that two hundred nicker you're in line for?' he demanded.

'How did you find out?'

'Mum told me all about it last night when you were out on the town getting laid by your American fancy man.'

Maisie frowned at her mother, who looked embarrassed, but said nothing. 'For your information, Stan, Major Mulholland is a gentleman, and what I do in my spare time is none of your business.'

'If he's an American, you stupid bitch, let me warn you – they don't wait to be asked, they think everythin's theirs by right.'

'You speak with your usual first-hand knowledge on the subject, no doubt,' said Maisie, trying to remain calm.

'Yanks are all the same,' said Stan. 'They only want one thing, and once they've got it, they bugger off back home and leave us to finish the job, just like they did in the first war.'

Maisie realized there was no point in continuing the conversation, so she just sat there, hoping this particular storm would blow over quickly.

'You still haven't told me what you're doin' about the two hundred quid,' said Stan.

'I haven't made up my mind yet,' said Maisie. 'In any case, how I spend my money has got nothing to do with you.'

'It's got everything to do with me,' said Stan, 'because half of it's mine.'

'And how do you work that out?' asked Maisie.

'On account of the fact that you're livin' in my house for a start, so I'm entitled. And let me warn you, girl, in case you're thinkin' of double-crossin' me, if I don't get my fair share, I'll beat you so black and blue, even an American negro won't give you a second look.'

'You make me sick, Stan,' said Maisie.

'Not half as sick as I'll make you if you don't cough up, because then I'll—'

Maisie stood up, marched out of the kitchen, ran down the hall, grabbed her coat and was out of the front door before Stan had come to the end of his tirade.

◄◦►

When she checked the lunch bookings that Sunday, Maisie quickly realized she'd have to make sure that two of her customers were seated as far away from each other as possible. She put Mike Mulholland on his usual table, and Patrick Casey on the far side of the room, so there wasn't any chance of them bumping into each other.

She hadn't set eyes on Patrick for nearly three years, and wondered if he'd changed. Did he still have those irresistible good looks and Irish charm that had so captivated her when they'd first met?

One of her questions was answered the moment he entered the room.

'How nice to see you after all this time, Mr Casey,' she said before accompanying him to his table. Several middle-aged women took a second look at the handsome Irishman as he crossed the room. 'Will you be staying with us for long this time, Mr Casey?' Maisie asked as she passed him a menu.

'That depends on you,' said Patrick. He opened the menu, but didn't study its contents.

Maisie hoped that no one noticed her blush. She turned, to see Mike Mulholland waiting by reception; he would never allow anyone but Maisie to show him to his table. She hurried across and whispered, 'Hello, Mike. I've reserved your usual table. Would you like to follow me?'

'I sure would.'

Once Mike had turned his attention to the menu – although he always had the same two dishes every Sunday, soup of the day followed by boiled beef and Yorkshire pudding – she walked back across the room to take Patrick's order.

During the next two hours, Maisie kept a close eye on both men, while at the same time trying to supervise a hundred other customers. When the dining-room clock struck three, there were only two people left in the room; John Wayne and Gary Cooper, thought Maisie, waiting to see who would draw first at the OK Corral. She folded Mike's bill, put it on a plate and took it across to him. He paid it without checking.

'Another great meal,' he said, before adding in a whisper, 'I hope we're still on for the theatre Tuesday night?'

'We sure are, honey,' said Maisie, teasing him.

'Then I'll see you at the Old Vic at eight,' he said as a waitress passed by his table.

'I'll look forward to that, sir, and you can be sure I'll pass on your compliments to the chef.'

Mike stifled a laugh, before leaving the table and strolling out of the dining room. He looked back at Maisie and smiled.

Once he was out of sight, Maisie took Patrick's bill across to him. He checked every item and left a large tip. 'Are you doing anything special tomorrow evening?' he asked, giving Maisie that smile she remembered so well.

'Yes, I'm attending an evening class.'

'You're kidding me,' said Patrick.

'No, and I mustn't be late, because it's the first lesson of a twelve-week course.' She didn't tell him that she hadn't finally decided whether to go through with it or not.

'Then it will have to be Tuesday,' said Patrick.

'I already have a date on Tuesday.'

'Do you really, or are you just saying that to get rid of me?'

'No, I'm going to the theatre.'

'Then what about Wednesday, or is that your night for algebraic equations?'

'No, composition and reading out loud.'

'Thursday?' said Patrick, trying not to sound exasperated.

'Yes, I'm free on Thursday,' said Maisie, as another waitress passed by their table.

'That's a relief,' said Patrick. 'I was beginning to think I'd have to book in for a second week, just to get an appointment.'

Maisie laughed. 'So what do you have in mind?'

'I thought we'd start by going to—'

'Mrs Clifton.' Maisie swung round to find the hotel manager, Mr Hurst, standing behind her. 'When you've finished with this customer,' he said, 'perhaps you'd be kind enough to join me in my office?'

Maisie thought she'd been discreet, but now she feared she might even get the sack, because it was against company policy for members of staff to fraternize with the customers. That was how she'd lost her previous job, and Pat Casey had been the customer in question on that occasion.

She was grateful that Patrick slipped out of the restaurant without another word, and once she'd checked the till, she reported to Mr Hurst's office.

'Take a seat, Mrs Clifton. I have a rather serious matter to discuss with you.' Maisie sat down and gripped the arms of the chair to stop herself shaking. 'I could see you were having another busy day.'

'A hundred and forty-two covers,' said Maisie. 'Almost a record.'

'I don't know how I'm going to replace you,' he said before adding, 'but management make these decisions, not me, you understand. It's out of my hands.'

'But I enjoy my job,' said Maisie.

'That may well be the case, but I have to tell you that on this occasion I agree with head office.' Maisie sat back, ready to accept her fate. 'They have made it clear,' continued Mr Hurst, 'that they no longer want you to work in the dining room, and have asked me to replace you as soon as possible.'

'But why?'

'Because they're keen for you to go into management. Frankly, Maisie, if you were a man, you'd already be running one of our hotels. Congratulations!'

'Thank you,' said Maisie, as she began to think about the implications.

'Let's get the formalities out of the way, shall we?' said Mr Hurst as he pulled open his desk drawer and extracted a letter. 'You'll need to study this carefully,' he said. 'It details your new terms of employment. Once you've read it, sign it, return it to me, and I'll send it back to head office.'

That was when she made the decision.

29

MAISIE WAS FEARFUL of making a fool of herself.

When she reached the school gate, she nearly turned back, and would have done, if she hadn't seen another woman older than herself entering the building. She followed her through the front door and along the corridor, stopping when she reached the classroom. She peeped inside, hoping to find the room so full that no one would notice her. But there were only seven other people present: two men and five women.

She crept to the back of the classroom and took a seat behind the two men, hoping she couldn't be seen. Maisie immediately regretted her decision, because if she'd taken a seat by the door, she could have escaped more easily.

She bowed her head when the door opened and Mr Holcombe swept into the room. He took his place behind the desk in front of the blackboard, tugged the lapels of his long black gown and peered down at his pupils. He smiled when he spotted Mrs Clifton seated near the back.

'I'm going to start by writing out all twenty-six letters of the alphabet,' he began, 'and I want you to call them out as I write them down.' He picked up a piece of chalk and turned his back on the class. He wrote the letter A on the blackboard, and several voices could be heard in unison, B, a veritable chorus, C, everyone except Maisie. When he came to Z, Maisie mouthed the letter.

'I'm now going to point to a letter at random and see if you can still identify it.' The second time round, Maisie called out over half of them, and on her third attempt she was leading the chorus. When the hour was up, only Mr Holcombe would have realized it was her first lesson in twenty years and Maisie wasn't in any hurry to go home.

'By the time we meet again on Wednesday,' said Mr Holcombe, 'you must all be able to write the twenty-six letters of the alphabet, in their correct order.'

Maisie intended to have the alphabet mastered by Tuesday, so there would be no possibility of her making a mistake.

'To those of you who are unable to join me in the pub for a drink, I'll see you on Wednesday.'

Maisie assumed you had to be invited to join Mr Holcombe, so she slipped out of her chair and headed for the door, while the others surrounded the schoolmaster's desk with a dozen questions.

'Will you be coming to the pub, Mrs Clifton?' asked the schoolmaster just as Maisie reached the door.

'Thank you, Mr Holcombe. I'd like that,' she heard herself saying, and joined the others as they left the room and strolled across the road to the Ship Inn.

One by one, the other pupils drifted off, until only the two of them were seated at the bar.

'Do you have any idea just how bright you are?' asked Mr Holcombe after he'd bought her another orange juice.

'But I left school at twelve, and I still can't read or write.'

'You may have left school too early, but you've never stopped learning. And as you're Harry Clifton's mother, you'll probably end up teaching me.'

'Harry taught you?'

'Daily, without realizing it. But then, I knew very early

on that he was brighter than me. I only hoped I could get him to Bristol Grammar School before he found it out for himself.'

'And did you?' asked Maisie, smiling.

'It was a damn close-run thing,' admitted Holcombe.

'Last orders!' shouted the barman.

Maisie looked at the clock behind the bar. She couldn't believe it was already 9.30, and blackout regulations had to be adhered to.

It seemed natural that Mr Holcombe should walk her home; after all, they'd known each other for so many years. On the way through the unlit streets, he told her many more stories about Harry, which made her both happy and sad. It was clear that Mr Holcombe also missed him, and she felt guilty for not thanking him many years before.

When they reached the front door of her home in Still House Lane, Maisie said, 'I don't know your first name.'

'Arnold,' he said shyly.

'It suits you,' she said. 'May I call you Arnold?'

'Yes, of course.'

'And you must call me Maisie.' She took out her front door key and placed it in the lock. 'Goodnight, Arnold. See you on Wednesday.'

◄○►

An evening at the theatre brought back many happy memories for Maisie of the days when Patrick Casey would take her to the Old Vic whenever he visited Bristol. But just as the memory of Patrick had faded and she'd begun to spend time with another man with whom she felt there might be a future, the damned leprechaun bounced back into her life. He'd already told her that there was a reason he wanted to see her, and she wasn't in much doubt what that reason was. She didn't need him to throw her life into turmoil yet again. She thought about Mike, one of the kindest and most decent men she'd ever come across, and guileless in his attempts to hide his feelings for her.

One thing Patrick had instilled in her was never to be late for the theatre. He felt there was nothing more embarrassing than treading on people's toes as you made your way in darkness to the inevitable centre seats after the curtain had risen.

Mike was already standing in the foyer holding a programme when Maisie walked into the theatre ten minutes before the curtain was due to rise. As soon as she saw him she smiled, and couldn't help thinking how he always raised her spirits. He returned her smile, and gave her a gentle kiss on the cheek.

'I don't know a lot about Noël Coward,' he admitted as he handed her the programme, 'but I've just been reading a synopsis of the play, and it turns out to be about a man and a woman who can't make up their mind who they should marry.'

Maisie said nothing as they entered the stalls. She began to follow the letters of the alphabet backwards until she reached H. When they made their way to the centre of the row, she wondered how Mike had managed to get such superb seats for a sold-out show.

Once the lights faded and the curtain rose, he took her hand. He only let go when Owen Nares made his entrance, and the audience burst into applause. Maisie became entranced by the story, even if it was a little too close for comfort. But the spell was broken when the loud whine of a siren drowned out Mr Nares's words. An audible groan went up around the auditorium, as the actors hurried off stage to be replaced by the theatre manager, who efficiently organized an exit strategy that would have gladdened the heart of a regimental sergeant major. Bristolians had long been familiar with flying visits from Germans who had no intention of paying for their theatre tickets.

Mike and Maisie made their way out of the theatre and down the steps to a bleak but familiar shelter that had become a home from home for regular theatregoers. The audience grabbed any place that was available for the unticketed performance. The great social equalizer, as Clement Attlee had described life in an air-raid shelter.

'Not my idea of a date,' said Mike, placing his jacket on the stone floor.

'When I was young,' said Maisie, as she sat down on the jacket, 'many a young fellow tried to get me down here, but you're the first one who's succeeded.' Mike laughed, as she began to scribble something on the cover of the programme.

'I'm flattered,' he said, placing an arm gently around her shoulder as the ground started to shake with bombs that sounded perilously close. 'You've never been to America, have you, Maisie?' he asked, trying to take her mind off the air raid.

'I've never been to London,' admitted Maisie. 'In fact, the furthest I've ever travelled is to Weston-super-Mare and Oxford, and as both trips turned out to be disastrous, I'd be perhaps better off staying at home.'

Mike laughed. 'I'd love to show you America,' he said, 'particularly the south.'

'I think we'd have to ask the Germans to take a few nights off before we could consider doing that,' said Maisie as the all-clear sounded.

A ripple of applause burst out in the shelter, and everyone emerged from the unscheduled interval and made their way back into the theatre.

Once they'd taken their seats, the theatre manager walked on to the stage. 'The performance will continue with no interval,' he announced. 'But should the Germans decide to pay us another visit, it will have to be cancelled. I'm sorry to say there will be no refunds. German regulations,' he announced. A few people laughed.

Within moments of the curtain going back up, Maisie once again lost herself in the story, and when the actors finally took their bows, the whole audience rose in appreciation, not only for the performance, but for another small victory over the Luftwaffe, as Mike described it.

'Harvey's or the Pantry?' asked Mike as he picked up the programme, on which each letter of the play's title had been crossed out and rewritten below, arranged in alphabetical order, A E E I I L P R S T V V.

'The Pantry,' said Maisie, not wanting to admit that on the one occasion she'd been to Harvey's with Patrick, she'd spent the entire evening glancing around the tables dreading the thought that Lord Harvey's daughter Elizabeth might be dining there with Hugo Barrington.

Mike took a long time studying the menu, which surprised Maisie, because the choice of dishes was so limited. He usually chatted about what was taking place back at camp, or the fort as he liked to call it, but not tonight; not even the oft-repeated grumbles about limeys not understanding baseball. She began to wonder if he wasn't feeling well.

'Is everything all right, Mike?' she asked.

He looked up. 'They're sending me back to the States,' he said as a waiter appeared by their side and asked if they would like to order. Great timing, thought Maisie, but at least it gave her a little time to think, and not about what she wanted to eat. Once they'd ordered and the waiter had left them, Mike tried again.

'I've been assigned to a desk job in Washington.'

Maisie leaned across the table and took his hand.

'I pressed them to let me stay for another six months . . . so I could be with you, but they turned my request down.'

'I'm sorry to hear that,' said Maisie, 'but—'

'Please don't say anything, Maisie, because I'm finding this difficult enough already. Though God knows I've given it enough thought.' This was followed by another long silence. 'I realize we've only known each other for a short time, but my feelings haven't changed since the first day I set eyes on you.' Maisie smiled. 'And I wondered,' he continued, 'hoped, prayed, that you might consider coming back to America with me . . . as my wife.'

Maisie was speechless. 'I'm so very flattered,' she eventually managed, but couldn't think of anything else to say.

'Of course, I realize you'll need time to think it over. I'm sorry that the ravages of war don't allow for the niceties of a long courtship.'

'When do you go home?'

'At the end of the month. So if you did say yes, we could get married at the base and fly back together as man and wife.' He leant forward and took her hand. 'I've never felt more certain about anything in my whole life,' he said as the waiter reappeared by their side.

'So which one of you is the chopped liver?'

—◦—

Maisie didn't sleep that night, and when she came down to breakfast the following morning, she told her mother that Mike had proposed to her.

'Jump at it,' was Mrs Tancock's immediate response. 'You'll never get a better chance to begin a new life. And, let's face it,' she added, glancing sadly at the photograph of Harry on the mantelpiece, 'there's no longer any reason for you to stay here.'

Maisie was about to express her one reservation when Stan burst into the room. She got up from the table. 'I'd better get a move on if I'm not going to be late for work.'

'Don't think I've forgotten about that 'undred quid you owe me!' he shouted as she left the room.

—◦—

Maisie was sitting on the edge of her seat in the front row when Mr Holcombe entered the classroom at seven that evening.

Her hand shot up several times during the next hour, like a tiresome schoolgirl who knows all the answers and wants teacher to notice her. If he did, he didn't let on.

'Could you start coming in on Tuesdays and Thursdays in future, Maisie?' Mr Holcombe asked as they strolled across to the pub with the rest of the class.

'Why?' asked Maisie. 'Aren't I good enough?'

'Am I not good enough,' corrected the schoolmaster without thinking. 'On the contrary,' he added, 'I've decided to put you into the intermediate class, before this lot,' he said, indicating her fellow classmates with the sweep of an arm, 'become overwhelmed.'

'But won't I be out of my depth, Arnold?'

'I do hope so, but no doubt you'll have caught up by the end of the month, by which time I'll have to put you into the advanced class.'

Maisie didn't respond, as she knew it wouldn't be too long before she would have to tell Arnold that she'd made other plans for the end of the month.

Once again, they ended up sitting alone together at the bar, and once again he accompanied her back to Still House Lane, only this time, when Maisie took the front-door key out of her bag, she thought he looked as if he might be trying to summon up the courage to kiss her. Surely not. Hadn't she got enough problems to cope with?

'I was just wondering,' he said, 'which book you ought to read first.'

'It won't be a book,' said Maisie as she placed the key in the lock, 'it will be a letter.'

30

PATRICK CASEY had breakfast, lunch and dinner in the hotel restaurant on Monday, Tuesday and Wednesday.

Maisie assumed that he would take her to dinner at the Plimsoll Line in the hope that it might evoke past memories. In fact, she hadn't been back to the restaurant since Patrick had disappeared off to Ireland. She was right, and it did.

Maisie was determined that she would not be seduced once again by Patrick's charm and good looks, and she intended to tell him about Mike and their plans for the future. But as the evening progressed, she found it more and more difficult to raise the subject.

'So, what have you been up to since I was last in Bristol?' Patrick asked her over a pre-dinner drink in the lounge bar. 'Not that anyone could miss the fact that you're running the best hotel restaurant in the city while somehow managing to fit in evening classes at the same time.'

'Yes, I shall miss all that when . . .' she began wistfully.

'When what?' asked Patrick.

'It's only a twelve-week course,' said Maisie, trying to recover.

'In twelve weeks' time,' said Patrick, 'my bet is you'll be the one who's giving the classes.'

'What about you? What have you been up to?' she asked

as the head waiter came over to tell them their table was ready.

Patrick didn't answer the question until they'd sat down at a quiet table in the corner of the room.

'You may remember I was promoted to deputy manager of the company about three years ago, which is why I had to go back to Dublin.'

'I haven't forgotten why you had to go back to Dublin,' said Maisie with some feeling.

'I tried to return to Bristol several times, but once war broke out, it proved almost impossible, and it didn't help that I couldn't even write to you.'

'Well, that problem may well be solved in the near future.'

'Then you can read to me in bed.'

'And how has your company fared during these hard times?' asked Maisie, steering the conversation back on to safer ground.

'Actually, a lot of Irish companies have done rather well out of the war. Because of the country's neutrality, we've been able to deal with both sides.'

'You're willing to do business with the Germans?' said Maisie in disbelief.

'No, as a company we've always made it clear where our allegiances lie, but you won't be surprised to know that quite a few of my countrymen are happy to do business with the Germans. Because of that, we had a couple of tough years, but once the Americans entered the war, even the Irish began to believe the Allies might end up on the winning side.'

That was her chance to tell Patrick about one American in particular, but she didn't take it. 'So what brings you to Bristol now?' she asked.

'The simple answer is, you.'

'Me?' Maisie quickly tried to think of a convincing way

of bringing the conversation back on to a less personal footing.

'Yes. Our managing director will be retiring at the end of the year, and the chairman has asked me to take his place.'

'Congratulations,' said Maisie, relieved to be back on safer ground. 'And you want me to take over as your deputy,' she added, trying to make light of it.

'No, I want you to be my wife.'

Maisie's tone changed. 'Didn't it cross your mind, Patrick, just for one moment during the past three years, that someone else might have come into my life?'

'Daily,' said Patrick, 'which is why I came over to find out if there was someone else.'

Maisie hesitated. 'Yes, there is.'

'And has he asked you to marry him?'

'Yes,' she whispered.

'Have you accepted his proposal?'

'No, but I've promised to let him have my answer before he returns to America at the end of the month,' she said more firmly.

'Does that mean I'm still in with a chance?'

'Frankly, Patrick, the odds are stacked against you. You haven't been in touch for nearly three years, and suddenly you turn up out of the blue as if nothing's changed.'

Patrick made no attempt to defend himself, while a waiter served their main courses. 'I wish it was that easy,' he said.

'Patrick, it was always that easy. If you'd asked me to marry you three years ago, I would have happily jumped on the first boat to Ireland.'

'I couldn't ask you then.'

Maisie put down her knife and fork without taking a bite. 'I always wondered if you were married.'

'Why didn't you say something at the time?'

'I was so much in love with you, Patrick, I was even willing to suffer that indignity.'

'And to think I only returned to Ireland because I couldn't ask you to be my wife.'

'And has that changed?'

'Yes. Bryony left me over a year ago. She met someone who took more interest in her than I did, which wouldn't have been difficult.'

'Oh my God,' said Maisie, 'why is my life always so complicated?'

Patrick smiled. 'I'm sorry if I've disrupted your life again, but I won't give in so easily this time, not while I still believe there's even the slightest chance.' He leant across the table and took her hand. A moment later the waiter reappeared by their side, an anxious look on his face as he looked at the two untouched plates of food that had been allowed to go cold.

'Is everything all right, sir?' he asked.

'No,' said Maisie. 'It's not.'

◄◦►

Maisie lay awake and thought about the two men in her life. Mike, so reliable, so kind, who she knew would be faithful until his dying day, and Patrick, so exciting, so alive, with whom there would never be a dull moment. She changed her mind several times during the night, and it didn't help that she had so little time to make her decision.

When she came down to breakfast the following morning, her mother didn't mince her words when Maisie asked her, if given the choice, which of the two men she should marry.

'Mike,' she said without hesitation. 'He'll be far more reliable in the long run, and marriage is for the long run. In any case,' she added, 'I've never trusted the Irish.'

Maisie considered her mother's words, and was about to

ask another question when Stan barged into the room. Once he'd gulped down his porridge, he barged into her thoughts.

'Aren't you seeing the bank manager today?'

Maisie didn't reply.

'I thought so. Just make sure you come straight home with my 'undred quid. If you don't, my girl, I'll come looking for you.'

'How nice to see you again, madam,' said Mr Prendergast as he ushered Maisie into a chair just after four o'clock that afternoon. He waited for Maisie to settle before he ventured, 'Have you been able to give my client's generous offer some thought?'

Maisie smiled. With one word, Mr Prendergast had given away whose interests he was looking after.

'I most certainly have,' Maisie replied, 'and I would be obliged if you would tell your client that I wouldn't consider accepting a penny less than four hundred pounds.'

Mr Prendergast's mouth opened.

'And as it's possible that I might be leaving Bristol at the end of the month, perhaps you'd also be kind enough to tell your client that my *generous* offer will only remain on the table for one week.'

Mr Prendergast closed his mouth.

'I'll try to drop by again at the same time next week, Mr Prendergast, when you can let me know your client's decision.' Maisie rose from her place and gave the manager a sweet smile, before adding, 'I do hope you have a pleasant weekend, Mr Prendergast.'

Maisie was finding it difficult to concentrate on Mr Holcombe's words, and not just because the intermediate class was proving far more demanding than the beginners, which she already regretted forsaking. When her hand did go up, it was more often to ask a question than to answer one.

Arnold's enthusiasm for his subject was contagious, and he had a real gift for making everyone feel equal and the most insignificant contribution seem important.

After twenty minutes of going back over what he called the basics he invited the class to turn to page 72 of *Little Women*. Numbers weren't a problem for Maisie, and she quickly turned to the correct page. He then invited a woman in the third row to stand and read the first paragraph, while the rest of the class followed each sentence word for word. Maisie placed a finger at the top of the page and tried desperately to follow the narrative, but she soon lost her place.

When the schoolmaster asked an elderly man in the front row to read the same passage a second time, Maisie was able to identify some of the words, but she was praying that Arnold wouldn't ask her to be next. She breathed a sigh of relief when someone else was invited to read the paragraph again. When the new reader sat down, Maisie bowed her head, but she didn't escape.

'And finally, I'm going to ask Mrs Clifton to stand up and read us the same passage.'

Maisie rose uncertainly from her place and tried to concentrate. She recited the entire paragraph almost word for word, without once looking down at the page. But then, she had spent so many years having to remember long, complicated restaurant orders.

Mr Holcombe gave her a warm smile as she sat down. 'What a remarkable memory you have, Mrs Clifton.' No one else seemed to pick up the significance of his words. 'I would now like to move on and discuss the meaning of certain words in that paragraph. In the second line, for example, you'll see the word betrothal, an old-fashioned word. Can anyone give me a more modern example, that has the same meaning?'

Several hands shot up, and Maisie's would have been among them if she hadn't recognized a familiar heavy step heading towards the classroom door.

'Miss Wilson,' said the schoolmaster.

'Marriage,' said Miss Wilson as the door burst open and Maisie's brother barged into the room. He stopped in front of the blackboard, his eyes darting from person to person.

'Can I help you?' asked Mr Holcombe politely.

'No,' said Stan. 'I've come to collect what's rightfully mine, so keep your mouth shut, schoolmaster, if you know what's good for you, and mind your own business.' His eyes settled on Maisie.

Maisie had intended to tell him at breakfast that it would be another week before she found out if Mr Prendergast's valued customer had accepted her counter-offer. But as Stan walked purposefully towards her, she knew she wasn't going to be able to convince him that she didn't have the money.

'Where's my cash?' he demanded long before he'd reached her desk.

'I haven't got it yet,' said Maisie. 'You're going to have to wait another week.'

'Like hell I am,' said Stan, who grabbed her by the hair and began to drag her, screaming, out from behind her desk. As he moved towards the door, the rest of the class sat mesmerized. Only one man stood in his path.

'Get out of my way, schoolmaster.'

'I suggest you let go of your sister, Mr Tancock, if you don't want to be in even more trouble than you already are.'

'From you and whose army?' laughed Stan. 'If you don't fuck off, mate, I'll knock your teeth right down your throat, and I promise you, that won't be a pretty sight.'

Stan didn't see the first punch coming, and when it landed in his solar plexus, he bent double, so he could be excused for not recovering before the second blow landed on his chin. The third sent him sprawling to the ground like a felled oak.

Stan lay on the floor, clutching his stomach, expecting a boot to be put in. The schoolmaster towered over him, and waited for him to recover. When he finally did, Stan rose unsteadily to his feet, never once taking his eyes off the schoolmaster as he edged slowly towards the door. When he thought he was at a safe distance, he looked back at Maisie, who was still lying on the floor, curled up in a ball, sobbing quietly.

'You'd better not come home till you've got my money, my girl,' he growled, 'if you know what's good for you!' Without another word he stormed out into the corridor.

Even after Maisie heard the door slam, she was still too frightened to move. The rest of the class gathered up their books and slipped quietly out of the room. No one would be visiting the pub that night.

Mr Holcombe walked quickly across the room, knelt down beside his charge and gathered her trembling body in his arms. It was some time before he said, 'You'd better come home with me tonight, Maisie. I'll make up a bed in the spare room. You can stay for as long as you want to.'

EMMA BARRINGTON

1941–1942

31

'SIXTY-FOURTH AND PARK,' said Emma as she jumped into a taxi outside Sefton Jelks's Wall Street office.

She sat in the back of the cab and tried to think about what she would say to Great-aunt Phyllis when, or if, she got past her front door, but the car radio was so loud that she couldn't concentrate. She thought about asking the driver to turn the volume down, but she had already learnt that New York cabbies are deaf when it suits them, although rarely dumb and never mute.

While listening to the commentator describe in an excited voice what had taken place at somewhere called Pearl Harbor, Emma accepted that her great-aunt's first question was bound to be, what brings you to New York, young lady, followed by, how long have you been here, and then, why has it taken you so long to come and see me? To none of these questions did she have a plausible answer, unless she was willing to tell Great-aunt Phyllis everything – something she wanted to avoid because she hadn't even told her own mother *everything*.

She might not even realize she has a great-niece, thought Emma. And was it possible there was a long-standing family feud that Emma didn't know about? Or perhaps her great-aunt was a recluse, divorced, remarried, or insane?

All Emma could remember was once seeing a Christmas

card signed Phyllis, Gordon and Alistair. Was one a husband and the other a son? To make matters worse, Emma didn't have any proof that she really was Phyllis's great-niece.

Emma was even less confident about facing her by the time the cab drew up outside the front door and she'd handed over another quarter.

Emma stepped out of the cab, looked up at the imposing, four-storey brownstone and changed her mind several times about knocking on the door. She finally decided to walk round the block, in the hope that she would feel more confident by the time she returned. As she walked down 64th Street, Emma couldn't help noticing that New Yorkers were scurrying back and forth at an unusually frantic pace, with shocked and anxious looks on their faces. Some were looking up at the sky. Surely they didn't believe the next Japanese air raid would be on Manhattan?

A paperboy standing on the corner of Park kept shouting out the same headline, 'America declares war! Read the latest!'

By the time Emma arrived back outside the front door, she had decided she couldn't have picked a worse day to call on her great-aunt. Perhaps it might be wise to return to her hotel and leave it until tomorrow. But why would tomorrow be any different? Her money had almost run out, and if America was now at war, how would she get back to England and, more important, to Sebastian, whom she'd never intended to be apart from for more than a couple of weeks?

She found herself climbing the five steps to face a shiny black door with a large, highly polished brass knocker. Perhaps Great-aunt Phyllis was out. Perhaps she'd moved. Emma was about to knock when she noticed a bell in the wall with the word 'Tradesmen' printed underneath. She pressed the bell, took a pace back and waited, far happier to face the person who dealt with tradesmen.

A few moments later a tall, elegantly dressed man, wearing a black jacket, striped trousers, a white shirt and grey tie, opened the door.

'How may I help you, ma'am?' he enquired, clearly having decided that Emma wasn't a tradesman.

'My name is Emma Barrington,' she told him. 'I wondered if my great-aunt Phyllis is at home.'

'She is indeed, Miss Barrington, Monday being her bridge afternoon. If you'll be kind enough to step inside, I'll let Mrs Stuart know you're here.'

'I could always come back tomorrow, if it isn't convenient,' stammered Emma, but he'd closed the door behind her and was already halfway down the corridor.

As Emma stood waiting in the hall, she couldn't have missed which country the Stuarts hailed from: a portrait of Bonnie Prince Charlie above crossed swords and a Stuart Clan shield hung on the wall at the far end of the hall. Emma walked slowly up and down, admiring paintings by Peploe, Fergusson, McTaggart and Raeburn. She remembered that her grandfather Lord Harvey owned a Lawrence that hung in the drawing room of Mulgelrie Castle. She had no idea what her great-uncle did for a living, but he clearly did it well.

The butler returned a few minutes later, the same impassive look on his face. Perhaps he hadn't heard the news about Pearl Harbor.

'Madam will receive you in the drawing room,' he said.

How like Jenkins he was: no surplus words, an even pace that never varied, and somehow he managed to display deference without being deferential. Emma wanted to ask him which part of England he came from, but knew he would consider that an intrusion, so she followed him along the corridor without another word.

She was about to start climbing the stairs when the butler stopped, pulled back a lift grille and stood aside to

allow her to step in. A lift in a private house? Emma wondered if Great-aunt Phyllis was an invalid. The lift shuddered
as it reached the third floor and she stepped out into a
beautifully furnished drawing room. If it were not for the
noise of traffic, blaring horns and police sirens coming from
the street below, one might have been in Edinburgh.

'If you'll wait here please, madam.'

Emma remained by the door while the butler walked
across the room to join four elderly ladies who were seated
around a log fire, enjoying tea and crumpets while listening
intently to a radio that had never blared.

When the butler announced, 'Miss Emma Barrington,'
they all turned and looked in Emma's direction. She
couldn't mistake which one of them was Lord Harvey's
sister, long before she rose to greet her: the flaming-red
hair, the impish smile and the unmistakable air of someone
who isn't first generation.

'It surely can't be little Emma,' she declared, as she left
the group and sailed across to her great-niece, the hint of a
Highland lilt still in her voice. 'The last time I saw you, dear
girl, you were wearing a gymslip, short white socks and daps
and carrying a hockey stick. I felt quite concerned for the
little boys playing in the opposing team.' Emma smiled;
the same sense of humour as her grandfather. 'And now look
at you. You've blossomed into such a beautiful creature.'
Emma blushed. 'So what brings you to New York, my dear?'

'I'm sorry to intrude like this, Great-aunt,' Emma began,
glancing nervously towards the other three ladies.

'Don't worry about them,' she whispered. 'After the
President's announcement, they've got more than enough to
keep themselves occupied. Now, where are your bags?'

'My bag is at the Mayflower Hotel,' Emma told her.

'Parker,' she said, turning to the butler, 'send someone
round to pick up Miss Emma's things from the Mayflower,
and then prepare the main guest bedroom because, after

today's news, I have a feeling my great-niece is going to be with us for quite some time.' The butler melted away.

'But, Great-aunt—'

'No buts,' she said, raising a hand. 'And I must insist that you stop calling me Great-aunt, it makes me sound like an old battleaxe. Now it's quite possible that I am an old battleaxe, but I do not wish to be reminded of it on a regular basis, so, please, call me Phyllis.'

'Thank you, Great-aunt Phyllis,' Emma said.

Phyllis laughed. 'I do so love the English,' she said. 'Now come and say hello to my friends. They will be fascinated to meet such an independent young lady. So frightfully modern.'

◄○►

'Quite some time' turned out to be more than a year, and as each day passed, Emma was more and more desperate to be reunited with Sebastian, but was only able to follow her son's progress from letters sent by her mother, and occasionally Grace. Emma wept when she learned of the death of 'Gramps', because she'd thought he'd live for ever. She tried not to think about who would take over the company, and assumed her father wouldn't have the nerve to show his face in Bristol.

Phyllis couldn't have made Emma feel more at home if she'd been her own mother. Emma quickly discovered that her great-aunt was a typical Harvey, generous to a fault, and the page defining the words impossible, implausible and impractical must have been torn out of her dictionary at an early age. The main guest bedroom, as Phyllis called it, was a suite of rooms overlooking Central Park, which came as a pleasant surprise after Emma's cramped single room at the Mayflower.

Emma's second surprise was when she came down for dinner on her first evening and found her great-aunt dressed in a flaming-red gown, drinking a glass of whiskey and smoking a cigarette in a long holder. She smiled at the thought of being described as modern by this woman.

'My son Alistair will be joining us for dinner,' she announced before Parker had been given a chance to pour Emma a glass of Harvey's Bristol Cream. 'He's a lawyer and a bachelor,' she added. 'Two disadvantages from which he's most unlikely to recover. But at times he can be quite amusing, if somewhat dry.'

Cousin Alistair arrived a few minutes later, dressed in a dinner jacket for a meal with his mother, thus embodying 'the British abroad'.

Emma guessed that he was around fifty, and a good tailor had disguised the fact that he was carrying a few surplus pounds. His humour may have been a little dry, but he was unquestionably bright, fun and well informed, even if he did go on a bit about the case he was currently working on. It came as no surprise when his proud mother told Emma over dinner that Alistair was the youngest partner in his law firm, since the death of her husband. Emma assumed that Phyllis knew why he wasn't married.

She couldn't be sure if it was the delicious food, the excellent wine or simply American hospitality that caused her to relax so much that she ended up telling them everything that had happened to her since Great-aunt Phyllis had last seen her on a hockey field at Red Maids' School.

By the time Emma had explained why she crossed the Atlantic despite the risks involved, they were both staring at her as if she'd just landed from another planet.

Once Alistair had devoured the last morsel of his fruit tart and turned his attention to a large brandy, he spent the next thirty minutes cross-examining their unexpected guest, as if he were opposing counsel and she a hostile witness.

'Well, I must say, Mother,' he said as he folded his

napkin, 'this case looks far more promising than Amalgamated Wire versus New York Electric. I can't wait to cross swords with Sefton Jelks.'

'What's the point of wasting our time on Jelks,' Emma said, 'when it's far more important to find Harry and clear his name?'

'I couldn't agree more,' said Alistair. 'But I have a feeling that one will lead to the other.' He picked up Emma's copy of *The Diary of a Convict*, but didn't open it, just studied the spine.

'Who's the publisher?' asked Phyllis.

'Viking Press,' said Alistair, removing his glasses.

'Harold Guinzburg, no less.'

'Do you think he and Max Lloyd might have collaborated in this deception?' Alistair asked, turning to his mother.

'Certainly not,' she replied. 'Your father once told me he'd come up against Guinzburg in court. I remember he described him as a formidable adversary, but a man who would never consider bending the law, let alone breaking it.'

'Then we're in with a chance,' said Alistair, 'because if that's the case, he won't be pleased to discover what's been perpetrated in his name. However, I'll need to read the book before I arrange a meeting with the publisher.' Alistair looked across the table and smiled at Emma. 'I shall be fascinated to discover what Mr Guinzburg makes of you, young lady.'

'And I,' said Phyllis, 'will be equally fascinated to discover what Emma makes of Harold Guinzburg.'

'Touché, Mama,' Alistair conceded.

After Parker had poured Alistair a second brandy and relit his cigar, Emma ventured to ask him what he thought her chances were of being allowed to visit Harry in Lavenham.

'I'll make an application on your behalf tomorrow,' he promised between puffs. 'Let's see if I can't do a little better than your helpful detective.'

'My helpful detective?' repeated Emma.

'Unusually helpful,' said Alistair. 'Once he realized Jelks was involved, I'm amazed Detective Kolowski even agreed to see you.'

'I'm not at all surprised that he was helpful,' said Phyllis, winking at Emma.

32

'AND YOU SAY your husband wrote this book?'

'No, Mr Guinzburg,' said Emma. 'Harry Clifton and I are not married, although I am the mother of his child. But yes, Harry did write *The Diary of a Convict* while he was incarcerated at Lavenham.'

Harold Guinzburg removed the half-moon spectacles from the end of his nose and took a closer look at the young woman seated on the opposite side of his desk. 'I do have a slight problem with your claim,' he said, 'and I feel I should point out that every sentence of the diary was written in Mr Lloyd's hand.'

'He copied Harry's manuscript word for word.'

'For that to be possible, Mr Lloyd would have had to share a cell with Tom Bradshaw, which shouldn't be difficult to check.'

'Or they could have worked together in the library,' suggested Alistair.

'If you were able to prove this,' said Guinzburg, 'it would place my company, and by that I mean me, in an invidious position to say the least, and in the circumstances, I might be wise to seek legal advice.'

'We would like to make it clear from the start,' interjected Alistair, who was sitting on Emma's right, 'that we came here in a spirit of goodwill, as we felt you would wish to be acquainted with my cousin's story.'

'It was the only reason I agreed to see you,' said Guinzburg, 'as I was a great admirer of your late father.'

'I didn't realize you knew him.'

'I didn't,' said Guinzburg. 'He appeared for the other side in a dispute my company was involved in, and I left the courtroom wishing he'd been on my side. However, if I am to accept your cousin's story,' he continued, 'I hope you won't mind if I ask Miss Barrington one or two questions.'

'I'm happy to answer any questions you might have, Mr Guinzburg,' said Emma. 'But may I ask if you've read Harry's book?'

'I make a point of reading every book we publish, Miss Barrington. I can't pretend I find all of them enjoyable, or even finish every one, but in the case of *The Diary of a Convict*, I knew the moment I'd finished the first chapter that it would be a bestseller. I also made a note in the margin on page two-eleven.' Guinzburg picked up the book and flicked through its pages before beginning to read. *'I've always wanted to be an author, and am currently working on an outline plot for the first in a series of detective novels based in Bristol.'*

'Bristol,' said Emma, interrupting the old man. 'How could Max Lloyd possibly know anything about Bristol?'

'There is a Bristol in Mr Lloyd's home state of Illinois, Miss Barrington,' said Guinzburg, 'as Max pointed out when I told him I'd be interested in reading the first in the series.'

'You never will,' Emma promised him.

'He's already submitted the opening chapters of *Mistaken Identity*,' said Guinzburg, 'and I have to say, they're rather good.'

'And were those chapters written in the same style as the diary?'

'Yes. And before you ask, Miss Barrington, they are also written in the same hand, unless you're suggesting that they were also copied.'

'He's got away with it once. Why wouldn't he try it on a second time?'

'But do you have any real proof that Mr Lloyd didn't write *The Diary of a Convict*?' said Guinzburg, beginning to sound a little irritated.

'Yes, sir. I am the "Emma" in the book.'

'If that is the case, Miss Barrington, I agree with the author's judgement that you are indeed a great beauty, and you have already proved, to quote him, to be both spirited and combative.'

Emma smiled. 'And you're an old flatterer, Mr Guinzburg.'

'As he wrote, spirited and combative,' said Guinzburg, placing his half-moon spectacles back on his nose. 'Nevertheless, I doubt your claim would stand up in a court of law. Sefton Jelks could put half a dozen Emmas on the witness stand who would swear blind they had known Lloyd all their lives. I need something more substantial.'

'Don't you find it a little too much of a coincidence, Mr Guinzburg, that the day Thomas Bradshaw arrives at Lavenham just happens to be the first day of the diary?'

'Mr Lloyd explained that he didn't start writing the diary until he became the prison librarian, when he had more time on his hands.'

'But how do you explain there being no mention of his last night in prison, or the morning he's released? He just has breakfast in the canteen, and reports to the library for another day's work.'

'What explanation do you have?' asked Guinzburg, peering at her over the top of his glasses.

'Whoever wrote the diary is still in Lavenham, and probably working on the next volume.'

'That shouldn't be difficult for you to verify,' said Guinzburg, raising an eyebrow.

'I agree,' said Alistair, 'and I've already submitted an application for Miss Barrington to visit Mr Bradshaw on compassionate grounds, and am waiting for the warden of Lavenham to give his approval.'

'May I be allowed to ask a few more questions, Miss Barrington, in the hope of removing any lingering doubts?' asked Guinzburg.

'Yes, of course,' said Emma.

The old man smiled, pulled his waistcoat down, pushed up his spectacles and studied a list of questions on a notepad in front of him. 'Who is Captain Jack Tarrant, sometimes known as Old Jack?'

'My grandfather's oldest friend. They served in the Boer War together.'

'Which grandfather?'

'Sir Walter Barrington.'

The publisher nodded. 'And did you consider Mr Tarrant to be an honourable man?'

'Like Caesar's wife, he was beyond reproach. He was probably the single biggest influence in Harry's life.'

'But isn't he to blame for the fact that you and Harry are not married?'

'Is that question relevant?' asked Alistair, jumping in.

'I suspect we're about to find out,' said Guinzburg, not taking his eyes off Emma.

'Jack felt it was his duty to alert the vicar to the possibility that my father, Hugo Barrington, might also be Harry's father,' said Emma, her voice breaking.

'Was that necessary, Mr Guinzburg?' snapped Alistair.

'Oh yes,' said the publisher, picking up the copy of *The Diary of a Convict* from his desk. 'I am now convinced that it was Harry Clifton, and not Max Lloyd, who wrote this book.'

Emma smiled. 'Thank you,' she said, 'even if I'm not sure what I can do about it.'

'I know exactly what I'm going to do about it,' said Guinzburg. 'To start with, I shall release a revised edition as quickly as the presses can print it, with two major changes: Harry Clifton's name will replace Max Lloyd's on the front cover, and his photograph will appear on the back cover, assuming you have one, Miss Barrington.'

'Several,' said Emma, 'including one of him on the *Kansas Star* as it sailed into New York harbour.'

'Ah, that would also explain—' began Guinzburg.

'But if you were to do that,' interrupted Alistair, 'all hell will break loose. Jelks will issue a writ on behalf of his client for defamation, and claim punitive damages.'

'Let's hope so,' said Guinzburg, 'because if he does, the book will undoubtedly go back to number one on the bestseller lists, and remain there for several months. However, if he does nothing, as I suspect will be the case, it will show that he believes he's the only person who has seen the missing exercise book Harry Clifton wrote about ending up in Lavenham.'

'I knew there was another one,' said Emma.

'There certainly is,' said Guinzburg, 'and it was your mention of the *Kansas Star* that made me realize the manuscript Mr Lloyd submitted as the opening chapters of *Mistaken Identity* is nothing more than an account of what happened to Harry Clifton before he was sentenced for a crime he didn't commit.'

'May I be allowed to read it?' said Emma.

—◦—

The moment Emma walked into Alistair's office, she knew something had gone badly wrong. The familiar warm welcome and gracious smile had been replaced by a furrowed brow.

'They're not going to let me visit Harry, are they,' she said.

'No,' said Alistair. 'Your application was turned down.'

'But why? You told me I was well within my rights.'

'I phoned the warden earlier this morning and asked him exactly the same question.'

'And what reason did he give?'

'You can hear for yourself,' said Alistair, 'because I made a tape recording of our conversation. Listen carefully, because it gives us three very important clues.' Without another word, he leant forward and pressed the play button on his Grundig. Two spools began to whirl.

'Lavenham Correctional Facility.'

'I'd like to speak to the warden.'

'Who's calling?'

'Alistair Stuart. I'm a New York attorney.'

Silence, followed by another ringing tone. A longer silence, then, 'I'll put you through, sir.'

Emma was sitting on the edge of her seat when the warden came on the line.

'Good morning, Mr Stuart. This is Warden Swanson. How can I help you?'

'Good morning, Mr Swanson. I made an application ten days ago on behalf of my client, Miss Emma Barrington, requesting a visit on compassionate grounds to an inmate, Thomas Bradshaw, at the earliest possible opportunity. I received a letter from your office this morning saying the application has been turned down. I can find no legal reason for—'

'Mr Stuart, your application was processed in the usual way, but I was unable to grant your request because Mr Bradshaw is no longer being held at this establishment.'

Another long silence followed, although Emma could see that the tape was still turning. Alistair eventually said, 'And which institution has he been transferred to?'

'I am not at liberty to disclose that information, Mr Stuart.'

'But under the law, my client has the right to—'

'The prisoner has signed a document waiving his rights, a copy of which I'd be happy to send to you.'

'But why would he do that?' said Alistair, casting a line into the water.

'I am not at liberty to disclose that information,' repeated the warden, not rising to the bait.

'Are you at liberty to divulge anything at all concerning Thomas Bradshaw?' asked Alistair, trying not to sound exasperated.

Another long silence followed and, although the tape was still running, Emma wondered if the warden had put his phone down. Alistair placed a finger to his lips, and suddenly the voice was back on the line.

'Harry Clifton was released from prison, but continued to serve his sentence.' Another long pause. 'And I lost the best librarian this prison's ever had.'

The phone went dead.

Alistair pressed the stop button before he spoke. 'The warden went as far as he could to assist us.'

'By mentioning Harry by name?' said Emma.

'Yes, but also by letting us know he served in the prison library until very recently. That explains how Lloyd got his hands on the diaries.'

Emma nodded. 'But you said there were *three* important clues,' she reminded him. 'What was the third?'

'That Harry was released from Lavenham, but continues to serve his sentence.'

'Then he must be in another prison,' said Emma.

'I don't think so,' said Alistair. 'Now we're at war, my bet is that Tom Bradshaw will be serving the rest of his sentence in the navy.'

'What makes you think that?'

'It's all in the diaries,' said Alistair. He picked up a copy of *The Diary of a Convict* from his desk, turned to a page marked by a bookmark and read: *'The first thing I'll do when I get back to Bristol is join the navy and fight the Germans.'*

'But they'd never have allowed him to return to England before he'd completed his sentence.'

'I didn't say he'd joined the British Navy.'

'Oh God,' said Emma as the significance of Alistair's words sank in.

'At least we know Harry's still alive,' said Alistair cheerfully.

'I wish he was still in prison.'

HUGO BARRINGTON

1942–1943

33

SIR WALTER'S FUNERAL was held at St Mary's Redcliffe, and the late chairman of Barrington's Shipping Line would surely have been proud to see such a packed congregation and to hear the heartfelt eulogy delivered by the Bishop of Bristol.

After the service, the mourners lined up to offer their condolences to Sir Hugo as he stood at the north door of the church, alongside his mother. He was able to explain to those who asked that his daughter Emma was marooned in New York, although he couldn't tell them why she'd gone there in the first place, and his son Giles, of whom he was inordinately proud, was interned in a German PoW camp in Weinsberg; information his mother had passed on to him the previous evening.

During the service, Lord and Lady Harvey, Hugo's ex-wife Elizabeth and their daughter Grace had all been seated in the front row of the church, on the opposite side of the aisle from Hugo. All of them had paid their respects to the grieving widow, and had then pointedly left without acknowledging his presence.

Maisie Clifton had sat at the back of the church, her head bowed throughout the service, and left moments after the bishop had delivered the final blessing.

When Bill Lockwood, the managing director of

Barrington's, stepped forward to shake hands with his new chairman and to express his condolences, all Hugo had to say was, 'I expect to see you in my office at nine o'clock tomorrow morning.'

Mr Lockwood gave a slight bow.

A reception was held at Barrington Hall after the funeral, and Hugo mingled among the mourners, several of whom were about to discover that they no longer had a job with Barrington's. When the last guest had departed, Hugo went up to his bedroom and changed for dinner.

He entered the dining room with his mother on his arm. Once she was seated, he took his father's place at the head of the table. During the meal, while there were no servants in attendance, he told his mother that, despite his father's misgivings, he was a reformed character.

He went on to assure her that the company was in safe hands, and that he had exciting plans for its future.

—◦—

Hugo drove his Bugatti through the gates of Barrington's shipyard for the first time in over two years, at 9.23 the following morning. He parked in the chairman's space before making his way up to his father's old office.

As he stepped out of the lift on the fourth floor, he saw Bill Lockwood pacing up and down the corridor outside his office, a red folder under his arm. But then Hugo had always intended to keep him waiting.

'Good morning, Hugo,' said Lockwood, stepping forward.

Hugo strolled past him without responding. 'Good morning, Miss Potts,' he said to his old secretary, as if he'd never been away. 'I'll let you know when I'm ready to see Mr Lockwood,' he added, before walking through to his new office.

He sat down at his father's desk – that was how he still thought of it, and he wondered how long that feeling would last – and began to read *The Times*. Once the Americans and Russians had entered the war, far more people were beginning to believe in an Allied victory. He put down the paper.

'I'll see Mr Lockwood now, Miss Potts.'

The managing director entered the chairman's office with a smile on his face. 'Welcome back, Hugo,' he said.

Hugo gave him a fixed stare and said, 'Chairman.'

'I'm sorry, chairman,' said a man who had served on the board of Barrington's when Hugo was in short trousers.

'I'd like you to bring me up to date on the company's financial position.'

'Of course, chairman.' Lockwood opened the red folder he'd been carrying under his arm.

As the chairman hadn't invited him to sit, he remained standing. 'Your father,' he began, 'managed to guide the company prudently through troubled times, and despite several setbacks, not least the Germans continually targeting the docks during their nightly bombing raids in the early part of the war, with the help of government contracts, we have managed to weather the storm, so we should be in good shape once this dreadful war is over.'

'Cut the waffle,' said Hugo, 'and get to the bottom line.'

'Last year,' continued the managing director turning a page, 'the company made a profit of thirty-seven thousand, four hundred pounds and ten shillings.'

'Wouldn't want to forget the ten shillings, would we,' said Hugo.

'That was always your father's attitude,' said Lockwood, missing the sarcasm.

'And this year?'

'Our half yearly results suggest that we're well placed to equal, possibly even surpass, last year's results.' Lockwood turned another page.

'How many places are currently available on the board?' asked Hugo.

The change of subject took Lockwood by surprise, and he had to turn several pages before he could respond. 'Three, as unfortunately Lord Harvey, Sir Derek Sinclair and Captain Havens all resigned following your father's death.'

'I'm glad to hear that,' said Hugo. 'It will save me the trouble of sacking them.'

'I presume, chairman, you would not wish me to record those sentiments in my minutes of this meeting?'

'I don't give a damn if you do or don't,' Hugo said.

The managing director bowed his head.

'And when are you due to retire?' was Hugo's next question.

'I'll be sixty in a couple of months' time, but if you felt, chairman, given the circumstances—'

'What circumstances?'

'As you will only just have got your feet under the table, so to speak, I could be persuaded to stay on for a couple more years.'

'That's good of you,' said Hugo, and the managing director smiled for the second time that morning. 'But please don't put yourself out on my account. Two months will be just fine by me. So what's the biggest challenge we're facing at the moment?'

'We have recently applied for a major government contract to lease out our merchant fleet to the navy,' said Lockwood once he'd recovered. 'We're not the favourites, but I think your father gave a good account of himself when the inspectors visited the company earlier this year, so we should be taken seriously.'

'When will we find out?'

'Not for some time, I fear. Civil servants aren't built for speed,' he added, laughing at his own joke. 'I have also prepared several discussion papers for your consideration, chairman, so that you will be well briefed before you chair your first board meeting.'

'I don't anticipate holding that many board meetings in the future,' said Hugo. 'I believe in leading from the front, making decisions and standing by them. But you can leave your briefing papers with my secretary, and I'll get round to them when I find the time.'

'As you wish, chairman.'

Within moments of Lockwood leaving his office, Hugo was on the move. 'I'm going to visit my bank,' he said as he passed Miss Potts's desk.

'Shall I call Mr Prendergast and let him know you'd like to see him?' Miss Potts asked as she hurried after him down the corridor.

'Certainly not,' said Hugo. 'I want to take him by surprise.'

'Is there anything you need me to do before you return, Sir Hugo?' Miss Potts enquired as he stepped into the lift.

'Yes, see that the name on my door is changed before I get back.'

Miss Potts turned round to look at the office door. *Sir Walter Barrington, Chairman* was displayed in gold leaf.

The lift door closed.

As Hugo drove into the centre of Bristol, he felt that his first few hours as chairman could not have gone better. All was finally right with the world. He parked his Bugatti outside the National Provincial Bank in Corn Street, leant across and picked up a packet he'd left under the passenger seat.

He strolled into the bank, past the reception desk and headed straight for the manager's office, giving a little tap on the door before marching in. A startled Mr Prendergast leapt up as Hugo placed a shoebox on his desk and sank into the chair opposite him.

'I hope I'm not interrupting anything important,' said Hugo.

'Of course not, Sir Hugo,' said Prendergast, staring at the shoebox. 'I'm available for you at any time.'

'That's good to know, Prendergast. Why don't you begin by bringing me up to date on Broad Street?'

The bank manager scurried across the room, pulled open the drawer of a filing cabinet and extracted a thick folder, which he placed on the table. He sorted through some papers before he spoke again.

'Ah yes,' he said eventually. 'Here's what I was looking for.'

Hugo was tapping the arm of his chair impatiently.

'Of the twenty-two businesses which have ceased to trade in Broad Street since the bombing began, seventeen have already accepted your offer of two hundred pounds or less for their freehold, namely Roland the florist, Bates the butcher, Makepeace—'

'What about Mrs Clifton? Has she accepted my offer?'

'I'm afraid not, Sir Hugo. Mrs Clifton said she wouldn't settle for less than four hundred pounds, and has only given you until next Friday to accept her offer.'

'Has she, be damned. Well, you can tell her that two hundred pounds is my final offer. That woman has never had a brass farthing to her name, so I don't expect we'll have to wait too much longer before she comes to her senses.'

Prendergast gave a slight cough that Hugo remembered well.

'If you succeed in purchasing every property in the street except Mrs Clifton's, four hundred pounds might turn out to be quite reasonable.'

'She's bluffing. All we have to do is bide our time.'

'If you say so.'

'I do say so. And in any case, I know exactly the right man to convince the Clifton woman that she'd be wise to settle for two hundred pounds.'

Prendergast didn't look convinced, but satisfied himself by asking, 'Is there anything else I can do to assist you?'

'Yes,' said Hugo, removing the lid from the shoebox. 'You can deposit this money into my personal account and issue me with a new cheque book.'

'Of course, Sir Hugo,' said Prendergast, looking into the box. 'I'll count it and issue you with a receipt and a cheque book.'

'But I'll need to make an immediate withdrawal, as I have my eye on a Lagonda V12.'

'Winner of Le Mans,' said Prendergast, 'but then, you've always been a pioneer in that particular field.'

Hugo smiled as he rose from his chair.

'Give me a call the moment Mrs Clifton realizes that two hundred pounds is all she's going to get.'

--◦--

'Do we still employ Stan Tancock, Miss Potts?' Hugo asked as he marched back into the office.

'Yes, Sir Hugo,' replied his secretary, following him into the room. 'He works as a loader in the stock yard.'

'I want to see him immediately,' said the chairman, as he slumped down behind his desk.

Miss Potts hurried out of the room.

Hugo stared at the files piled on his desk which he was supposed to have read before the next board meeting. He flicked open the cover of the top one: a list of the union's demands following their last meeting with management. He had reached number four on the list, two weeks' paid holiday each year, when there was a tap on the door.

'Tancock to see you, chairman.'

'Thank you, Miss Potts. Send him in.'

Stan Tancock walked into the room, removed his cloth cap and stood in front of the chairman's desk.

'You wanted to see me, guv?' he said, looking a little nervous.

Hugo glanced up at the squat, unshaven docker, whose beer belly didn't leave much doubt where most of his wage packet went on a Friday night.

'I've got a job for you, Tancock.'

'Yes, guv,' said Stan looking more hopeful.

'It concerns your sister, Maisie Clifton, and the plot of land she owns on Broad Street, where Tilly's tea shop used to stand. Do you know anything about it?'

'Yes, guv, some geezer offered her two hundred quid for it.'

'Is that right?' said Hugo, removing his wallet from an inside pocket. He extracted a crisp five-pound note and laid it on the desk. Hugo remembered the same licking of the lips and the same piggy eyes the last time he'd bribed the man. 'I want you to make sure, Tancock, that your sister accepts the offer, without the suggestion that I'm in any way involved.'

He slid the five-pound note across the desk.

'No problem,' said Stan, no longer looking at the chairman, only at the five-pound note.

'There will be another of those,' Hugo said, tapping his wallet, 'the day she signs the contract.'

'Consider it done, guv.'

Hugo added casually, 'I was sorry to hear about your nephew.'

'Don't make much odds to me,' said Stan. 'Got far too big for his boots, in my opinion.'

'Buried at sea, I was told.'

'Yeah, more'n two years back.'

'How did you find out?'

'Ship's doctor came to visit me sister, didn't he.'

'And was he able to confirm that young Clifton was buried at sea?'

'Sure did. Even brought a letter from some mate who was on board the ship when Harry died.'

'A letter?' said Hugo leaning forward. 'What did this letter say?'

'No idea, guv. Maisie never opened it.'

'So what did she do with the letter?'

'Still on the mantelpiece isn't it?'

Hugo extracted another five-pound note.

'I'd like to see that letter.'

34

HUGO THREW ON the brakes of his new Lagonda when he heard a paperboy shouting his name from a street corner.

'Sir Hugo Barrington's son decorated for gallantry at Tobruk. Read all about it!'

Hugo leapt out of his car, handed the paperboy a halfpenny and looked at a photograph of his son when he was school captain of Bristol Grammar that dominated the front page. He climbed back into his car, turned off the ignition and read all about it.

> Second Lieutenant Giles Barrington of the 1st Battalion, the Wessex, son of Sir Hugo Barrington Bt, has been awarded the Military Cross following action in Tobruk. Lt Barrington led a platoon across eighty yards of open desert, killing a German officer and five other soldiers, before over-running an enemy dugout and capturing 63 German infantry men from Rommel's crack Afrika Korps. Lt/Col. Robertson of the Wessex described Lt Barrington's action as displaying remarkable leadership and selfless courage in the face of overwhelming odds.
>
> 2/Lt Barrington's platoon commander, Captain Alex Fisher, also an Old Bristolian, was involved in the same action, and mentioned in dispatches, as was Corporal Terry Bates, a local butcher from Broad Street. Lt Giles Barrington MC was later

captured by the Germans when Rommel sacked Tobruk. Neither Barrington, nor Bates, is aware of their award for gallantry, because both of them are currently prisoners of war in Germany. Captain Fisher has been reported as missing in action. Full story pages 6 & 7.

Hugo sped home to share the news with his mother.

'How proud Walter would have been,' she said once she'd finished reading the report. 'I must call Elizabeth immediately, in case she hasn't heard the news.'

It was the first time anyone had mentioned his former wife's name for a long while.

<o>

'I thought you'd be interested to know,' said Mitchell, 'that Mrs Clifton is wearing an engagement ring.'

'Who would want to marry that bitch?'

'A Mr Arnold Holcombe, it seems.'

'Who's he?'

'A schoolmaster. Teaches English at Merrywood Elementary. In fact, he used to teach Harry Clifton before he went to St Bede's.'

'But that was years ago. Why haven't you mentioned his name before?'

'They've only recently met up again, when Mrs Clifton began attending evening classes.'

'Evening classes?' repeated Hugo.

'Yes,' said Mitchell. 'She's been learning to read and write. Seems she's a chip off the young block.'

'What do you mean?' snapped Hugo.

'When the class took their final exam at the end of the course, she came top.'

'Did she now?' said Hugo. 'Perhaps I should visit Mr Holcombe and let him know exactly what his fiancée was up to during the years he lost touch with her.'

'Perhaps I should mention that Holcombe boxed for Bristol University, as Stan Tancock found to his cost.'

'I can handle myself,' said Hugo. 'Meanwhile I want you to keep an eye on another woman, who just might prove every bit as dangerous for my future as Maisie Clifton.'

Mitchell removed a tiny notebook and pencil from an inside pocket.

'Her name is Olga Piotrovska, and she lives in London, at number forty-two Lowndes Square. I need to know everyone she comes into contact with, particularly if she's ever interviewed by any members of your former profession. Spare no details, however trivial or unpleasant you may consider them.'

Once Hugo had finished speaking, the notebook and pencil disappeared. He then handed Mitchell an envelope, a sign that the meeting was over. Mitchell slipped his pay packet into his jacket pocket, stood up and limped away.

◄○►

Hugo was surprised how quickly he became bored with being chairman of Barrington's. Endless meetings to attend, countless papers to read, minutes to be circulated, memos to be considered, and a stack of mail that should have been replied to by return of post. And on top of that, before he left every evening, Miss Potts would hand him a briefcase bulging with even more papers that had to be gone over by the time he was back behind his desk at eight the following morning.

Hugo invited three chums to join the board, including Archie Fenwick and Toby Dunstable, in the hope that they would lessen his load. They rarely showed up for meetings, but still expected to receive their stipend.

As the weeks passed, Hugo began turning up at the office later and later, and after Bill Lockwood reminded the chairman that it was only a few days to his sixtieth birthday, when he would be retiring, Hugo capitulated and said that he'd decided Lockwood could stay on for another couple of years.

'How kind of you to reconsider my position, chairman,' said Lockwood. 'But I feel that, having served the company for almost forty years, the time has come for me to make way for a younger man.'

Hugo cancelled Lockwood's farewell party.

That younger man was Ray Compton, Lockwood's deputy, who had only been with the company for a few months, and certainly hadn't got his feet under the table. When he presented Barrington's year results to the board, Hugo accepted for the first time that the company was only just breaking even, and agreed with Compton that the time had come to start laying off some of the dock labourers before the company couldn't afford to pay their wages.

As Barrington's fortunes dwindled, the nation's future looked more hopeful.

With the German army retreating from Stalingrad the British people began to believe for the first time that the Allies could win the war. Confidence in the future started to seep back into the nation's psyche as theatres, clubs and restaurants began to reopen all over the country.

Hugo longed to be back in town and to rejoin his social set, but Mitchell's reports continued to make it clear that London was one city he'd be wise to steer clear of.

─◦─

The year 1943 didn't begin well for Barrington's.

There were several cancelled contracts from customers who became exasperated when the chairman couldn't be bothered to answer their letters, and several creditors began demanding payment, one or two of them even threatening writs. And then one morning, a ray of sunlight appeared that Hugo believed would solve all of the immediate cash-flow problems.

It was a call from Prendergast that raised Hugo's hopes.

The bank manager had been approached by the United Dominion Real Estate Company, who were showing an interest in purchasing the Broad Street site.

'I think, Sir Hugo, it would be prudent not to mention the figure over the phone,' Prendergast intoned slightly pompously.

Hugo was sitting in Prendergast's office forty minutes later, and even he gasped when he heard how much they were willing to offer.

'Twenty-four thousand pounds?' repeated Hugo.

'Yes,' said Prendergast, 'and I'm confident that's their opening bid, and I can push them up to nearer thirty. Remembering that your original outlay was less than three thousand pounds, I think we can consider it a shrewd investment. But there's a fly in the ointment.'

'A fly?' said Hugo, sounding anxious.

'In the form of Mrs Clifton,' said Prendergast. 'The offer is conditional on you obtaining the freehold for the entire site, including her plot.'

'Offer her eight hundred,' Hugo barked.

The Prendergast cough followed, although he didn't remind his client that had he taken his advice, they could have closed a deal with Mrs Clifton for four hundred pounds some months ago, and if she were ever to find out about United Dominion's offer . . .

'I'll let you know the moment I've heard from her,' was all Prendergast said.

'Do that,' said Hugo, 'and while I'm here, I need to withdraw a little cash from my private account.'

'I'm sorry, Sir Hugo, but that account is overdrawn at the present time . . .'

Hugo was sitting in the front seat of his sleek royal blue Lagonda when Holcombe pushed through the school door and began to walk across the playground. He stopped to speak to a handyman who was giving the front gates a fresh coat of lilac and green paint, the Merrywood school colours.

'That's a fine job you're doing, Alf.'

'Thank you, Mr Holcombe,' Hugo heard the handyman say.

'But I still expect you to concentrate more on your verbs, and do try not to be late on Wednesday.'

Alf touched his cap.

Holcombe began walking along the pavement and pretended not to see Hugo sitting behind the wheel of his car. Hugo allowed himself a smirk; everyone gave his Lagonda V12 a second look. Three young lads loitering on the pavement opposite hadn't been able to take their eyes off it for the past half hour.

Hugo stepped out of the car and stood in the middle of the pavement, but Holcombe still ignored him. He couldn't have been more than a stride away when Hugo said, 'I wonder if we could have a word, Mr Holcombe. My name is—'

'I'm well aware of who you are,' said Holcombe, and walked straight past him.

Hugo chased after the schoolmaster. 'It's just that I felt you ought to know—'

'Know what?' said Holcombe, stopping in his tracks and turning to face him.

'What your fiancée did for a living, not so very long ago.'

'She was forced into prostitution because you wouldn't pay for her son's –' he looked Hugo straight in the eye – '*your* son's school fees, when he was in his last two years at Bristol Grammar School.'

'There's no proof that Harry Clifton is my son,' said Hugo defiantly.

'There was enough proof for a vicar to refuse to allow Harry to marry your daughter.'

'How would you know? You weren't there.'

'How would you know? You ran away.'

'Then let me tell you something you certainly don't know,' said Hugo, almost shouting. 'This paragon of virtue that you're planning to spend the rest of your life with has swindled me out of a piece of land I owned in Broad Street.'

'Let me tell you something you do know,' said Holcombe. 'Maisie paid off every penny of your loan, with interest, and all you left her with was less than ten pounds to her name.'

'That land's now worth four hundred pounds,' said Hugo, immediately regretting his words, 'and it belongs to me.'

'If it belonged to you,' said Holcombe, 'you wouldn't be trying to buy the site for twice that amount.'

Hugo was livid that he had allowed himself to reveal the extent of his interest in the site, but he wasn't finished. 'So when you have sex with Maisie Clifton, do you have to pay for it, schoolmaster, because I certainly didn't.'

Holcombe raised a fist.

'Go on, hit me,' goaded Hugo. 'Unlike Stan Tancock, I'd sue you for every penny you're worth.'

Holcombe lowered his fist and marched off, annoyed with himself for having allowed Barrington to rile him.

Hugo smiled. He felt he had delivered the knockout blow.

He turned round to see the lads on the other side of the road sniggering. But then they'd never seen a lilac and green Lagonda before.

35

WHEN THE FIRST cheque bounced, Hugo simply ignored it and waited a few days before he presented it a second time. When it came back again, stamped 'Refer to Drawer', he began to accept the inevitable.

For the next few weeks, Hugo found several different ways of getting around the immediate cash problem.

He first raided the office safe and removed the £100 that his father always kept for a rainy day. This was a thunderstorm, and the old man had certainly never had to resort to the cash reserve to pay his secretary's wages. Once that had run out, he reluctantly let go of the Lagonda. However, the dealer politely pointed out that lilac and green weren't this year's colours, and as Sir Hugo required cash, he could only offer him half the original purchase price, because the bodywork would have to be stripped and repainted.

Hugo survived for another month.

With no other available assets to dispose of, he began to steal from his mother. First, any loose change left lying about the house, followed by coins in purses and then notes in bags.

It wasn't long before he bagged a small silver pheasant that had graced the centre of the dining-room table for years, followed by its parents, all of which flew to the nearest pawn shop.

Hugo then moved on to his mother's jewellery. He started with items she wouldn't notice. A hat pin and a Victorian brooch were quickly followed by an amber necklace she rarely wore, and a diamond tiara which had been in the family for over a century and was only worn at weddings or ceremonial occasions. He didn't anticipate there being many of those in the near future.

He finally turned to his father's art collection, first taking off the wall a portrait of his grandfather by a young John Singer Sargent, but not before the housekeeper and the cook had handed in their notice, having received no wages for over three months. Jenkins conveniently died a month later.

His grandfather's Constable (*The Mill at Dunning Lock*) was followed by his great-grandfather's Turner (*Swans on the Avon*), both of which had been in the family for over a century.

Hugo was able to convince himself that it wasn't theft. After all, his father's will had stated *and all that therein is*.

This irregular source of funds ensured that the company survived and only showed a small loss for the first quarter of the year, that is, if you didn't count the resignation of three more directors and several other senior members of staff who hadn't received their pay cheques on the last day of the month. When asked, Hugo blamed the temporary setbacks on the war. One elderly director's parting words were, 'Your father never found it necessary to use that as an excuse.'

Soon, even the removable assets began to dwindle.

Hugo knew that if he were to put Barrington Hall and its 72 acres of parkland on the market, it would announce to the world that a company that had declared a profit for over a hundred years was insolvent.

His mother continued to accept Hugo's assurances that the problem was only temporary, and that given time everything would sort itself out. After a time, he started to believe his own propaganda. When the cheques started to bounce again, Mr Prendergast reminded him that there was an offer of £3,500 on the table for his properties in Broad Street, which, Prendergast pointed out, would still show him a profit of £600.

'What about the thirty thousand I was promised?' Hugo shouted down the phone.

'That offer is also still on the table, Sir Hugo, but it remains subject to your purchasing Mrs Clifton's freehold.'

'Offer her a thousand,' he barked.

'As you wish, Sir Hugo.'

Hugo slammed the phone down and wondered what else could go wrong. The phone rang again.

◄◦►

Hugo was hidden away in a corner alcove of the Railway Arms, a hotel he'd never frequented before, and never would again. He nervously checked his watch every few minutes, while he waited for Mitchell to arrive.

The private detective joined him at 11.34 a.m., only minutes after the Paddington express had pulled into Temple Meads station. Mitchell slipped into the chair opposite his only client, although he hadn't received any remuneration for several months.

'What is so urgent that it couldn't wait?' demanded Hugo, once a half pint of beer had been placed in front of the private detective.

'I'm sorry to report, sir,' Mitchell began after taking a sip, 'that the police have arrested your friend Toby Dunstable.' Hugo felt a shiver shoot through his body. 'They've charged him with the theft of the Piotrovska diamonds along with several paintings, including a Picasso and a Monet, that he tried to offload on Agnew's, the Mayfair art dealer.'

'Toby will keep his mouth shut,' said Hugo.

'I fear not, sir. I am reliably informed that he has turned

King's evidence in exchange for a lighter sentence. It seems Scotland Yard are more interested in arresting the man behind the crime.'

Hugo's beer went flat while he tried to take in the significance of Mitchell's words. After a long silence, the private detective continued. 'I thought you'd also want to know that Miss Piotrovska has hired Sir Francis Mayhew KC to represent her.'

'Why doesn't she just leave the police to deal with the case?'

'She did not seek Sir Francis's advice on the burglary, but on two other matters.'

'Two other matters?' repeated Hugo.

'Yes. I understand a writ is about to be served on you for breach of promise, and Miss Piotrovska is also lodging a paternity suit, naming you as the father of her daughter.'

'She'll never be able to prove it.'

'Among the evidence that will be presented to the court is the receipt for an engagement ring purchased from a Burlington Arcade jeweller, and both her resident housekeeper and her lady's maid have signed affidavits confirming that you resided at forty-two Lowndes Square for over a year.'

For the first time in ten years, Hugo asked Mitchell for his advice. 'What do you think I should do?' he almost whispered.

'If I found myself in your position, sir, I'd leave the country as soon as possible.'

'How long do you think I've got?'

'A week, ten days at the most.'

A waiter appeared by their side. 'That will be one shilling and nine pence, sir.'

As Hugo didn't move, Mitchell handed the waiter a florin and said, 'Keep the change.'

Once the private detective had left to return to London,

Hugo sat alone for some time, considering his options. The waiter came over again and asked if he'd like another drink, but Hugo didn't even bother to reply. Eventually he heaved himself up from his chair and made his way out of the bar.

Hugo headed towards the city centre, slower and slower with each pace, until he'd finally worked out what he had to do next. He marched into the bank a few minutes later.

'Can I help you, sir?' asked the young man on reception. But Hugo was halfway across the hall before he'd had time to call the manager and warn him that Sir Hugo Barrington was heading towards his office.

Prendergast was no longer surprised that Sir Hugo always assumed he would be available at a moment's notice, but he was shocked to see that the chairman of Barrington's hadn't bothered to shave that morning.

'I have a problem that needs to be dealt with urgently,' Hugo said as he sank into the chair opposite the manager.

'Yes of course, Sir Hugo. How can I be of assistance?'

'What's the most you could hope to raise for my properties on Broad Street?'

'But only last week I sent a letter advising you that Mrs Clifton has rejected your latest offer.'

'I'm well aware of that,' said Hugo. 'I meant without her site.'

'There is still an offer on the table of three thousand five hundred, but I have reason to believe that were you to offer Mrs Clifton a little more, she would release her site and the thirty-thousand-pound bid would still be valid.'

'I don't have any more time,' said Hugo without explanation.

'If that is the case, I'm confident that I could press my client to raise his bid to four thousand, which would still show you a handsome profit.'

'If I were to accept that offer, I would need your assurance on one thing.' Mr Prendergast allowed himself a raised eyebrow. 'That your client does not have, and never has had, any connection with Mrs Clifton.'

'I am able to give you that assurance, Sir Hugo.'

'If your client was to pay me four thousand, how much would that leave in my current account?'

Mr Prendergast opened Sir Hugo's file and checked the balance sheet. 'Eight hundred and twenty-two pounds and ten shillings,' he said.

Hugo no longer joked about the ten shillings. 'In which case, I require eight hundred pounds in cash immediately. And I'll instruct you later where to send the proceeds of the sale.'

'The proceeds of the sale?' repeated Prendergast.

'Yes,' replied Hugo. 'I've decided to place Barrington Hall on the market.'

36

No one saw him leave the house.

He was carrying a suitcase and was dressed in a warm tweed suit, a pair of stout brown shoes that had been made to last, a heavy topcoat and a brown felt hat. A casual glance, and you would have taken him for a commercial traveller.

He walked to the nearest bus stop, which was just over a mile away, most of it his own land. Forty minutes later he boarded a green single-decker bus – a mode of transport he'd never used before. He sat in the back seat, not letting the suitcase out of his sight. He handed the clippie a ten-shilling note, despite the fact that he was only asked for thruppence; his first mistake if he hoped to avoid drawing attention to himself.

The bus continued on its way into Bristol, a journey he would normally cover in about twelve minutes in the Lagonda, but today it took over an hour before they finally pulled into the bus station. Hugo was neither the first nor the last passenger to get off. He checked his watch: 2.38 p.m. He'd left himself enough time.

He walked up the slope to Temple Meads station – he'd never noticed the slope, but then he'd never had to carry his own suitcase before – where he joined a long queue and purchased a third-class single to Fishguard. He asked which platform the train would be leaving from, and once he'd found it, stood at the far end, under an unlit gas light.

When the train eventually pulled in, he climbed aboard and found a seat in the middle of a third-class compartment, which quickly filled up. He placed his suitcase on the rack opposite him, and rarely took his eyes off it. A woman pulled open the carriage door and glanced into the crowded compartment, but he didn't offer her his seat.

As the train pulled out of the station, he let out a sigh of relief, delighted to see Bristol disappearing into the distance. He sat back and thought about the decision he'd made. By this time tomorrow, he'd be in Cork. He wouldn't feel safe until his feet were treading on Irish soil. But they had to arrive in Swansea on schedule if he hoped to link up with the train for Fishguard.

The train pulled into Swansea with half an hour to spare; time for a cup of tea and a Chelsea bun in the station buffet. It wasn't Earl Grey or Carwardine's, but he was too tired to care. As soon as he'd finished, he exchanged the buffet for another dimly lit platform and waited for the Fishguard train to appear.

The train was late, but he was confident that the ferry wouldn't leave the harbour before all the passengers were on board. After an overnight stay in Cork, he would book a passage on a ship, any ship, that was sailing to America. There he would begin a new life, with the money he made from the sale of Barrington Hall.

The idea of his ancestral home going under the hammer made him think about his mother for the first time. Where would she live, once the house had been sold? She could always join Elizabeth at the Manor House. After all, it had more than enough room. Failing that, she could move in with the Harveys, who had three houses, not to mention numerous cottages on their estates.

His thoughts then turned to the Barrington Shipping Line – a business that had been built up by two generations of the family, while the third had managed to bring it to its knees quicker than a bishop's blessing.

For a moment, he thought about Olga Piotrovska, thankful that he would never see her again. He even spared a passing thought for Toby Dunstable, who had been the cause of all his trouble.

Emma and Grace crossed his mind, but not for very long: he'd never seen the point of daughters. And then he thought about Giles, who had avoided him after escaping from Weinsberg PoW camp and returning to Bristol. People regularly asked after his war hero son, and Hugo had to make up some new story every time. That would no longer be necessary, because once he was in America the umbilical cord would finally be severed, although in time – and Hugo was still determined it would be some considerable time – Giles would inherit the family title, even if *all that therein is* was no longer worth the paper it was written on.

But most of the time he thought about himself, an indulgence that was only interrupted when the train arrived at Fishguard. He waited for everyone else to leave the carriage before he took his suitcase down from the rack and stepped out on to the platform.

He followed the megaphone directions, 'Buses to the harbour. Buses to the harbour!' There were four. He chose the third. This time it was only a short journey, and he couldn't miss the terminal, despite the blackout; another long third-class queue, this time for the Cork ferry.

After buying a one-way ticket, he walked up the gangway, stepped on board and found a nook that no self-respecting cat would have curled up in. He didn't feel safe until he heard two blasts on the foghorn and, in the gentle swell, felt the ship drifting away from the quayside.

Once the ferry had passed the harbour wall, he relaxed for the first time, and was so exhausted he rested his head on the suitcase and fell into a deep sleep.

Hugo couldn't be sure how long he'd been asleep when he felt a tap on his shoulder. He looked up to see two men towering over him.

'Sir Hugo Barrington?' one of them asked.

There didn't seem much point in denying it. They yanked him up by the shoulders and told him he was under arrest. They took their time reading out a long list of the charges.

'But I'm on my way to Cork,' he protested. 'Surely we must be beyond the twelve-mile limit?'

'No, sir,' said the second officer, 'you're on your way back to Fishguard.'

Several passengers leaned over the ship's railings to get a closer view of the handcuffed man being escorted down the gangway, who had been the cause of them being delayed.

Hugo was bundled into the back of a black Wolseley car, and moments later he began the long journey back to Bristol.

◄○►

When the cell door opened a uniformed man brought in some breakfast on a tray – not the kind of breakfast, not the kind of tray and certainly not the kind of uniformed man Sir Hugo was accustomed to seeing first thing in the morning. One look at the fried bread and tomatoes bathed in oil, and he pushed the tray to one side. He wondered how long it would be before this became part of his staple diet. The constable returned a few minutes later, took away the tray and slammed the cell door closed.

The next time the door opened, two officers entered the cell and escorted Hugo up the stone steps to the charge

room on the first floor. Ben Winshaw, the Barrington Shipping Line's company solicitor, was waiting for him.

'I'm so very sorry, chairman,' he said.

Hugo shook his head, a look of resignation on his face.
'What happens next?' he asked.

'The superintendent told me they'll be charging you in
the next few minutes. You'll then be taken to court, where
you'll appear before a magistrate. All you have to do is plead
not guilty. The superintendent made it clear that they would
oppose any request for bail, and would point out to the
magistrate that you were arrested while trying to leave the
country in possession of a suitcase containing eight hundred
pounds. The press, I fear, are going to have a field day.'

Hugo and his solicitor sat alone in the charge room and
waited for the superintendent to appear. The solicitor
warned Hugo that he should be prepared to spend several
weeks in prison before the trial opened. He suggested the
names of four KCs who might be retained to defend him.
They had just settled on Sir Gilbert Gray, when the door
opened and a sergeant walked in.

'You are free to leave, sir,' he said, as if Hugo had committed some minor traffic offence.

It was some time before Winshaw recovered enough to
ask, 'Will my client be expected to return later in the day?'

'Not that I'm aware of, sir.'

Hugo walked out of the police station a free man.

━◦━

The story only made a small paragraph on page 9 of the
*Bristol Evening News. The Hon Toby Dunstable, second son
of the eleventh Earl of Dunstable, died of a heart attack,
while in custody at Wimbledon Police Station.*

It was Derek Mitchell who later filled in the details
behind the story.

He reported that the earl had visited his son in his cell,

just a couple of hours before Toby took his own life. The officer on duty overheard several sharp exchanges between father and son, during which honour, the family's reputation and the decent thing to do in the circumstances were repeated again and again by the earl. At the inquest held a fortnight later at Wimbledon Crown Court, the magistrate asked the officer in question if he'd seen any pills pass between the two men during the earl's visit.

'No, sir,' he replied, 'I did not.'

Death by natural causes was the verdict delivered by the magistrate's panel at Wimbledon Crown Court later that afternoon.

37

'Mr Prendergast has telephoned several times this morning, chairman,' said Miss Potts as she followed Sir Hugo into his office, 'and on the last occasion he emphasized that it was urgent.' If she was surprised to see the chairman unshaven and wearing a tweed suit that looked as if he'd slept in it, she said nothing.

Hugo's first thought on hearing that Prendergast wanted to speak to him urgently was that the Broad Street deal must have fallen through and the bank would expect him to return its £800 forthwith. Prendergast could think again.

'And Tancock,' said Miss Potts, checking her notepad, 'says he has some news that you'll want to hear.' The chairman didn't comment. 'But the most important thing,' she continued, 'is the letter I've left on your desk. I have a feeling you'll want to read it immediately.'

Hugo began reading the letter even before he'd sat down. He then read it a second time, but still couldn't believe it. He looked up at his secretary.

'Many congratulations, sir.'

'Get Prendergast on the phone,' barked Hugo, 'and then I want to see the managing director, followed by Tancock, in that order.'

'Yes, chairman,' said Miss Potts, and hurried out of the room.

While Hugo waited for Prendergast to come on the line, he read the Minister of Shipping's letter a third time.

Dear Sir Hugo,

I am delighted to inform you that Barrington Shipping has been awarded the contract for . . .

The phone on Hugo's desk rang. 'Mr Prendergast on the line,' announced Miss Potts.

'Good morning, Sir Hugo.' The deference was back in the voice. 'I thought you'd want to know that Mrs Clifton has finally agreed to sell her site on Broad Street, for a thousand pounds.'

'But I've already signed a contract to sell the rest of my property in the street to United Dominion for four thousand.'

'And that contract is still on my desk,' said Prendergast. 'Unfortunately for them, and more fortunately for you, the earliest time they could make an appointment to see me was at ten o'clock this morning.'

'Did you exchange contracts?'

'Yes, Sir Hugo, I most certainly did.'

Hugo's heart sank.

'For forty thousand pounds.'

'I don't understand.'

'Once I was able to assure United Dominion that you were in possession of Mrs Clifton's plot, as well as the deeds for every other freehold in the street, they wrote out a cheque for the full amount.'

'Well done, Prendergast. I knew I could rely on you.'

'Thank you, sir. All you need to do now is countersign Mrs Clifton's agreement, and then I can bank United Dominion's cheque.'

Hugo glanced at his watch. 'As it's already gone four, I'll drop in to the bank first thing tomorrow morning.'

The Prendergast cough. 'First thing, Sir Hugo, is nine

o'clock. And may I ask if you still have the eight hundred pounds I advanced to you in cash yesterday?'

'Yes I do. But how can that still be of any significance?'

'I do consider it would be prudent, Sir Hugo, to pay Mrs Clifton her thousand pounds before we bank United Dominion's cheque for forty thousand. We wouldn't want any embarrassing questions from head office at a later date.'

'Quite so,' said Hugo as he looked at his suitcase, relieved that he hadn't spent one penny of the £800.

'There's nothing more for me to say,' said Prendergast, 'other than to congratulate you on closing a most successful contract.'

'How do you know about the contract?'

'I beg your pardon, Sir Hugo?' said Prendergast sounding a little puzzled.

'Oh, I thought you were referring to something else,' said Hugo. 'It's of no importance, Prendergast. Forget I mentioned it,' he added as he put the phone down.

Miss Potts came back into the room. 'The managing director is waiting to see you, chairman.'

'Send him straight in.'

'You've heard the good news, Ray?' said Hugo as Compton entered the room.

'I have indeed, chairman, and it couldn't have come at a better time.'

'I'm not sure I understand,' said Hugo.

'You're due to present the company's annual results at next month's board meeting, and although we'll still have to declare a heavy loss this year, the new contract will guarantee that we go into profit next year.'

'And for five years after that,' Hugo reminded him, waving the minister's letter triumphantly. 'Why don't you prepare the agenda for the board meeting, but don't include the news about the government contract. I'd rather like to make that announcement myself.'

'As you wish, chairman. I'll see that all the relevant papers are on your desk by noon tomorrow,' Compton added before leaving the room.

Hugo read the minister's letter a fourth time. 'Thirty thousand a year,' he said out loud, just as the phone on his desk rang again.

'A Mr Foster from Savills, the estate agency, is on the line,' said Miss Potts.

'Put him through.'

'Good morning, Sir Hugo. My name is Foster. I'm the senior partner of Savills. I thought perhaps we ought to get together to discuss your instructions to sell Barrington Hall. Perhaps a spot of lunch at my club?'

'No need to bother, Foster. I've changed my mind. Barrington Hall is no longer on the market,' Hugo said, and put the phone down.

He spent the rest of the afternoon signing a stack of letters and cheques his secretary put in front of him, and it was just after six o'clock when he finally screwed the cap back on his pen.

When Miss Potts returned to collect all the correspondence, Hugo said, 'I'll see Tancock now.'

'Yes, sir,' said Miss Potts with a hint of disapproval.

While Hugo waited for Tancock to appear, he fell on his knees and opened the suitcase. He stared at the £800 that would have made it possible for him to survive in America while he waited for the funds raised by the sale of Barrington Hall. Now, that same £800 would be used to make him a fortune on Broad Street.

When he heard a knock on the door, he snapped the lid of the suitcase closed and quickly returned to his desk.

'Tancock to see you,' said Miss Potts before closing the door behind her.

The docker marched confidently into the room and approached the chairman's desk.

'So what's this news that can't wait?' asked Hugo.

'I've come to collect the other five quid what you owe me,' Tancock said, with a look of triumph in his eyes.

'I owe you nothing,' said Hugo.

'But I talked my sister into selling that land you wanted, didn't I?'

'We agreed on two hundred pounds, and I ended up having to pay five times that amount, so as I said, I owe you nothing. Get out of my office, and go back to work.'

Stan didn't budge. 'And I've got that letter you said you wanted.'

'What letter?'

'The letter what our Maisie got from that doctor off the American ship.'

Hugo had completely forgotten about the letter of condolence from Harry Clifton's shipmate, and couldn't imagine that it would be of any significance now Maisie had agreed to the sale. 'I'll give you a pound for it.'

'You said you'd give me a fiver.'

'I suggest you leave my office while you've still got a job, Tancock.'

'OK, OK,' said Stan, backing down, 'you can have it for a quid. What's it to me?' He took a crumpled envelope out of his back pocket and handed it over to the chairman. Hugo extracted a ten-shilling note from his wallet and placed it on the desk in front of him.

Stan stood his ground as Hugo put his wallet back in an inside pocket and stared defiantly at him.

'You can have the letter or the ten-bob note. Take your choice.'

Stan grabbed the ten-bob note and left the room grumbling under his breath.

Hugo put the envelope to one side, leant back in his chair and thought about how he would spend some of the profit he'd made on the Broad Street deal. Once he'd been to the bank and signed all the necessary documents, he would walk across the road to the car saleroom. He had his eye on a 1937 2-litre 4-seater Aston Martin. He would then drive it across town and visit his tailor – he hadn't had a suit made for longer than he cared to remember – and after the fitting, lunch at the club, where he would settle his outstanding bar bill. During the afternoon, he would set about replenishing the wine cellar at Barrington Hall, and might even consider redeeming from the pawnbroker some of the jewellery his mother seemed to miss so much. In the evening— there was a tap at the door.

'I'm just leaving,' said Miss Potts. 'I want to get to the post office before seven to catch the last delivery. Do you need anything else, sir?'

'No, Miss Potts. But I may be in a little late tomorrow, as I have an appointment with Mr Prendergast at nine o'clock.'

'Of course, chairman,' said Miss Potts.

As the door closed behind her, his eyes settled on the crumpled envelope. He picked up a silver letter opener, slit the envelope open and pulled out a single sheet of paper. His eyes impatiently scanned the page, searching for relevant phrases.

> *New York,*
> *September 8th, 1939*
>
> *My dearest mother,*
>
> *. . . I did not die when the Devonian was sunk . . . I was plucked out of the sea . . . the vain hope that at some time in the future I might be able to prove that Arthur Clifton and not Hugo Barrington was my father . . .*
> *I must beg you to keep my secret as steadfastly as you kept your own for so many years.*
> *Your loving son,*
>
> *Harry*

Hugo's blood ran cold. All the triumphs of the day evaporated in an instant. This was not a letter he wanted to read a second time or, more important, that he wished anyone else to become aware of.

He pulled open the top drawer of his desk and took out a box of Swan Vestas. He lit a match, held the letter over the wastepaper basket and didn't let it go until the frail black cinders had evaporated into dust. The best ten shillings he'd ever spent.

Hugo was confident that he was the only person who knew Clifton was still alive, and he intended it to remain that way. After all, if Clifton kept his word and continued to go by the name of Tom Bradshaw, how could anyone else find out the truth?

He suddenly felt sick when he remembered that Emma was still in America. Had she somehow discovered that Clifton was alive? But surely that wasn't possible if she hadn't read the letter. He needed to find out why she'd gone to America.

He had picked up the phone and begun to dial Mitchell's number when he thought he heard footsteps in the corridor. He replaced the receiver, assuming it must be the night watchman checking to see why his light was still on.

The door opened, and he stared at a woman he had hoped never to see again.

'How did you get past the guard on the gate?' he demanded.

'I told him we had an appointment to see the chairman; a long overdue appointment.'

'We?' said Hugo.

'Yes, I've brought you a little present. Not that you can give something to someone when it's already theirs.' She placed a wicker basket on Hugo's desk, and removed a thin muslin cloth to reveal a sleeping baby. 'I felt it was about time you were introduced to your daughter,' Olga said, standing aside to allow Hugo to admire her.

'What makes you think I would have the slightest interest in your bastard?'

'Because she's also your bastard,' said Olga calmly, 'so I will assume you want to give her the same start in life you gave Emma and Grace.'

'Why would I even consider making such a ridiculous gesture?'

'Because Hugo,' she said, 'you bled me dry, and now it's your turn to face up to your responsibility. You can't assume you will always get away with it.'

'The only thing I got away from was you,' said Hugo with a smirk. 'So you can bugger off and take that basket with you, because I won't be lifting a finger to help her.'

'Then perhaps I'll have to turn to someone who just might be willing to lift a finger to help her.'

'Like who?' snapped Hugo.

'Your mother might be a good place to start, although she's probably the last person on earth who still believes a word you say.'

Hugo leapt up from his seat, but Olga didn't flinch. 'And if I can't convince her,' she continued, 'my next stop would be the Manor House, where I would take afternoon tea with your ex-wife, and we could talk about the fact that she'd already divorced you long before we even met.'

Hugo stepped out from behind his desk, but it didn't stop Olga continuing. 'And if Elizabeth is not at home, I can always pay a visit to Mulgelrie Castle and introduce Lord and Lady Harvey to yet another of your offspring.'

'What makes you think they'd believe you?'

'What makes you think they wouldn't?'

Hugo moved towards her, only stopping when they were a few inches apart, but Olga still hadn't finished.

'And then finally, I'd feel I owe it to myself to visit Maisie Clifton, a woman I greatly admire, because if all I've heard about her—'

Hugo grabbed Olga by the shoulders and began to shake her. He was only surprised that she made no attempt to defend herself.

'Now you listen to me, you Yid,' he shouted. 'If you so much as hint to anyone that I'm the father of that child, I'll make your life so miserable that you'll wish you'd been dragged off by the Gestapo with your parents.'

'You don't frighten me any longer, Hugo,' said Olga, with an air of resignation. 'I only have one interest left in life, and that's to make sure you don't get away with it a second time.'

'A second time?' repeated Hugo.

'You think I don't know about Harry Clifton, and his claim to the family title?'

Hugo let go of her and took a step back, clearly shaken. 'Clifton is dead. Buried at sea. Everyone knows that.'

'You know he's still alive, Hugo, however much you want everyone else to believe he isn't.'

'But how can you possibly know—'

'Because I've learnt to think like you, behave like you, and more important, act like you, which is why I decided to hire my own private detective.'

'But it would have taken you years—' began Hugo.

'Not if you come across someone who's out of work, whose only client has run away a second time and who hasn't been paid for six months.' Olga smiled when Hugo clenched his fists, a sure sign that her words had hit home. Even when he raised his arm she didn't flinch, just stood her ground.

When the first blow came crashing into her face, she toppled back, clutching her broken nose, just as a second punch landed in her stomach, causing her to double up.

Hugo stood back and laughed while she swayed from side to side, trying to stay on her feet. He was about to hit her a third time when her legs crumpled and she collapsed to the ground in a heap, like a puppet whose strings have been cut.

'Now you know what you can expect if you're ever foolish enough to bother me again,' shouted Hugo, as he towered over her. 'And if you don't want more of the same, you'll get out while you've still got the chance. Just be sure to take that bastard with you back to London.'

Olga slowly pushed herself up off the floor and on to her knees, blood still pouring from her nose. She attempted to stand, but was so weak that she stumbled forward, only breaking her fall by clinging on to the edge of the desk. She paused for a moment and took several deep breaths as she tried to recover. When she finally raised her head, she was distracted by a long, thin silver object that glistened in a circle of light thrown out by the desk lamp.

'Didn't you hear what I said?' Hugo hollered as he stepped forward, grabbed her by the hair and yanked her head back.

With all the force she could muster, Olga jerked her leg back and rammed the heel of her shoe into his groin.

'You bitch,' screamed Hugo as he let go of her hair and fell back, allowing Olga a split second to grab the letter opener and conceal it inside the sleeve of her dress. She turned to face her tormentor. When Hugo had caught his breath, he once again moved towards her. As he passed a side table, he grabbed a heavy glass ashtray and raised it high above his head, determined to deliver a blow from which she would not so easily recover.

When he was only a pace away, she pulled up her sleeve, gripped the letter opener with both hands and pointed the blade towards his heart. Just as he was about to bring the ashtray crashing down on her head, he spotted the blade for the first time, tried to swerve to one side, tripped and lost his balance, falling heavily on top of her.

There was a moment's silence before he sank slowly to

his knees and let out a scream that would have woken all Hades. Olga watched as he grabbed at the handle of the letter opener. She stood mesmerized, as if she was watching a slow-motion clip from a film. It must have been only a moment, although it felt interminable to Olga, before Hugo finally collapsed and slumped to the floor at her feet.

She stared down at the blade of the letter opener. The tip was sticking out of the back of his neck and blood was spurting in every direction, like an out-of-control fire hydrant.

'Help me,' Hugo whimpered, trying to raise a hand.

Olga knelt by his side and took the hand of a man she'd once loved. 'There is nothing I can do to help you, my darling,' she said, 'but then there never was.'

His breathing was becoming less regular, although he still gripped her hand tightly. She bent down to be sure that he could hear her every word. 'You only have a few more moments to live,' she whispered, 'and I wouldn't want you to go to your grave without knowing the details of Mitchell's latest report.'

Hugo made one last effort to speak. His lips moved, but no words came out.

'Emma has found Harry,' said Olga, 'and I know you'll be pleased to hear he's alive and well.' Hugo's eyes never left her as she leant even closer, until her lips were almost touching his ear. 'And he's on his way back to England to claim his rightful inheritance.'

It wasn't until Hugo's hand went limp that she added, 'Ah, but I forgot to tell you, I've also learnt how to lie like you.'

—◦—

The *Bristol Evening Post* and the *Bristol Evening News* ran different headlines on the first editions of their papers the following day.

SIR HUGO BARRINGTON
STABBED TO DEATH

was the banner headline in the *Post*, while the *News* preferred to lead with

UNKNOWN WOMAN THROWS HERSELF
IN FRONT OF LONDON EXPRESS

Only Detective Chief Inspector Blakemore, the head of the local CID, worked out the connection between the two.

EMMA BARRINGTON

1942

38

'GOOD MORNING, MR GUINZBURG,' said Sefton Jelks as he rose from behind his desk. 'It is indeed an honour to meet the man who publishes Dorothy Parker and Graham Greene.'

Guinzburg gave a slight bow, before shaking hands with Jelks.

'And Miss Barrington,' said Jelks, turning to Emma. 'How nice to see you again. As I am no longer representing Mr Lloyd, I hope we can be friends.'

Emma frowned, and sat down without shaking Jelks's outstretched hand.

Once the three of them were settled, Jelks continued. 'Perhaps I might open this meeting by saying I thought it would be worthwhile for the three of us to get together and have a frank and open discussion, and see if it were possible to come up with a solution to our problem.'

'Your problem,' interjected Emma.

Mr Guinzburg pursed his lips, but said nothing.

'I am sure,' continued Jelks, focusing his attention on Guinzburg, 'that you will want to do what is best for all concerned.'

'And will that include Harry Clifton this time?' asked Emma.

Guinzburg turned to Emma and gave her a disapproving grimace.

'Yes, Miss Barrington,' said Jelks, 'any agreement we might reach would certainly include Mr Clifton.'

'Just as it did last time, Mr Jelks, when you walked away at the time he most needed you?'

'Emma,' said Guinzburg reproachfully.

'I should point out, Miss Barrington, that I was doing no more than carrying out my client's instructions. Mr and Mrs Bradshaw both assured me that the man I was representing was their son, and I had no reason to believe otherwise. And of course I did prevent Tom from being tried for—'

'And then you left Harry to fend for himself.'

'In my defence, Miss Barrington, when I finally discovered that Tom Bradshaw was in fact Harry Clifton, he begged me to keep my counsel, as he didn't want *you* to discover that he was still alive.'

'That's not Harry's version of what happened,' said Emma, who appeared to regret her words the moment she'd said them.

Guinzburg made no attempt to mask his displeasure. He looked like a man who realizes his trump card has been played too soon.

'I see,' said Jelks. 'From that little outburst, I must assume you have both read the earlier notebook?'

'Every word,' said Emma. 'So you can stop pretending you only did what was in Harry's best interests.'

'Emma,' said Guinzburg firmly, 'you must learn not to take things so personally, and try to consider the bigger picture.'

'Is that the one where a leading New York lawyer ends up in jail for falsifying evidence and perverting the course of justice?' said Emma, her eyes never leaving Jelks.

'I apologize, Mr Jelks,' said Guinzburg. 'My young friend gets quite carried away when it comes to—'

'You bet I do,' said Emma, now almost shouting, 'because I can tell you exactly what this man –' she pointed at Jelks – 'would have done if Harry had been sent to the electric chair. He would have pulled the lever himself if he thought it would save his own skin.'

'That is outrageous,' said Jelks, jumping up from his seat. 'I had already prepared an appeal that would have left the jury in no doubt that the police had arrested the wrong man.'

'So you did know it was Harry all along,' said Emma, sitting back in her chair.

Jelks was momentarily stunned by Emma's rebuke. She took advantage of his silence.

'Let me tell you what's going to happen, Mr Jelks. When Viking publishes Harry's first notebook in the spring, not only will your reputation be shattered and your career in ruins, but, like Harry, you'll discover at first hand what life is like at Lavenham.'

Jelks turned to Guinzburg in desperation. 'I would have thought it in both our interests to reach an amicable settlement before this whole affair gets out of hand.'

'What do you have in mind, Mr Jelks?' asked Guinzburg, trying to sound conciliatory.

'You're not going to give this crook a lifeline, are you?' said Emma.

Guinzburg raised a hand. 'The least we can do, Emma, is hear him out.'

'Just as he heard Harry out?'

Jelks turned to Guinzburg. 'If you felt able *not* to publish the earlier notebook, I can assure you I would make it worth your while.'

'I can't believe you're taking this seriously,' said Emma.

Jelks continued to address Guinzburg as if Emma wasn't in the room. 'Of course, I realize that you stand to lose a considerable amount of money if you decide not to go ahead.'

'If *The Diary of a Convict* is anything to go by,' said Guinzburg, 'over a hundred thousand dollars.'

The figure must have taken Jelks by surprise, because he didn't respond.

'And there's also the twenty-thousand-dollar advance that was paid to Lloyd,' continued Guinzburg. 'That will have to be reimbursed to Mr Clifton.'

'If Harry were here, he'd be the first to tell you that he's not interested in the money, Mr Guinzburg, only in making sure that this man ends up in jail.'

Guinzburg looked appalled. 'My company has not built its reputation on scandal-mongering, Emma, so before I make a final decision on whether or not to publish the notebook, I have to consider how my more distinguished authors might react to a publication of that kind.'

'How right you are, Mr Guinzburg. Reputation is everything.'

'How would you know?' demanded Emma.

'While we're on the subject of distinguished authors,' continued Jelks a little pompously, ignoring the interruption, 'you may be aware that my firm has the privilege of representing the F. Scott Fitzgerald estate.' He leaned back in his chair. 'I remember so well Scotty telling me that if he were to change publishers, he would want to move to Viking.'

'You're not going to fall for that line, are you?' said Emma.

'Emma, my dear, there are times when it is wise to take the long view.'

'How long have you got in mind? Six years?'

'Emma, I'm only doing what is in everyone's best interests.'

'It sounds to me as if what you're doing will end up in your best interests. Because the reality is that once money becomes involved, you're no better than him,' she said, pointing at Jelks.

Guinzburg appeared wounded by Emma's accusation, but quickly recovered. He turned to the lawyer and asked, 'What do you have in mind, Mr Jelks?'

'If you'll agree not to publish the first notebook in any form, I would be happy to pay compensation, equivalent to the sum you have earned for *The Diary of a Convict* and, on top of that, I would repay in full the twenty thousand dollars you advanced to Mr Lloyd.'

'Why don't you just kiss me on the cheek, Mr Guinzburg,' said Emma, 'and then he'll know who to give the thirty pieces of silver to.'

'And Fitzgerald?' said Guinzburg, ignoring her.

'I will grant you the publishing rights of the F. Scott Fitzgerald estate for a period of fifty years, on the same terms as his current publisher.'

Guinzburg smiled. 'Draw up a contract, Mr Jelks, and I'll be happy to sign it.'

'And what pseudonym will you use when you sign the contract?' asked Emma. 'Judas?'

Guinzburg shrugged his shoulders. 'Business is business, my dear. And you and Harry won't go unrewarded.'

'I'm glad you mention that, Mr Guinzburg,' said Jelks, 'because I've been holding a cheque for ten thousand dollars made payable to Harry Clifton's mother for some time, but because of the outbreak of war I had no way of getting it to her. Perhaps, Miss Barrington, you would be kind enough to give it to Mrs Clifton when you return to England.' He slid the cheque across the table.

Emma ignored it. 'You would never have mentioned that cheque if I hadn't read about it in the first notebook, when you gave Harry your word that you'd send Mrs Clifton ten thousand dollars once he agreed to take the place of Tom Bradshaw.' Emma stood up, before adding, 'You both disgust me, and I only hope I never come across either of you again in my life.'

She stormed out of the office without another word, leaving the cheque on the desk.

'Headstrong girl,' said Guinzburg, 'but I'm sure, given time, I'll be able to convince her we made the right decision.'

'I feel confident, Harold,' said Jelks, 'that you'll handle this minor incident with all the skill and diplomacy that have become the hallmark of your distinguished company.'

'That's kind of you to say so, Sefton,' said Guinzburg as he rose from his chair and picked up the cheque. 'And I'll make sure that Mrs Clifton gets this,' he added, placing it in his wallet.

'I knew I could rely on you, Harold.'

'You most certainly can, Sefton, and I look forward to seeing you again, once the contract has been drawn up.'

'I'll have it ready by the end of the week,' Jelks said as they left the room together and walked down the corridor. 'Surprising we haven't done any business before.'

'I agree,' said Guinzburg, 'but I have a feeling this is just the beginning of a long and fruitful relationship.'

'Let's hope so,' said Jelks when they reached the lift. 'I'll be in touch as soon as the contract is ready to sign,' he added as he pressed the down button.

'I'll look forward to that, Sefton,' said Guinzburg, and shook Jelks warmly by the hand before stepping into the lift.

When the lift reached the ground floor, Guinzburg stepped out, and the first thing he saw was Emma heading straight for him.

'You were brilliant, my dear,' he said. 'I confess that for a moment I wondered if you'd gone a little too far with your comment about the electric chair, but no, you'd got the measure of the man,' he added as they strolled out of the building arm in arm.

◄○►

Emma spent most of the afternoon sitting alone in her room rereading the first exercise book, in which Harry had written about the time before he was sent to Lavenham.

As she turned each page and was made aware once again what he had been willing to put himself through in order to release her from any obligation she might feel she owed him, Emma resolved that if she ever found the idiotic man again, she wouldn't let him out of her sight.

With Mr Guinzburg's blessing, Emma became involved with every aspect of publishing the revised edition of *The Diary of a Convict*, or the first edition, as she always referred to it. She attended editorial meetings, discussed the cover lettering with the head of the art department, chose the photograph that would go on the back cover, wrote the blurb about Harry for the inside flap and even addressed a sales conference.

Six weeks later, boxes of books were transported from the printer by rail, truck and plane to depositories all across America.

On publication day, Emma was standing on the pavement outside Doubleday's waiting for the doors of the bookstore to open. She was able to report to Great-aunt Phyllis and Cousin Alistair that evening that the book had been running out of the shop. Confirmation of this came in the form of the *New York Times* bestseller list the following Sunday, when the revised edition of *The Diary of a Convict* appeared in the top ten after only a week's sales.

Journalists and magazine editors from all over the country

were desperate to interview Harry Clifton and Max Lloyd. But Harry couldn't be found in any penal establishment in America, while Lloyd, to quote *The Times*, was unavailable for comment. The *New York News* was less prosaic when it ran the headline, **LLOYD ON THE LAM**.

On the day of publication, Sefton Jelks's office issued a formal statement making it clear that the company no longer represented Max Lloyd. Although *The Diary of a Convict* hit the number one spot on the *New York Times* bestseller list for the next five weeks, Guinzburg kept to his agreement with Jelks and did not publish any extracts from the earlier notebook.

However, Jelks did sign a contract giving Viking the exclusive right to publish all of F. Scott Fitzgerald's works for the next fifty years. Jelks considered that he'd honoured his side of the bargain and that, given time, the press would become bored with the story and move on. And he might have been right if *Time* magazine hadn't run a full-page interview with the recently retired Detective Karl Kolowski of the New York Police Department.

'And I can tell you,' Kolowski was quoted as saying, 'that so far they've only published the boring bits. Just wait until you read what happened to Harry Clifton before he arrived at Lavenham.'

The story hit the wires around 6 p.m. Eastern Time, and Mr Guinzburg had received over a hundred calls by the time he walked into his office the following morning.

Jelks read the article in *Time* as he was driven to Wall Street. When he stepped out of the lift on the twenty-second floor, he found three of his partners waiting outside his office.

39

'WHICH DO YOU want first?' asked Phyllis, holding up two letters. 'The good news or the bad news?'

'The good news,' said Emma without hesitation, as she buttered another piece of toast.

Phyllis placed one letter back on the table, adjusted her pince-nez and began to read the other.

Dear Mrs Stuart,

I've just finished reading The Diary of a Convict *by Harry Clifton. There was an excellent review of the book in the* Washington Post *today, which towards the end posed a question about what happened to Mr Clifton after he left Lavenham Correctional Facility seven months ago, having completed only a third of his sentence.*

For reasons of national security, which I am sure you will appreciate, I am unable to go into any great detail in this letter.

If Miss Barrington, who I understand is staying with you, would like any further information concerning Lieutenant Clifton, she is welcome to contact this office, and I will be happy to make an appointment to see her.

As it does not breach the Official Secrets Act, may I

315

add how much I enjoyed Lieutenant Clifton's diary.
If the rumours in today's New York Post *are to be*
believed, I can't wait to find out what happened to him
before he was shipped off to Lavenham.
Yours sincerely

John Cleverdon (Col.)

Great-aunt Phyllis looked across to see Emma bouncing up
and down like a bobbysoxer at a Sinatra concert. Parker
poured Mrs Stuart a second cup of coffee, as if nothing
unusual was taking place a few feet behind him.

Emma suddenly stood still. 'So what's the bad news?'
she asked, sitting back down at the table.

Phyllis picked up the other letter. 'This one is from
Rupert Harvey,' she declared. 'A second cousin, once
removed.' Emma stifled a laugh. Phyllis observed her criti-
cally over her pince-nez. 'Don't mock, child,' she said.
'Being a member of a large clan can have its advantages, as
you're about to discover.' She turned her attention back to
the letter.

Dear cousin Phyllis,

How nice to hear from you after all this time. It was
kind of you to draw my attention to The Diary of a
Convict *by Harry Clifton, which I thoroughly enjoyed.*
What a formidable young lady cousin Emma must be.

Phyllis looked up.
'Twice removed in your case,' she said before returning
to the letter.

I'd be delighted to assist Emma in her current
dilemma. To that end: the Embassy has an aircraft
that will be flying to London next Thursday, and the

Ambassador has agreed that Miss Barrington can join him and his staff on the flight.

If Emma would be kind enough to drop by my office on Thursday morning, I will make sure that all the necessary paperwork is completed. Do remind her to bring her passport with her.

Yours affectionately,

Rupert

PS. Is cousin Emma half as beautiful as Mr Clifton suggests in his book?

Phyllis folded the letter and placed it back in the envelope.

'So what's the bad news?' demanded Emma.

Phyllis bowed her head, as she did not approve of displays of emotion, and said quietly, 'You have no idea, child, how much I shall miss you. You are the daughter I never had.'

—◇—

'I signed the contract this morning,' said Guinzburg, raising his glass.

'Congratulations,' said Alistair, as everyone else around the dinner table raised their glasses.

'Do forgive me,' said Phyllis, 'if I appear to be the only one among us who doesn't fully understand. If you signed a contract that prevents your company from publishing Harry Clifton's earlier work, what exactly are we celebrating?'

'The fact that I put one hundred thousand dollars of Sefton Jelks's money into my company's bank account this morning,' Guinzburg replied.

'And I,' said Emma, 'have received a cheque for twenty thousand dollars from the same source. Lloyd's original advance for Harry's book.'

'And don't forget the cheque for ten thousand you failed

to pick up for Mrs Clifton, which I retrieved,' said Guinz-burg. 'Frankly, we've all done very well out of it, and now the contract has been signed, there will be even more to come, for the next fifty years.'

'Possibly,' said Phyllis, taking the high ground, 'but I'm more than a little irked that you've allowed Jelks to get away with murder.'

'I think you'll find he's still on Death Row, Mrs Stuart,' said Guinzburg, 'though I accept we've granted him a three-month stay of execution.'

'I'm even more confused,' said Phyllis.

'Then allow me to explain,' said Guinzburg. 'You see, the contract I signed this morning wasn't with Jelks, but with Pocket Books, a company who have bought the rights to publish all Harry's diaries in softback.'

'And what, may I ask, is a softback?' said Phyllis.

'Mama,' said Alistair, 'softbacks have been around for years now.'

'So have ten-thousand-dollar bills, but I've never seen one.'

'Your mother makes a fair point,' said Guinzburg. 'In fact, it could explain why Jelks was taken in, because Mrs Stuart represents an entire generation who will never come to terms with books being published in softback, and would only ever consider reading a hardback.'

'What made you realize that Jelks was not fully acquainted with the concept of a softback?' asked Phyllis.

'F. Scott Fitzgerald was the clincher,' said Alistair.

'I do wish you wouldn't use slang at the dinner table,' said Phyllis.

'It was Alistair who advised us,' said Emma, 'that if Jelks was willing to hold a meeting in his office without his legal assistant present, it must mean he hadn't alerted his partners to the fact there was a missing notebook, and that if it were published it would be even more damning to the firm's reputation than *The Diary of a Convict*.'

'Then why didn't Alistair attend the meeting,' said Phyllis, 'and make a record of everything Jelks said? After all, that man is one of the slipperiest lawyers in New York.'

'Which is precisely why I didn't attend the meeting, Mother. We didn't want anything on the record, and I was convinced that Jelks would be arrogant enough to think that all he was up against was a slip of a girl from England and a publisher he was sure he could bribe, which meant we had him by the short and curlies.'

'Alistair.'

'However,' Alistair continued, now in full flow, 'it was just after Emma had stormed out of the meeting that Mr Guinzburg displayed a moment of true genius.' Emma looked puzzled. 'He told Jelks, "I look forward to seeing you again, once the contract has been drawn up."'

'And that's exactly what Jelks did,' said Guinzburg, 'because once I'd gone over his contract, I realized it was modelled on one that had originally been drawn up for F. Scott Fitzgerald, a man who was only ever published in hardback. There was nothing in that contract to suggest that we couldn't publish in softback. So the sub-contract I signed this morning will allow Pocket Books to publish Harry's earlier diary, without breaking my agreement with Jelks.' Guinzburg allowed Parker to refill his glass with champagne.

'How much did you make?' demanded Emma.

'There are times, young lady, when you push your luck.'

'How much did you make?' asked Phyllis.

'Two hundred thousand dollars,' admitted Guinzburg.

'You'll need every penny of it,' said Phyllis, 'because once that book goes on sale, you and Alistair will be spending the next couple of years in court defending yourself against half a dozen libel writs.'

'I don't think so,' said Alistair after Parker had poured him a brandy. 'In fact, I'd be willing to bet that ten-thousand-dollar bill you've never seen, Mama, that Sefton Jelks is now spending his last three months as the senior partner of Jelks, Myers and Abernathy.'

'What makes you so sure of yourself?'

'I have a feeling Jelks didn't tell his partners about the first notebook, so when Pocket Books publish the earlier diary, he will be left with no choice but to hand in his resignation.'

'And if he doesn't?'

'Then they'll throw him out,' said Alistair. 'A firm which is that ruthless with its clients won't suddenly become humane with its partners. And don't forget, there's always someone else who wants to be senior partner ... So, I'm bound to admit, Emma, you're far more interesting than Amalgamated Wire—'

'—versus New York Electric,' said the others in unison, as they raised their glasses to Emma.

'And should you ever change your mind about staying in New York, young lady,' said Guinzburg, 'there'll always be a job for you at Viking.'

'Thank you, Mr Guinzburg,' said Emma. 'But the only reason I came to America was to find Harry, and now I discover that he's in Europe while I'm stranded in New York. So once I've had my meeting with Colonel Cleverdon, I'll be flying home to be with our son.'

'Harry Clifton's a damn lucky man to have you in his corner,' said Alistair wistfully.

'If you ever meet either of them, Alistair, you'll realize that I'm the lucky one.'

40

EMMA WOKE EARLY the following morning and chatted happily to Phyllis over breakfast about how much she was looking forward to being reunited with Sebastian and her family. Phyllis nodded, but said very little.

Parker collected Emma's bags from her room, took them down in the lift and left them in the hall. She'd acquired another two since arriving in New York. Does anyone ever go home with less than they started out with? she wondered.

'I'll not come downstairs,' said Phyllis after several attempts to say goodbye. 'I'll only make a fool of myself. It's better that you simply remember an old battleaxe who didn't like to be disturbed during her bridge parties. When you visit us next time, my dear, bring Harry and Sebastian with you. I want to meet the man who captured your heart.'

A taxi blasted its horn in the street below.

'Time to go,' said Phyllis. 'Go quickly.'

Emma gave her one last hug and then she didn't look back.

When she stepped out of the lift Parker was standing by the front door waiting for her, the bags already stowed away in the boot of the taxi. The moment he saw her, he walked out on to the pavement and opened the back door of the cab.

'Goodbye, Parker,' said Emma, 'and thank you for everything.'

'My pleasure, ma'am,' he replied. Just as she was about to step into the taxi, he added, 'If it's not inappropriate, ma'am, I wondered if I might be allowed to make an observation?'

Emma stepped back, trying to mask her surprise. 'Of course, please do.'

'I so enjoyed Mr Clifton's diary,' he said, 'that I hope it will not be too long before you return to New York accompanied by your husband.'

<o>

It wasn't long before the train was speeding through the countryside and New York was no more, as they headed towards the capital. Emma found she couldn't read or sleep for more than a few minutes at a time. Great-aunt Phyllis, Mr Guinzburg, Cousin Alistair, Mr Jelks, Detective Kolowski and Parker all made their exits and entrances.

She thought about what needed to be done once she arrived in Washington. First, she had to go to the British Embassy and sign some forms so she could join the ambassador on his flight to London, as arranged by Rupert Harvey, a second cousin twice removed. 'Don't mock, child,' she could hear her great-aunt remonstrating, and then she fell asleep. Harry entered her dreams, this time in uniform, smiling, laughing, and then she woke with a jolt, quite expecting him to be in the carriage with her.

When the train pulled into Union Station five hours later, Emma had trouble lugging her suitcases on to the platform, until a porter, an ex-serviceman with one arm, came to her rescue. He found a taxi for her, thanked her for the tip and gave her a salute with the wrong arm. Someone else whose destiny had been decided by a war he didn't declare.

'The British Embassy,' Emma said as she climbed into the cab.

She was dropped on Massachusetts Avenue, outside a pair of ornate iron gates displaying the Royal Standard. Two young soldiers ran across to help Emma with her bags.

'Who are you visiting, ma'am?' An English accent, an American word.

'Mr Rupert Harvey,' she said.

'Commander Harvey. Certainly,' said the corporal, who picked up her bags and guided Emma to an office at the rear of the building.

Emma entered a large room in which the staff, most dressed in uniform, scurried about in every direction. No one walked. A figure appeared out of the melee and greeted her with a huge smile.

'I'm Rupert Harvey,' he said. 'Sorry about the organized chaos, but it's always like this when the ambassador is returning to England. It's even worse this time, because we've had a visiting cabinet minister with us for the past week. All your paperwork has been prepared,' he added, returning to his desk. 'I just need to see your passport.'

Once he'd flicked through the pages, he asked her to sign here, here and here. 'A bus will be leaving from the front of the embassy for the airport at six this evening. Please make sure you're on time as everyone's expected to be on board the plane before the ambassador arrives.'

'I'll be on time,' said Emma. 'Would it be possible to leave my bags here while I go sightseeing?'

'That won't be a problem,' said Rupert. 'I'll have someone put them on the bus for you.'

'Thank you,' said Emma.

She was about to leave when he added, 'By the way, I loved the book. And just to warn you, the minister is hoping to have a private word with you when we're on the plane. I think he was a publisher before he went into politics.'

'What's his name?' Emma asked.

'Harold Macmillan.'

Emma recalled some of Mr Guinzburg's sage advice. 'Everyone is going to want this book,' he'd told her. 'There isn't a publisher who won't open their doors for you, so don't be easily flattered. Try and see Billy Collins and Allen Lane of Penguin.' He'd made no mention of a Harold Macmillan.

'Then I'll see you on the bus around six,' said her second cousin twice removed, before he disappeared back into the melee.

Emma left the embassy, walked out on to Massachusetts Avenue and checked her watch. Just over two hours to spare before her appointment with Colonel Cleverdon. She hailed a cab.

'Where to, miss?'

'I want to see everything the city has to offer,' she said.

'How long have you got, a couple of years?'

'No,' Emma replied, 'a couple of hours. So let's get moving.'

The taxi sped away from the kerb. First stop: the White House – 15 minutes. On to the Capitol – 20 minutes. Circling the Washington, Jefferson and Lincoln Memorials – 25 minutes. Dashing into the National Gallery – another 25 minutes. Ending up at the Smithsonian – but there was only 30 minutes left until her appointment, so she didn't make it past the first floor.

When she jumped back into the cab, the driver asked, 'Where to now, miss?'

Emma checked the address on Colonel Cleverdon's letter. '3022 Adams Street,' she replied, 'and I'm cutting it fine.'

When the cab drew up outside a large white marble building that occupied the entire block, Emma handed the cabbie her last five-dollar note. She would have to walk back to the embassy after her meeting. 'Worth every cent,' she told him.

He touched the rim of his cap. 'I thought it was only us Americans who did that sort of thing,' he said with a grin.

Emma walked up the steps, past two guards who stared right through her, and on into the building. She noticed that almost everyone was dressed in different shades of khaki, although few of them wore battle ribbons. A young woman behind the reception desk directed her to room 9197. Emma joined a mass of khaki uniforms as they headed towards the lifts, and when she stepped out on the ninth floor, she found Colonel Cleverdon's secretary waiting to greet her.

'I'm afraid the colonel has got caught up in a meeting, but he should be with you in a few minutes,' she said as they walked along the corridor.

Emma was shown into the colonel's office. Once she had sat down, she stared at a thick file on the centre of the desk. As with the letter on Maisie's mantelpiece and the note-books on Jelks's desk, she wondered how long she would have to wait before its contents were revealed.

The answer was twenty minutes. When the door eventually swung open, a tall, athletic man, around the same age as her father, burst into the room, a cigar bobbing up and down in his mouth.

'So sorry to have kept you,' he said, shaking hands, 'but there just aren't enough hours in the day.' He sat down behind his desk and smiled at her. 'John Cleverdon, and I would have recognized you anywhere.' Emma looked surprised, until he explained. 'You're exactly as Harry described you in his book. Would you like coffee?'

'No, thank you,' said Emma, trying not to sound impatient as she glanced at the file on the colonel's desk.

'I don't even have to open this,' he said, tapping the file. 'I wrote most of it myself, so I can tell you everything

Harry's been up to since he left Lavenham. And now, thanks to his diaries, we all know he should never have been there in the first place. I can't wait to read the next instalment and find out what happened to him before he was sent to Lavenham.'

'And I can't wait to find out what happened to him after he left Lavenham,' Emma said, hoping she didn't sound impatient.

'Then let's get on with it,' said the colonel. 'Harry volunteered to join a special services unit, which I have the privilege of commanding, in exchange for his prison sentence being commuted. Having begun his life in the United States Army as a GI, he was recently commissioned in the field, and is currently serving as a lieutenant. He's been behind enemy lines now for several months,' he continued. 'He's been working with resistance groups in occupied countries and helping to prepare for our eventual landing in Europe.'

Emma didn't like the sound of that. 'What does behind enemy lines actually mean?'

'I can't tell you exactly, because it's not always easy to track him down when he's on a mission. He often cuts off communication with the outside world for days on end. But what I can tell you is that he and his driver, Corporal Pat Quinn, another Lavenham graduate, have turned out to be two of the most effective operatives to come out of my group. They're like two schoolboys who've been given a giant chemistry set and told they can go and experiment on the enemy's communications network. They spend most of their time blowing up bridges, dismantling railway lines and bringing down electricity pylons. Harry's specialty is disrupting German troop movements, and on one or two occasions the Krauts have nearly caught up with him. But so far he's managed to stay a step ahead of them. In fact, he's proved such a thorn in their flesh that they've put a price on his head, which seems to go up every month. Thirty thousand francs when I last checked.'

The colonel noticed that Emma's face had gone as white as a sheet.

'I'm so sorry,' he said. 'I didn't mean to alarm you but I sometimes forget, when I'm sitting behind a desk, just how much danger my boys face every day.'

'When will Harry be released?' asked Emma quietly.

'I'm afraid he's expected to serve out his sentence,' said the colonel.

'But now that you know he's innocent, can't you at least send him back to England?'

'I don't think that would make a great deal of difference, Miss Barrington, because if I know Harry, the moment he set foot in his homeland he'd only swap one uniform for another.'

'Not if I have anything to do with it.'

The colonel smiled. 'I'll see what I can do to help,' he promised as he rose from behind his desk. He opened the door and saluted her. 'Have a safe journey back to England, Miss Barrington. I hope it won't be long before the two of you end up in the same place, at the same time.'

HARRY CLIFTON

1945

41

'I'LL REPORT BACK, SIR, as soon as I've located them,' said Harry, before putting the field phone down.

'Located who?' asked Quinn.

'Kertel's army. Colonel Benson seems to think they could be in the valley on the other side of that ridge,' he said, pointing to the top of the hill.

'There's only one way we're going to find out,' said Quinn, shifting the Jeep noisily into first gear.

'Take it easy,' Harry told him, 'if the Hun are there, we don't need to alert them.'

Quinn remained in first as they crept slowly up the hill.

'That's far enough,' said Harry when they were less than fifty yards from the brow of the hill. Quinn put the hand-brake on and turned the ignition off, and they jumped out and ran on up the incline. When they were only a few yards from the top, they fell flat on their stomachs, then, like two crabs scurrying back into the sea, they crawled until they stopped just below the crest.

Harry peeped over the top and caught his breath. He didn't need a pair of binoculars to see what they were up against. Field Marshal Kertel's legendary Nineteenth Armoured Corps was clearly preparing for battle in the valley below. Tanks were lined up as far as the eye could see, and the support troops would have filled a football stadium. Harry estimated that the Second Division of the Texas Rangers would be outnumbered by at least three to one.

'If we get the hell out of here,' whispered Quinn, 'we might just have enough time to prevent Custer's second-to-last stand.'

'Not so fast,' said Harry. 'We might be able to turn this to our advantage.'

'Don't you think we've used up enough of our nine lives during the past year?'

'I've counted eight so far,' said Harry. 'So I think we can risk just one more.' He began to crawl back down the hill before Quinn could offer an opinion. 'Have you got a handkerchief?' Harry asked as Quinn climbed behind the wheel.

'Yes, sir,' he said, taking one out of his pocket and passing it to Harry, who tied it to the Jeep's radio mast.

'You're not going to—'

'—surrender? Yes, it's our one chance,' said Harry. 'So drive slowly to the top of the ridge, corporal, and then on down into the valley.' Harry only ever called Pat 'corporal' when he didn't want to prolong the discussion.

'Into the valley of death,' suggested Quinn.

'Not a fair comparison,' said Harry. 'There were six hundred in the Light Brigade, and we are but two. So I see myself more like Horatius than Lord Cardigan.'

'I see myself more like a sitting duck.'

'That's because you're Irish,' said Harry, as they crested the ridge and began the slow journey down the other side. 'Don't exceed the speed limit,' he said, trying to make light of it. He was expecting a hail of bullets to greet their impudent intrusion, but clearly curiosity got the better of the Germans.

'Whatever you do, Pat,' Harry said firmly, 'don't open

your mouth. And try to look as if this has all been planned in advance.'

If Quinn had an opinion, he didn't express it, which was most unlike him. The corporal drove at a steady pace, and didn't touch the brake until they reached the front line of tanks.

Kertel's men stared at the occupants of the Jeep in disbelief, but no one moved until a major pushed his way through the ranks and headed straight for them. Harry leapt out of the Jeep, stood to attention and saluted, hoping his German would be up to it.

'What in God's name do you imagine you're doing?' asked the major.

Harry thought that was the gist of it. He maintained a calm exterior.

'I have a message for Field Marshal Kertel, from General Eisenhower, Supreme Commander of the Allied Forces in Europe.' Harry knew that when the major heard the name Eisenhower, he couldn't risk not taking it to a higher level.

Without another word the major climbed into the back of the Jeep, tapped Quinn on the shoulder with his baton and pointed in the direction of a large, well-camouflaged tent that stood to one side of the assembled troops.

When they reached the tent, the major leapt out. 'Wait here,' he ordered, before going inside.

Quinn and Harry sat there, surrounded by thousands of wary eyes.

'If looks could kill . . .' whispered Quinn. Harry ignored him.

It was several minutes before the major returned.

'What's it going to be, sir,' mumbled Quinn, 'the firing squad, or will he ask you to join him for a glass of schnapps?'

'The field marshal has agreed to see you,' said the major, not attempting to hide his surprise.

'Thank you, sir,' Harry said as he got out of the Jeep and followed him into the tent.

Field Marshal Kertel rose from behind a long table that was covered in a map that Harry recognized immediately, but this one had models of tanks and soldiers all heading in his direction. He was surrounded by a dozen field officers, none below the rank of colonel.

Harry stood rigidly to attention and saluted.

'Name and rank?' the field marshal asked after he had returned Harry's salute.

'Clifton, sir, Lieutenant Clifton. I am General Eisenhower's ADC.' Harry spotted a bible on a small folding table by the field marshal's bed. A German flag covered the canvas of one side of the tent. Something was missing.

'And why would General Eisenhower send his ADC to see me?'

Harry observed the man carefully before answering his question. Unlike Goebbels's or Goering's, Kertel's battle-worn face confirmed that he had seen frontline action many times. The only medal he wore was an Iron Cross with oakleaf cluster, which Harry knew he'd won as a lieutenant at the Battle of the Marne in 1918.

'General Eisenhower wishes you to know that on the far side of Clemenceau, he has three full battalions of thirty thousand men, along with twenty-two thousand tanks. On his right flank is the Second Division of the Texas Rangers, in the centre, the Third Battalion of the Green Jackets, and on their left flank, a battalion of the Australian Light Infantry.'

The field marshal would have made an excellent poker player, because he gave nothing away. He would have known that the numbers were accurate, assuming those three regiments were actually in place.

'Then it should prove a most interesting battle, lieutenant. But if your purpose was to alarm me, you have failed.'

'That is no part of my brief, sir,' Harry said, glancing

down at the map, 'because I suspect I haven't told you anything you didn't already know, including the fact that the Allies have recently taken control of the airfield at Wilhelmsberg.' A fact that was confirmed by a small American flag pinned on the airport on the map. 'What you may not know, sir, is that lined up on the runway is a squadron of Lancaster bombers, awaiting an order from General Eisenhower to destroy your tanks, while his battalions advance in battle formation.'

What Harry knew was that the only planes at the airfield were a couple of reconnaissance aircraft stranded because they'd run out of fuel.

'Get to the point, lieutenant,' said Kertel. 'Why did General Eisenhower send you to see me?'

'I will try to recall the general's exact words, sir.' Harry attempted to sound as if he were reciting a message. 'There can be no doubt that this dreadful war is fast drawing to a close, and only a deluded man with a limited experience of warfare could still believe victory is possible.'

The allusion to Hitler did not go unnoticed by the officers who surrounded their field marshal. That was when Harry realized what was missing. There was no Nazi flag or picture of the Führer in the field marshal's tent.

'General Eisenhower holds you and the Nineteenth Corps in the highest regard,' Harry continued. 'He has no doubt that your men would lay down their lives for you, whatever the odds. But in the name of God, he asks, for what purpose? This engagement will end with your troops being decimated, while we will undoubtedly lose vast numbers of men. Everyone knows that the end of the war can only be a matter of weeks away, so what can be gained by such unnecessary carnage? General Eisenhower read your book, *The Professional Soldier*, when he was at West Point, sir, and one sentence in particular has remained indelibly fixed in his memory throughout his military career.'

Harry had read Kertel's memoirs a fortnight before, when he realized they might be up against him, so he was able to recite the sentence almost word for word.

'"Sending young men to an unnecessary death is not an act of leadership, but of vainglory, and unworthy of a professional soldier." That, sir, is something you share with General Eisenhower, and to that end, he guarantees that if you lay down your arms, your men will be treated with the utmost dignity and respect, as set out in the Third Geneva Convention.'

Harry expected the field marshal's response to be, 'Good try, young man, but you can tell whoever it is commanding your puny brigade on the other side of that hill that I am about to wipe them off the face of the earth.' But what Kertel actually said, was, 'I will discuss the general's proposal with my officers. Perhaps you would be kind enough to wait outside.'

'Of course, sir.' Harry saluted, left the tent and returned to the Jeep. Quinn didn't speak when he climbed back into the front seat and sat beside him.

It was clear that Kertel's officers were not of one opinion, as raised voices could be heard from inside the tent. Harry could imagine the words, honour, commonsense, duty, realism, humiliation and sacrifice being bandied about. But the two he feared most were 'he's bluffing'.

It was almost an hour before the major summoned Harry back into the tent. Kertel was standing apart from his most trusted advisers, a world-weary look on his face. He had made his decision, and even if some of his officers didn't agree with it, once he had given the order they would never question him. He didn't need to tell Harry what that decision was.

'Do I have your permission, sir, to contact General Eisenhower and inform him of your decision?'

The field marshal gave a curt nod, and his officers quickly left the tent to see that his orders were carried out.

Harry returned to his Jeep accompanied by the major, and watched 23,000 men lay down their arms, climb out of their tanks and line up in columns of three as they prepared to surrender. His only fear was that having bluffed the field marshal, he wouldn't be able to pull off the same trick with his area commander. He picked up his field phone and only had to wait a few moments before Colonel Benson came on the line. Harry hoped the major hadn't noticed the bead of sweat that was trickling down his nose.

'Have you discovered how many of them we're up against, Clifton?' were the colonel's first words.

'Could you put me through to General Eisenhower, colonel? This is Lieutenant Clifton, his ADC.'

'Have you gone out of your mind, Clifton?'

'Yes, I will hold on, sir, while you go and look for him.' His heart couldn't have beaten faster if he'd just run a hundred yards, and he began to wonder how long it would be before the colonel worked out what he was up to. He nodded at the major, but the major didn't respond. Was he standing there hoping to find a chink in his armour? As he waited, Harry watched thousands of fighting men, some perplexed, while others looked relieved, joining the ranks of those who had already abandoned their tanks and laid down their arms.

'It's General Eisenhower here. Is that you, Clifton?' said Colonel Benson when he came back on the line.

'Yes, sir. I'm with Field Marshal Kertel, and he has accepted your proposal that the Nineteenth Corps lay down their arms and surrender under the terms of the Geneva Convention, in order to avoid, if I remember your words correctly, sir, unnecessary carnage. If you bring forward one of our five battalions, they should be able to carry out the operation in an orderly fashion. I anticipate coming over Clemenceau ridge, accompanied by the Nineteenth Corps –' he looked at his watch – 'at approximately 1700 hours.'

'We'll be waiting for you, lieutenant.'

'Thank you, sir.'

Fifty minutes later Harry crossed the Clemenceau ridge for the second time that day, the German battalion following him as if he were the Pied Piper, over the hill and into the arms of the Texas Rangers. As the 700 men and 214 tanks surrounded the Nineteenth Corps, Kertel realized he had been duped by an Englishman and an Irishman, whose only weapons were a Jeep and a handkerchief.

The field marshal pulled a pistol from inside his tunic, and Harry thought for a moment that he was going to shoot him. Kertel stood to attention, saluted, placed the pistol to his temple and pulled the trigger.

Harry felt no pleasure in his death.

Once the Germans had been rounded up, Colonel Benson invited Harry to lead the nineteenth un-armoured corps in triumph to the compound. As they drove at the head of the column, even Pat Quinn had a smile on his face.

They must have been about a mile away when the Jeep passed over a German landmine. Harry heard a loud explosion, and remembered Pat's prophetic words, *Don't you think we've used up enough of our nine lives during the past year?*, as the Jeep cartwheeled into the air before bursting into flames.

And then, nothing.

42

Do you know when you're dead?

Does it happen in an instant, and then suddenly you're no longer there?

All Harry could be sure of was the images that appeared before him were like actors in a Shakespearian play, each making their exits and entrances. But he couldn't be sure if it was a comedy, a tragedy or a history.

The central character never changed, and was played by a woman who gave a remarkable performance, while others seemed to flit on and off the stage at her bidding. And then his eyes opened, and Emma was standing by his side.

When Harry smiled, her whole face lit up. She bent down and kissed him gently on the lips. 'Welcome home,' she said.

That was the moment when he realized not only how much he loved her, but also that now nothing would ever keep them apart. He took her gently by the hand. 'You're going to have to help me,' he began. 'Where am I? And how long have I been here?'

'Bristol General, and just over a month. It was touch and go for a while, but I wasn't going to lose you a second time.'

Harry gripped her hand firmly and smiled. He felt exhausted, and drifted back into a deep sleep.

⏤◦▸

When he woke again it was dark, and he sensed that he was alone. He tried to imagine what might have happened to all those characters during the past five years, because, as in *Twelfth Night*, they must have believed he'd died at sea.

Had his mother read the letter he wrote to her? Had Giles used his colour-blindness as an excuse not to be called up? Had Hugo returned to Bristol once he was convinced Harry was no longer a threat? Were Sir Walter Barrington and Lord Harvey still alive? And one other thought kept returning again and again. Was Emma waiting for the right moment to tell him there was someone else in her life?

Suddenly, the door to his room was thrown open and a little boy came running in, shouting, 'Daddy, Daddy, Daddy!' before leaping on to his bed and throwing his arms around him.

Emma appeared moments later and watched as the two men in her life met for the first time.

Harry was reminded of the photograph of himself as a boy that his mother kept on the mantelpiece in Still House Lane. He didn't have to be told that this was his child and he felt a thrill he couldn't have begun to imagine before. He studied the boy more closely as he leapt up and down on the bed – his fair hair, blue eyes and square jaw, just like Harry's father.

'Oh my God,' said Harry, and fell into a deep sleep.

◄○►

When he woke again, Emma was sitting on the bed beside him. He smiled and took her hand.

'Now I've met my son, any other surprises?' he asked. Emma hesitated, before adding with a sheepish grin, 'I'm not sure where to start.'

'At the beginning possibly,' said Harry, 'like any good

story. Just remember that the last time I saw you was on our wedding day.'

Emma began with her trip to Scotland and the birth of their son Sebastian. She'd just pressed the doorbell of Kristin's apartment in Manhattan, when Harry fell asleep.

—◦—

When he woke again, she was still with him.

Harry liked the sound of Great-aunt Phyllis and her cousin Alistair, and although he could only just remember Detective Kolowski, he would never forget Sefton Jelks. When Emma came to the end of her story she was on a plane crossing the Atlantic back to England, sitting next to Mr Harold Macmillan.

Emma presented Harry with a copy of *The Diary of a Convict*. All Harry said was, 'I must try and find out what happened to Pat Quinn.'

Emma found it difficult to find the right words.

'Was he killed by the landmine?' Harry asked quietly.

Emma bowed her head. Harry didn't speak again that night.

—◦—

Each day produced new surprises because, inevitably, everyone's life had moved on in the five years since Harry had seen them.

When his mother came to visit him the following day, she was on her own. He was so proud to learn that she was excelling at reading and writing, and was deputy manager of the hotel, but was saddened when she admitted she had never opened the letter delivered by Dr Wallace before it disappeared.

'I thought it was from a Tom Bradshaw,' she explained.

Harry changed the subject. 'I see you're wearing an engagement ring, as well as a wedding ring.'

His mother blushed. 'Yes, I wanted to see you on my own, before you met your stepfather.'

'My stepfather?' said Harry. 'Anyone I know?'

'Oh yes,' she said, and would have told him who she'd married, if he hadn't fallen asleep.

-◄o►-

The next time Harry woke it was the middle of the night. He switched on the bedside light and began to read *The Diary of a Convict*. He smiled several times before he reached the last page.

Nothing Emma told him about Max Lloyd came as a surprise, especially after Sefton Jelks had made a reappearance. However, he was surprised when Emma told him that the book had been an instant bestseller, and that the follow-up was doing even better.

'The follow-up?' enquired Harry.

'The first diary you wrote, about what happened to you before you were sent to Lavenham, has just been published in England. It's racing up the charts here, as it did in America. That reminds me, Mr Guinzburg keeps asking when he can expect your first novel, the one you hinted at in *The Diary of a Convict*?'

'I've got enough ideas for half a dozen,' Harry said.

'Then why don't you get started?' asked Emma.

-◄o►-

When Harry woke that afternoon, his mother and Mr Holcombe were standing by his side, holding hands as if they were on their second date. He'd never seen his mother looking so happy.

'You can't be my stepfather,' Harry protested, as the two shook hands.

'I most certainly am,' said Mr Holcombe. 'Truth is, I

should have asked your mother to be my wife twenty years ago, but I simply didn't think I was good enough for her.'

'And you're still not good enough, sir,' said Harry with a grin. 'But then, neither of us ever will be.'

'Truth be known, I married your mother for her money.'

'What money?' said Harry.

'The ten thousand dollars Mr Jelks sent, which made it possible for us to buy a cottage in the country.'

'For which we will be eternally grateful,' chipped in Maisie.

'Don't thank me,' said Harry. 'Thank Emma.'

If Harry was taken by surprise when he discovered that his mother had married Mr Holcombe, it was nothing compared to the shock when Giles walked into the room, dressed in the uniform of a lieutenant in the Wessex Regiment. If that wasn't enough, his chest was covered in combat medals, including the Military Cross. But when Harry asked how he'd won it, Giles changed the subject.

'I'm planning to stand for Parliament at the next election,' he announced.

'To which seat have you granted this honour?' asked Harry.

'Bristol Docklands,' Giles replied.

'But that's a safe Labour seat.'

'And I intend to be the Labour candidate.'

Harry made no attempt to hide his surprise. 'What caused this Saint Paul-like conversion?' he asked.

'A corporal I served with on the frontline called Bates—'

'Not Terry Bates?' said Harry.

'Yes, did you know him?'

'Sure did. The brightest kid in my class at Merrywood Elementary, and the best sportsman. He left school at twelve to work in his father's business: Bates and Son, butchers.'

'That's why I'm standing as a Labour candidate,' said

Giles. 'Terry had just as much right to be at Oxford as you or me.'

-<o>-

The following day, Emma and Sebastian returned, armed with pens, pencils, pads and an India rubber. She told Harry the time had come for him to stop thinking and start writing.

During the long hours when he couldn't sleep, or was simply alone, Harry's thoughts turned to the novel he had intended to write if he hadn't escaped from Lavenham.

He began to make outline notes of the characters that must turn the page. His detective would have to be a one-off, an original, who he hoped would become part of his readers' everyday lives, like Poirot, Holmes or Maigret.

He finally settled on the name William Warwick. The Hon. William would be the second son of the Earl of Warwick, and have turned down the opportunity to go to Oxford, much to his father's disgust, because he wanted to join the police force. His character would be loosely based on his friend Giles. After three years on the beat, walking the streets of Bristol, Bill, as he was known to his colleagues, would become a detective constable, and be assigned to Chief Inspector Blakemore, the man who'd intervened when Harry's uncle Stan had been arrested and wrongly charged with stealing money from Hugo Barrington's safe.

Lady Warwick, Bill's mother, would be modelled on Elizabeth Barrington; Bill would have a girlfriend called Emma, and his grandfathers Lord Harvey and Sir Walter Barrington would make the occasional entrance on the page but only to offer sage advice.

Every night, Harry would read over the pages he'd written that day, and every morning his wastepaper basket needed emptying.

-<o>-

Harry always looked forward to Sebastian's visits. His young son was so full of energy, so inquisitive and so good-looking, just like his mother, as everyone teased him.

Sebastian often asked questions no one else would have dared to: what's it like being in prison? How many Germans did you kill? Why aren't you and Mama married? Harry sidestepped most of them, but he knew Sebastian was far too bright not to work out what his father was up to, and feared it wouldn't be long before the boy trapped him.

—◦—

Whenever Harry was alone he continued to work on the outline plot for his novel.

He'd read over a hundred detective novels while he was working as deputy librarian at Lavenham, and he felt that some of the characters he'd come across in prison and in the army could provide material for a dozen novels: Max Lloyd, Sefton Jelks, Warden Swanson, Officer Hessler, Colonel Cleverdon, Captain Havens, Tom Bradshaw and Pat Quinn – especially Pat Quinn.

During the next few weeks, Harry became lost in his own world, but he had to admit that the way some of his visitors had spent the last five years had also turned out to be stranger than fiction.

—◦—

When Emma's sister Grace paid him a visit, Harry didn't comment on the fact that she looked so much older than when he'd last seen her, but then she'd only been a schoolgirl at the time. Now Grace was in her final year at Cambridge and about to sit her exams. She told him with pride that for a couple of years she'd worked on a farm, not going back up to Cambridge until she was convinced the war was won.

It was with sadness that Harry learnt from Lady Barrington that her husband, Sir Walter, had passed away, a man Harry had admired second only to Old Jack.

His uncle Stan never visited him.

As the days went by, Harry thought about raising the subject of Emma's father, but he sensed that even the mention of his name was off-limits.

And then one evening, after Harry's doctor had told him that it wouldn't be too long before they released him, Emma lay down next to him on the bed and told him that her father was dead.

When she came to the end of her story, Harry said, 'You've never been good at dissembling, my darling, so perhaps the time has come to tell me why the whole family is so on edge.'

43

HARRY WOKE the next morning to find his mother, along with the whole Barrington family, seated around his bed.

The only absentees were Sebastian and his uncle Stan, neither of whom it was felt would have made a serious contribution.

'The doctor has said you can go home,' said Emma.

'Great news,' said Harry. 'But where's home? If it means going back to Still House Lane and living with Uncle Stan, I'd prefer to stay in hospital – even go back to prison.' No one laughed.

'I'm now living at Barrington Hall,' said Giles, 'so why don't you move in with me? Heaven knows there are enough rooms.'

'Including a library,' said Emma. 'So you'll have no excuse not to continue working on your novel.'

'And you can come and visit Emma and Sebastian whenever you want to,' added Elizabeth Barrington.

Harry didn't respond for some time.

'You're all being very kind,' he eventually managed, 'and please don't think I'm not grateful, but I can't believe it needed the whole family to decide where I'm going to live.'

'There's another reason we wanted to talk to you,' said Lord Harvey, 'and the family have asked me to speak on their behalf.'

Harry sat bolt upright, and gave Emma's grandfather his full attention.

'A serious issue has arisen concerning the future of the Barrington estate,' began Lord Harvey. 'The terms of Joshua Barrington's will have turned out to be a legal nightmare, rivalled only by Jarndyce and Jarndyce, and could end up being just as financially crippling.'

'But I have no interest in either the title or the estate,' said Harry. 'My only desire is to prove that Hugo Barrington was not my father, so I can marry Emma.'

'Amen to that,' said Lord Harvey. 'However, complications have arisen that I must acquaint you with.'

'Please do, sir, because I can't see that there's any problem.'

'I'll try to explain. Following Hugo's untimely death, I advised Lady Barrington that as she had recently suffered two onerous demands for death duties, and remembering that I am over seventy, it might be wise for our two companies, Barrington's and Harvey's, to join forces. This, you understand, was at a time when we still believed you were dead. Therefore, it seemed that any dispute over who would inherit the title and the estate had, however unhappily, been resolved, making it possible for Giles to take his place as head of the family.'

'And he still can, as far as I'm concerned,' said Harry.

'The problem is that other interested parties have become involved and the implications now go far beyond the people in this room. When Hugo was killed, I took over as chairman of the newly merged company, and asked Bill Lockwood to return as managing director. Without blowing my own trumpet, Barrington Harvey has paid its shareholders a handsome dividend for the past two years, despite Herr Hitler. Once we realized you were still alive, we took legal advice from Sir Danvers Barker KC, to be sure that we were not in breach of the terms of Joshua Barrington's will.'

'If only I'd opened that letter,' said Maisie, almost to herself.

'Sir Danvers assured us,' continued Lord Harvey, 'that as long as you renounce any claim to the title or the estate, we could continue trading as we had for the previous two years. And indeed, he drew up a document to that effect.'

'If someone hands me a pen,' said Harry, 'I'll happily sign it.'

'I wish it were that easy,' said Lord Harvey. 'And it might have been if the *Daily Express* hadn't picked up the story.'

'I'm afraid I'm to blame for that,' Emma interrupted, 'because following the success of your book on both sides of the Atlantic, the press have become obsessed with finding out who will inherit the Barrington title – will it be Sir Harry or Sir Giles?'

'There's a cartoon in the *News Chronicle* this morning,' said Giles, 'of the two of us on horseback, jousting, with Emma sitting in the stands offering you her handkerchief, while the men in the crowd boo and the women cheer.'

'What are they alluding to?' asked Harry.

'The nation is divided right down the middle,' said Lord Harvey. 'The men only seem interested in who'll end up with the title and the estate, while the women all want to see Emma walking up the aisle a second time. In fact, between you, you're keeping Cary Grant and Ingrid Bergman off the front pages.'

'But once I've signed the document renouncing any claim to the title or the estate, surely the public will lose interest and turn their attention to something else?'

'This might well have been the case had the Garter King of Arms not become involved.'

'And who's he?' asked Harry.

'The King's representative when it comes to deciding who is next in line for any title. Ninety-nine times out of a hundred, he simply sends letters patent to the next of kin. On the rare occasions when there's a disagreement between two parties, he recommends that the matter be settled by a judge in chambers.'

'Don't tell me it's come to that,' said Harry.

'I'm afraid it has. Lord Justice Shawcross ruled in favour of Giles's claim, but only on the condition that once you were fully fit, you signed a disclaimer, waiving your rights to the title and the estate, while allowing the succession to progress from father to son.'

'Well, I am fully fit now, so let's make an appointment to see the judge and get this settled once and for all.'

'I'd like nothing more,' said Lord Harvey, 'but I'm afraid the decision has been taken out of his hands.'

'By who this time?' asked Harry.

'A Labour peer called Lord Preston,' said Giles. 'He picked up the story in the press and tabled a written question to the Home Secretary, asking him to make a ruling on which one of us was entitled to inherit the baronetcy. He then held a press conference, at which he claimed that I had no right to succeed to the title, because the real candidate was lying unconscious in a Bristol hospital, unable to put his case.'

'Why would a Labour peer give a damn if it was me or Giles who inherited the title?'

'When the press asked him the same question,' said Lord Harvey, 'he told them if Giles inherited the title it would be a classic example of class prejudice, and that it was only fair that the docker's son should be able to put forward his claim.'

'But that defies logic,' said Harry, 'because if I am a docker's son, then Giles would inherit the title anyway.'

'Several people wrote to *The Times* making exactly that point,' said Lord Harvey. 'However, as we're so close to a general election, the Home Secretary ducked the issue, and told his noble friend that he would refer the matter to the Lord Chancellor's office. The Lord Chancellor passed it on to the Law Lords, and seven learned men took their time deliberating and came down by four votes to three. In favour of you, Harry.'

'But this is madness. Why wasn't I consulted?'

'You were unconscious,' Lord Harvey reminded him, 'and in any case, they were debating a point of law, not your opinion, so the verdict will stand, unless it's overturned on appeal in the House of Lords.'

Harry was speechless.

'So as things stand,' continued Lord Harvey, 'you are now *Sir* Harry, and the major shareholder in Barrington Harvey, as well as owner of the Barrington estate and, to quote the original will, all that therein is.'

'Then I'll appeal against the Law Lords' judgment, making it clear that I wish to renounce the title,' said Harry firmly.

'That's the irony,' said Giles, 'you can't. Only I can appeal against the verdict, but I have no intention of doing so unless I have your blessing.'

'Of course you have my blessing,' said Harry. 'But I can think of a far easier solution.'

They all looked at him.

'I could commit suicide.'

'I don't think so,' said Emma, sitting down on the bed beside him. 'You've tried that twice, and look where it got you.'

44

EMMA BURST INTO the library clutching a letter. As she rarely interrupted Harry when he was writing, he knew it had to be important. He put down his pen.

'Sorry, darling,' she said as she pulled up a chair, 'but I've just had some important news that I had to come across and share with you.'

Harry smiled at the woman he adored. Her idea of important could range from Seb pouring water over the cat, to 'it's the Lord Chancellor's office on the phone and they need to speak to you urgently'. He leaned back in his chair and waited to see which category this would fall into.

'I've just had a letter from Great-aunt Phyllis,' she said.

'Whom we all hold in such awe,' teased Harry.

'Don't mock, child,' said Emma. 'She's raised a point that may help us prove Papa wasn't your father.'

Harry didn't mock.

'We know that your blood group and your mother's are Rhesus negative,' continued Emma. 'If *my* father is Rhesus positive, he can't be *your* father.'

'We've discussed this on numerous occasions,' Harry reminded her.

'But if we were able to *prove* that my father's blood group wasn't the same as yours, we could get married. That is assuming you still want to marry me?'

'Not this morning, my darling,' said Harry, feigning boredom. 'You see, I'm in the middle of committing a murder.' He smiled. 'In any case, we have no idea which blood type your father was, because despite considerable pressure from your mother and Sir Walter, he always refused to be tested. So perhaps you ought to write back, explaining that it will have to remain a mystery.'

'Not necessarily,' said Emma, unbowed. 'Because Great-aunt Phyllis has been following the case closely, and thinks she may have come up with a solution neither of us has considered.'

'Picks up a copy of the *Bristol Evening News* from a newsstand on the corner of sixty-fourth street every morning, does she?'

'No, but she does read *The Times*,' said Emma, still unbowed, 'even if it is a week out of date.'

'And?' said Harry, wanting to get on with his murder.

'She says it's now possible for scientists to identify blood groups long after the person has died.'

'Thinking of employing Burke and Hare to exhume the body, are we, darling?'

'No, I am not,' said Emma, 'but she also points out that when my father was killed, an artery was severed, so a great deal of blood would have been spilt on the carpet and the clothes he was wearing at the time.'

Harry stood up, walked across the room and picked up the phone.

'Who are you calling?' asked Emma.

'Detective Chief Inspector Blakemore, who was in charge of the case. It may be a long shot, but I swear I'll never mock you or your great-aunt Phyllis again.'

◄○►

'Do you mind if I smoke, Sir Harry?'

'Not at all, chief inspector.'

Blakemore lit a cigarette and inhaled deeply. 'Dreadful habit,' he said. 'I blame Sir Walter.'

'Sir Walter?' said Harry.

'Raleigh, not Barrington, you understand.'

Harry laughed as he sat down in the chair opposite the detective.

'So how can I help you, Sir Harry?'

'I prefer Mr Clifton.'

'As you wish, sir.'

'I was hoping you might be able to supply me with some information concerning the death of Hugo Barrington.'

'I'm afraid that will depend on whom I'm addressing, because I can have that conversation with Sir Harry Barrington, but not with Mr Harry Clifton.'

'Why not with Mr Clifton?'

'Because I can only discuss details of a case like this with a member of the family.'

'Then on this occasion, I shall revert to being Sir Harry.'

'So how can I help, Sir Harry?'

'When Barrington was murdered—'

'He was not murdered,' said the chief inspector.

'But the newspaper reports led me to believe—'

'It is what the newspapers didn't report that is significant. But to be fair, they were unable to study the crime scene. Had they done so,' said Blakemore before Harry could ask his next question, 'they would have spotted the angle at which the letter opener entered Sir Hugo's neck and severed his artery.'

'Why is that significant?'

'When I examined the body, I noticed that the blade of the letter opener was pointing upwards, not down. If I wanted to murder someone,' continued Blakemore, rising from his chair and picking up a ruler, 'and I was taller and heavier than that person, I would raise my arm and strike down into his neck, like this. But if I was shorter and lighter than him, and, more important, if I was defending myself –' Blakemore knelt down in front of Harry and looked up at him, pointing the ruler towards his neck – 'that would explain the angle at which the blade entered Sir Hugo's neck. It is even possible from that angle that he fell on to the blade, which led me to conclude that he was far more likely to have been killed in self-defence than murdered.'

Harry thought about the chief inspector's words before he said, 'You used the words "shorter and lighter", chief inspector, and "defending myself". Are you suggesting that a woman might have been responsible for Barrington's death?'

'You'd have made a first-class detective,' said Blakemore.

'And do you know who that woman is?' asked Harry.

'I have my suspicions,' admitted Blakemore.

'Then why haven't you arrested her?'

'Because it's quite difficult to arrest someone who later throws herself under the London express.'

'Oh my God,' said Harry. 'I never made any connection between those two incidents.'

'Why should you? You weren't even in England at the time.'

'True, but after I was released from hospital I trawled through every newspaper that even mentioned Sir Hugo's death. Did you ever find out who the lady was?'

'No, the body was in no state to be identified. However, a colleague from Scotland Yard who was investigating another case at the time informed me that Sir Hugo had been living with a woman in London for over a year, and she gave birth to a daughter not long after he returned to Bristol.'

'Was that the child discovered in Barrington's office?'

'The same,' said Blakemore.

'And where is that child now?'

'I have no idea.'

'Can you at least tell me the name of the woman Barrington was living with?'

'No, I am not at liberty to do so,' said Blakemore, stubbing out his cigarette in an ashtray full of butts. 'However, it's no secret that Sir Hugo employed a private detective who is now out of work and might be willing to talk, for a modest remuneration.'

'The man with the limp,' said Harry.

'Derek Mitchell, a damn fine policeman, until he was invalided out of the force.'

'But there's one question Mitchell won't be able to answer, which I suspect you can. You said the letter opener severed an artery, so there must have been a great deal of blood?'

'There was indeed, sir,' replied the chief inspector. 'By the time I arrived, Sir Hugo was lying in a pool of blood.'

'Do you have any idea what happened to the suit Sir Hugo was wearing at the time, or even the carpet?'

'No, sir. Once a murder enquiry is closed, all the personal belongings of the deceased are returned to the next of kin. As for the carpet, it was still in the office when I'd completed my investigation.'

'That's very helpful, chief inspector. I'm most grateful.'

'My pleasure, Sir Harry.' Blakemore stood up and accompanied Harry to the door. 'May I say how much I enjoyed *The Diary of a Convict*, and although I don't normally deal in rumour, I've read that you might be writing a detective novel. After our chat today, I shall look forward to reading it.'

'Would you consider looking at an early draft and giving me your professional opinion?'

'In the past, Sir Harry, your family haven't cared too much for my professional opinion.'

'Let me assure you, chief inspector, that Mr Clifton does,' Harry replied.

—◦—

Once Harry had left the police station, he drove over to the Manor House to tell Emma his news. Emma listened attentively and when he'd come to the end, she surprised him with her first question.

'Did Inspector Blakemore tell you what happened to the little girl?'

'No, he didn't seem that interested, but then why should he be?'

'Because she might just be a Barrington, and therefore my half-sister!'

'How thoughtless of me,' said Harry, taking Emma into his arms. 'It never crossed my mind.'

'Why should it?' asked Emma. 'You have enough to cope with. Why don't you start by calling my grandfather and asking him if he knows what happened to the carpet, and leave me to worry about the little girl.'

'I'm a very lucky man, you know,' said Harry as he reluctantly released her.

'Get on with it,' said Emma.

When Harry telephoned Lord Harvey to ask him about the carpet, he was once again taken by surprise.

'I replaced it within days of the police completing their investigation.'

'What happened to the old one?' Harry asked.

'I personally threw it into one of the shipyard's furnaces and watched it burn until there was nothing left but ashes,' Lord Harvey said with considerable feeling.

Harry wanted to say 'damn', but held his tongue.

When he joined Emma for lunch, he asked Mrs Barrington if she knew what had happened to Sir Hugo's clothes.

Elizabeth told Harry that she'd instructed the police to dispose of them in any way they considered appropriate.

After lunch, Harry returned to Barrington Hall and called the local police station. He asked the desk sergeant if he could remember what had happened to Sir Hugo Barrington's clothes once the investigation had been closed.

'Everything will have been entered in the log book at the time, Sir Harry. If you give me a moment, I'll check.'

It turned out to be several moments before the sergeant came back on the line. 'How time flies,' he said. 'I'd forgotten how long ago that case was. But I've managed to track down the details you wanted.' Harry held his breath. 'We threw out the shirt, underwear and socks, but we gave one overcoat, grey, one hat, brown felt, one suit, lovat-green tweed, and one pair of brogues, brown leather, to Miss Penhaligon, who distributes all unclaimed goods on behalf of the Sally Army. Not the easiest of women,' the sergeant added without explanation.

—◇—

The sign on the counter read 'Miss Penhaligon'.

'This is most irregular, Sir Harry,' said the woman standing behind the name. 'Most irregular.'

Harry was glad that he'd brought Emma along with him. 'But it could prove incredibly important for both of us,' he said, taking Emma's hand.

'I don't doubt that, Sir Harry, but it's still most irregular. I can't imagine what my supervisor will make of it.'

Harry couldn't imagine Miss Penhaligon having a supervisor. She turned her back on them and began to study a neat row of box files on a shelf dust was not allowed to settle on. She finally pulled out one marked 1943 and placed it on the counter. She opened it, and had to turn several pages before she came across what she was looking for.

'No one seemed to want the brown felt hat,' she

announced. 'In fact, my records show that we still have it in store. The overcoat was allocated to a Mr Stephenson, the suit to someone who goes by the name of Old Joey, and the brown brogues to a Mr Watson.'

'Do you have any idea where we might find any of those gentlemen?' asked Emma.

'They are rarely to be found apart,' said Miss Penhaligon. 'In the summer, they never stray far from the municipal park, while in the winter we accommodate them in our hostel. I feel confident that at this time of year you'll find them in the park.'

'Thank you, Miss Penhaligon,' said Harry, giving her a warm smile. 'You couldn't have been more helpful.'

Miss Penhaligon beamed. 'My pleasure, Sir Harry.'

'I could get used to being addressed as Sir Harry,' he said to Emma as they walked out of the building.

'Not if you're still hoping to marry me,' she said, 'because I have no desire to be Lady Barrington.'

◄○►

Harry spotted him lying on a park bench with his back to them. He was wrapped up in a grey overcoat.

'I'm sorry to bother you, Mr Stephenson,' said Harry, touching him gently on the shoulder, 'but we need your help.'

A grimy hand shot out, but he didn't turn over. Harry placed a half crown in the outstretched palm. Mr Stephenson bit the coin, before cocking his head to take a closer look at Harry. 'What do you want?' he asked.

'We're looking for Old Joey,' said Emma softly.

'The corporal's got bench number one, on account of his age and seniority. This is bench number two, and I'll take over bench number one when Old Joey dies, which shouldn't be long now. Mr Watson's got bench number three, so he'll get bench number two when I get bench number one. But I've already warned him he's going to have to wait a long time.'

'And do you, by any chance, know if Old Joey is still in possession of a green tweed suit?' asked Harry.

'Never takes it off,' said Mr Stephenson. 'Grown attached to it, you might say,' he added with a slight chuckle. 'He got the suit, I got the overcoat and Mr Watson got the shoes. He says they're a bit tight, but he doesn't complain. None of us wanted the hat.'

'So where will we find bench number one?' asked Emma.

'Where it's always been, in the bandstand, under cover. Joey calls it his palace. But he's a bit soft in the head on account of the fact he still suffers from shellshock.' Mr Stephenson turned his back on them, on account of the fact that he felt he'd earned his half crown.

It wasn't difficult for Harry and Emma to find the bandstand, or Old Joey, who turned out to be its only occupant. He was sitting bolt upright in the middle of bench number one as if he were seated on a throne. Emma didn't need to see the faded brown stains to recognize her father's old tweed suit, but how would they ever get him to part with it, she wondered.

'What do you want?' said Old Joey suspiciously as they walked up the steps and into his kingdom. 'If it's my bench you're after, you can forget it, because possession is nine-tenths of the law, as I keep reminding Mr Stephenson.'

'No,' said Emma gently, 'we don't want your bench, Old Joey, but we wondered if you'd like a new suit.'

'No thank you, miss, very happy with the one I got. It keeps me warm, so I don't need no other one.'

'But we'd give you a new suit that would be just as warm,' said Harry.

'Old Joey's done nothing wrong,' he said, turning to face him.

Harry stared at the row of medals on his chest: the Mons

Star, the long service medal and the Victory Medal, and a single stripe that had been sewn on to his sleeve. 'I need your help, corporal,' he said.

Old Joey sprang to attention, saluted and said, 'Bayonet fixed, sir, just give the order and the lads are ready to go over the top.'

Harry felt ashamed.

Emma and Harry returned the next day with a herring-bone overcoat, a new tweed suit and a pair of shoes for Old Joey. Mr Stephenson paraded around the park in his new blazer and grey flannels, while Mr Watson, bench number three, was delighted with his double-breasted sports jacket and cavalry twills, but as he didn't need another pair of shoes, he asked Emma to give them to Mr Stephenson. She handed the rest of Sir Hugo's wardrobe to a grateful Miss Penhaligon.

Harry left the park with Sir Hugo Barrington's blood-stained lovat-green tweed suit.

◄○►

Professor Inchcape studied the blood stains under a microscope for some time before he offered an opinion.

'I'll need to carry out several more tests before I make a final assessment, but on a preliminary inspection, I'm fairly confident that I'll be able to tell you which blood group these samples came from.'

'That's a relief,' said Harry. 'But how long will it be before you know the results?'

'A couple of days would be my guess,' said the professor, 'three at the most. I'll give you a call as soon as I find out, Sir Harry.'

'Let's hope you have to make the call to Mr Clifton.'

◄○►

'I've phoned the Lord Chancellor's office,' said Lord Harvey, 'and let them know that blood tests are being carried out on Hugo's clothes. If the blood group is Rhesus positive, I'm sure he'll ask the Law Lords to reconsider their verdict in light of the fresh evidence.'

'But if we don't get the result we're hoping for,' said Harry, 'then what?'

'The Lord Chancellor will schedule a debate in the parliamentary calendar soon after the House is reconvened after the general election. But let's hope Professor Inchcape's findings make that unnecessary. By the way, does Giles know what you're up to?'

'No, sir, but as I'm spending the afternoon with him, I'll be able to bring him up to date.'

'Don't tell me he's talked you into doing a stint of canvassing?'

'I'm afraid so, although he's well aware I'll be voting Tory at the election. But I have assured him that my mother and Uncle Stan will both be supporting him.'

'Don't let the press find out that you won't be voting for him, because they'll be looking for any opportunity to drive a stake between the two of you. Bosom pals is not on their agenda.'

'All the more reason to hope that the professor comes up with the right result and we're all put out of our misery.'

'Amen to that,' said Lord Harvey.

◄○►

William Warwick was just about to solve the crime when the phone rang. Harry still had the gun in his hand as he walked across the library and picked up the receiver.

'It's Professor Inchcape. Can I have a word with Sir Harry?'

Fiction was replaced by fact in a cruel moment. Harry didn't need to be told the results of the blood tests. 'Speaking,' he said.

'I'm afraid my news isn't what you were hoping for,' said

the professor. 'Sir Hugo's blood type turns out to be Rhesus negative, so the possibility of him being your father can't be eliminated on those grounds.'

Harry telephoned Ashcombe Hall.

'Harvey here,' said the voice he knew so well.

'It's Harry, sir. I'm afraid you're going to have to phone the Lord Chancellor and tell him the debate will be going ahead.'

45

GILES HAD BECOME so preoccupied with getting elected to the House of Commons as the Member of Parliament for Bristol Docklands, and Harry was so involved with the publication of *William Warwick and the Case of the Blind Witness*, that when they received an invitation to join Lord Harvey at his country home for Sunday lunch, they both assumed it would be a family gathering. But when they turned up at Ashcombe Hall, there was no sign of any other member of the family.

Lawson did not escort them to the drawing room, or even the dining room, but to his lordship's study, where they found Lord Harvey seated behind his desk with two empty leather chairs facing him. He didn't waste any time on small talk.

'I've been informed by the Lord Chancellor's office that Thursday September 6th has been reserved in the parliamentary calendar for a debate that will determine which of you will inherit the family title. We have two months to prepare. I will be opening the debate from the front bench,' said Lord Harvey, 'and I expect to be opposed by Lord Preston.'

'What's he hoping to achieve?' asked Harry.

'He wants to undermine the hereditary system, and to do him justice, he doesn't make any bones about it.'

'Perhaps if I could get an appointment to see him,' said Harry, 'and let him know my views . . .'

'He's not interested in you or your views,' said Lord Harvey. 'He's simply using the debate as a platform to air his well-known opinions on the hereditary principle.'

'But surely if I were to write to him—'

'I already have,' said Giles, 'and even though we're in the same party, he didn't bother to reply.'

'In his opinion, the issue is far more important than any one individual case,' said Lord Harvey.

'Won't such an intransigent stance go down badly with their lordships?' asked Harry.

'Not necessarily,' replied Lord Harvey. 'Reg Preston used to be a trade union firebrand, until Ramsay MacDonald offered him a seat in the Lords. He's always been a formidable orator, and since joining us on the red benches, has become someone you can't afford to underestimate.'

'Do you have any sense of how the House might divide?' asked Giles.

'The government whips tell me it will be a close-run thing. The Labour peers will get behind Reg because they can't afford to be seen supporting the hereditary principle.'

'And the Tories?' asked Harry.

'The majority will support me, not least because the last thing they'll want is to see the hereditary principle being dealt a blow in their own back yard, although there are still one or two waverers I'll have to work on.'

'What about the Liberals?' asked Giles.

'Heaven alone knows, although they've announced that it will be a free vote.'

'A free vote?' queried Harry.

'There will be no party whip,' explained Giles. 'Each member can decide which corridor to go into as a matter of principle.'

'And finally, there are the cross-benchers,' continued

Lord Harvey. 'They will listen to the arguments on both sides and then go where their conscience guides them. So we'll only discover how they intend to vote when the division is called.'

'So what can we do to help?' asked Harry.

'You, Harry, as a writer and you, Giles, as a politician can start by assisting me with my speech. Any contribution either of you would care to make will be most welcome. Let's start by drawing up an outline plan over lunch.'

Neither Giles nor Harry thought it worth mentioning to their host such frivolous matters as forthcoming general elections or publication dates, as the three of them made their way through to the dining room.

◆◇◆

'When's your book being published?' Giles asked as they drove away from Ashcombe Hall later that afternoon.

'July twentieth,' said Harry. 'So it won't be out until after the election. My publishers want me to do a tour of the country, and carry out some signing sessions as well as a few press interviews.'

'Be warned,' said Giles, 'the journalists won't ask you any questions about the book, only your views on who should inherit the title.'

'How often do I have to tell them that my sole interest is Emma, and I'll sacrifice anything to be allowed to spend the rest of my life with her?' asked Harry, trying not to sound exasperated. 'You can have the title, you can have the estate, you can have all that therein is, if I can have Emma.'

◆◇◆

William Warwick and the Case of the Blind Witness was well received by the critics, but Giles turned out to be right. The press didn't seem to be particularly interested in the ambitious young detective constable from Bristol, only the writer's alter ego, Giles Barrington, and his chances of regaining the family title. Whenever Harry told the press that he had no interest in the title, it only made them more convinced he did.

In what the journalists regarded as the battle for the Barrington inheritance, all the newspapers, with the exception of the *Daily Telegraph*, supported the handsome, brave, self-made, popular, smart grammar-school boy, who, they repeatedly reminded their readers, had been raised in the back streets of Bristol.

Harry took every opportunity to remind the same journalists that Giles had been a contemporary at Bristol Grammar School, was now the Labour MP for Bristol Docklands, just happened to have won the MC at Tobruk, a cricket blue in his first year at Oxford, and certainly wasn't responsible for which cot he was born in. Harry's loyal support of his friend only made him even more popular, with both the press and the public.

Despite the fact that Giles had been elected to the House of Commons by over three thousand votes and had already taken his place on the green benches, he knew it would be a debate that was due to take place on the red benches at the other end of the corridor in just over a month's time that would decide both his and Harry's future.

46

HARRY WAS USED TO being woken by birds chirping happily in the trees that surrounded Barrington Hall, and Sebastian charging into the library uninvited and unannounced or the sound of Emma arriving for breakfast after her early morning gallop.

But today it was different.

He was woken by street lights, the noise of traffic and Big Ben chiming relentlessly every fifteen minutes, to remind him how many hours were left before Lord Harvey would rise to open a debate after which men he'd never met would cast a vote that would decide his and Giles's futures, for a thousand years.

He had a long bath, as it was too early to go down for breakfast. Once he was dressed, he phoned Barrington Hall, only to be told by the butler that Miss Barrington had already left for the station. Harry was puzzled. Why would Emma catch the early train when they hadn't planned to meet up until lunch? When Harry walked into the morning room just after seven, he wasn't surprised to find Giles already up and reading the morning papers.

'Is your grandfather up?' asked Harry.

'Long before either of us, I suspect. When I came down, just after six, the light was on in his study. Once this dreadful business is behind us, whatever the result, we must get him to spend a few days in Mulgelrie Castle, and take a well-earned rest.'

'Good idea,' said Harry as he slumped into the nearest armchair, only to shoot back up again a moment later when Lord Harvey entered the room.

'Time for breakfast, chaps. Never wise to go to the gallows on an empty stomach.'

Despite Lord Harvey's advice, the three of them didn't eat a great deal as they considered the day ahead. Lord Harvey tried out a few key phrases, while Harry and Giles made some last-minute suggestions to be added or taken away from his script.

'I wish I could tell their lordships how much of a contribution both of you have made,' said the old man, once he'd added a couple of sentences to his peroration. 'Right, chaps, time to fix bayonets and go over the top.'

◄o►

Both of them were nervous.

'I was hoping you might be able to help me,' said Emma, unable to look him in the eye.

'I will if I can, miss,' he said.

Emma looked up at a man who, although he was clean-shaven and his shoes must have been polished that morning, wore a shirt with a frayed collar, and the trousers of his well-worn suit were baggy.

'When my father died –' Emma could never bring herself to say 'was killed' – 'the police found a baby girl in his office. Do you have any idea what happened to her?'

'No,' said the man, 'but as the police weren't able to contact her next of kin, she would have been placed in a church mission and put up for adoption.'

'Do you have any idea which orphanage she ended up in?' asked Emma.

'No, but I could always make some enquiries if . . .'

'How much did my father owe you?'

'Thirty-seven pounds and eleven shillings,' said the private detective, who took out a wad of bills from an inside pocket.

Emma waved a hand, opened her purse and extracted two crisp five-pound notes. 'I'll settle the balance when we meet again.'

'Thank you, Miss Barrington,' Mitchell said as he rose from his place, assuming the meeting was now over. 'I'll be in touch as soon as I have news.'

'Just one more question,' said Emma, looking up at him. 'Do you know the little girl's name?'

'Jessica Smith,' he replied.

'Why Smith?'

'That's the name they always give a child nobody wants.'

◄○►

Lord Harvey locked himself in his office on the third floor of the Queen's Tower for the rest of the morning. He didn't leave his room even to join Harry, Giles and Emma for lunch, preferring a sandwich and a stiff whisky, while he went over his speech once again.

◄○►

Giles and Harry sat on the green benches in the central lobby of the House of Commons and chatted amiably as they waited for Emma to join them. Harry hoped that anyone who saw them, peers, commoners and press alike, would be left in no doubt that they were the closest of friends.

Harry kept checking his watch as he knew they had to be seated in the visitors' gallery of the House of Lords before the Lord Chancellor took his place on the Woolsack at two o'clock.

Harry allowed himself a smile when he saw Emma come

rushing into the central lobby just before one. Giles gave his sister a wave, as both men rose to greet her.

'What have you been up to?' asked Harry, even before he'd bent down to kiss her.

'I'll tell you over lunch,' promised Emma as she linked arms with both of them. 'But first I want to be brought up to date on your news.'

'Too close to call, seems to be the general consensus,' said Giles as he guided his guests towards the visitors' dining room. 'But it won't be long now before we all learn our fates,' he added morbidly.

◄◦►

The House of Lords was full long before Big Ben struck twice, and by the time the Lord High Chancellor of Great Britain entered the chamber, there wasn't a place to be found on the packed benches. In fact, several members were left standing at the bar of the House. Lord Harvey glanced across to the other side of the chamber to see Reg Preston smiling at him like a lion who had just spotted his lunch.

Their lordships rose as one when the Lord Chancellor took his place on the Woolsack. He bowed to the assembled gathering, and they returned the compliment before resuming their seats.

The Lord Chancellor opened his gold-tasselled red leather folder.

'My lords, we are gathered to give judgment as to whether Mr Giles Barrington or Mr Harry Clifton is entitled to inherit the title, estate and accoutrements of the late Sir Hugo Barrington, Baronet, defender of the peace.'

Lord Harvey looked up to see Harry, Emma and Giles seated in the front row of the visitors' gallery. He was greeted with a warm smile from his granddaughter and could lip-read her words, 'Good luck, Gramps!'

'I call upon Lord Harvey to open the debate,' said the Lord High Chancellor, before taking his seat on the Woolsack.

Lord Harvey rose from his place on the front bench and gripped the sides of the dispatch box to help steady his nerves, while his colleagues on the benches behind him greeted their noble and gallant friend with cries of 'Hear, hear!' He looked around the House, aware that he was about to deliver the most important speech of his life.

'My lords,' he began, 'I stand before you today representing my kinsman, Mr Giles Barrington, a member of the other place, in his lawful claim to the Barrington title and all the possessions of that lineage. My lords, allow me to acquaint you with the circumstances that have brought this case to your lordships' attention. In 1877, Joshua Barrington was created a baronet by Queen Victoria, for services to the shipping industry, which included the Barrington Line, a fleet of ocean-going vessels that are, to this day, still based in the port of Bristol.

'Joshua was the fifth child in a family of nine, and left school at the age of seven, unable to read or write, before he began life as an apprentice at the Coldwater Shipping Company, where it soon became clear to all those around him that this was no ordinary child.

'By the age of thirty, he had gained his master's certificate, and at forty-two he was invited to join the board of Coldwater's, which was experiencing difficult times. During the next ten years, he rescued the company virtually single-handed, and for the next twenty-two years, served as its chairman.

'But, my lords, you need to know a little more about Sir Joshua the man, to understand why we are gathered here today, because it certainly would not have been at his bidding. Above all, Sir Joshua was a God-fearing man, who considered his word was his bond. A handshake was enough for Sir Joshua to accept that a contract had been signed. Where are such men today, my lords?'

'Hear, hear' echoed around the chamber.

'But like so many successful men, my lords, Sir Joshua took a little longer than the rest of us to accept his own mortality.' A ripple of laughter greeted this statement. 'So when the time came for him to make his first and only will, he had already fulfilled the maker's contract of three score years and ten. That did not stop him approaching the task with his usual vigour and vision. To that end, he invited Sir Isaiah Waldegrave, the leading QC in the land, to represent him, an advocate who, like you, my lord,' he said, turning to face the Woolsack, 'ended his judicial days as Lord High Chancellor. I mention this, my lords, to emphasize that Sir Joshua's testament bears a legal weight and authority that does not allow it to be questioned by his successors.

'In that will, he left everything to his first born and next of kin, Walter Barrington, my oldest and dearest friend. That included the title, the shipping company, the estates and, I quote the exact words of the will, "all that therein is". This debate, my lords, is not about the validity of Sir Joshua's last will and testament, but only about who can rightfully claim to be his heir. At this point, my lords, I would like you to take something into consideration that would never have crossed Sir Joshua's God-fearing mind; the possibility that an heir of his could ever father an illegitimate son.

'Hugo Barrington became next in line when his elder brother Nicholas was killed fighting for his country at Ypres in 1918. Hugo succeeded to the title in 1942 on the death of his father, Sir Walter. When the House divides, my lords, you will be called upon to decide between my grandson, Mr Giles Barrington, who is the legitimate son of a union between the late Sir Hugo Barrington and my only daughter, Elizabeth Harvey, and Mr Harry Clifton, who, I would suggest, is the legitimate son of Mrs Maisie Clifton and the late Arthur Clifton.

'May I at this point, my lords, seek your indulgence and speak for a moment a little about my grandson, Giles Barrington. He was educated at Bristol Grammar School, from where he went on to win a place at Brasenose College, Oxford. However, he did not complete his degree, rather he decided to abandon the life of an undergraduate to join the Wessex Regiment soon after the outbreak of war. While serving in Tobruk as a young lieutenant, he won the Military Cross defending that place against Rommel's Afrika Korps. He was later captured and taken to Weinsberg prisoner of war camp in Germany, from where he escaped to return to England and rejoin his regiment for the remainder of the hostilities. In the general election he stood for, and indeed won, a seat in another place as the honourable member for Bristol Docklands.'

Loud 'Hear, hear's came from the benches opposite.

'On the death of his father, he inherited the title, without dispute, as it had been widely reported that Harry Clifton had been buried at sea, not long after the declaration of war. It is one of the ironies of life, my lords, that my granddaughter, Emma, through her diligence and determination, was the person who discovered that Harry was still alive, and she unwittingly set in motion the train of events that has brought your lordships to this House today.' Lord Harvey looked into the gallery, and gave his granddaughter a warm smile.

'There is, my lords, no dispute that Harry Clifton was born before Giles Barrington. However, there is, I would submit, no definite or conclusive proof that Harry Clifton is the result of a liaison between Sir Hugo Barrington and Miss Maisie Tancock, later to become Mrs Arthur Clifton.

'Mrs Clifton does not deny that she had sexual intercourse with Hugo Barrington on one occasion in 1919, and one occasion only. However, a few weeks later she married Mr Arthur Clifton, and a child was later born whose name was entered on the birth certificate as Harry Arthur Clifton.

'You therefore have, my lords, on the one hand, Giles Barrington, the legitimate offspring of Sir Hugo Barrington. On the other, you have Harry Clifton, who, perchance, could possibly be the progeny of Sir Hugo, while there can be no doubt that Giles Barrington is. And is that a risk you are willing to take, my lords? If it is, allow me to add just one more factor that might help your lordships decide which lobby they should enter at the conclusion of this debate. Harry Clifton, who is seated in the visitors' gallery this afternoon, has made his own position clear again and again. He has no interest in being burdened – I use his own word – with the title, but would far rather it was inherited by his close friend, Giles Barrington.'

Several peers looked up into the gallery to see Giles and Emma Barrington seated on either side of Harry Clifton, who was nodding. Lord Harvey did not continue until he had regained the attention of the whole House.

'And so, my lords, when you cast your votes later tonight, I urge you to take into consideration the wishes of Harry Clifton, and the intentions of Sir Joshua Barrington, and give the benefit of the doubt to my grandson Giles Barrington. I am grateful to the House for its indulgence.'

Lord Harvey lowered himself on to the bench, to be greeted with loud cheers and the waving of order papers. Harry felt confident that he had won the day.

When the House had regained its composure, the Lord Chancellor rose from his place, and said, 'I call upon Lord Preston to respond.'

Harry looked down from the gallery and watched as a man he'd never seen before rose slowly from the opposition benches. Lord Preston could not have been an inch above five foot, and his squat, muscular body and furnace-lined face would have left no one in any doubt that he had been a labourer all his working life, while his pugnacious expression suggested that he feared no man.

Reg Preston spent a moment surveying the benches opposite, like a private soldier who puts his head above the parapet to take a closer look at the enemy.

'My lords, I would like to open my remarks by congratulating Lord Harvey on a brilliant and moving speech. However, I would suggest that its very brilliance was its weakness, and bears the seeds of its downfall. The noble lord's contribution was indeed moving, but as it progressed, he sounded more and more like an advocate who's only too aware that he's defending a weak case.' Preston had created a silence in the chamber that Lord Harvey had not managed.

'Let us, my lords, consider some of the facts so conveniently papered over by the noble and gallant Lord Harvey. No one disputes that the young Hugo Barrington had sexual relations with Maisie Tancock some six weeks before she married Arthur Clifton. Or that nine months later, almost to the day, she gave birth to a son whose name was conveniently entered on the birth certificate as Harry Arthur Clifton. Well, that's sorted out that little problem, hasn't it, my lords? Except for the inconvenient fact that if Mrs Clifton conceived that child on the day she married, he was born seven months and twelve days later.

'Now, my lords, I'd be the first to accept that's a possibility, but as a betting man, if I was given the choice between nine months and seven months and twelve days, I know where I'd place my wager, and I don't think the bookies would offer me very long odds.'

A little laughter broke out on the Labour benches.

'And I should add, my lords, that the child weighed in at nine pounds four ounces. That doesn't sound premature to me.'

The laughter was even louder.

'Let us next consider something else that must have slipped Lord Harvey's agile mind. Hugo Barrington, like his father and his grandfather before him, suffered from a hereditary condition known as colour-blindness, as does his son, Giles. And so does Harry Clifton. The odds are shortening, my lords.'

More laughter followed, and muttered discussion broke out on both sides of the House. Lord Harvey looked grimly on, as he waited for the next punch to land.

'Let us shorten those odds still further, my lords. It was the great Dr Milne of St Thomas' Hospital who discovered that if parents shared the same Rhesus negative blood type, then their children will also be Rhesus negative. Sir Hugo Barrington was Rhesus negative. Mrs Clifton is Rhesus negative. And surprise, surprise, Harry Clifton is Rhesus negative, a blood type that only twelve per cent of the British people share. I think the bookies are paying out, my lords, because the only other horse in the race didn't reach the starting gate.'

More laughter followed, and Lord Harvey slumped even lower on the bench, angry that he hadn't pointed out that Arthur Clifton was also Rhesus negative.

'Now allow me to touch on one thing, my lords, on which I am whole-heartedly in agreement with Lord Harvey. No one has the right to question Sir Joshua Barrington's will, when it has such a fine legal pedigree. Therefore, all we have to decide is what the words "first born" and "next of kin" actually mean.

'Most of you in this House will be well aware of my strongly held views on the hereditary principle.' Preston smiled before adding, 'I consider it to be *without* principle.'

This time the laughter only came from one side of the House, while those on the benches opposite sat in stony silence.

'My lords, should you decide to ignore legal precedent and tamper with historical tradition, simply to suit your own convenience, you will bring the hereditary concept into disrepute, and in time the whole edifice will surely come crashing down on your lordships' heads,' he said, pointing to the benches opposite.

'So let us consider the two young men involved in this sad dispute, not, I might say, my lords, a dispute of their making. Harry Clifton, we are told, would prefer that his friend Giles Barrington inherit the title. How very decent of him. But then Harry Clifton is, without question, a decent man. However, my lords, should we travel down that road, every hereditary peer in the land would, in future, be able to decide which of his offspring he would prefer to succeed him, and that, my lords, is a road with a dead-end sign.'

The House had fallen silent and Lord Preston was able to lower his voice to barely a whisper.

'Did this decent young man, Harry Clifton, have any ulterior motive when he told the world that he wanted his friend Giles Barrington to be acknowledged as the first-born?'

Every eye was on Lord Preston.

'You see, my lords, the Church of England would not allow Harry Clifton to marry the woman he loved, Giles Barrington's sister Emma Barrington, because they weren't in much doubt that they shared the same father.'

Harry had never loathed a man more in his life.

'I see the bishops' benches are packed today, my lords,' continued Preston, turning to face the churchmen. 'I shall be fascinated to discover the ecclesiastical view on this matter, because they cannot have it both ways.' One or two of the bishops looked uneasy. 'And while I am on the subject of Harry Clifton's pedigree, may I suggest that as a candidate in the lists, he is every bit the equal of Giles Barrington. Brought up in the back streets of Bristol, against

all the odds he wins a place at Bristol Grammar School, and
five years later an exhibition to Brasenose College, Oxford.
And young Harry didn't even wait for war to be declared
before he left the university with the intention of joining up,
only being prevented from doing so when his ship was
torpedoed by a German U-boat, leading Lord Harvey and
the rest of the Barrington family to believe that he had been
buried at sea.

'Anyone who has read Mr Clifton's moving words in his
book *The Diary of a Convict*, knows how he ended up
serving in the US Army, where he won the Silver Star
before being badly wounded by a German landmine only
weeks before peace was declared. But the Germans couldn't
kill off Harry Clifton quite that easily, my lords, and neither
should we.'

The Labour benches erupted as one, and Lord Preston
waited until the House had fallen silent once again.

'Finally, my lords, we should ask ourselves why we are
here today. I will tell you why. It is because Giles Barrington
is appealing against a judgment made by the seven leading
legal minds in the land, something else Lord Harvey failed
to mention in his heartfelt speech. But I will remind you
that, in their wisdom, the Law Lords came down in favour
of Harry Clifton inheriting the baronetcy. If you are thinking
of reversing that decision, my lords, before you do so, you
must be certain that they have made a fundamental error of
judgment.

'And so, my lords,' said Preston as he began his peroration, 'when you cast your votes to decide which of these
two men should inherit the Barrington title, do not base
your judgment on convenience, but on strong probability.
Because then, to quote Lord Harvey, you will give the
benefit of the doubt not to Giles Barrington, but to Harry
Clifton, as the odds, if not the pedigree, are stacked in his
favour. And may I conclude, my lords,' he said, staring

defiantly at the benches opposite, 'by suggesting that when you enter the division lobby, you should take your consciences with you, and leave your politics in the chamber.'

Lord Preston sat down to loud acclamation from his own benches, while several peers on the opposite side of the House could be seen nodding.

Lord Harvey wrote a note to his opponent, congratulating him on a powerful speech that was made even more persuasive by its obvious conviction. Following the tradition of the House, both opening speakers remained in their places to listen to the views of fellow members who followed them.

There turned out to be several unpredictable contributions delivered from both sides of the House, which only left Lord Harvey even more unsure what the outcome would be when the votes were finally cast. One speech that was listened to with rapt attention from all quarters of the chamber was delivered by the Bishop of Bristol, and was clearly endorsed by his noble and ecclesiastical friends, who sat on the benches beside him.

'My lords,' said the bishop, 'if, in your wisdom, you vote tonight in favour of Mr Giles Barrington inheriting the title, my noble friends and I would be left with no choice but to withdraw the church's objection to a lawful marriage taking place between Mr Harry Clifton and Miss Emma Barrington. Because, my lords, were you to decide that Harry is not the son of Hugo Barrington, there can be no objection to such a union.'

'But how will they vote?' Lord Harvey whispered to the colleague sitting beside him on the front bench.

'My colleagues and I will not be casting a vote in either lobby when the division is called, as we feel we are not qualified to make either a political or a legal judgment on this issue.'

'What about a moral judgment?' said Lord Preston, loud

enough to be heard on the bishops' benches. Lord Harvey had at last found something on which the two of them were in agreement.

Another speech that took the House by surprise was delivered by Lord Hughes, a cross-bencher and a former president of the British Medical Association.

'My lords, I must inform the House that recent medical research, carried out at the Moorfields Hospital, has shown that colour-blindness can only be passed down through the female line.'

The Lord Chancellor opened his red folder and made an emendation to his notes.

'And therefore, for Lord Preston to suggest that because Sir Hugo Barrington was colour-blind, it is more likely that Harry Clifton is his son, is bogus, and should be dismissed as nothing more than a coincidence.'

When Big Ben struck ten times, there were still several members who wished to catch the Lord Chancellor's eye. In his wisdom, he decided to allow the debate to run its natural course. The final speaker sat down a few minutes after three the following morning.

When the division bell finally rang, rows of dishevelled and exhausted members trooped out of the chamber and into the voting lobby. Harry, still seated in the gallery, noticed that Lord Harvey was fast asleep. No one commented. After all, he hadn't left his place for the past thirteen hours.

'Let's hope he wakes up in time to vote,' said Giles with a chuckle, which he stifled as his grandfather slumped further down on to the bench.

A badge messenger quickly left the chamber and called for an ambulance, while two ushers rushed on to the floor of the House and gently lowered the noble lord on to a stretcher.

Harry, Giles and Emma left the visitors' gallery and ran

down the stairs, and reached the peers' lobby just as the stretcher bearers came out of the chamber. The three of them accompanied Lord Harvey out of the building and into a waiting ambulance.

Once members had cast their votes in the lobby of their choice, they slowly made their way back into the chamber. No one wanted to leave before they'd heard the result of the count. Members on both sides of the House were puzzled not to see Lord Harvey in his place on the front bench.

Rumours began to circulate around the chamber, and when Lord Preston was told the news, he turned ashen-white.

It was several more minutes before the four whips on duty returned to the chamber to inform the House of the result of the division. They marched up the centre aisle in step, like the guards officers they had been, and came to a halt in front of the Lord Chancellor.

A hush descended on the House.

The chief whip raised the voting slip and declared in a loud voice, 'Contents to the right, two hundred and seventy-three votes. Non-contents to the left, two hundred and seventy-three votes.'

Pandemonium broke out in the chamber and in the gallery above, as members and visitors sought guidance as to what would happen next. Old hands realized that the Lord Chancellor would have the casting vote. He sat alone on the Woolsack, inscrutable and unmoved by the noise and clamour all around him as he waited patiently for the House to come to order.

Once the last whisper had died away, the Lord Chancellor rose slowly from the Woolsack, adjusted his full-bottomed wig and tugged the lapels of his black and gold-braided robe, before he addressed the House. Every eye in the chamber was fixed upon him. In the packed gallery overlooking the chamber, those who had been fortunate enough to acquire a ticket leant over the railings in anticipation. There were three empty seats in the distinguished guests' gallery: those of the three people whose future the Lord Chancellor held in his gift.

'My lords,' he began. 'I have listened with interest to each and every contribution your lordships have made during this long and fascinating debate. I have considered the arguments so eloquently and so passionately delivered from all parts of the House and find myself facing something of a dilemma. I would like to share my concerns with you all.

'In normal circumstances, being presented with a tied vote, I would not hesitate to support the Law Lords in their earlier judgment, when they came down in favour by four votes to three, of Harry Clifton inheriting the Barrington title. Indeed, it would have been irresponsible of me not to do so. However, your lordships may not be aware that just after the division was called, Lord Harvey, the proposer of the motion, was taken ill, and therefore unable to cast his vote. None of us can be in any doubt which corridor he would have entered, ensuring that he would have won the day even if it was by the slimmest of margins, and the title would therefore have passed to his grandson Giles Barrington.

'My lords, I am sure the House will agree that given these circumstances, my final judgment will require the wisdom of Solomon.'

Muffled 'hear, hear's could be heard from both sides of the House.

'However, I have to tell the House,' the Lord Chancellor continued, 'that I have not yet decided which son I should cut in half, and which son I should restore to his birthright.'

A ripple of laughter followed these remarks, which helped break the tension in the chamber.

'Therefore, my lords,' he said, once he had again captured the attention of the whole House, 'I will announce my judgment in the case of Barrington versus Clifton at ten o'clock this morning.' He resumed his seat on the Woolsack without uttering another word. The chief usher banged his rod on the ground three times, but could barely be heard above the clamour.

'House will reconvene at ten o'clock in the forenoon,' he bellowed, 'when the Lord Chancellor will deliver his judgment in the case of Barrington versus Clifton. House will rise!'

The Lord Chancellor rose from his place, bowed to the assembled gathering, and their lordships repaid the compliment.

The chief usher once again banged his rod three times on the ground.

'House is adjourned!'